The BOOK of MAGIC

Alice Hoffman

SCRIBNER

LONDON NEW YORK SYDNEY TORONTO NEW DELHI

First published in the United States by Simon & Schuster Inc., 2021
First published in Great Britain by Scribner,
an imprint of Simon & Schuster UK Ltd, 2021
This paperback edition published 2022

1 3 5 7 9 10 8 6 4 2

Simon & Schuster UK Ltd
1st Floor
222 Gray's Inn Road
London WC1X 8HB

Simon & Schuster Australia, Sydney
Simon & Schuster India, New Delhi

www.simonandschuster.co.uk
www.simonandschuster.com.au
www.simonandschuster.co.in

A CIP catalogue record for this book
is available from the British Library

Paperback ISBN: 978-1-3985-0997-9
eBook ISBN: 978-1-3985-0996-2
Audio ISBN: 978-1-3985-0998-6

Interior design by Carly Loman

Printed and bound by CPI Group (UK) Ltd, Croydon CR0 4YY

To all the librarians who changed my life

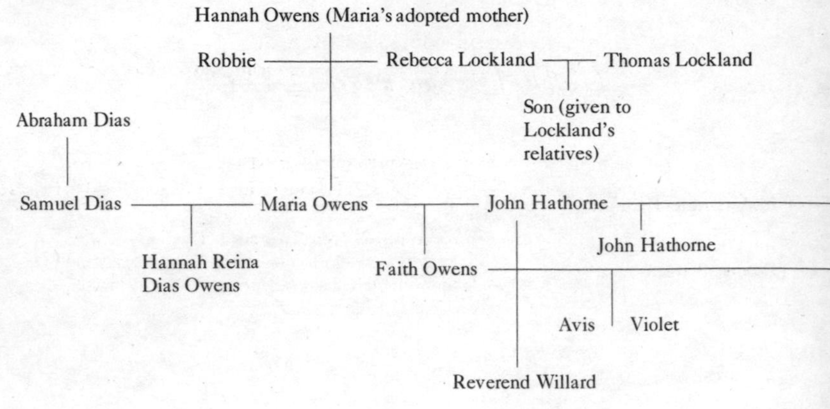
Hannah Owens (Maria's adopted mother)
Robbie
Rebecca Lockland
Thomas Lockland
Son (given to Lockland's relatives)
Abraham Dias
Samuel Dias
Maria Owens
John Hathorne
Hannah Reina Dias Owens
Faith Owens
John Hathorne
Avis
Violet
Reverend Willard

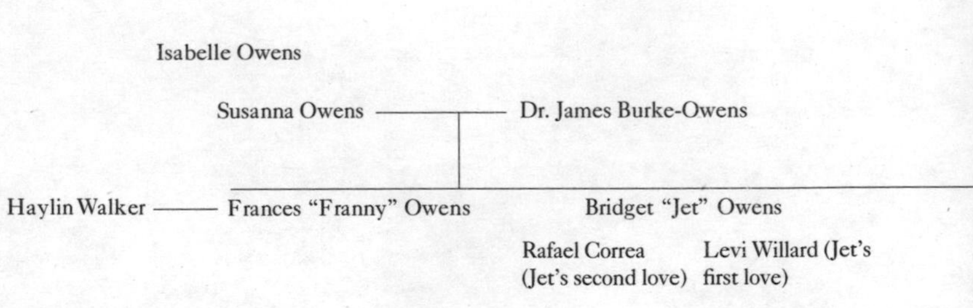
Isabelle Owens
Susanna Owens
Dr. James Burke-Owens
Haylin Walker
Frances "Franny" Owens
Bridget "Jet" Owens
Rafael Correa (Jet's second love)
Levi Willard (Jet's first love)

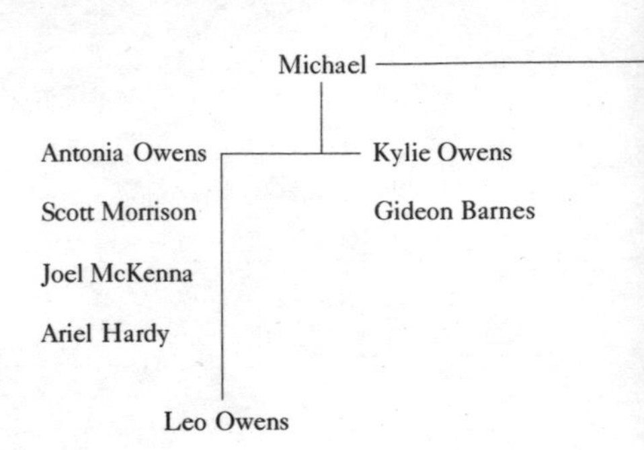
Michael
Antonia Owens
Kylie Owens
Scott Morrison
Gideon Barnes
Joel McKenna
Ariel Hardy
Leo Owens

Owens Family Tree

OTHER OWENS

— Jinx Owens – cousin of Franny, Jet & Vincent
— Boston Owenses
— Cousins from Maine

OTHER IMPORTANT CHARACTERS

— James "Jimmy" Hawkins – Gillian's ex-boyfriend in Practical Magic
— David Ward – Vincent's partner in The Book of Magic
— Tom Lockland – 13th grandson of Thomas Lockland
— John Hathorne's granddaughter married John Proctor who is related to The Willard family

—— Ruth Gardner Hathorne

—— Thomas Brattle

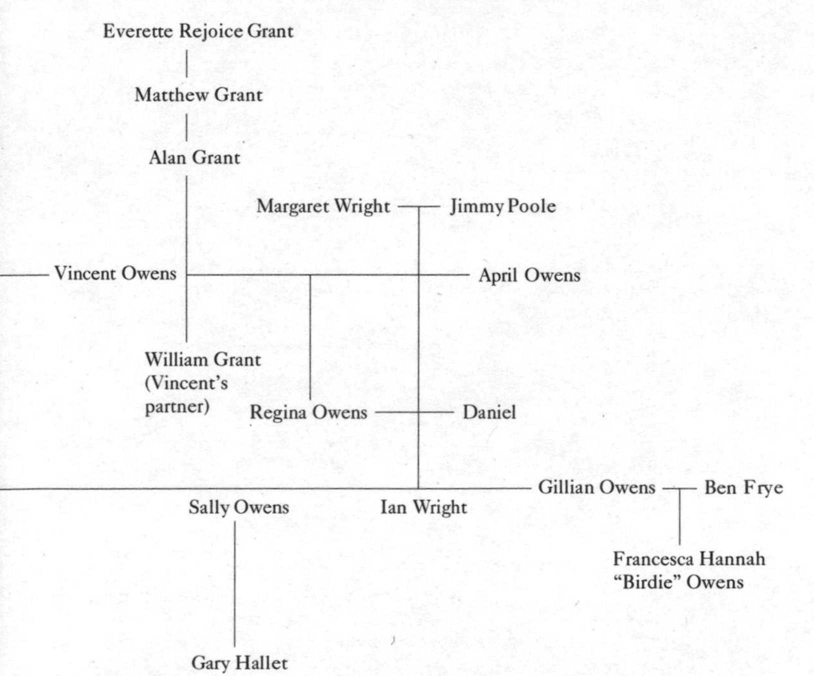

PART ONE

The Book of Shadows

I.

Some stories begin at the beginning and others begin at the end, but all the best stories begin in a library. It was there that Jet Owens saw her fate in a mirror behind the reference desk. Even in her eighties, Jet was still beautiful. Each day she washed with the black soap the family prepared in March during the dark phase of the moon, with every bar then wrapped in crinkly cellophane. Jet had no aches or pains and had never been ill a day in her life, but fate is fate and it can often be what you least expect it to be. On this day, when the daffodils had begun to bloom, Jet saw that she had seven days to live.

The deathwatch beetle had begun to call from within the walls of the Owens Library, a sound that often went unnoticed until it was so loud it was all a person could hear. When your time came, the black beetle would withdraw from hiding and follow you everywhere, no matter where you went. Its presence meant that the past was over and the future no longer existed. This was the moment that revealed how you had walked through the world, with kindness or with fear, with your heart open or closed. It had taken this long for Jet to appreciate that every instant was a marvel. Now everything she saw was illuminated. The sun streaming through the library windows in fierce bands of orange light. A moth tapping at the glass. The sweep of the branches of one of the last elm trees in the commonwealth, which shadowed the library's lawn. Some people unravel or run for shelter when their time has come, they curse their fate or hide under their beds, but Jet knew exactly what she wished to do in the last days she'd been granted. She didn't have to think twice.

Long ago, the library had been a jail where Maria Owens, the first woman in their family to set foot in Massachusetts in 1680, had been confined until the judges announced she would be hanged. Those were the days when witchery was forbidden and women were harshly punished, judged to be dangerous creatures if they talked too much, or read books, or did their best to protect themselves from harm. People said Maria could turn herself into a crow, that she had the ability to enchant men without ever speaking to them directly and to compel other women to do as they pleased, so that they were willing to forsake their proper place in society and in their own families. The court set out to destroy Maria and nearly did, but she could not be drowned, and she did not back down. She blamed love for her undoing, for she'd chosen the wrong man, with dire consequences. Just before the rope that was meant to end her life snapped, and she was miraculously saved, Maria called out a curse upon love.

Beware of love, she had written on the first page of her journal, now exhibited in the library, a display mothers in town often brought their teenaged daughters to view before they started dating. Beware of love that was dishonest and disloyal, love that would lie to you and trick you, love that could break you and condemn you to sorrow, love that could never be trusted. If Maria Owens had been less rash, she might have realized that when you curse another, you curse yourself as well. Curses are like knots, the more you struggle to be free, the tighter they become, whether they're made of rope or spite or desperation. Maria invoked an enchantment to protect the generations to follow, with her daughters' and great-granddaughters' best interests at heart. For their own safety, they must avoid love. Those who failed to abide by this rule would find that engagements would be tragic, and marriages would end with funerals. Over the years, many of those in the Owens family had found ways to outwit the curse, always an intricate and risky endeavor. All the same, a person could trick fate if she dared, she could change her name, never admit her love, skip a legal union, vanish from view, or, for those who were careless and wild, simply plunge in and hope for the best, knowing that sooner or later everyone had to face her own destiny.

Maria's journal pages had been up on the wall of the library for more years than anyone could remember. Certainly, they had been there when Jet and her sister, Franny, were girls, and came here on muggy heat-laden summer days, waiting for their lives to begin, learning the truth about themselves from the town records and from their beloved aunt Isabelle. The family had a history of witchery, inherited in every generation, and had practiced the Nameless Art. They were bloodline witches, genetically predisposed to magic, with a lineage to ancestors who possessed the same sacred gifts. For those who tried to escape their heritage, it soon became clear that they couldn't run away from who they were. A person could do her best to be ordinary and fit in, but the past could not be refuted, even when it was hidden from children thought to be too tender to know the truth. You didn't choose magic, it chose you; it bloomed inside you, blood and bones. And a curse, once spoken, could not be denied. All the same, fate was what you made of it. You could make the best of it, or you could let it make the best of you. On this evening when she saw the truth in the library, Jet Owens decided she would do her best to change her family's destiny.

It was dusk when Jet and her niece Sally walked home from the library, as they did nearly every evening. Sally and her husband and daughters had moved into the old family house when the aunts' aging became noticeable, and she had been happy to settle into the place she couldn't wait to escape from as a girl. Sally had two wonderful girls, Kylie and Antonia, but both were now off at school, and her sister, Gillian, lived in Cambridge quite near to the girls, where she worked in a lab at MIT, so it was only Sally, now a widow, who still resided with her aunts in that big tilted house with the black shutters on Magnolia Street, where a fierce iron fence circled an enormous parcel of land the gardeners in town all envied, for it was here that the first daffodils pushed through the earth and where herbs grew between patches of ice in March, a month before they appeared anywhere else. Already the bramble of blackberries along the gate was beginning to green, and the lilacs, which would bloom in shades of violet and deep purple and white, were filling in with their flat heart-shaped leaves.

Unfortunately, Sally Owens couldn't hold on to love and everyone knew it. She'd been a victim of her family's curse, not once but twice. She was quite young when she first married, a forbidden act that could only end badly. Her husband Michael, a school friend and the father of her girls, had been a local boy and the first to ask her out; he was cursed with an untimely death, a victim of bad luck and bad weather, struck by lightning. Sally didn't speak for a year after his death, but she tried again with her second husband, Gary Hallet, a man she could depend on until he'd passed on a few years after their marriage. Gary had been afflicted with a childhood congenital heart disease that had finally caught up to him, but Sally was convinced his death had been activated by the family curse, for Gary had always seemed to be as healthy as he was strong. He had come from Arizona to work on the local police force, preferring a horse to a patrol car, and he and his tall good-natured bay, Jack, were known and beloved in town. Gary would rather give someone a second chance than arrest him, and the children in town begged to visit old Jack at the police stable on the far side of Endicott Street, bringing sugar cubes and carrots.

How was it possible for a man like Gary Hallet to kiss his wife good night, close his eyes, and never wake again? His horse had died of grief two nights later, lying down on the earthen floor of the stable. Sally was stunned and devastated, and some people said she had lost a piece of her heart. Certainly, she seemed transformed. When she did say hello to her neighbors, which was rare, she made it perfectly clear she preferred to be left in peace. Sally had returned to school for her degree in library science at Simmons University, and now, at the age of forty-four, she was the director of the Owens Library. The only other employee was Sarah Hardwick, who had worked at the library for over sixty years, and who still made it a point of leaving every day at five o'clock on the dot, which allowed her to stop by the Black Rabbit Inn and have a cocktail at her regular time. Often, she didn't report back until ten in the morning, especially if she'd had more than one drink. Sally didn't begrudge Miss Hardwick the need to come in late and leave early at her age, and she didn't mind the hours she spent working alone in the library, late into the evenings. She did her best to be helpful when she checked out books, or assisted students from the local high school, but everyone knew Sally Owens was embittered, and even more standoffish than she'd been as a girl.

The curse had ruined Sally's life, and she had decided not to reveal the Owens fate to her daughters. They knew bits, of course, and there was a scrim of magic over the house on Magnolia Street; the famous garden, the dangerous plants locked away in the greenhouse, the sparrow that arrived at midsummer. Still, the word *witchery* was never spoken out loud. Sally knew that her great-grandmother Susannah Owens had also kept the truth of their heritage from her children, setting out a series of rules to ensure they would avoid magic. Sally felt a kinship with Susannah, and when she found her great-grandmother's rules jotted down in an old diary, she made use of them. No swimming, no books about magic, no candles, no sitting out on the roof and gazing at stars, no wearing black, no walking in the moonlight. In Sally's opinion a life without magic was preferable, and she had done her best to ensure that her daughters wouldn't live with the cloud of the curse above them, spying danger in every kiss. When the time came, if and when one of the girls teetered on the verge of falling in love, Sally would step in and put a stop to it, as she wished she had done when her sister, Gillian, had fallen for the man whose name was never said aloud for fear he'd be called back from the dead. Thankfully, neither Antonia nor Kylie seemed to have any romantic inclinations. Perhaps the curse would never be a problem for them and they'd be safe after all. Kylie spent all her time with her best friend, Gideon Barnes, and Antonia was clearly a workaholic, even now that she was pregnant. There was no partner in the picture and when asked who the father of her unborn child was, Antonia merely shrugged and said it was a long story, which in truth it was not. She had dated Scott Morrison in high school, but she had always preferred women and had several girlfriends, many of whose hearts were broken without Antonia even trying to accomplish that task. Antonia was a confident, calm young woman of twenty-three, a redhead who didn't possess the same fierce temperament as Franny, the sort of person you would want beside you in an emergency, and no one was surprised when she announced that emergency medicine was the specialty she wished to pursue. Whenever she heard a siren on the street, she broke into a run, ready to offer help, for she was and always had been a natural healer; the more urgent the problem, the more focused she was on a cure.

Antonia didn't understand why people thought she was a bit tone deaf in matters of the heart when she was simply more preoccupied by her studies. To be honest, she wasn't even sure if she believed in love, but she definitely believed in children, as did Scott, who was two years ahead of her at med school, in a long-term relationship with another doctor, Joel McKenna. They agreed they would all make terrific parents, especially if they raised the child together.

As for Sally, she had worn black ever since her husband Gary's death and had a closet filled with dark, austere dresses, cotton for spring and summer, wool for the colder seasons. With her silky black hair pinned up, and her black coat flaring out behind her, Sally looked like a ghost on evenings when she walked home from the Owens Library with her aunt, with heaps of new leaves falling from the trees as she passed by. She closed the shutters on sunshiny days and favored large dark glasses that made her expression impenetrable. When she lingered on the porch in the evenings, not wishing to go up to her lonely bedroom, she rocked back and forth in an old wicker chair as the dusk settled around her, not realizing that she was frightening the neighborhood children who came upon her in the falling dark. The children who glimpsed Sally Owens on cold, crisp evenings shared their opinion that she was a witch who could turn herself into whatever she wished to be—a cat or a crow or a she-wolf—and that they had best not talk too much or have too much fun when she had them in her sights. Most people in town considered Sally to be unpredictable and irritable and there were those who insisted it was best not to cross her or she would hex you in the blink of an eye. Sally paid no attention. Let the neighbors gossip, let them cross the street when they spied her, she couldn't care less. The Owens women had a habit of doing as they pleased no matter what people might say, and she would continue to do so.

This week, as spring neared, Sally had decided to turn out the light on the porch, which had been kept on for three hundred years, assuring women in need of assistance that they were welcome to call. Enough was enough, in Sally's estimation. Let the neighbors go elsewhere for cures. Soon after, the gate was latched, the front door bolted, and thorny vines clung to the skirts of anyone who tried to pass by on the bluestone path. If a remedy was needed, for health or love or revenge, the best clients could do was wait on the sidewalk outside the fence, hoping that Franny Owens, or more likely dear Jet, would venture out on the way to the market or the drugstore and stop long enough to listen to their woes. Perhaps, if they were lucky, one of the aunts would grant them an elixir, stored in the pantry or in the greenhouse, well out of Sally's sight. Star tulip to decipher dreams, blue beads for protection, garlic, salt, and rosemary to dispel evil, or the most sought-after cure, Love Potion Number Nine, which consisted of anise, rosemary, honey, and cloves, all simmered for nine hours and always costing $9.99. Jet would never charge a penny more, and she made certain to remind the buyer that the spell worked best on the ninth hour of the ninth day of the ninth month. On some nights, neighborhood women stood in the dark in front of the Owens house, their hands clutching the iron fence, with jewelry or cash in their purses, in need of assistance in matters of love or health or revenge. Often the aunts were already in bed, still the women stayed, ever hopeful, and there were times when Sally had to step over them on her way to work in the morning, for some truly desperate clients fell asleep on the sidewalk, dreaming of cures they would never receive.

Sally had become so closed off that she had recently lost the ability to see the color red, a side effect of severing one's emotions. One morning she woke and that color was simply gone from the palette of her vision. Anything that had once been scarlet or crimson or cherry or coral had turned a splotchy gray. As far as Sally was concerned, good riddance. She didn't mind the loss of red in her life one bit. Who needed a color as bright and disturbing as red? Red blossoms, red heart, red magic, red love. Even though spring had begun, for Sally the month of March was muted and blurry, a world of black and white. She didn't care that she could no longer spy cardinals perched in the trees, or that the red tulips in the greenhouse forced into an early bloom were the color of dust. Sally felt quite sensible observing the world through a scrim of gloom.

Though Jet didn't work in the library officially, she was a great favorite with the youngest patrons. She had the ability to know what people were thinking, and therefore understood that boys who were rude were usually fearful and that quiet girls often had a lot to say. She frequently stopped by to help young people choose books, guiding them to stories that contained magic of the best sort, practical magic that was folded into the everyday world, tales in which people stumbled into enchantments, often while walking down the street in their own hometown, or when they stepped into closets that contained other worlds, or waited for a train that would take them to a place they'd never before imagined.

"All you need is patience," Jet told Sally when she threw up her hands each time she was faced with disruptive behavior from middle-school visitors who gathered in groups, lounging at the tables as if they were in their own homes.

Sally had been an excellent mother, but nowadays she was strict and rarely smiled anymore, and children are always put off by a rigid sensibility. Her own daughters had chafed under the household rules, but the rules were the rules, and Sally would not have them be broken. She'd taped up a laminated list at the reference desk in the library. No running, no shouting, no gathering in groups, no pets, no bare feet, no crying when you didn't get the book you most wanted to read. She didn't blame the children for avoiding her, preferring Jet or Miss Hardwick. She had turned away from the world and its sorrows and there were times when she walked past a mirror and could have sworn she saw the image of her aunt Franny rather than her own. Those cold gray eyes; that frown. Surely, she had inherited Frances Owens's no-nonsense attitude; she was curt and didn't easily suffer fools. She sometimes heard Franny's voice inside her head, or worse, she heard herself speaking phrases Franny had long ago imparted to her, blunt advice that pulled no punches. *Courage or caution? Why on earth would you want to be normal? What fun would that be?*

When their parents had died, and Sally and Gillian had come to the house on Magnolia Street, they'd both been terrified of Franny, intimidated by her wild hair and her red boots and her freckled complexion and her clipped conversation, and they'd secretly called her the mean aunt. But when Sally wept in bed at night, it was Franny who came upstairs to sit beside her. She didn't offer silly, meaningless words of comfort, but instead stroked Sally's long, dark hair and told her that in the morning they would have chocolate cake for breakfast, and they always did.

Although Sally considered herself to be a logical woman, she knew there was more to this world than could be seen with the naked eye. Ever since childhood she'd been convinced that a dark brand of bad luck followed at her heels, a wicked spell she couldn't diffuse, not with sage or garlic or salt. It was after her, there was no doubt about it. The Owens curse stalked her even though she was determined to avoid magic. Oh, she had tried, but no matter how ordinary her life might be, the curse hung on as if it were an obstinate dog that refused to loosen its bite even when she tried to shake it off. Now, as Sally and Jet walked through town, Sally realized that a little dog was, indeed, pursuing them, as though it had read her mind, validating her theory that a hex and a wild dog were equally difficult to be rid of. The one following them was a scraggly white thing with sharp black eyes. Sally soon recognized it as the stray that had been hanging around trash barrels behind the library for several days, one wily enough to escape every time animal control was called in.

"I can't seem to catch that dog," Sally said. Now that her girls were grown, with Kylie a sophomore and Antonia in her second year of medical school, both at Harvard, and with Antonia pregnant, nearly a mother herself, Sally often stayed at the library after hours. What was the point of leaving? She would have preferred to eat a sandwich at her desk and would likely have forgotten to come home entirely, choosing to work through the night, had Jet not come for her at the end of the day.

"I think it's Daisy," Jet said thoughtfully as she observed the dog.

Once you knew that death was walking alongside you, things came into focus, as they now did for Jet. With only seven days left she had best pay attention to every detail. She had already taken note that the lines on her right palm, showing the fate that she'd been given, and those on the left hand, the fate she had made for herself, were exactly the same; they had converged, as they always do at the end of a life. Jet's gift of the sight had intensified. She could envision the dog's heart beating under its tangled fur, just as she saw the slow unfolding of black leaves on the last surviving elm trees in Essex County. The Reverend Willard had owned a dog resembling this one before he'd been forced into residing at the retirement home on Endicott Street. The Willards and the Owenses were all descendants of a witch-finder and a witch, John Hathorne and Maria Owens on the Owens' side, and a granddaughter of Hathorne and a relation of John Proctor, hanged as a witch when he tried to protect an innocent woman brought to trial, on the Willards' side. Although there had been centuries of distrust, Jet had managed to change that after her beloved Levi Willard's death when she knocked at the Reverend's door, refusing to allow him to turn her away until they set the situation right. The Reverend had passed his hundredth birthday and could no longer care for himself, let alone a dog, and it was said that his little Maltese had run off and was now dodging around town, eating from garbage cans, sleeping on porches, begging for food from children exiting the school bus. Wary, the dog ducked beneath the thickets, but Jet stopped and waved cheerfully. "Come here, Daisy," she called. "I think she belongs to the Reverend."

"You don't want a dog," Sally reminded her aunt. "You're a cat person."

True enough. Jet had had a series of adored black cats when she was younger, all named for birds, including Magpie and Goose and Crow. Yet when Daisy, if indeed it was she, began to approach, Jet felt something prick her heart. She bent to pick up the dog and when she held it she could feel its jumpy heartbeat next to her own. She remembered being told that you didn't choose a familiar, it chose you. In truth, Jet felt comforted by Daisy's presence. Life of any sort was marvelous. She saw that now.

"Are you sure?" Jet murmured to the dog. She had only a few days left, after all, and couldn't pledge to oversee Daisy's future. All the same, the Reverend's dog settled in against her, clearly pleased to be carried along, although it didn't make eye contact. That was curious. A familiar saw inside you. It was then Jet realized she was only a temporary caretaker. Daisy was meant for someone else.

"Here we go." Sally's tone was gloomy. She had no patience for anything these days. Although she looked far younger than her age, likely due to the miraculous black soap the Owenses had concocted from a family recipe since the 1600s, when it had been useful in treating those infected with the plague in a time when simply washing one's hands made a world of difference, with ingredients that were disinfectants, including rosemary, lavender, and mint. Sally distrusted the world, an attitude that aged a person beyond her years. Soap couldn't fix that. "One thing will lead to another," Sally told her aunt, "and the end result will likely be fleas."

Jet patted the dog and didn't argue. She had always loved the month of March, though it was wild and unpredictable, evoking hope as the wintry brown world began to flourish. Jet felt extremely grateful to experience it this one last time. Everything was greening and the hedges had a fresh, peppery scent. There was a chill in the blue air, yet daffodils were pushing up through the damp, black earth, and in the Owenses' garden they had already bloomed. Oh, what a beautiful, unexpected world this was.

"Be prepared. Franny will have a fit if you bring a dog home,"

Sally continued to warn her aunt as they walked along past the Black Rabbit Inn. Tonight the special was chicken pot pie, but most of the regulars were concentrating on whiskey. A fiddler was playing enthusiastically in the bar. It was the kind of rousing, rowdy song Gary would have liked. Once he'd moved to Massachusetts, he'd missed the desert where he'd grown up, and the untamed country he'd known. He enjoyed standing outside with Sally before they went to bed to gaze at the stars and point out constellations, even in the dead of winter. Gary had never believed in curses or bad luck, and he'd considered fairy tales to be stories for children. Sally had loved his fearless attitude and the way he'd made her feel so safe, even though she knew that the world was, and always had been, a dangerous place. What was wicked grew with the ferocity of the bramble; cut it down, and it rose up again with even deeper roots.

Now, on the way home, Sally linked an arm through Jet's. She always softened when in the presence of her aunt Jet, who was the most kindhearted among them. Gillian had voiced a hunch that there must be an irregularity in Jet's DNA, and some unexpected genes had rendered her a huge heart, absent in most of their relations. Gillian should know; she worked in a lab at MIT researching genetics, a subject that had come to obsess her. She was convinced that somewhere in their past there had been an ancestor who had been as kind as their aunt, perhaps the same person from whom Jet had inherited her striking good looks.

Warmer weather was predicted for the rest of the week, and Jet's seven days marked the start of a season that was always a delight in Massachusetts. All through the long winter people waited for a sign for the first surge of spring. The green bark of a lilac. The murmur of a dove in the yard. While there was still a scrim of ice on Leech Lake, people came down with spring fever that made them act as if they were young again; they took risks, they stayed out late, they fell in love unexpectedly. This was the month when teams began to play softball in the high school field and music flooded out from open windows as children practiced scales at pianos that had been ignored all winter long. There was an extra hour of daylight, so glorious and so needed after the many months of darkness.

Jet could hear the hum of the first of the season's bees as they neared the house on Magnolia Street with its black shutters and tilted roof slates and dozens of windows made of old, wavering green glass. She came to a halt when they turned a corner, well aware that people had long believed that whenever bees swarmed outside a house, a resident was sure to die. Hundreds were now circling the porch in a buzzing whirlwind of yellow. There was Franny, out in the chilly dusk without a coat, a broom in her hands, doing her best to bat them away.

"You're going to be stung!" Sally called to her tall, fearsome aunt who had always shone with a beauty all her own. Franny Owens was in her eighties but her hair had a red tone, and although people whispered she had it dyed in a salon in Boston or magicked away the gray with a mixture of blood and potent herbs, all it took to keep the color was a rinse of madder root every once in a while.

Jet set down the dog and went directly to her sister. "We need the bees," Jet said in a no-nonsense voice. She pried the broom from Franny's hands and let it drop to the ground. "Franny, that's enough."

The sisters gazed into one another's eyes. They'd always been able to read each other but now Franny was baffled by what she saw. She glimpsed herself in the future, there in their garden alone, and then, with a quickening breath, she understood.

"No," she said.

This is how it happened, on an ordinary night when Franny had planned to read a book after supper, she had Virginia Woolf's *The Waves* on her night table, then go early to bed. She had assumed life would remain as it was, with nothing daring to change, but all at once it had become an anguished night of bees, of a mad swarm around them, of her sister already wrested away from her, gazing into the world to come that was written in the constellations spinning above them. There was the Winter Triangle, which would fade away by the end of the month, as it always did at this time of year. Franny understood this was how loss began. She had been here before, but then, like anyone else, she had forgotten this is what happened, that things ended when you least expected them to, that you could not protect those you loved from nature and fate.

Sally had come up beside her aunts. She would likely have to call the exterminator in the morning, for once bees got into a house they might just decide to stay there and then honey would be dripping through the ceiling and down the walls. In the garden, the sprouting herbs were already letting off clouds of scent: marjoram, lavender, rosemary. There was always plenty of Spanish garlic, traditional to harvest in great abundance. There was chickweed, and feverfew, and juniper with the last of its berries. The dog was sniffing around, making itself at home.

"Did you see what we picked up on the way home?" Sally asked Franny. When her aunt looked blank, Sally laughed. Franny did have a way of ignoring the townspeople, as did she, and she'd likely never noticed the dog before. "Daisy. The Reverend's dog?"

"To hell with the Reverend's dog," Franny said, turning to stalk past the plumy weeds on her way into the rear of the garden where they kept a beehive. It was empty. When she tapped on the sides it rattled and then Franny knew. Their very own bees had announced the death to come. There was no denying what would happen. One of their family. One of their own.

"I told you she wouldn't be happy about this." Sally glared at the dog, but Jet was no longer beside her. She had gone after her sister, her dear Franny, who was as different from her as night was from day, but whom she had always loved beyond all reason.

On the first day of her last week on earth, Jet went to New York, taking the train from Boston's South Station. Because it was a lovely afternoon when she arrived in Manhattan, she walked uptown to the Plaza Hotel on Fifth Avenue and Fifty-Ninth Street. She'd brought Daisy along, tucked into a shoulder bag on the train, now leashed and free to gleefully smell the scents that greeted her when they left Penn Station. Jet had made this trip once a month for the past sixty years, and the older employees who worked at the hotel always recognized her and were happy to greet her. When she'd first come here, the Oak Room had refused to serve women at lunch, but that all changed in 1969 when Betty Friedan and fifteen other members of National Organization for Women decided enough was enough and refused to leave. For years afterward, Jet would frequent the Oak Bar, lingering until it was time to go upstairs for the one night she waited for all month long.

When she walked in with the dog under her arm, no one behind the desk asked any questions. They never had. She was always without a suitcase, and simply packed a nightgown, some undergarments, and a change of clothes into her purse. This time she had brought along a tote bag containing dog food. She always paid cash.

More than six decades earlier, Jet had been a bewitching, dark-haired girl who had registered at this very hotel in order to do away with herself. She had lost her first love, Levi, the Reverend's son, in a car accident that seemed triggered by the curse, a horrific collision that had claimed her parents' lives as well. She'd seen no reason to go on and was certain that the world no longer was a place in which she wished to reside.

Her fate changed when a young bellman noticed she had checked into the Plaza without a suitcase. People without luggage most often had one of two things in mind: an affair or suicide, although occasionally there was a third possibility when a novelist arrived, desperate for inspiration, and always asking for the cheapest room. Rafael Correa was the bellman who had noticed Jet. He had stopped her, begging her to reconsider her plans and have room service with him instead. Jet told him from the start she would never belong to him; she mentioned a curse, but he was head over heels after their first encounter, and he didn't argue. When you save someone's life, they belong to you, no matter what they might say.

This time Jet had reserved the room for two nights. If she didn't do as she pleased this week, when would she ever? The one good thing about her death to come was that the curse could no longer claim the man she loved. She had taken a suite, damn the expense, and for two nights and days they could pretend they lived together, or maybe it wasn't pretense, maybe this was the realest time they had ever known.

Rafael had been a principal of a high school in Queens and since his retirement he had tutored ESL students in his neighborhood. He had a wide social circle, but he went home alone every night. Despite his friends' concerns about the solitary life he led, Rafael never married. He'd wanted more, but it wasn't possible, and in many ways they were more fortunate than most. They never quarreled and any disagreements were brief; they wanted to make the best of the time they had together and use it wisely. But when Rafael arrived at the Plaza, his instinct that there was bad news kicked in, left over from his years as a principal. For one thing, Jet had brought a stray dog along, a white scruffy pup who sat at Rafael's feet when he took off his shoes, staring into his eyes as if he were a long-lost friend.

"She'll cheer you up," Jet said.

"All I need is you," Rafael said mournfully, sensing that something wasn't right.

Jet sat down beside him and took his hand. For all these years she had been protecting Rafael every time she claimed she didn't love him, but now Jet told him the truth. She had loved him and only him.

"I know," Rafael assured her.

"And that's why Daisy is here. She'll be a companion."

That was when he'd known something terrible and unbreakable was about to befall them. They considered getting married that afternoon, since the curse could no longer do them any harm, but in the end they decided they didn't need a witness to their love. Instead, they did things any couple might have done on an ordinary day. That was what Jet wanted most. To be just another couple on the streets of New York. Oh, she knew it wasn't really possible, it never had been, but during this last time they spent together, she wanted them to be people who weren't afraid of love, who believed that the future belonged to them.

The next morning they walked through Central Park to Belvedere Castle, with Daisy tugging at her leash. From the height of the castle's craggy ledge they observed the greening canopy below. The sky turned lemon-colored, and they huddled in the castle during a quick blast of rain. Then they went arm in arm to the Boathouse for brunch, the dog hidden in Jet's purse and fed bits of toast. Jet went so far as to kiss Rafael in public, curse be damned. After that, they took the subway to Queens so that Jet could see the high school in Forest Hills where Rafael had worked. He'd had a life without her, he'd made a world for himself as a teacher and as a man, but on the train back into Manhattan she could see how lonely he would be once she was gone.

In the evening, they left the dog at the hotel and took a taxi to Waverly Place, where they sat holding hands at the best Italian restaurant in the Village. When they could eat and drink no more, they did so anyway, and ordered the famous olive oil cake with gelato. There was a mackerel sky dotted with clouds as they walked down Greenwich Avenue to number 44, the small townhouse where Jet had lived with Franny and their much-loved brother Vincent when they were young and anything seemed possible. The literary agent who'd had an office there after they'd moved out was now sadly gone, but there were still scraggly lilacs in the tiny yard. Jet closed her eyes and remembered everything. Her room on the third floor where she read so many novels, including *Wuthering Heights*, which she devoured three times over, Franny sitting at the kitchen table sorting out how to pay the bills when she was all of nineteen, Vincent playing guitar in his room, his reedy voice echoing.

When Jet and Rafael looked at each other in bed, they saw one another as they had been when they were young and beautiful, both with dark hair and flushed olive skin. Perhaps this was why they were still burning for each other. Or perhaps it was that the last time is beautiful and somber when it's finally understood every instant counts.

Whenever they were together, Jet thought of their first time, when she was certain that she'd lost everything and that life wasn't worth living. Each time Jet encountered young women crying in the library, or on the porch of the house on Magnolia Street, convinced there was no point in going on, she always told them that you never knew who might walk through the door. Fate worked that way. Some of what was to come was fixed, true enough, as shown in the lines on your right hand. But the lines on your left hand changed, day by day, for that was the fate you made for yourself.

When it was time to leave, Jet couldn't bring herself to wake Rafael. She wished she could stay all week, but if she remained with him for too long her heart would break; it was breaking already. She watched him sleep for a few moments, grateful to have known love despite the curse. She wasn't normal, she never could be, but Rafael hadn't seemed to mind. She left a note on the bedside table, a quote from her favorite poet. Rafael would understand. He always had. They would never be parted.

Unable are the Loved to die
For Love is Immortality.

On the train back to Boston, Daisy sat on Jet's lap and gazed out the window as they passed through the pale green marshes in Connecticut. "Service dog," Jet told the conductor, and who would argue with such a dear, old lady who appeared to be crying black tears, the tears that witches cry no matter that lore says they have no hearts and are incapable of love. There were osprey nests on the tallest utility poles and one huge bird with a wingspan of five feet swooped over the lowering tide in search of fish. Tall tawny grass was growing in the rivulets, and the clouds reflected in the water. Had there ever been a marsh as beautiful?

Everything you did for the last time was a miracle, no matter how ordinary. Jet had been beside Rafael while he brushed his teeth, she had taken the subway with him to Queens, she had seen the way he looked at her, as if nothing else mattered. This is the way their real life might have been if she hadn't been forced to keep vigil over the curse.

"You don't have to worry about the curse anymore," she'd reassured him as they'd walked along the landscape of their past, so that it almost seemed as if they were young again and had all the time in the world.

"I was never worried," Rafael told her. "I've been lucky and I know it."

Franny came in from the garden with a basket of fresh parsley and mint. She stopped when she saw that her sister had returned. She could see an ashy shadow around Jet, visible only if you knew what death looked like, if you dared to peer into a black mirror and see the future of those you loved most. It was the evening of the second day and by tomorrow the color of the shadow would be more ink than ash.

"Back at last," Franny said crisply. Her heart was breaking, but what good would it do to let it show?

"Here I am," Jet replied. "Yours for the next five days."

Mine alone, Franny thought. *Beautiful, darling, dear sister*. "Then we should make supper," she said. *We should make the most of every minute we have.*

They spent nearly every moment together during the next few days, linked in thought and deed, as sisters often are. Who can you trust if not your sister? Who knows your story better than she? If you saw one Owens sister at the grocery, the other would be right beside her. If one was working in the garden, making certain the rows of herbs were weeded, her sister would be there as well, carrying a basket to collect the dandelion greens. When Jet went to visit Reverend Willard at the retirement home, Franny tagged along, even though she was the least social creature in town and had certainly never visited anyone there before. Daisy was with them, and no one at the retirement home considered giving them any trouble concerning a canine visitor, knowing if they did they'd have Franny to deal with, who had already cast a domination spell in the entry hall to ensure that people on the premises would bend to her will.

The Reverend had performed the marriage ceremony for Franny and her beloved Haylin Walker soon after Haylin was diagnosed with cancer, and due to that kindness, Franny had made allowances for the way he'd treated Jet when she was a girl, which, in point of fact, had been all but unforgivable. But forgiveness was one thing, a social call was another, and Franny simply couldn't fathom holding a cheerful conversation wedged in between emergency alerts going off for failing residents and Reverend Willard's labored breathing, for spring always affected his asthma. Franny remained on the threshold while Jet went to sit at the Reverend's bedside. That was as social as Franny got. She pursed her lips as she gazed at Reverend Willard. Things didn't look good for the old man and he had been despondent for some time. Once you are over a hundred you stop counting days. Once you've lost your son you glimpse death everywhere. All the same the Reverend let out a whoop when Daisy jumped onto his bed.

"Here's my girl." He patted the dog, wholly absorbed, turning to Jet only when she politely coughed. "And my other girl!"

"She's a grown woman." Franny reminded the Reverend, still not venturing any farther than the doorway. "An old one at that."

One who was spending precious time with a man who had made her life miserable long ago, but that was clearly water under the bridge to everyone but Franny. The Reverend hadn't wanted his son to have any dealings with an Owens girl because of her family, but he'd realized he'd been a bigot and over these many years he'd come to think of Jet as a daughter. Today she looked sadder than usual.

"Am I dying?" he asked her. They had loved the same person, that was their lasting bond.

"Not yet," Jet told him. "It's me this time."

"So, you won't be coming to visit anymore?" The Reverend was struck by emotion, his eyes and nose running.

"No." Jet smiled at him with tenderness. "That will be Franny from now on."

"What!" Franny said sharply. She'd only been half listening, but she'd paid attention when she heard her sister's remark. "Not me. I'm not one for social calls."

"Then one of my grand-nieces will come," Jet reassured the Reverend. "Kylie or Antonia. Someone will always look in on you. And don't worry about Daisy. I've found her the perfect home."

As Jet was leaving, Reverend Willard seized her hand. "Make sure it's not your sister." He spoke in a low voice, eyeing the fearsome figure at the door who was gesturing for Jet to hurry. Jet ignored Franny rushing her and took her time. Why not? She had grown to love this old man who, if fate had taken a different route, would have been her father-in-law.

"It won't be," she promised.

"Whoever it is, she won't be as good as you."

Franny looped her arm through her sister's as they were leaving. The world was still beautiful and they stood in the front yard of the retirement home while Daisy nosed around. There were old people sitting on wooden benches, gazing at the pink-tinged sky. "Did you ever imagine you'd forgive him?" Franny asked, remembering how the Reverend had made Jet's and Levi's lives intolerable when he flatly refused to allow his son to see her. He'd been a fool who judged Jet by her family's history of witchery.

"I still can't forgive myself." Levi had loved her and she had brought the curse to him. "Forgiveness is the most difficult undertaking."

"I forgave you for being the better sister," Franny said bluntly.

"Nonsense," Jet said, and because she didn't have all the time in the world, she threw her arms around her sister even though Franny was always uncomfortable in an embrace. "Dear sister, that was always you."

On the fourth day, Jet and Franny went out to the greenhouse to read through the *Grimoire*, the thick book that was the repository of the family's magical knowledge. Their treasured *Grimoire* had been created in Essex, England, by Maria Owens's adopted mother, Hannah, a birthday gift when Maria was ten, old enough to study magic. The cover was the cool green-black skin of some strange leather that was said to be toad skin, a material that was both delicate and strong. Maria's original cures and spells could be found in these pages, learned in England and Curaçao, and it was here in this book that the original curse had been written down years after it had been set when Maria stood upon the gallows, having been judged to be a witch by the man she imagined she loved. There were also several pages written by Maria's daughter, Faith, who had assisted her mother in opening the library and a well-respected girls' school, thanks to the most loyal wealthy patron, Thomas Brattle, the treasurer of Harvard College who had helped to thwart the witchcraft trials, publicly refuting Cotton Mather's unprovable beliefs in spectral evidence, calling the entire episode a delusion, a man who was also rumored to be the father of Faith's two little girls, Avis and Violet.

The women in the following generations had added to the family's knowledge, including their cherished aunt Isabelle, who had invited Franny and Jet to Magnolia Street when they had no idea who they were. They'd been kept in the dark by their mother, Susannah, who had abandoned the family and its history when she was little more than a girl. The most recent pages in the *Grimoire* had been written over a period of fifty years by Franny and Jet, and there were remedies and enchantments Gillian had added, even though Gillian had always had less talent for magic than the others and had been mortified by her lack of skill. She was frankly jealous that magic had come to Sally so naturally, when Sally clearly had no use for such things and only craved to be normal. Sally had never written a word in the *Grimoire*. "I'm not interested," she always said when the topic of magic was broached. "I've got better things to do."

Stored beside the book was the black mirror Jet and Franny had been shown during their first summer on Magnolia Street. It was possible to see the future in this mirror, if you dared. You'd know if you had the sight when the mirror was presented; you'd see your future in bits and pieces and begin to unravel the story of your life. But stories change, depending on who tells them, and stories are nothing if you don't have someone to tell them to. Fortunately, they'd had each other. When they put the book away, they held hands and listened to the riotous birdsong in the trees. How lucky to have a sister.

They had a brother as well, one they loved dearly, the darling of their family, wild and talented, the sort of man who could do no harm and dared to fall in love when everything in their history told him he should not. That evening Jet wrote a letter to Vincent, who had disappeared after being called up to fight in Vietnam. He had managed to avoid the curse with a false death, tricking fate and setting off with his beloved William to a life that couldn't be shared with his family. Jet kept a photograph of Vincent in her bedside table drawer, along with her treasured packet of letters from Rafael. She took out her best stationery and a pen with red ink that made the white paper flush the color of roses.

Darling boy, Jet began, *we have missed you every day. Whenever you can come home, do.*

She addressed the letter to Vincent's great friend Agnes Durant, in Paris, then slipped the key to the house on Magnolia Street into the envelope. She and Franny walked through the gusty night to the post office, where the letter was sent off in the mailbox.

"Unlikely he'll get the letter," Franny chimed in. She had written to Vincent several times and had never heard a word in return, although every year she received a card from Agnes with a bright greeting—*All is fine here in France*—which she supposed meant Vincent was well.

"I don't know about that," Jet responded. "He could always find anything. He had that talent."

"When he wanted to use it," Franny sniffed. Her brother's absence still pained her. "He never found us."

"He couldn't, darling," Jet said. "There was the curse. He had William to think of."

On the fifth day, after Sally had gone off to the library, Jet turned on the porch light and threw open the door. When the news got out that Jet was available to her neighbors, a line formed along the path and down the street. People wanted cures for rashes and indigestion, enchantments for runaway daughters and for sons who had made a wrong turn, tinctures for forgetfulness and for mean-spirited husbands, and, as always, they came for love. Jet was so busy that she enlisted Franny, who grumbled but set about gathering ingredients from the garden: leaves from their ginkgo tree, one of the oldest varieties on earth, for anxiety; turmeric as an anti-inflammatory; primrose, whose essence would be pressed into an oil that helped skin conditions and lifted the spirts; echinacea, best for the common cold; lavender, to bring wayward children home. In tall glass jars in the pantry there was mandrake, belladonna, mushrooms of all sorts, blue beads, black feathers, apple seeds, the hollow bones of birds, dove's hearts. The rush lasted until five, and by the time it was through most of the daffodils had been trampled by people who wanted to make certain they got their turn bringing their problems to Jet. Before Sally arrived home to chastise them for practicing magic, Franny chased the last of the visitors from the path and once they were gone, she switched off the light. She agreed with Sally; let the porch light be turned down forevermore.

Jet sat at the table, exhausted, in need herself of a cup of Courage Tea.

"I hope you're happy," Franny said. "Half the neighborhood has been here today."

Jet smiled and poured more tea. She was, indeed, happy, and because Franny couldn't fight that, she had a cup of tea as well, for courage was what they both needed now.

On the sixth day, the aunts fell silent, in a haze of disbelief. The future was less than forty-eight hours away. Still, no one had ever called them lazy, and they made good use of their time, setting about cleaning the house, which, frankly, had not been seen to for some time, so that the woodwork and drapes were dusty and the carpets had to be taken out to the porch and beaten with a broom. It was traditional to do so after a death, to prepare for the mourners and clear out anything the deceased might wish to keep private, but knowing what they knew, they had the opportunity to complete the task together before the funeral. They covered the mirrors and opened the windows to let in fresh air. Sparrows were nesting in the shrubbery and buds had appeared on the magnolias that lined the street. The sisters packed up Jet's clothing and her collection of novels, along with the batch of letters Levi had sent her when she was a girl, mostly concerning how they might manage to meet without the Reverend catching on. There was another correspondence that Jet treasured, letters tied up with blue ribbon. These were Rafael's. She gazed at them, on the brink of tears.

"His?" Franny said. She'd never questioned Jet about her love life. Still, she'd been curious.

Jet nodded. She thought about what might have happened if Rafael hadn't taken a part-time job as a bellman while he was going to college. "Life is luck."

"That it is," Franny agreed.

When they were through with the house, and the woodwork shone and the cobwebs were all swept away with a broom, they had a picnic lunch that included splurging on all of their favorite childhood foods which were too rich for them now: jam sandwiches, scones with lavender honey, cheese and chive biscuits, sliced apples with cream. Later, they walked to the cemetery where Jet wrote out a check, the final payment for the plot beside Levi Willard, whom she had loved when she was so young and hadn't any idea of what love meant. Then they went out grocery shopping for the ingredients they needed. In the morning, when

Sally came into the kitchen, ready to head to the library, her aunts were baking a Chocolate Tipsy Cake, a family tradition for birthdays, weddings, and funerals ever since Maria Owens's time.

"Do you know how many calories are in that?" Sally said. All the same, she sat down at the table and ate the leftover batter with a spoon. "What are we celebrating?" she asked.

Sally looked exhausted, with dark bluish circles under her eyes. She worked too much and she hadn't conditioned her hair for ages, but she was still beautiful and, in the aunts' eyes, still their little girl.

"If you can't eat chocolate cake for breakfast, what is the point of being alive?" Franny said.

On the morning of the seventh day, when the ashy circle around Jet closed so that she was surrounded by a black aura and time was running out, they did exactly that. For reasons Sally could never explain to herself, nor understand, she joined her aunts at the breakfast table, and instead of her usual yogurt and blueberries, she had the biggest slice of all.

Jet insisted they all have dinner in the taproom at the Black Rabbit Inn that evening. She'd already phoned Gillian, who would fetch Kylie and Antonia and drive them up from Cambridge. Jet had made reservations as well, the rear table, far away from the fiddler who played there after six, whose mother had often come to them for a success elixir for her son, though, due to the level of his talent, there was none to be had.

"Are you certain you want them all here on the seventh day?" Franny asked with concern.

"They'll need to be here on the eighth day, won't they? I don't want you to have to handle everything alone."

Franny had little choice but to agree. She couldn't yet bring herself to think about the eighth day and a world without Jet. Perhaps just this one time, she might need help dealing with what was to come. Although the Black Rabbit certainly would not have been *her* choice for a last supper; she couldn't stand the cheerful dining room, with its red-checked tablecloths and a menu of second-rate New England food: boiled potatoes, baked cod, macaroni and cheese, always burned on top, along with salads that included only shredded iceberg lettuce, and all manner of puddings for dessert, the specialty being something called cheesecake upside-down, which the kitchen had been serving to mixed reviews for more than a hundred years.

At the close of the afternoon, before the others arrived, Jet grabbed her spring coat and set out for the library.

"Where do you think you're going?" Franny wanted to know. The truth was she didn't wish to let her sister out of her sight. The deathwatch beetle had situated itself in the linen closet on the second floor and its clacking was louder all the time. Franny had used bug spray and set out traps laced with sugar with no success. When it came down to it, she knew this was one insect it was impossible to be rid of.

"What I want most is for this to be an ordinary day," Jet explained. "On an ordinary day I'd go get Sally to be certain she left the library at a decent hour."

"Fine. But be at the inn by five. I'll bring the girls. Don't leave me stranded there."

Time was everything, and there was so little of it. Jet walked the long way around, stopping at the cemetery to visit Levi Willard, bringing a bunch of daffodils from the garden, yellow with orange centers dotted with inky black marks. She lay down in the grass next to his headstone and looked up at a sky clotted with clouds. She was beginning to say good-bye to the world, to all the things she loved, grass and sky, the lanes in town that were so shady and green, the library where she and Franny and Vincent would go on sultry days during their first summer in town. When she arrived, Sally was still working even though it was nearly five and they certainly didn't want to keep Franny waiting at the inn.

"I need fifteen minutes to close up," Sally called when Jet came through the door. Sally was in a hurry, as always, but something made her stop and gaze into Jet's eyes. They seemed darker than usual, the pale gray flecked with black. Dear Jet, whose love and good heart were constant, appeared to be quite exhausted. "Are you all right?" Sally smoothed down her aunt's hair. "Is that mud on your shoes?"

"I've been for a walk in the cemetery." On Jet's last night in the world she saw everything with clear eyes, including her beloved niece. How kindhearted Sally was. How vulnerable beneath all that bluster. Sally had been the one who had found the aunts listed in their mother's phone book, and had called clear across the country to inform them that she and Gillian would be coming to stay. Their aunts had loved them beyond measure ever since.

Sally narrowed her eyes, wondering if Jet was trying to pull a fast one. She had always been wary, certain that Jet wasn't exactly what she seemed to be. Once, in the year when she'd turned thirteen, Sally had gone so far as to follow Jet into Manhattan, breaking into a run to catch up with her outside Penn Station. Jet had surprised her by being furious.

"I want one day a month to myself," Jet had said as they stood on Eighth Avenue, nearly deafened by the roar of the traffic. "If I want to go to a museum or take a walk in Central Park, it's no one's business but my own."

Sally had been embarrassed and had quickly apologized. They'd gone to a coffee shop where Sally had been treated to an ice-cream soda, then she had taken the train home, leaving Jet to do as she pleased. But Sally had the sight, and she knew there was more to the story, then and now. She so rarely used her bloodline talents, that the sight came to her in little sparks, almost as if she'd had a slight electric shock. She blinked and took a step closer to her aunt. There was the scent of smoke and the ceiling above them was shadowed with a black smudge. Could it be that the room needed to be repainted? Hadn't they had the Merrill brothers do so only two years earlier?

"There's something you're not telling me," Sally mused.

"Gillian and the girls are joining us for the evening," Jet explained. "Isn't that a lovely surprise?"

"Why didn't you mention it this morning? I have nothing to serve for dinner other than canned soup!" Antonia was such a picky eater now that she was pregnant and Kylie was a vegetarian, and lately Sally and the aunts had mostly eaten pasta and tomato soup, quick easy meals that took no care or thought.

"We're meeting Franny and having dinner at the inn."

"Franny loathes the inn," Sally said, even more suspicious.

"We want it to be a special night," Jet explained. "We'll all be together."

"Well, then, the inn it is," Sally agreed.

While Sally saw to her end of the day's duties, Jet sat down and observed the room. She took in everything she usually would have ignored: the skittering sound of mice beneath the floorboards, the clock ticking off seconds, the wind hitting against the cloudy windows. There were fingerprints on the glass cases of the rare books, and the ceiling fan spun in a cockeyed circle. She noticed that the hems of the curtains that were original to the library were decorated with an intricate pattern of moons in every phase. Funny how she'd never seen that before; she'd never looked deeply enough. Jet gazed around the room, wondering what else she had never noticed, and there it was. The bricks directly beneath Maria's framed journal page were not fitted properly. The mortar was a dark crimson. Jet crossed the room so she might place a hand on the wall. You can live a whole lifetime without knowing what was right in front of you. Seeing has little to do with opening your eyes; it's what you feel inside that counts, it's what you know without anyone telling you.

Behind the bricks there was a steady rhythm, the pulse of a book that had been hidden for more than three hundred years. Jet loosened one of the bricks by scraping a pen against mortar. She wriggled the brick back and forth until it gave way and could be pried loose. The space behind the wall was dank and icy cold. It appeared to be empty until Jet reached her hand inside. A shiver ran through her as she brought forth a small black book. *The Book of the Raven*.

Maria Owens might have rid the world of this slim volume, for it had nearly ruined her daughter Faith's life, but to destroy a book seemed an unnatural act, especially one written by a woman of great talent and skill. Instead of burning it, Maria had come here to the library, then set to work hiding *The Book of the Raven*, a dark spell book that had brought her daughter to the left-handed side of magic long ago. She'd deposited this *Grimoire* behind the loose bricks, mixing in three drops of her blood to seal the mortar, well aware that some things should stay hidden until they were meant to be found, for the knowledge this book held was so dark it was intended for a reader who possessed the ability to handle its power. Maria had just had a child with the man she loved and was in no position to use *The Book of the Raven*. In time, however, an Owens woman would discover the book, and use it as it should be used, with love and courage.

This was that time. The seventh day. Jet's last day on earth.

When she reached for the book, the binding scalded her fingertips. She could feel the darkness within the text. She knew left-handed magic when she saw it, black magic so perilous that every page was inflamed. She thought of the time her brother, Vincent, had discovered *The Magus*, a compilation of the history of magic first published in 1801. *The Magus* had shaken the bureau drawer whenever it was locked away, as if it had a life and a mind of its own. At the turn of the century it had been deemed so fearsome that copies had been burned on bonfires in Washington Square.

The Book of the Raven had been written by the first woman to publish a book in England, Amelia Bassano. *Salve Deus Rex Judaeorum*, her volume of poems, had been written from a woman's point of view, defending Eve, thought to have caused sin in the mortal world. Bassano had gone largely unrecognized due to her gender, but that hadn't stopped her from writing. Jet had now rediscovered this second book no one but its users knew about, Amelia Bassano's private *Grimoire*, an ode to the Dark Art sometimes referred to as a Book of Shadows. It was a volume made up of equal parts love and revenge, meant to help a woman in need, a woman who'd been cursed, who was in love, who was desperate, who was at the end of her life and the end of her rope. On the very first page *Un desiderio* was written in pale blue ink. One wish. That was what the book promised to grant its reader.

Amelia Bassano was the daughter of a Jew from Venice, from a family of musicians who had lived on the outskirts of power, attached to the court of England, where she learned more than most educated men about politics and falconry and music and myth. At the age of thirteen she'd been a mistress to Lord Hunsdon, the Queen's patron of the theater, said to be Anne Boleyn's son, and she was said to have had an affair with Christopher Marlowe, who had taught her the art of writing for the theater. *Language was everything. Trust was for fools. Love came and went. Words could be stolen.* There were those who said she was the Dark Lady William Shakespeare wrote about and that it was she who taught him to write plays. There had always been rumors that he had loved her, but in this book she claimed even more. She had not only taught him how to write, she had written the plays.

The last chapter of *The Book of the Raven* was titled "How to End a Curse."

> *I didn't know that what you sent into the world came back to you threefold, and that I would be the one to suffer. To begin a curse is done with ease, to break it takes a great sacrifice.*
>
> *Everything worthwhile is dangerous.*

Jet could hear Sally returning books to the shelves in the travel section; fortunately she was too far away for her to observe Jet slip the slim volume into her coat pocket, then hastily replace the brick in the wall, her hands now stained with blood and mortar. Sally might have seen the abnormality in the wall had she been able to see the color red, but as it was, she was still disconnected from her emotions, and had walked past it daily without a glance. She'd never once noticed what was right in front of her.

Gillian and her nieces drove up from Cambridge, leaving before rush-hour traffic set in. The sky was bright and blue and the magnolias were so spectacular that people from all over the commonwealth came to gawk as soon as the buds began to bloom in creamy cups.

"Home sweet home," Gillian said when she and Antonia and Kylie unfolded themselves from her black and white Mini, which, considering how huge Antonia was in the seventh month of her pregnancy, could not have fit anything more than the three women and a tray of heirloom tomato seedlings called Blue Zebra that Gillian had brought for her aunt Jet.

Jet had always been especially fond of Gillian, despite the fact that Gilly had been a wild girl who had looked for trouble in her youth, and had made certain to find it. Sally had pulled her back from the brink, and Gillian would always be grateful to her sister.

But that was long ago, and Gillian had learned her lesson. She blushed when recalling her mistakes and all those dreadful men she'd taken up with; she had long ago come to understand she was entitled to kindness and comfort. Gillian had thought she was through with love, until she'd met Ben Frye. He'd been her niece's science teacher, the opposite of the men she'd gone for in the past, steady and earnest and kindhearted. She still laughed to think he'd been attracted to her because of her ability to work complex figures in her head. Halfway through her life, she'd been lucky in love. She'd avoided the curse by following the rules. *Don't live together, don't declare your love, no wedding rings, no displays of affection in public.* Ben had been puzzled and somewhat hurt by these strange traditions.

"Your aunt Franny didn't hide the fact that she was married," he reminded her.

Yes, but that was after her beloved Haylin had been diagnosed with stage four cancer, and once there was no cure the curse couldn't touch them.

"And Sally!" Ben had said. "She was married twice."

And look at her, twice a widow and brokenhearted. And look at me, without a daughter, what I want most in the world.

To do their best to trick the curse, Gillian and Ben had wed simply and quietly at the courthouse and Gillian refused to have their marriage officially recorded. Whether or not they were legally married was up for debate; certainly Gillian refused to wear a ring. They lived in a two-family house in Central Square, where Gillian resided on the ground floor, while Ben took the upstairs apartment. Whenever he asked why they must live separately—neither earned much of a salary—Ben was a science teacher at Cambridge Rindge and Latin School and MIT didn't pay lab technicians a fortune and clearly it would have made more sense to live in one apartment and rent out the other—Gillian asserted that too much togetherness was certain to ruin a relationship, especially in the Owens family. In truth, they spent most nights together, and when they didn't Ben would often spy Gillian out in their small garden, sleepless and shivering, scanning the heavens, as if she might find an answer there in the night sky above them as to how the curse had found her despite her deception.

When she saw Antonia blooming in the last trimester of her pregnancy, her red hair pinned up, her freckled skin rosy and flushed, Gillian felt her heart jolt. Her one wish was to have a daughter, but now that she was forty-three she'd begun to wonder if her inability to have a child was the work of the curse. She had been to infertility specialists at Mass General and when that didn't work, she'd begged the aunts for a cure. Franny and Jet had done their best, attempting any number of traditional botanical remedies. Myrrh, juniper berries, licorice, skullcap, pennyroyal, hemlock, chamomile flowers, unicorn root taken in small doses, butterfly weed, a tea of stinging nettle to strengthen the uterus, motherwort to bolster Gillian's immune system. She had tried red clover and evening primrose oil, and the oddly named chasteberry, along with black cohosh. She ate pomegranates and olive oil, honey and cinnamon, and had even tried the ancient ritual of bringing a toad to sleep in her bed, all to no avail. Now, to explain her brimming eyes as they stood in front of the old house, Gillian told her nieces she was affected by the spring pollen in the air. Antonia and Kylie exchanged a look, for both had read that the pollen count on this day was zero.

Franny was out on the porch waiting, which wasn't at all like her. Usually, she was the last to be ready for anything. "Come in. Come in," she called.

Antonia held on to Kylie's arm so she wouldn't trip on the bluestone path that led through the falling shadows. "Why do they keeping turning off the porch light?" Antonia muttered.

"That's your mother's decision," Gillian informed them. "No neighbors need come to call."

"Call for what?" Kylie asked. The family had kept secrets from Kylie and Antonia, at Sally's insistence. To them, magic was little more than a story in a book of fairy tales.

A small dog came out, yapping at them.

"What's going on here?" Antonia wanted to know. "Who is this creature?"

It was explained that Jet was watching over Reverend Willard's dog, and that she had gone to fetch Sally and would meet them at the inn. The tomato seedlings were left in the garden, and they all traipsed into the kitchen, where half a Chocolate Tipsy Cake sat on a platter on the marble counter.

"Why wait for dinner?" Gillian grinned, getting some cake

plates from the cabinet. "We can have chocolate cake as an appetizer."

"I can't eat that," Antonia scolded. "All that rum? It's much too alcoholic."

"Sorry." Gillian felt like a fool. Of course, a pregnant woman couldn't have rum, not the amount that was in this recipe. In many ways Antonia reminded her of Sally, so sure of herself, so logical and matter-of-fact, always wanting clear-cut evidence before she made a decision. "Of course you can't," Gillian apologized.

"I can," Kylie said, looping one arm around Gillian's waist. "I'll have her slice, too."

Dear Kylie, who had grown so tall so fast, reaching her full height by the time she was ten, coming to her aunt Gillian to ask in a small voice if she might be a giant. In fact, she was a true beauty, with long hair that glinted copper in certain slants of light, and gray-green eyes, but she had a nervous disposition and couldn't sit still. She had been a runner in high school and it often seemed as if she might take off at a fast clip at any given moment. Men stopped on the street when they saw her, mouths open, but she never even noticed.

Kylie ate her cake with her fingers, as she had when she was five years old, in heaven from the very first bite. She still considered Chocolate Tipsy Cake to be the best dessert in the world. She wished that Gideon were here with her. He would have probably finished the rest of the cake with ease.

"What are you thinking about?" Franny asked her great-niece. "Your face is all lit up."

"Nothing," Kylie was quick to say. She was discreet about all things, taught to be so by living in a town where people tended to judge the Owenses and gossip was rampant. Her love life was her own business, not that she was making that sort of admission to anyone, not even to members of her own family. "No one," she insisted even though Franny was giving her that stern look she always had when she didn't believe a word you said.

They had the best table in the dining room, thanks to Jet having helped the host with his love life several years ago. When the fiddler started up they could barely hear him, which was all for the best. "Yoo-hoo," Jet called when the family arrived. "We've already ordered the macaroni and cheese as a starter."

There was a great deal of hugging, but Franny was out of sorts. "Seriously? The macaroni and cheese?"

"We never eat that," Sally said, agreeing with her aunt. "It's totally unhealthy."

"Well, just tonight, as a lark," Jet said. "Just this once."

Jet was so apologetic and sweet, Franny felt guilty complaining about the food, which was known far and wide to be terrible, and she buried her head in the oversized menu, lest anyone see that her eyes were brimming with tears. She couldn't remember the last time she'd been to the inn, and most of the customers were nervous in her presence, convinced she could perceive their wrongdoings and transgressions and that they would be made to atone for thoughtless deeds by the use of witchery. One fool went so far as to send Franny a bottle of wine, hoping to win her favor, but she sent it right back, with a note scribbled on a napkin. *Be faithful to your wife and you have nothing to fear.*

Jet, on the other hand, was delighted to see her neighbors, many of whom had found their way to the Owenses' front door over the years in search of tonics and remedies, receiving their fair share of green magic, horseradish and cayenne for coughs, Fever Tea for flu, black mustard seed for those plagued by nightmares.

Several members of the waitstaff had waved, delighted to see her, for many had been clients as well.

"I wish someone had told me you were coming for dinner," Sally murmured to Gillian.

"I thought you knew. Anyway, we're here now and we're staying the night."

"I'm never included," Sally said, stealing a glance at her daughters.

"You could be if you wanted to be," Gillian said. "You're always working."

"Of course, I want to be." It was true, Sally had been more and more distant, and she regretted it. She was grouchy and had become something of a loner, and that was not who she wanted to be. "Let's kick the girls out of the attic and sleep up there." Long ago, Sally and Gillian had shared the attic; they'd sat out on the roof on summer nights counting stars.

"Don't you look wonderful," Jet said to Antonia, who frankly was relieved that there was something to eat set out on the table. She didn't understand how it was possible for her to be so hungry, but she was and she spooned up the macaroni and cheese.

"I'm uber-healthy," Antonia told her aunt. "No sugar, no coffee, no alcohol."

"You don't wish there was someone to help you when the baby comes?" Jet wanted to know.

"Women have been having babies on their own since the beginning of time, Jetty. And besides, I have Scott and Joel. We're in this together, and they're constantly on my case. I don't eat enough, apparently." Antonia took note of the worry on Jet's face. "I don't need someone special, if that's what you're thinking. I'm too busy to fall in love. Besides, I'm not even sure I believe in it."

"You will," Jet assured her. "It will make a mess of things and your life will never be the same, but it will happen. No one is immune."

It was lovely to all be together, but as time wore on, Jet realized that the beetle had followed her and was now directly beneath her chair. She could hear it chirping, more softly now, as if it barely had any energy. The time had nearly come.

Jet would never know the end of Kylie's story, her darling great-niece who had been such a charming, awkward child, who loved to work in the garden and get dirty, who borrowed Jet's novels and sprawled out on the window seat below Maria Owens's portrait to read *Wide Sargasso Sea* and *Jane Eyre*. She would never get to meet Antonia's child, or spend summer afternoons with her beloved Gillian, canning tomatoes or making soap as they did every year in the old cauldron they set up at the rear of the garden. She wouldn't get to see Sally fall in love, the sort of love that would take up her whole heart, so that she didn't hold anything back the way she had even with that wonderful Gary, the kind of love Jet had found with Rafael, despite the fact that they were forced to hide from the curse. Life was like a book, Jet thought, but one you would never finish. You would never know how people would wind up; the good often suffered and the wicked prospered and there was no explanation for the way in which fate was meted out as there was in novels. Fiction made sense of the world, perhaps that was why Jet had been a fanatical reader as a girl. When Levi Willard died, so tragically and before his time, novels had saved her. Sometimes, when the world looked especially gloomy, Jet returned to the ones that had helped her through her darkest hours. *Wuthering Heights*, *The Scarlet Letter*, and *Fahrenheit 451*, her favorite, a love letter to books.

"I'm tired." Jet explained as she called for the check. "We've had a long day."

Franny paled when she heard this. It was the evening of the seventh day, the time she had dreaded ever since the bees appeared. They left through the bar and perhaps Jet couldn't quite bear for their night to end. She stopped to order a whiskey. For what was to come, she needed strength.

"Good idea," Gillian said, calling over the bartender, a fellow named Jed who swore they had dated in high school, though Gillian, for the life of her, couldn't remember him.

"Seriously?" Sally said to Jet, disbelieving. "You don't drink."

"Now and then." Jet shrugged. "It helps me sleep." As a matter of fact, the whiskey was delightful, tasting of smoke and wood.

"Why not?" Franny, who had never once ordered anything at the bar of the Black Rabbit, relented and joined her sister in a toast. It was their last night after all. They might as well do as they pleased. "To us," Franny said.

Jet nodded. "Always and forever."

Antonia and Kylie stood at the bar, Antonia because her belly wouldn't fit in the space allotted when perched on a barstool, and Kylie to keep her company.

"Something for you, ladies?" Jed the bartender asked, though he was still gazing at Gillian.

"I'm pregnant and she's underage," Antonia answered. "So, no."

"Thanks," Kylie said to her sister. "I was just about to get my first Black Rabbit martini."

Gillian overheard and came over to order one, letting Kylie have a sip. "Happy now?" Gillian asked. The martinis at the Black Rabbit were especially dreadful.

Kylie made a face and pushed the glass away. "Why do people drink these?"

"To get drunk," Gillian said. "There's no other reason."

"Do you get the feeling something isn't right?" Antonia asked their aunt.

Gillian looked past Sally, who was paying for the drinks, to the end of the bar where the aunts were on their second round of whiskeys.

"It all ends," she said for some reason. There was no point in getting moody, so she shook her head, snapped her fingers, and grinned. "Even a night at the Black Rabbit."

By the time they turned onto Magnolia Street, the aunts were tipsy. The magnolias had bloomed early this year, the white and mauve cups of petals high above them in the dark on twisted black branches.

How lucky, Jet thought. *How I wish I had all the time in the world*.

Franny and Jet walked slowly, their arms linked, taking so long to reach their corner, Sally had a feeling of dread when she turned to look over her shoulder. Her beloved aunts were old. She'd thought they were old when she was a little girl, for back then anyone over forty had seemed ancient. Now she was nearly to the middle of her forties, likely the age the aunts had been when she and Gillian arrived, and Jet and Franny were in their eighties. Franny carried an umbrella these days for she'd be damned if she used a cane and her knee had been bothering her, despite applications of lavender oil. As for Jet, she seemed both exhausted and jittery, a worrisome combination.

"I'll just have a little rest," Jet said once they reached home.

"What is wrong with her?" Gillian asked Sally after Jet had retired to her room, the Reverend's dog at her heels. It was barely seven.

"I don't know," Sally said. "I'm worried." If she had allowed herself to call up the sight, she might have known exactly what was happening, but it had been many years since she'd accessed any magic, and like all things that aren't used, her talent had begun to waste away.

Franny reached to stroke Sally's hair, which was not at all like her. She was not the touchy-feely sort. Not one bit. "She just needs some peace and quiet."

Jet was already behind her locked bedroom door, sitting at her desk, another woman's spell book open before her, a rare occurrence, for such books were meant to be burned upon the death of the writer, unless there was a family member to inherit the text. Jet understood that the Owens family beginnings were in England, in a rural area they referred to as the first Essex County since they lived in the second, which had been named by the Pilgrims for the home across the sea they had left.

The Book of the Raven had escaped destruction since the time it had been hand-printed in London, in 1615. On the first page, in sloping script, was the name Faith Owens, for Faith had found the volume in a New York City market. *It begins at the beginning*, had been written on the very first page. Below that line there was a quote from William Shakespeare, who had written of his admiration and desire for Amelia Bassano.

Love's fire heats water, water cools not love.

How to exact revenge, how to break another's heart, how to cause a rival to fall ill, how to escape from a cruel man, how to set fires without touching a candle, how to make figures of wax and cloth and blackthorn and scarlet thread that would cause grave results to an intended enemy, how to bring on a curse, and more important, how to end it. Near the end of the book, there was a warning. *To end a curse, be prepared to give up everything.* There was always a price to pay, one higher than anyone might have imagined. All the same, there would always be women in such dire situations they were willing to yield to the left side, those who had no choice, who had been trapped, chained, reviled, cast aside, cursed.

There were blisters on Jet's fingers that had risen from touching the last page. A line of invisible writing revealed itself.

> *When you are ready and have nothing to lose. When you are unafraid. When you wish to save someone else more than you wish to save yourself.*

It was only when Jet read the last line of the curse-breaker that she realized just how dangerous the book was. The price of using it was far too dear for most practitioners. In good faith, she could not leave this book in her room for Franny to find. She wished she could be the one to break the curse, but because it was her seventh day, only someone else could complete what she had begun. She did what she must with great haste, knowing that time would not wait. She took a pot of paste she used whenever she attached samples of herbs or plants to the *Grimoire*. It was strong stuff, made of bird bones and black stones and, once it had set, was impossible to remove unless you knew the secret to doing so. She glued the last two pages together, so that the dangerous remedy would be hidden, and set a privacy spell upon the last section of the book so that no one would accidentally stumble upon it. At last, she scrawled a note that she folded in between the pages of *The Poems of Emily Dickinson*, always kept on her night table. If Franny ever did use the curse-breaker, she would have to search for it, and perhaps it would be better if *The Book of the Raven* was never found again.

Jet left the dog behind and went downstairs, and while Sally was asking Franny what might have caused Jet to retire so early, with Gillian assuring her that it was likely the effects of the whiskey, and Franny keeping her knowledge of the future to herself, Jet lifted her coat from the peg in the hallway. She could hear the deathwatch beetle clacking at her feet as she swept up Sally's set of keys to the library before stepping outside. Jet felt she had never been as wide awake nor as focused on her surroundings. The rustling of the gauzy leaves on the trees. The birds in the thickets, waking as she passed by. She hurried as fast as she could. The beautiful world was already slipping away.

Jet was gone less than an hour, the beetle following along on the dark, windy street, a shadow it was impossible to dodge. Franny was waiting at the gate when her sister returned. Daisy was beside her waiting as well, barking, comforted only when Jet lifted her up. Both Sally and Gillian had gone up to bed, sharing the attic room where they'd grown up, with Kylie and Antonia each taking spare bedrooms on the second floor that were usually considered too fancy for family, not that they ever had any other guests.

Franny had been out on the porch the entire time, pacing. "You weren't in your bed," she said accusingly. She didn't usually fuss, but her deep worry showed now.

"One last look around town. Remember the day we first came here with Vincent? When everyone on the street stared at us?"

"We were worth staring at," Franny said. "We were marvelous."

They went into the garden. There were the old wicker chairs, near the herb garden. There was the beehive, empty now. Long ago their aunt Isabelle had raised brown and white chickens and they'd loved to collect the blue speckled eggs, warm in their hands. They'd had a dozen cats, every single one black, but all had grown old and died. The greenhouse was padlocked shut and the cloudy glass shone. Everything was white as parchment in the light of the moon. They held hands and scanned the sky as pale moths flitted up from the damp grass. Once upon a time there were two sisters, as different from each other as night and day. In their family a sister was everything, your heart and soul, and here they were together on the last evening of Jet's life, grateful to be so. Oh, seven days. Oh, beautiful world. Oh, how lucky they were.

II.

The funeral was held on a bright blue morning. By now the bees were quiet, having returned to take up residence in their hive where they were working away as if the world was still the same, which, for them, perhaps, it was. The family had gathered earlier in the garden to partake in old family recipes, Honesty Cake and Courage Tea, then had walked en masse to the graveyard. When Franny and Jet and Vincent first arrived in town, more than sixty years earlier, people had, indeed, come to stand at the windows and stare. They'd been tall, moody New York teenagers dressed in black. Vincent had carried a guitar, Franny had blood-red hair that left scarlet pools on the cement when she was out in the rain, and every black cat came yowling out onto the street when Jet approached. Now, Jet was leaving, and people in town did the very same thing, stepping out of their houses to observe the family's procession to the cemetery, only this time many of their neighbors were moved to tears. Jet Owens had been a lovely person, both kind and practical, the one woman people in town could go to when their lives were in shambles or when love was out of reach.

The mourners weren't headed to the Owens family cemetery,

a small patch of land most people avoided, especially on dark nights, for Jet had decided to be buried in the town cemetery, beside Levi Willard, her first sweetheart, the Reverend's only son. Franny and Jet had seen to the arrangements together, choosing a white marble headstone. Beneath Jet's chiseled name and the date of her birth and death was a quotation that had been her favorite, written by the poet she most admired.

Unable are the Loved to die

For Love is Immortality.

Unbeknownst to Jet, Franny had added another line beneath her sister's name.

Beloved by all.

It was easy to praise Jet, and many in the gathering came forward to do so on this sorrowful day. The crowd was far larger than anyone in the family had expected. The Owens cousins from Maine were in attendance, along with family members from Boston, and a few distant cousins from New York, who were sulky and standoffish, the men known to be rakish heartbreakers, the women doctors and nurses. The town doctor, who had taken over Dr. Haylin Walker's practice, and was himself now poised to retire, recalled the packets of tea Jet left on his doorstep each New Year's Day, a blend that gave him courage. The postman stood up to confide that Miss Owens always tipped him a hundred dollars on Midsummer's Eve, reciting an incantation that she vowed would ensure he would be safe in every storm. Even the children who gathered around Jet during the library's story hour were in attendance; boys and girls held books in their hands and had tears running down their solemn faces, and several carried collections of fairy tales to set beside the gravesite, favoring Andrew Lang's *Blue Fairy Book*.

Jet had passed away on March 21, the date some people believe to be the unluckiest day of the year, Franny's birthday, a day that had always proved inauspicious for her, now more than ever. Still, March had been Jet's favorite month, and another Emily Dickinson poem had been read at the graveside, the verses shared by Antonia and Kylie, who spoke in hushed voices.

Dear March— Come in—
How glad I am—
I hoped for you before—
Put down your Hat—
You must have walked—
How out of Breath you are—
Dear March, how are you, and the Rest—
Did you leave Nature well—
Oh March, Come right upstairs with me—
I have so much to tell—

At the edge of the crowd, Rafael Correa stood alone without introducing himself. He had never encountered anyone in the Owens family, though he had been involved with Jet for more than sixty years. Rafael didn't mind that she was laid to rest beside Levi, who'd been little more than a boy when he'd met his sad fate. On a night of too much champagne, Jet had slipped, allowing that Rafael was her true love, then in a panic that she might have activated the curse, she had mixed up a concoction of vinegar and lemon juice, which she drank down in gulps to cleanse her confession. Rafael had listened in disbelief when she first told him that her family had been cursed; all the same, he'd agreed to do his best to trick the hex, a lifetime of love kept secret.

Rafael wept during the service, and came to help shovel the crumbling earth over the simple pine box. Everyone noticed him when he returned to his place at the rear of the gathering. Gillian gazed behind her to study the stranger who stood beside a stone angel that honored local boys who had fought in the Civil War. "Who do you think he is?" she asked her aunt Franny.

Franny looked over her shoulder. She knew about Rafael, of course. Jet had been quite good at keeping secrets, but once, long ago, Franny followed her sister to the Plaza Hotel, although she'd never seen Rafael before. He was handsome, even at his age, and he was grieving as a husband would. "A man in love with Jet," she told Gillian.

Sally shushed the two of them. "Must you?" she said.

Reverend Willard had been driven over from the retirement home so that he could officiate the service. There were so many of their shared relations in the town cemetery no one had ever counted them all. The Reverend was crying, even as he spoke. Jet had made it a point to stop by to visit him every day. She brought him oat biscuits on a regular basis, and, occasionally, a slice of her Chocolate Tipsy Cake that he wasn't allowed to eat. Far too sweet, the doctors said, but life was short and getting shorter, and sometimes a person needed to simply enjoy himself. Jet covered the cake with a handkerchief when she smuggled it in, and brought along a fork and a napkin. She and the Reverend always laughed to think they'd pulled one over on the nurses, who, of course, knew about the deviation in the old man's dietary regime all along, but who weren't about to argue with Jet Owens, for as lovely as she was, the family had a reputation, and considering that the Reverend was over a hundred, it was best to let him do as he pleased.

The service after the burial was brief, due to Reverend Willard's inability to stand for more than a few minutes at a time, and of course there was the appearance of the raindrops, the soft green shower Jet always called Daffodil Rain. And then it happened.

The very last speaker, a plain-spoken second cousin from Maine who thought of herself as the family historian, read a letter composed by Faith Owens.

As the rain began, the cousin read Faith's note in her flat New England speaking voice.

"We who are cursed in love are born to fight that curse in every way we can until the one among us who can break it appears. Until that time, we must love as best we can. Our fates may already be determined, but each day is ours to live as we see fit."

"What is she talking about? Who's cursed in love?" Kylie asked her sister. She was wearing the silver locket her mother had given her on her last birthday. Just last night, she had slipped in a small photograph of Jet, taken long ago when her great-aunt was a girl sitting on the rocks beside Leech Lake.

Antonia shrugged. She had been deflecting questions about her pregnancy all morning and was in a foul mood. Why did people want to pat your stomach, as if you were a dog? Why was the identity of the father so fascinating? "Your guess is as good as mine."

Antonia often didn't understand Owens family traditions, many of which seemed far more irrational than falling in love, a state of being she'd never experienced. Chasing a sparrow from the house every Midsummer's Eve instead of simply checking earlier in the day to make certain the windows were closed; concocting soap in the dark of the moon when there was perfectly good bars of the stuff to buy at the pharmacy, brewing Aunt Franny's special Courage Tea at family get-togethers; when store-bought tea bags were so much more practical; using the greenhouse to grow poisonous seedlings—such as belladonna, hemlock, black nightshade, and henbane, plants so toxic that Antonia didn't think they should be grown anywhere at all. And now here was this message from an ancestor who was convinced that the reasons for unhappiness lay in the power of a curse.

"The letter was written in the 1700s, when people believed in nonsense," Antonia told her younger sister. "I wouldn't pay it the slightest bit of attention." She knew that Kylie, a sophomore studying classics, was suggestible and sensitive, a reader of novels, which left her a target to wrought-up emotions. Right now, Kylie appeared overheated, her face flushed even though they were standing in the cool spring rain. She never revealed the skills she possessed, for her odd talents made her nervous. Her mother always looked at her sharply from the corner of her eye when Kylie seemed the least bit abnormal. She kept her uncanny abilities to herself, and never told a soul that she could glimpse an aura of color around individuals that revealed their personalities and their fates. Far worse, she could feel the pricking stab of other people's pain, and therefore avoided crowds.

Kylie had tried to follow Antonia's lead, for in a town where the Owenses were considered oddities, Antonia had always done her best to be superior. "Take that," Antonia would say cheerfully when she was at the top of her class. After receiving her acceptance to Harvard as an undergraduate, she'd worn a crimson T-shirt for an entire summer, just to make sure everyone knew where she was headed once autumn rolled around. She had also made certain to write an announcement for the local paper when she was accepted to medical school.

Kylie had tried; she had done her best to be ordinary, but that charade had always ended in failure. At one point, when she was already too old for such things, she had joined the 4-H and raised a calf for an entire season before realizing that its prescribed fate was to be sold to a butcher. She and Gideon had stolen it and brought it to an Audubon preserve where it still resided; having reached the weight of half a ton, Beanbag, called Beanie by most, had become a great favorite with the children who visited, offering handfuls of grain and stalks of grass. Kylie and Gideon still laughed about that day, how they'd risked getting into serious trouble for the sake of a calf, how he'd never thought it peculiar that she'd wanted to steal it, no matter the consequences.

"Did you ever hear Jet mention a curse?" Kylie asked her mother.

Sally was not a liar by nature, but when it came to the curse, she had her reasons for never telling her daughters about that particular portion of the Owens history. Once you knew, you could never act freely in the world again. Let them have fun and be young; there would be time enough to live in fear.

"Let's not talk about family gossip on the day of your aunt's funeral," Sally insisted. She went up to the cousin from Maine who thought she was so clever and hissed, "Bring that up again, and you won't be speaking much."

Sally could feel her frantic heart at the very mention of the curse. You can hope that the following generations will be immune to whatever plagued their ancestors, you can do your best to keep your children safe, but you can't entirely change their fate. The only ones with the potential for doing so are the individuals in question themselves, according to the choices they make. Sally had insisted that Gillian and the aunts never mention the curse, and because of this rule, her girls had grown up without its threat hanging over them. But what is meant to be will be, and truth has a way of revealing itself. It's said aloud at the most unexpected time, when defenses are down, when Honesty Cake is served, cut up on a platter, there for anyone to taste.

Antonia and Kylie walked side by side on the way home, wearing black coats, holding up wide black umbrellas to protect against the pale spring rain that was spattering down. The world was dizzy with new leaves and the scent of the rain, sweet and fresh and green. It was their task to get to the house and set up lunch before the mourners arrived. It was the sort of damp, soft weather their aunt had always loved. The striking canopy of leaves opening above them could not console the sisters as they walked back to Magnolia Street. Rather, they were even more shocked postfuneral that their aunt had been taken from them. Kylie was hunched over, a habit she'd acquired so that she didn't seem as tall as she was, nearly six feet, the same height as her imposing aunt Frances, who, in her eighties, still frightened people in the neighborhood when she walked along Main Street. Franny, however, didn't seem the least bit fearsome now. She stood holding a bunch of rain-drenched daffodils. They were Jet's favorite flower and for years children in town had called Jet the daffodil lady, for she grew hundreds in the Owenses' garden and always brought a bouquet tied with blue ribbon when she visited Levi Willard's grave. Witches were said never to cry, but Franny's face was puffy and she wore sunglasses in the rain. She could not imagine the world without her sister, who had been wounded terribly in her youth and had still managed to love more, not less.

After the service, Sally came to take Franny's arm. It was a good thing, for the world had shifted and now seemed a trickier, more slippery place. Franny accepted her niece's assistance as they trekked over the sodden ground. She was glad that one of the Merrill brothers—George, Franny thought his name was, after all these years she still got them confused—had come in his truck to drive her home, for the path was soggy and Franny felt off-kilter. Her knees were soft, as if she might collapse, not that she was the sort of person who would ever do so. Somehow, while her back was turned she had become old and had lost her husband and her sister and her dear brother, Vincent.

Once home, Franny went up to her large bedroom and closed the door before any of the cousins could trap her in conversation. Long ago, her room had belonged to her aunt Isabelle, who had always favored Franny and had insisted she be the next occupant of the best room in the house. Franny recalled getting into bed beside her sister after her beloved Haylin had passed away. She remembered how Jet had held her hand, and how the telephone had rung and dear little Sally had been on the other end of the line insisting that she and her sister, Gillian, were coming to stay. That is how love worked, Jet had assured Franny. It arrived when you least expected it. *But what happened when it disappeared*, Franny wondered as she lay in the old bed that had long ago belonged to Aunt Isabelle.

She could hear people filing into the house. The brass bell, a family heirloom set beside the door, rang as guests came up the bluestone path, bringing casseroles and Bundt cakes to be set out on willowware platters. Soon, the family was all accounted for. Gillian and that Ben Frye, whom she never wanted to introduce to anyone, but who was always ready to perform a few magic tricks if any children were gathered. Kylie and that tall fellow Gideon Barnes, a friend of hers who had been hanging around ever since they were twelve. Antonia and her med school pals, those two handsome men, Scott Morrison and Joel McKenna. Members of the library board, and neighborhood women Jet had invited into their home, no matter the weather, at whatever hour they knocked on the door in search of a cure. Franny didn't care to see a single one of them, so she stayed where she was, stretched out in bed.

Sally looked for Franny, who was nowhere to be found. She came upstairs to check on her aunt, passing by Maria's portrait on the landing. She stopped at Franny's door and called her name, but there was no answer. When Sally pushed open the door a crack and spied the rumpled figure in bed, she felt like breaking down. But as always, she pulled herself together and asked if Franny would like a sandwich or a cup of tea. Franny failed to answer; she had the blanket pulled over her head and pretended to be napping. Thankfully, Sally let her be so that she might grieve alone.

What happens next? Franny wondered. *How do I walk through this world without my sister beside me?*

Gillian was in the kitchen, putting the finishing touches on a Chocolate Tipsy Cake. Ben was helping her, measuring out the rum to mix into the last of the frosting that would be piped into a decorative border. He was concentrating hard and his face was smeared with chocolate and he was still just as handsome as he'd been when Gillian first met him, which for some reason made her feel like crying. There was a chill in the house and Gillian had the shivers, caused by both the cold and her raw emotions. "Can you find me one of Jet's sweaters?" she asked Kylie, who seemed lost and in need of an errand to run.

Kylie took the stairs up to Jet's room, pausing before she opened the door. Jet had been the one Kylie had always turned to, in good times and bad. She forced herself to go forward, into the lovely large room with floral wallpaper and white painted furniture. Jet had been a great reader, and there were books piled everywhere, even on the bureau. Kylie found a sweater for Gillian to wear, black cashmere with pearl buttons, a cardigan so carefully stored away it looked brand-new. The windows were old, green glass, but it was possible to see the lilacs when Kylie looked out, her eyes brimming with tears. *The Poems of Emily Dickinson* remained open on Jet's night table. Without thinking twice, Kylie took the volume, her aunt's favorite, knowing it was Jet's habit to read one of the poems each and every night, as if the words of that great poet equaled a prayer. Perhaps it was a habit that Kylie herself might acquire.

Rafael Correa had never been to Magnolia Street and he wanted to see where his darling Jet had lived. He walked through the gathering of Owens relatives and the neighbors who were indebted to Jet for the help she provided in their times of need. He noticed a blond woman in the kitchen wearing a sweater that had been a birthday gift he'd given Jet one year, long ago. Rafael remembered choosing it at Saks, something that would, in some small way, let Jet know what she meant to him. She'd worn it that very night, when they went to the Oak Bar at the Plaza Hotel. Their room was always reserved under an assumed name, often E. Dickinson but, occasionally, when Jet was feeling perverse, registered to N. Hawthorne, a distant relation.

At first, Rafael had been jealous of Levi Willard, even after Levi had been dead and buried for years. He'd wondered if Levi was the reason Jet could never fully commit herself to him, but in time, he'd come to understand it was because of a family curse that she feared. She'd been a dark-haired girl when they were first together, barely a woman, gentle and tender, yet she'd warned him to be careful on the night they'd met. "I'm dangerous," Jet had said. It seemed far-fetched. She had a heart-shaped serious face and silver-gray eyes and she cut her own pitch-black hair so that it was always choppy. He'd been madly in love with her in no time, but he made a solemn promise to never say so, a vow he now regretted. He would say it out loud, he would shout it, but what good would it do?

He stopped in the hall to observe the portrait of the Owens

ancestor Maria on the stairwell, staring back at him with her clear gray eyes. Despite her gaze, which seemed to track his movements, he went upstairs when no one was looking. That scruffy little white dog who'd come to New York with Jet on her last visit had been ignored ever since her death and now tagged after him, shadowing him to the topmost stair. Annoyed, Rafael did his best to chase it away. "Go on, scat," he told the dog, but there it was, escorting him along the second-floor hall, gazing up at Rafael to make certain he was following along.

It was easy to tell which was Jet's room, for she had often described it to him in great detail as they lay side by side in their hotel bed. There were the windows made of wavering glass that overlooked the garden where the daffodils bloomed in bunches of yellow and white. He could see the potting shed and the greenhouse.

When we were young, we were taught to beware of the plants that grew there, Jet had whispered. *But of course, that made us all the more interested.*

Along the porch, twisted branches of wisteria wound up toward the roof, thick with purple buds. The dog had made itself comfortable on the carpet despite Rafael's admonitions that it should get out. He had no choice but to ignore the wretched little thing. Daisy, Jet had called it. *She'll watch over you,* she'd said.

Rafael sat heavily on the edge of the bed, his head in his hands. He didn't hear Franny enter the room or know she was there until the bed sank down as she sat beside him.

"Let me apologize," Rafael began, but Franny pushed a cup of steaming hot tea into his hands. She had sneaked downstairs to make a cup for herself, but clearly the strong brew was even more necessary for this man.

"You need this," she insisted.

Rafael took a sip and recognized it immediately. Courage. Jet always gave him a box of this mixture on the first day of the year.

"The damn curse," he said.

"Didn't seem to have stopped you," Franny responded.

Rafael laughed at her matter-of-fact tone. Jet had told him Franny could stand up to anyone and anything, including the curse. He didn't realize he was still crying until Franny handed him a handkerchief. One of Jet's.

"You seem to have done just fine." Franny patted his shoulder with awkward compassion. "You knew how to love her."

"And this dog," Rafael declared, eyeing Daisy. The pup gazed back at him and for some reason he felt like weeping all over again. How could it be that this mutt understood him? How could she know his pain? "What am I supposed to do with it?"

"I suspect Jet left it for you so you wouldn't be alone. Now you're stuck with it." Franny stared at the dog. "But what of me?"

Rafael patted Franny's hand. She nodded her thanks for his attempt to comfort her, then lifted her hand away. They sat there for a while in a haze of grief until they heard a ruckus downstairs.

"Shall we?" Franny said.

"Of course."

Rafael knew he would never be in Jet's room again. He would never meet her at the Plaza Hotel or walk through the park with her on a November night or slip into bed beside her. He handed the handkerchief to Franny, who shook her head, insisting he keep it, and so he did, tucking it into the pocket of his suit jacket. There was a rush of noise from downstairs, and some stray gasps. Franny was already on her way downstairs; she was spry for someone her age, despite her bad knee, and when Rafael reached the first floor he saw what the fuss was about. There was a sparrow in the dining room, flitting from one corner to the other, settling on the iron rod that held up the damask curtains.

"But it's not Midsummer's Eve," Rafael heard a tall young woman say. It was Kylie, who on this day realized there was a good deal she didn't know about her own family. She had taken many of their traditions for granted, not asking for explanations. Husbands and wives often didn't live together, mirrors were covered with white cloths, and a sparrow came through the window every Midsummer's Eve and had to be chased out with a broom or bad luck would follow them. Now it was here, out of time and season, an unexpected guest peering down at them all with its bright eye. "I don't understand," Kylie said to her sister. "Why is it here today?"

But Rafael understood and so did Franny, who reached out her hand so that the sparrow might come to perch. She'd always had a way with birds; the natural world had beckoned to her even when she was growing up on Eighty-Ninth Street in Manhattan, when the only nature nearby was Central Park, a preplanned swath of countryside on the other side of the wall running along Fifth Avenue. It was said that the Owens girls could levitate, and that Franny in particular had the talent for rising, and often had to check herself so that she would not do so in public.

"Dear girl," Franny said to the sparrow. She could hear its heart beating and she felt quite dazed with emotion. Franny knew that heartbeat; she'd heard it all her life and had never paid much attention. It's only when you're old that you truly appreciate those you have lost.

Franny went to the window and nodded to Rafael, who came to open it. The rain had stopped, and the air was fresh; as it turned out this day in March was the most beautiful day of the year. It would be like Jet to choose such a day to be interred, so that her family would be reminded of how glorious the world was. Franny breathed in the soft air. She wanted this moment to last. She was aware that spirits could return in the form of birds to let those they'd left behind know they have not been forgotten, and also to remind those who loved them that they must let go. Franny would be so alone, but what choice did she have? The sparrow flew through the open window to perch in one of the old magnolias, and then, before anyone could blink, it was gone, as was Rafael.

He walked the long way back to his parked car, left outside the cemetery gates. The dog was trailing him, and he understood that Jet had meant for this to happen. She hadn't wanted him to be alone, so he whistled, and Daisy walked beside him so he could take her home to Queens.

"How do I do this?" Rafael said aloud.

The dog looked up at him, but they kept walking, for that seemed to be the only answer. Rafael counted twenty-five magnolias as they went along, all abloom, each one planted in the name of love, a long time ago, when there was a man who refused to believe in curses and a woman who wished she had known love when she first saw it.

III.

For many years, Vincent Owens had lived on the Île de Ré, across the bridge from La Rochelle on the west coast of France, the scene of a bloody battle between Huguenot Protestants and Catholics, an island that in the past had belonged to England and then to France. Vincent had wanted to get as far away from his old life as possible and he had succeeded. Sometimes, when he woke, he had no idea where he was, not until he looked out at the flat blue sea. His residence was on the far side of the salt marshes, past the village of La Flotte, in an old stucco house where the ivy grew wild in the garden and every room was laden with sunlight. No one knew who he was. They had no idea that he'd been broken many times, and that love had saved him.

By now he was old, but he still had the charm he'd been born with when a nurse at the hospital had been so enchanted by him she'd tried to steal him from the nursery. Vincent's thick black hair was now white, but he still wore it long, and his handsome features were the same, even though he often had a dark expression. He was tall, and his form seemed that of a younger man, for his mother had drilled all of her children on the need for good posture. A half smile crossed Vincent's face when he thought of his mother; Susannah Owens had run away from love while he had run toward it. Vincent was the sort of man who loved completely. That was what he'd had with William, and it had been worth giving up his country and his family for that sort of love. It had been worth everything.

William's heart had stopped, suddenly, in his sleep, and when it did, it was the end of a life that had been bound with Vincent's, for they were made for each other, and had made one another's lives whole. Now that his life with William was over, Vincent's existence seemed pointless. His loneliness could not be soothed by words of comfort, there were no incantations to ease his pain, nowhere to take refuge. The family curse had ruled his fate and forced him to surrender one life and begin another in which he could be safe and anonymous, but the curse meant nothing now that he had been left with only his grief to sustain him. Nights and days alike were dark, and they had been ever since the instant he lost the only man he had ever loved.

Since that time, the doors and windows had been kept shut. For months Vincent had lived in gloom and he had wanted it that way. The house echoed his distress, and should anyone happen to pass, Vincent was pleased that his home was so shrouded in ivy it appeared forbidding; no one would think to stop by. This past winter, the ivy froze, then broke into cold green shards so that the garden seemed littered with glass. The sunflowers that had always been kept in jars to dry fell to pieces, with petals falling onto tabletops and dusting the corners of every room. Vincent often didn't rise from bed until the dark was settling. He lost weight. He drank. He sat in a metal chair on the stone patio at odd hours and smoked cigarettes, which he never would have done if William had been there. William, who had loved him completely, would have taken the cigarette from his hand and scolded him. How lucky they had been; how ruined he'd become.

They had deliberately kept to themselves, as people in love often do, but in the months since William's death, the other inhabitants who had homes on the narrow, curving road at the edge of the village began to worry about their solitary neighbor. Vincent walked at night, along the cliffs, a haunted man. There was debris piling up outside his house and the mossy smell of rotting plants. The rambler roses had no buds and only black leaves, the lawn had gone to seed, the paper lanterns William strung along the deck, always so charming, had been shredded by the wind. An expat American down the lane was chosen to look in on Vincent, and was startled by the ghost of a man who faced him when he came calling. If the neighbor wasn't mistaken, the handsome old man who peered out at him was someone who used to be famous.

"Do I know you?" the neighbor asked.

Vincent had disappeared from his music career, faking his death, in exchange for the freedom to love someone. He had been in hiding from the curse for so long, he'd never expected anyone to notice him or remember that once, long ago, he'd written a song whose words nearly everyone knew. It occurred to him that he'd become a grumpy old Frenchman.

"You don't know me," he said with a scowl, and then, as soon as the door had slammed closed, he packed up the house. He took the train to Paris the following morning, wearing his black coat and cap, a single suitcase in hand, going directly to his old friend Agnes Durant's elegant house on Boulevard de la Madeleine. His song, "I Walk at Night," recorded years ago, happened to be playing on the radio when he climbed into a taxi and Vincent was stunned by how moved he was by the sound of his own youth and innocence and by the depth of the love he had to give. His one regret in life was that he had not seen his family for all these years, his daughter Regina, now gone in a tragic accident, his granddaughters Sally and Gillian, and most especially his dear sisters, of whom he often dreamed. The time he and Franny and Jet had spent at 44 Greenwich Avenue in Manhattan was the landscape he walked through during his restless nights of tossing and turning in bed, and he remembered every street, Barrow and Bedford and Jones and Christopher. He remembered the first night he had spent with William, and how Franny was there for him when he was beaten in the street on the night of the Stonewall Uprising, ready to wrap her arms around him, and how Jet had stood in the garden beneath a lilac tree on the day that the boy she'd loved had died so young.

By this time, Vincent's dear friend Agnes Durant was well over one hundred. Women in her family had lives that often spanned a century. Her great-great-grandmother, Catherine, who had left Paris for New York, was said to have lived to be a hundred and twenty, although people swore she didn't look a day over eighty. As for Agnes, she had been a great friend to Vincent and William, the one to hatch the plan for Vincent to escape the curse by dying, officially at least, and becoming someone brand-new. Now, when he arrived, she greeted him at the door, gracious as she'd ever been. "Stay for as long as you'd like," she declared.

On his very first night in Paris, Vincent left the house as soon as darkness fell, walking at night as always, finding his way past pink-tinged streetlights, through deserted parks where goats ate grass in the dark hollows. He was drawn to the Père-Lachaise Cemetery, built by Napoleon in 1804, and went there to visit William's grave, which was beside his own falsified monument, for although his own grave was empty, it was marked by a headstone upon which his name and the date when he had disappeared had been engraved. He made his way there easily, for he had always been a finder, able to locate what was missing or lost.

Once at his grave, Vincent realized he had more fans now then he'd had when he was "alive." He'd become a cult figure, a personality, even though no one knew him. All they knew was that he'd come out about his sexuality at a time when few musicians had, and fans celebrated his integrity, as well as his one and only hit song, although no one recognized him now. Vincent wore his black cap pulled down and kept his eyes lowered when anyone passed by. His admirers hadn't vandalized his headstone, as Jim Morrison fanatics had, with graffitied messages and spilled bottles of alcohol. Instead, Vincent's fans left candles that glowed in the gloaming, and white roses tied in bouquets with red ribbon; he beheld scores of love notes, more than he could count, some left out in the wind and the rain for weeks or months. People still fell in love with him, stirred by his words and his story, even though he'd been presumed dead for sixty years. His grave was a pilgrimage site for those who believed they'd been cursed in love and saw their own plight reflected in Vincent's famed song. He collected the letters left on his empty tomb, which he read while sitting on a bench. Vincent wore reading glasses now, which galled him. He was old, but he remembered how young men's blood burned when he read the notes from his grave. *I am ruined by love,* someone had scrawled in blood. *I'm still trying even though I'm burned to ash,* wrote another, quoting from the song Vincent produced when he was lovestruck and confused about his fate.

William's name had been added beside his own on the gravestone, and Vincent's fans had noticed the addition and had begun to bring flowers for William as well. Somehow it had gotten out that irises had been William's favorite, and people often left stems of purple or yellow or ice-white blooms, named for the messenger of the gods who could travel freely back and forth to the underworld. When Iris wished to deliver a message, she could become a shape-shifter and take on the form of someone known to the mortal. *Know me, accept me, hear what I have to tell you.*

On this evening, Vincent wore the black overcoat given to him by William on the last Valentine's Day they had spent together. They were romantics who believed in love. The coat was meant to replace one Vincent had worn as a younger man and he adored this new, cashmere version. He kept his hands in his pockets, for the truth was he had a tremor in his hands that gave away his age. By the end of the evening, he seemed to have acquired a dog, or rather, the dog had acquired him, following at a distance at first, then side by side when Vincent shortened his usual long strides so the dog could catch up. They were an unlikely duo. This dog was the opposite of Harry, the German shepherd dog of Vincent's youth, a dignified creature who had lived out his last years on the porch of the Owens house on Magnolia Street after Vincent disappeared, leaving his post only to follow Franny's husband as he attended to his rounds, the last physician in town to make house calls.

The stray dog was a comic mix involving a corgi and half a dozen other breeds, a clown who jumped up on gravestones during their walk in the cemetery. Vincent decided to call the stray Dodger, in praise of his ability to have clearly lived for so long on the streets of Paris without being run over. Soon enough, Dodger wouldn't leave his side, and Vincent wondered if William had sent his new companion to him to make certain he wasn't alone.

When Vincent returned to the house, he went to bed in the chilly, elegant guest room with Dodger beside him on the crisp linen sheets, snuffling and stretched out as if he'd always lived a privileged existence. It was in those early morning hours that Jet came to Vincent in a dream, so real and present she took his breath away. She was young and beautiful, with her choppy black hair and her black eyebrows shaped like wings, wearing jeans and a black sweater. Vincent and his sisters had been able to communicate without speech when they were young.

Dear boy, she said in his dream. *It's time.* In her hands she held a map, one it was impossible for Vincent to read. *It's a treasure map*, Jet told him just before he woke. *When they find the lock, you have the key*.

At breakfast the next morning, Agnes Durant had forsaken wearing one of her sleek black dresses, and simply appeared in a bathrobe. She'd come down early to tell Vincent about his sister's death, having received a phone call from one of her cousins in New York. As it turned out, there was no need for her to inform Vincent of his loss. He already knew. He'd woken in tears from his dream, aware that his sister was gone. The world already seemed darker without her. Vincent wept black tears that morning, overwhelmed by Jet's passing. Agnes merely bowed her head in sympathy, then poured them two cups of Courage Tea, which they both needed. When Vincent steadied himself, he told Agnes about his dream, how beautiful Jet had been, just as she'd been that first summer when they'd gone to visit their aunt Isabelle in Massachusetts and discovered who they were. What was the treasure he was meant to find? What was the key? Agnes poured more tea and considered.

"A map is not for those who stay in one place," she told him. "You have the sight. Use it."

Dodger hopped onto Vincent's lap at the breakfast table—the dog could be a clown, but he was empathetic and could chart his new owner's moods—and Vincent stroked his head as he thought about his dream. A treasure map signified he was meant to find something, although he had no idea what that might be. Later that afternoon, when the post arrived, there was the letter with Jet's familiar sloping handwriting, written the day before she died. Vincent stood by the window and read his sister's last message to him. *I could not love you more. Come home if you wish. You have always been able to find the way.* Inside the envelope was the key to the front door of the house on Magnolia Street. He threaded the key through a silver chain he wore, looped around his neck. The key grazed his heart and he could feel its pressure and its warmth. He had not used the sight in more than fifty years, but he understood that this was the key in his dream.

The harsh sunlight of the day hurt his eyes and his battered soul; he winced in the glare of the day and waited for dusk before making his way to the stationery store where he bought a creamy white card and envelope edged in black. Paris was so beautiful at this violet hour that his heart ached. Dodger waited for him outside the shop while he made his purchase, then together they walked to the Tuileries, where they sat in the garden near the playground. The view was lovely here, with shafts of orange light streaming through the plane trees as the day fell away. The voices of children rose and fell in their last hour of play. The clouds moved slowly above them, turning gold and then red and finally ink blue. Time had not moved as slowly. It had been a whirlwind, and Vincent had been caught up in it. Had he really thought they'd be young forever? What was over, was over. What was to come was just beginning. He had written to his sisters after

William's passing. But he'd remained in hiding, not disclosing his whereabouts, used to being guarded. Now he wrote again, this time to one sister alone.

My darling Franny. I'm sorry I wasn't there for Jet. I was gone for all of it, and I have missed you.

On his way back to Agnes Durant's house, Vincent stopped at the post office and tapped on the window. The postman, who ignored most people, and could be downright rude, came to open the door for Vincent as if enchanted. Vincent still affected people that way, without even trying. At the last moment, before mailing the note to Franny, Vincent jotted down Madame Durant's address on the back of the envelope. Just in case he was meant to be found. There was no point in being vigilant anymore now that William was gone. He could peel away all of his deceit.

He decided to walk to a shop he'd discovered years ago, Amulette, set on a small winding street on the Left Bank beyond the Île de la Cité. It was a plain-looking shop, with a few books messily stacked in the window. If a passerby didn't bother to read the titles on the spines, he might think it to be an ordinary junk store that featured old volumes and antiques. But *The Magus* was there, in plain sight for anyone who stopped long enough to peer through the glass. This was the book that had first introduced Vincent to magic when he was young. He'd been a boy when a vender sold it to him, warning him that once he opened *The Magus* his life would never be the same.

Dodger accompanied him inside. Bells rang and there was the scent of mint, the green-black fresh aroma that signaled the start of spring in Paris, though the weather could still be blustery. A young handsome man was at the counter. He knew who Vincent was, everyone who practiced magic did, but in this shop it was a courtesy to give people their privacy.

"What can we do for you, monsieur?" the clerk asked.

You can set back time, Vincent thought. *You can make me twenty again. You can bring William and my sister back from the dead.*

Life all happened so quickly; people tell you it will, but you won't believe it until it happens to you. Cry all you want, being young will slip through your hands and you will be left standing there, you who were once so young, not recognizing yourself or your life.

"I'd like a mirror," Vincent said, already reaching for his wallet.

The clerk smiled. Vincent was still exceedingly handsome, of course he would want to gaze at himself. But Vincent shook his head when the clerk brought out a hand mirror. "A black one."

A black mirror was much more expensive and not for the faint-hearted. It was used for scrying, to glimpse what was to come. Only those who could see into the future would be able to use such an item. In Amulette, these things were kept in a locked drawer in the back of the shop.

"Perfect," Vincent said when the black mirror was at last presented to him.

The clerk wrapped Vincent's purchase in three sheets of brown paper, for safety's sake. Vincent carried it under his arm as he walked back to Agnes's house. The night was dark and for the first time in months, Vincent felt alive. Something was about to happen. It was beginning all over again, he could sense it in his bones. He'd felt this way on the bus to their aunt Isabelle's house when they were young, and when he'd first walked through the streets of Greenwich Village, and when he fell in love.

When Vincent arrived back at the apartment, Agnes was in the parlor having a glass of Pineau des Charentes, as she did each evening. She took one look at the parcel he carried and instantly knew what was inside.

"Are you sure about this?" she asked.

Black mirrors were dangerous. Look into one and you could never forget what you'd seen.

Vincent shrugged. "Who can be sure about anything?"

"That's the spirit," his old friend agreed wholeheartedly. Why not take a chance as long as you were still alive? At this age there wasn't much more to lose, only the beautiful world, only every morning and night.

They had a quick dinner, and then Vincent excused himself and went up to the guest room. He sat at the dressing table, seized a pair of scissors, and cut the string to unwrap the mirror, which he placed on the walnut table. He thought about the first time he'd looked into a black mirror, in the greenhouse of the Owens home in Massachusetts with his aunt Isabelle beside him. It was the first time he had truly seen who he was.

He used a handkerchief to clean the dust from the mirror, then gazed down. There was a black book and a girl he didn't recognize. Left-handed magic arose in a circle of smoke, the brand of the Art he'd been attracted to as a younger man. He'd been wise to give it up, yet he remembered the dark side's pull. It was there once again. Something was about to happen. Something that hadn't happened for years. The mirror told him that he would soon see his dear sister Franny, his protector from the time he'd been born, his coconspirator in all things, the person he'd missed most during his disappearance. A mirror such as this always told the truth about a person's fate, and that was why only a few had the courage to look. The future was an unsteady place where anything might happen, but Vincent intended to look no matter the cost. Whatever his flaws might have been, he had always had courage.

That was what he needed now as he observed the inside story of everything that would come to be.

He would see those he loved and the past would come back to him in three ways. His fate was before him and he now had the key. There was the treasure map, there was the treasure, there was the curse that had afflicted them all.

IV.

April had arrived, the most beautiful month of the year, but time had stood still for Franny ever since the funeral. It was the spring of sorrow when the beautiful world had turned dark. There was a scrim of ash over everything, covering the trees; black leaves fell onto sidewalks all over town. Death was in the air and the birds were hushed. Lilacs refused to bloom. People went through the cemetery gates to leave tokens of their respect on Jet's grave: apples, mint, sage, blue ribbons, photographs of babies who had grown up to be men and women because of Jet's tonics, wedding pictures of those who had found love after knocking at her door. Now that she was gone, there was no one to go to for help. On the day after her funeral, Franny brought out a stepladder and removed the bulb from the porch light.

"We can just keep it turned off," Sally suggested, but Franny wanted to make certain no one accidentally switched on the light. She might have offered her expertise in matters of the heart, as Jet had done, but she no longer had reason to do so. Without her sister, magic meant very little to her, and the problems of her neighbors even less. She went to bed before it was dark. She refused the dinners Sally insisted upon offering her. She saw death everywhere. Mice neighborhood cats had left on the doorstep. Spiders curled up in corners. Sparrows fallen from the sky.

The weather was warming, yet Franny had on her winter coat and her red boots when she went out to walk. It was a tradition among the Owens women to wear such footwear, and the wearing of red shoes had a long history. Louis XIV favored red heels to show his right to be king, and Kings Edward IV and Henry VIII were buried in red shoes. Dyed with madder or cochineal, they were worn by Roman senators as well, but it was women who dealt in magic who were best known for donning red shoes, and the idea of a scarlet woman who did as she pleased made wearing red shoes an act of defiance; they might just take the wearer places she would not otherwise go.

Though she was warmly dressed, Franny continued to be chilled to the bone. She was stuck in the past and she didn't care to go forward. She wished there was a door to open so that she might step back through time. The best she could do was to make her way into the woods, past the tangled saplings, down to Leech Lake, which was vast and blue, aglitter in the brilliance of the afternoon light. Franny and Jet and their brother, Vincent, came to swim here when they were young, splashing each other and dissolving into laughter when the toads followed Franny, gathering round as if she were their queen. Vincent was as brash as he was charming. He always dared Jet and Franny to leap from the highest ledge, and when his sisters refused, for they'd been warned by their mother to always avoid water, Vincent dove off the cliff by himself. Filled with courage and youth he would make a mad swan dive even though he knew he would land hard on the calm surface of the water, for the Owens bloodline didn't allow them to sink. They floated no matter what, as did all witches, which was both their salvation and their downfall, for it revealed who they were.

In their youth, only Vincent had been drawn to magic, why, he was made for it, while his sisters were still alarmed by their heritage. Now Franny understood that you must be yourself no matter what; anything else was a lie, and a denial of who you were would always cause grief. What you put out into the world came back to you threefold. If you could not accept yourself, you would be reviled and cast out, adrift in the world.

One afternoon, Franny had finally accepted Vincent's dare. She still remembered Jet calling for her to stop before she made her own wild leap, long arms and legs flailing in the blue summer air, her narrow shoulders pulled in as if to protect herself. It had indeed hurt to land on the surface, and her body ached from the force of impact, but even though she could not sink, the unfolding sensation of feeling the water against her skin was numbing and utterly delicious. When you couldn't drown, water was the element you were drawn to, and Franny had floated on her back all that afternoon, getting a wicked sunburn in the bargain, still, it had been worth it. Jet jumped in as well, a water nymph gliding through the lilies. "This is *the* most fun," she cried out, for she took to swimming immediately, vowing to never adhere to their mother's rules again.

"You should listen to me more often," Vincent had said as they tromped back to their aunt Isabelle's house, towels thrown over their shoulders. That year Franny had been seventeen, Jet sixteen, and Vincent fifteen. They were perfect and they didn't know it. They laughed at each other as they slipped and sank into the mud, making their way through tall weeds strung with spiderwebs. Franny tied her long hair in a knot and let the water puddle in red pools that stained the ground. Did she think then that she would ever see an old woman when she gazed into a mirror? Perhaps that was why the mirrors in the house were covered by white cloths, so that those among them of a certain age wouldn't have the shock of spying their own faces.

Franny recalled a story that the locals told which vowed that a sea monster of some sort had made its home in the lake. It had arrived at the docks on a wave from the harbor during a huge squall hundreds of years earlier, dazed and in need of water, and had managed to find its way to this deep, blue-green pool. Franny used to crouch on the water's edge with an offering of salt, which was said to draw such creatures to the shallows. Like was attracted to like, after all. She was eager to see something miraculous, and when she was married to Hay and he came home from Vietnam after losing his leg, they would sit here together in the evenings on canvas chairs, a picnic basket beside them. Hay was never impressed by the notion of wondrous beasts. "I've already seen monsters, another one doesn't interest me," he told her. "All I want to see is you."

But once when there was an unexpected ripple in the water, Hay had startled and fell off his chair and they had laughed themselves silly. They had loved each other madly for their whole lives, only Franny's life had been longer, and now here she was, walking home alone, with a single crazy wish, that she would spy Hay on the lane, waiting for her, calling out for her to hurry. As a girl, before Haylin, she'd been a loner, a defiant outsider, but now her aloneness haunted her; even when she was in a crowd at the bake sale to raise funds for the library, or in the kitchen with Sally and Kylie and Antonia at Sunday evening supper, she might as well have been locked in a room by herself. When you had a familiar you had a soul mate, but she'd never had another after her beloved crow, Lewis, had passed on. Their family had a passion for crows, creatures who were as intelligent as most men and smarter than many. Franny often wished that one would choose her again, but it had never happened. There are some things you have only once in a lifetime, and then only if you're lucky.

Franny's route home led her through a damp field where swamp cabbage grew in the ditches and celandine bloomed blue on tiny, wavering stems. The lake was in the migration path of scarlet tanagers who had recently returned to Massachusetts and there were flecks of red in the hedges, as if each branch had a beating heart. It was the time of year when the magnolias were fully abloom and the distance was riddled with a pink haze. The trees had been brought here for Maria Owens by the man who loved her, and some were now thirty feet tall, with lustrous black-green leaves. Franny made her way out of the woods, the green scent of the ferns clinging to her skirts. She walked past houses whose residents had come to see her and Jet for help over the years. Mostly they searched out Jet, it was true, for she was kinder and more compassionate. Franny often told people the harsh truth without any fudging or fabrications. *Are you sure?* she would say. *Everything has a cost.* Why on earth did so many of them want love charms to trick people who wanted nothing to do with them into falling head over heels? *Ridiculous,* Franny thought. *If that's being normal, then normal is madness.*

Franny rounded the corner onto Magnolia Street. Here the flowers on the trees were all a lustrous creamy white and there were sparrows in the branches, already nesting. There was mud on the soles of Franny's red boots, not very proper for someone of her age, as if she cared. What mattered now that so many of the people she loved were gone? Very little, it seemed, for it was more and more punishing to get out of bed in the morning and face the day.

But this was not a day like any other. Franny saw the mail truck and she knew. She could feel the thrum of her pulse. She would have run if she still could do so. Instead she walked at a brisker pace, carrying the umbrella that everyone knew was used as a cane, her coat flaring out behind her. She went up to the truck and pounded on the door, insisting that the flustered postman prop open his window, which he did immediately, though he was clearly nervous in her presence, as he always was, his large hands clammy.

"Well, come on," Franny said, impatient. "What do you have for me?"

"I already delivered the mail," the postman said. He was a big fellow, but he sounded like a boy who dreaded that his teacher had just discovered he'd made an error in his homework. "Was I not supposed to?"

In the past, the postman had dealt with Jet Owens, who was a lovely person no matter what people said about the family. He'd delivered boxes of herbs from India and seeds from Maine and once he'd brought a crate that had arrived airmail from Tennessee, in which there was a small black cat that had been abused, rescued from a shelter. Jet had run out to claim the poor creature while still in her bathrobe. "Oh, you'll be happy here!" the postman had remembered Jet saying to the little cat. She'd tipped him twenty dollars and told him to go to the Black Rabbit and have a drink on her, but of course she had been the cheerful aunt, and Franny was the one everyone feared.

Franny clicked her tongue disapprovingly. "You most certainly *are* supposed to deliver the mail," she said. "Isn't that your job?" She shook her head at the fellow's foolishness, then went up to the gate, in a hurry. She opened the black mailbox knowing what she would find. She could almost hear her brother's voice. A message from Vincent. Thrilled despite the black border around the envelope, she took the letter into the garden where she would have some privacy without Sally buzzing around.

All of the early seedlings had been planted, including Gillian's Zebra tomatoes, and the herb garden was flourishing in the mild April weather. She remembered when she and Vincent had sat knee to knee in the kitchen in their family's apartment on Eighty-Ninth Street and together they had made the table rise. Their very first act of magic. "We have it, Franny," he'd said, as enthralled as she was terrified. Now she sat in a garden chair that was damp with droplets from yesterday's rain shower. With the letter in hand she felt a swell of love for her brother. She swiftly opened the envelope, slipping her finger under the flap. In her hurry, the paper cut across her skin and a drop of blood flowed, staining the envelope with a dark, nearly black flush. She noticed that Vincent had written his return address in Paris. He hadn't done that when he sent the card about William's passing. Then she knew. He wanted to be found.

Franny scanned every word, then read the letter again. Vincent wrote that when they lost something dear to them, he would help find it again. As a boy he always managed to navigate without a guide or a map, and lost objects were his specialty. Their parents might hide books or clothing they found unacceptable, but Vincent always tracked down the confiscated belongings hidden in the cellar or in the back of a closet. All Franny could think of was

Vincent, whom she had missed terribly. She could feel the sun on her skin, and the breeze from the east. Her dear brother, back from the dead and the disappeared, a victim of the curse, a believer in love, the person she trusted most in the world, assuring her that fate would bring them together again.

V.

Four weeks after the funeral, Kylie remembered that she had her aunt's copy of *The Poems of Emily Dickinson*. She had planned to read a poem a day, but the loss of her aunt Jet continued to sting and she felt paralyzed by grief. She hadn't read a single one, still, there was the book on Kylie's night table. She reached to turn on her lamp, then let the pages fall open.

This is the Hour of Lead—
Remembered, if outlived,
As Freezing persons, recollect the Snow—
First—Chill—then Stupor—then the letting go—

It was then Kylie noticed that a letter had dropped from in between the pages. It was addressed to Franny, but here it was, a bird that had flown into her lap. Kylie unfolded it, her heart thudding against the cage of her ribs.

My darling girl,

If there be a cure, seek till you find it. If there be none, never mind it.

The curse Maria Owens placed on herself and us to protect us from love has nearly ruined our family. Look where we keep our books. There is a cure in The Book of the Raven.

But beware, it is the most dangerous book of all. It grants your heart's desire, but the price you pay is steep. I was already dying, so I couldn't be the one.

The one among us with the most courage will break the curse.

It's always been you.

Kylie thought of the cousin at the funeral, going on about an Owens curse. It was nothing, she'd been told. It was a myth. Clearly, her aunt Jet had thought otherwise. All the same, Kylie folded the note and stored it in her drawer. As far as she was concerned, she already possessed her heart's desire, and he was waiting for her just around the corner.

Kylie and Gideon Barnes were sprawled in the grass on the Cambridge Common where General George Washington had amassed his troops during the American Revolution. May had come at last, bringing with it the end of the term. Gideon was studying, and she was looking at the sky, thinking about the letter she'd found.

"Do you believe in curses?" Kylie asked.

"I believe Latin is an impossible language."

"Seriously."

He kissed her as his answer.

She drew away. "Does that mean no?"

"I believe in us," Gideon said.

"Do you?" Kylie grinned. It was a very good answer.

"Oh, I do," he assured her, better still.

She let it drop then. Her aunts had some strange practices, and surely the note from Jet must have another meaning, for curses were fairy tales, not part of real life. Kylie and Gideon were so young they didn't notice this spring was a season of darkness. All they saw was the world around them, the small triangle of Cambridge that contained their lives, and each other. They paid no attention to the fact that the sun often didn't break through till late afternoon. There were sudden frosts and the temperature rarely rose above fifty, most often lingering in the thirties so that squill and trout lilies turned to bruise-colored ice carpeting the gardens of tall Colonial-era houses. All along Brattle Street, the lilacs faded, their heart-shaped leaves turning black around the edges. People who had been married for thirty years suddenly filed for divorce, children refused to sleep and couldn't be comforted with warm milk and stories they'd heard a dozen times before. People knew something had gone wrong, not just with the weather but with fate itself. Yet all Kylie and Gideon saw was each other. They were in love and always had been, but they kept their love secret, it was theirs and theirs alone. They lounged beneath the canopy of the beech trees, studying for exams, longing for summer when they intended to travel through France, taking a route Gideon had planned, which included wineries and campgrounds.

"We'll sleep and we'll drink," he boasted.

Gideon gazed at her with hazel eyes speckled with green or yellow, depending on the light. When he did that, there really was no one else in the world. *Maybe we'll never come back*, Kylie thought, for she'd always considered her hometown to be provincial and did her best to stay away. She flicked at her waist-length braid of brown hair streaked with red and gold. If they ran off together, she wouldn't miss Harvard one bit; she felt she was an imposter who only pretended to care about her studies, an outsider yet again.

At this time of year, Cambridge was quiet, with only the coffeehouses jam-packed with bleary-eyed students in need of caffeine and sugar so they could pull all-nighters and prepare to pass or fail, win or lose. Kylie and Gideon had been best friends ever since they were twelve, which had made falling in love easy, once they gave in to it. Gideon had too many winning traits to ignore. He had large, handsome features and an open face that hid little. In high school, he had been the president of the chess club, the county spelling champion, the tallest boy in their class, which mattered greatly to Kylie, and the smartest, which mattered even more, and the one Kylie fell for once she stopped fighting her attraction to him. For years they told each other they didn't want to ruin their friendship with anything as complicated as sex, then went ahead and ruined it anyway. When they admitted that they were indeed in love, and likely always had been, it was a great relief to both. Kylie continued to tell her mother that she and Gideon were just friends; she didn't need anyone prying into her business, least of all her mother, who always looked so concerned when questioning Kylie about her love life. Kylie kept her thoughts and dreams and deeds to herself. She and her sister, Antonia, had made a pact never to tell their mother more than she needed to know.

Kylie always felt comfortable with Gideon; it was as if they were both members of a rare species, set apart from the rest of the world, striking, lanky creatures who managed to sleep together in the single beds in their dorm rooms, arms and legs thrown across one another, often dreaming the same dream, as Kylie clutched the black baby blanket her aunts had knitted for her when she was a newborn. Embarrassing to admit, but she couldn't sleep without it, even now as a sophomore in college.

On this gleaming day, when all the trees were a vivid green, Gideon was reading for his Latin exam, the one he feared most of all. *I can only speak one language*, he always said, and Kylie always teased, *And not well.* Then he would kiss her and she wouldn't have minded if he couldn't speak at all. He was awkward and endearing, and best of all, he was hers. It was a perfectly ordinary Cambridge afternoon, the sky flecked with pale clouds, the hum of bees rising and falling, the joyful cries of children echoing from the playground, until Kylie looked up from her copy of the *Odyssey* to catch sight of a circle of ashy black specks looming around Gideon. She had always seen auras of color around people, and usually there was an orange glow over Gideon's head, signifying good health and a full heart, but his aura had changed, with the ash becoming darker even though the afternoon was streaked with pale bands of light. *Something is about to happen*, she thought.

Kylie sat on her haunches and closed her book. Gideon gazed up from his text, concerned when he saw her expression. He knew Kylie was sensitive and could often tell what was to come. She could foretell when it would rain and when classes would be canceled. She'd phoned the school police before a fire started in the entranceway, and rang them again a few months later, a full hour before a quiet girl down the hall attempted to take her own life. Gideon didn't call it witchery, but instead referred to her premonitions as her *talent,* as if the sight was no different than an aptitude for music or dance.

"I'm going to fail, right?" Gideon said when he saw the dread on her face.

Kylie had a flash of vision. A blank paper, an empty chair, a day of scarlet rain, a lake with no bottom, a man with black hair.

From her expression it was clear the future contained something worse than a failed exam.

"I'll be expelled," Gideon guessed.

"No, it's nothing like that. Let's go." Kylie herself didn't know what it meant. She had never seen that sort of aura before. *Violet, gray, silver, ash, black, scarlet.* None of it boded well. She stood and reached out her hand to him. She didn't know if other people loved the way that she did, completely and utterly, and she didn't much care.

Gideon rose from the grass, and when he did his height blocked out the sun and he saw that there were black tears in Kylie's eyes. She never cried. Or at least rarely. He thought she'd shed tears at her aunt Jet's funeral, but that was to be expected.

"Did I do something wrong?" he asked.

Kylie looped her arms around him. "Never," she said. And then she leaned up to whisper that she loved him and always would. It was the first time she'd said so aloud, and she immediately felt flushed with raw emotion.

"I've always loved you," Gideon told her. "From the first day we met."

The weather was changing. It was turning wicked. As they crossed Mass Ave, Kylie had the chills, as if the west wind had cut right through her. The sky had begun to glaze over with windblown clouds, as if it were the witching hour rather than three in the afternoon. Kylie decided she wouldn't let Gideon out of her sight. Curse or not, nothing could happen if she watched over him.

They went to Dunster House, took three strides to cross the room, then fell into bed. That was when the rain started to pelt down on rooftops and roads, but Kylie didn't hear the torrents of rain because she was kissing him. She was kissing him the way you do when you're afraid you will lose someone, when you need their breath and life inside you, when your souls melt together in the act of kissing. The silence was broken by a slow, methodical clicking, somewhere in the wall, the sound anyone with any knowledge never wishes to hear.

Dunster House had been built in 1930 as a student residence, and people were charged by the floor they inhabited, with the poorer students required to walk up six flights. There was a great deal of old, dead wood, and deathwatch beetles were wood borers that could infest old buildings. Kylie heard one tapping now, a sound people said could portend a death. She had never been told about the deathwatch beetle, and was too young to remember her mother tearing the floor apart in search of just such a horrid creature before her own father met with his accident. Kylie hadn't been told that there had been the same clicking in the stable where Gary Hallet had kept his horse, although Gary had insisted it was the echo of wood settling, refusing to believe it marked the time of his death. Still, the sound itself was unnerving.

Kylie had once overheard her aunts discussing that a black aura meant death and destruction and danger, wickedness in a world where there had previously been none. When this happened, an individual must place salt on her windowsills and in the four corners of her house. Now a black cloud rose up toward the ceiling of Kylie's dorm room, but she didn't intend to search for packets of salt. She didn't believe in the curse, why should she? All the same, she would keep Gideon close to her, until the circle dissipated. If they missed finals, so be it. If they stayed in bed for a week, well, they'd done that before. While she slept Kylie dreamed of rain, for by now it was pouring buckets. The Common was flooded, and the birds hid in the bushes and under the eaves, doing their best to avoid the deluge. The women in the Owens family were attracted to water, even though it could be dangerous for them, for water always revealed the truth about who they were. That had been a problem for Kylie and Antonia Owens, for their mother feared that a single glimpse of the truth would rock their lives. Kylie and her sister had never been allowed to go to the town pool for swimming lessons, but every summer their aunt Gillian had brought them to Leech Lake on the sly, permitting them to break the rules and float in the cool, glassy water for hours. Still, there were some issues even she refused to discuss. When asked why they could never remain underwater and always popped up, as if made of cork, Gillian would tell them that some gifts should never be questioned. *Be happy you can't sink!* she would cry. *Enjoy every minute!*

Kylie slept fitfully, immersed in her dreams; try as she might, she couldn't wake, but instead fell even more deeply into a twilight she couldn't escape. In her dream she was in the garden at home sitting across from Jet, who had a book open on her lap. *If you want to know the cure*, Jet told her, *all you have to do is turn the page*.

Gideon left their bed so quietly, his long legs extended, that Kylie didn't notice his absence. He pulled on his clothes and found an umbrella that had been stuffed into the closet. It wasn't too late to go to the florist on Brattle Street. Kylie had been so sad and preoccupied ever since her aunt's death, he wanted to cheer her up and present her with something beautiful, roses that would erase the gloom of the day. He knew she preferred yellow and hoped they were in stock. Yellow, the color of courage and hope, loyalty and joy. He did not think of its other meanings, jealousy and sickness and deceit. He thought only of how lucky they were to be at school together. How lucky to have found each other when they were so young. He might have had to go through a dozen people before he found his true love, he might have never found her at all, but instead he had spotted her on a soccer field when they weren't yet thirteen. They both had a fierce dislike of sports, other than running, which they loved. On the day they met they'd walked toward one another with grins on their faces, their feet lifting off the grass, their hearts pounding, as if they had already run ten miles.

Let's get out of here, was the first thing Gideon had ever said to Kylie, and her first remark to him was *Yes.*

Yes, I'll love you. Yes, I'm yours. Now I've said it aloud.

He left Dunster House in the stinging rain, and headed over the wet pavement down Brattle Street, a fortunate young man who dreaded nothing more than Latin class. When he dashed across the street there was thunder and he looked up at the mottled sky when he should have been watching the traffic speeding down the road. He heard the horns blaring before everything around him was ashes, a world black as night.

When Gideon's mother called, the shrill wail of the phone woke Kylie from her terrible bottomless sleep. The garden in her dream had been on fire, and she'd been running through the flames. The moment she woke, she saw a smoky cloud on the ceiling of the room. Kylie scrambled to get to her phone, her chest tightening. She knew something terrible had happened even before his mother began to speak, only she didn't know how terrible until Mrs. Barnes began to talk about the accident. *He's been hit*, she said, and Kylie felt her world come apart. She could feel the curse lodged beside her heart, a black moth that had been inside her chest all along, waiting for the moment when she professed her love and it could at last rise. She'd told him today that she loved him. She'd opened the door to whatever came next.

Gideon's mother and stepfather lived in New York, and were heading for LaGuardia; they would be there as quickly as possible. But what was done was done. Gideon had been struck while crossing Brattle Street, while Kylie was dreaming. She flung his raincoat over her T-shirt and pajama pants, then jammed her feet into a pair of boots. The taxi ride was a blur, the hospital one corridor after another until she found him. Kylie scrambled into bed beside Gideon, slowing her breath to match his. She felt a rush of love for him, but for herself she felt only recriminations. She should have watched over him; she was meant to protect him and now here he was. There were wires and tubes and machines whose purpose Kylie didn't understand. Gideon was ghastly pale, his scalp and face bruised and cut; he was both there and not there, in a world of his own.

Wake up, she told him. *Wake up now*, she whispered, and when there was no response she shouted, but he couldn't hear her. She circled her arms around him and wept until his hospital gown was drenched. When the doctor came by, he told Kylie she could easily disrupt the electrodes attached to his skull; she had best leave him be. *Do not be so close to the patient*, she was told in a calm, measured tone. Caution was everything; courage was a fool's errand. The team didn't yet know how severe Gideon's head injuries might be. When the doctor left the room, the nurse murmured that Kylie could stay where she was as long as she was careful. But how was one to be careful when the world was in ruins, when it was no larger than a hospital room and the thrum of the pump assisting with each of Gideon's inhalations was so very loud she couldn't hear his heart? Usually Gideon's beating heart was all she could hear, whether they were in bed or on the street. She fancied she could hear it even when they were a hundred miles apart. Now there was nothing. As Kylie held his hand, which was limp in her own, she thought about her aunt Jet's letter. All at once she knew what had happened to Gideon had been the work of the curse.

As soon as the rainstorm lifted, Franny went into the garden, cringing to see the damage. There was a spell of protection over their house and even hurricanes passed by their address, but that wasn't the case in this dark spring. Leaves had been blasted from the trees by gusts of wet wind, the tomato seedlings had been washed away, the herb garden was flooded with murky pools, flowers that had bloomed had wilted in a matter of minutes. Jet had planted a rare variety in 1978, the Osiria rose, which had both white and red petals, but now the leaves were darkened and spotty, and the scarlet buds had cracked open to reveal that moths had devoured the petals from the inside out.

As Franny gathered several mud-slicked sprigs of mint, she heard a clacking that made her stand up straight. She recognized the deathwatch beetle, and immediately thought her time had come. She looked up through the branches, wondering what might happen next here in the center of the dark spring, where hope was all but impossible to find. But instead of death stalking her, the garden gate swung open and there was Kylie, who had taken the bus from Boston. Kylie's hair was in knots and her face ashen, so that her freckles stood out as if blood had flecked her pale complexion.

"Tell me what to do," she begged. Her face was swollen and tearstained. "There has to be a way to stop it."

The story came out in a rush. *Hit by a car. Unresponsive. A declaration of love.* Then Franny knew, the beetle was calling for Gideon. It was the curse. She could smell it, the stink of sorrow, and blood, and desperation, all braided together until it became one. "I don't know the answer," Franny told her distraught great-niece. "None of us do. Once the curse begins, there's nothing to stop it."

Kylie dug her nails into the palms of her hands until beads of burning-hot blood fell to the ground. "It's not a good enough answer." She sounded fierce, so much so that she frightened herself. She had no idea that she had risen off the ground until Franny took hold of the sleeve of Gideon's raincoat and tugged at her. "What is happening to me?" Kylie asked. The magic inside her was surfacing, like it or not, brought on by raw emotion.

"It's who we are," Franny said simply, no longer adhering to Sally's insistence that they keep silent about their heritage. Franny knew what it was like to be raised in a household of secrets; such an upbringing never boded well. Sooner or later you would find out the truth. Usually at the worst possible moment.

"What are you saying?" Kylie asked.

"Darling," Franny said, for this was never easy. "We have a history of magic."

Kylie let out a sharp laugh. "We're not witches."

Her aunt stared at her, a serious expression crossing her face.

"That's just what people say," Kylie insisted.

"Your mother didn't want you to know," Franny said. "So we kept quiet."

"Is that why those women always come here at night?" Kylie asked. As a girl she'd seen neighbors approach the door after dark at a time when they hoped their family or friends wouldn't spy them in the shadows of the Owenses' yard. Some had been crying, some carried babies, some brought gifts, baskets of fruit, caged birds, boxes of fancy chocolate; all made certain to latch the garden gate when they left.

"They don't come here anymore. Not without Jet. We've turned off the porch light. They know there's no one here to help them anymore. Certainly not Sally. Your mother stays away from magic. Always has. She meant the best. She wanted to protect you."

"But she didn't, did she?" Hot, black tears brimmed in Kylie's eyes.

"You should have told us you were in love," Franny said sadly.

"It wasn't your business! It was between us!"

It was then Kylie remembered the *Grimoire,* which she had stumbled upon in the greenhouse one summer. When she'd brought the heavy tome into the kitchen, her mother had pitched a fit and quickly returned it to its proper place, only this time under lock and key.

"What about the book in the greenhouse?"

"We've searched the *Grimoire* a thousand times," Franny assured her. "There's nothing there."

"There has to be. Jet said the cure is in a book," Kylie insisted.

"Jet?" Franny was truly puzzled. "When did she say that?"

"In her letter."

Franny felt a chill settle over her, the cold clasp of unfinished business. If it was Jet's concern, then it was hers as well. "I think you'd better show that to me." There was a wash of sooty ash above the rooftop, above the trees. The time had come when fate would make the best of them if they didn't make the best of it.

The letter had been written for Franny, but does a letter belong to the person it was written to or the one who finds it? It had made its way to Kylie and so, in her opinion, it belonged to her now. Instead of allowing Franny to see Jet's message, Kylie took off running through the muddy garden, Gideon's raincoat flapping out behind her in what had become a foul wind rising in the east.

"Kylie," Franny cried. "Where do you think you're going?"

"If you don't know the answer, maybe my mother does. Maybe this is one more thing she's been hiding."

The Owens School for Girls had been the first of its kind in Massachusetts. Grammar schools for boys were commonplace, the first in the commonwealth being the Boston Latin School, which opened in 1635. Soon thereafter there were Dame schools for girls, which taught reading and writing, as well as the domestic arts, but Maria Owens wanted more, and so did her daughter, Faith, who taught Latin and Greek. This was long before the radical notion of equal education for females became a reality in 1830 when a high school for girls opened in Boston and compulsory education laws were passed in 1852.

The school, situated in the library, had closed at the turn of the eighteenth century, and the former classroom was now the quiet corner of the circulation desk, where Sally was figuring out the monthly bills. The library was run as a private institution, depending on the yearly sum Maria's will provided, from a trust handled by the family's attorneys, the Hardys, on Beacon Street in Boston. All the same, the library had always been open to the public and even for those interested parties who lived one town over, or outside the limits of Essex County, Jet had always been happy to produce a library card.

Kylie was so agitated when she arrived that the books on the shelves responded in fear, with several flopping onto the floor in a flurry of pages.

"My goodness," Miss Hardwick cried as Kylie stormed by, not even noticing the elderly librarian.

Miss Hardwick was relieved that she could use her plastic grabber, newly purchased at the hardware store, to reach for and retrieve the fallen volumes, delighted to think of the many ways it could be put to use. Grabbing the newspaper, grabbing for toast, grabbing that annoying teenaged boy Ryan Heller who came to the library to stir up trouble and moon over girls and who'd never in his life once withdrawn a book.

Sally was concentrating on the bills, wondering if they would have to find a way to cut back on the charges for heat and electricity, when she glanced up to see that her daughter had arrived unexpectedly, dressed, it seemed, in a raincoat and pajamas. She wondered if she had somehow fallen asleep and if this were a dream, for she often had such deep visions in her sleep, ones so real that when she woke she was confused as to which was her real life. But no, Kylie was here, her face drawn and pale. The lights above them were flickering, never a good sign.

"I need to break the curse," Kylie said in a no-nonsense tone. She didn't seem like herself at all. Her voice was flat and more adult. "I need to do it now."

Two teenagers in the next room were paging through the newest graphic novels, unaware that several lights had blinked completely out. Nearby, Miss Hardwick was still intent on picking up books with her grabber.

"Got you!" Miss Hardwick said to the book she lifted off the floor. It was a copy of Grace Paley's short stories *Enormous Changes at the Last Minute.*

"It's Gideon," Kylie said. "He's in the hospital and I think you know why."

Sally had the sight despite herself and now a vision flashed as if she herself had stood on Brattle Street in the pouring rain. There was the slick pavement, and the muffled sounds of speeding cars, and Gideon dashing out, grinning when he spied yellow flowers in the window of the florist shop.

"Gideon?" Sally asked. "Your friend?"

"Mother, don't be an idiot."

They looked at one another. Was that the way it was?

Sally felt a stab of fear. "It can't be," she said.

"Well, it is," Kylie told her mother. She seemed much older

than her age. All of a sudden she had revealed herself to be someone Sally hadn't imagined her to be. A woman in love, held hostage by the curse.

"You didn't tell us about the curse," Kylie cried. Of course she knew they were different, some people crossed the street when the members of the Owens family passed by, but now she understood there were dark secrets that hadn't been shared.

"I intended to." Someday, of course, when it seemed necessary, when she was ready to break their hearts and divulge the Owens family history.

"When? At Gideon's funeral?"

"That's not fair." Sally was shivering, though she wore one of Jet's old sweaters, gray lambswool with pearl buttons, carefully stored in the bureau, wrapped in tissue with a note that read *R holiday gift 1983*.

"I need the book," Kylie said.

"The book is where it always is. In the greenhouse, where it belongs."

"You know what I mean. *The Book of the Raven*."

"I don't know what you're talking about." Sally truly didn't understand.

"You don't know anything about *The Book of the Raven*?" Kylie asked.

Sally piled up the bills in a messy tower, too concerned to finish her chore. "Let me close up and get my coat. We'll have dinner, then I'll go with you to the hospital in Boston."

Kylie glared at her mother.

"Wait here," Sally said.

Kylie remained where she was, unsure of what to do next. She wasn't about to eat dinner or go to Boston with her mother. There was something here that she was meant to find.

"Oh, Jetty," she moaned softly. "Tell me what to do."

Kylie looked around, and when she did she finally noticed Miss Hardwick, who, due to the day of the week, was wearing a dowdy old-fashioned dress with a blue bodice, along with a bonnet made of straw and ribbon. The librarian played the part of Marmee from *Little Women* every Thursday at the children's story hour and as usual she hadn't bothered to change her clothes. People at the Black Rabbit enjoyed seeing her in her costume on Thursday evenings. "Where's Jo?" they would call. "Amy's been asking for you," they would tease, which was all fine and good, for these jokers usually picked up the tab for her drink.

"I didn't realize you were here," Kylie said, embarrassed that Miss Hardwick had seen her outburst when she confronted her mother.

"I'm here all right, just as I was when Jet brought the book in." Kylie looked at her openmouthed, so Miss Hardwick went on. "The one about the raven that you mentioned. Jet said it was too special to be listed in the catalogue, so she put it on the magic shelf. I'm the only one who knows where it is."

Kylie was stopped cold. Her need for the book twisted inside her, a snake that circled her heart. That is how left-handed magic began, with a desire that matters more than anything else. "I'm the person who's come for it."

Miss Hardwick took a well-measured pause before she said, "I had the impression she meant Franny." Then the librarian shrugged. The less she had to do with crotchety Franny Owens the better. "But now it seems that someone is you."

Miss Hardwick led Kylie to the section that housed the oldest manuscripts set inside glass cases in the rear of the rare-books room. The temperature here was always set at sixty-five, with a humidity level of fifty percent, for such texts needed a cool, dark place. The library's greatest treasure was a first-edition copy of

Emily Dickinson's poems, published in 1890, of which only five hundred copies had been printed, found by Isabelle Owens at a flea market in Pittsfield. There was also an envelope on which the poet had scrawled the beginning of a poem in her birdlike scrawl, discovered at the same used-book stall one lucky October day.

One Heart instructed to be Two—
As Lightning splits a Tree—
Can be—but No one knows
The Truth of it—
Except for Thee and me.

Harvard University had done its best to claim the scrap for its Emily Dickinson Collection, but the Owens Library had refused to hand it over. There was also a rare first edition of *Wuthering Heights*, the same printing that had recently sold at auction in London for six figures. To see these volumes and other treasures, a patron must have Miss Hardwick sit beside them, for she alone could turn the pages, wearing white cotton gloves. As for Emily's scrap, the librarian visited it every day, merely to check on its well-being.

As they approached a glass case at the very rear of the room, Kylie heard something rustling, much like the wingbeats of a bird. There was a collection of magic books here, one that most of the library's patrons never noticed. Sally had considered ridding the library of all magical texts, but Franny and Jet had insisted they stay, and so they'd remained, uncatalogued and out of the way, collected by Maria Owens's daughter, Faith, who had traveled to New York and London in search of such volumes. Reginald Scot's *The Discoverie of Witchcraft*, written in 1584, contained lists of charms and conjurations, all while trying to convince the reader that there was no such creature as a witch. Charles Godfrey Leland's *Aradia or the Gospel of the Witches*, a feminist retelling of the creation story that included folk medicine and magic from Italy. *The Golden Bough* by Sir James George Frazer, filled with folktales, an exploration of witchcraft in the ancient world.

Kylie ran her hand along the books, but eager as she was to find the book Jet had hidden, the text escaped her.

"We made it difficult to find," Miss Hardwick said. "It's not for just anyone, you know."

Miss Hardwick led Kylie to the book Jet had placed on the shelf on her seventh day when she ran out of the house to attend to the last mission of her life. The library door had been unlocked, and Jet had discovered Miss Hardwick passed out at her desk; she often fainted when a dip occurred in her blood sugar before she could leave for the Black Rabbit and have her drink and a platter of fries. She sometimes forgot to eat lunch and the results were such spells. Jet had swiftly taken hold of the Owenses' first-aid kit, which included garlic and ginger and smelling salts.

"Can you keep a secret?" Jet had asked once Miss Hardwick had been revived.

The hour was late, and when Miss Hardwick nodded, Jet confided that she was adding a book to the library's acquisitions and that at some point her sister might come to retrieve it. It had been there waiting ever since, a black book meant for a woman in need, ready to be found by the person who was willing to do whatever was necessary to save someone she loved. The book was filled with Black Magic, dangerous not only to the intended subject of the Dark Art, but to the practitioner as well. What you send into the world would come back to you three times over, for good or for evil. Maria Owens could not bring herself to destroy the book, written with so much care and longing, and neither could Jet.

Kylie followed Miss Hardwick down the narrow aisle, until

the librarian paused. There it was, among the rarest of the rare. A slim book bound in black leather that had been tied together with knotted silk thread. The text had been shoved between two of John Hathorne's journals, which consisted of little more than financial details. His books were so mundane they had masked the power and magic of *The Book of the Raven*. The text had been waiting, quite impatiently, to be selected for more than three hundred years. The prose on the thin pages of vellum had been carefully crafted in alternating red and black inks.

"It doesn't look like much, does it?" Miss Hardwick said. "The best ones never do. I suggest you use gloves."

"Thank you, I can take it from here," Kylie assured the librarian as she accepted a pair of white cotton gloves.

"Good. It's nearly five and I have to wash up and get over to the inn." Miss Hardwick patted Kylie's shoulder before she went to collect her teacup to rinse.

The cover of the book did indeed burn Kylie's fingertips and she slipped on the gloves before sinking down on the floor. She sat back on her heels as she turned to the first page. There was an envelope tucked inside, another note in Jet's familiar sloping script.

Dear One,

Do not use The Book of the Raven unless you are prepared to lose everything. This book will lead you to the end of the curse. Start in the city where it was written.

Kylie examined the frontispiece on which the author had drawn a sketch of a raven in black ink. *1615, London.* When Faith Owens found the text at a market in Manhattan in the seventeenth century, she had written her name in the lower left-hand corner. *The Book of the Raven* by Amelia Bassano was a private journal, written for her own purposes, but she had others in mind as well, those she wished to help. Women who had no access to what they needed most in the world often turned to the left, and it was occurring once again here in the Owens Library as Kylie joined those who had walked the Crooked Path before her. It often began with women who were given away to men they didn't love, who were too poor to make their own decisions, who lived lives they would have never chosen, who couldn't be published but who wrote anyway, women who had been cursed, women who needed to save someone, no matter the cost. This was the dark side and to reach it a woman must take a chance, close her eyes, make the leap, do whatever must be done.

On the back of the envelope was Jet's last thought, hastily scrawled, in a shakier hand than usual, for she'd been in a great hurry on the seventh day.

Everything worthwhile is dangerous.

Kylie slipped the book into the pocket of her raincoat. She could feel it there, as though it had a beating heart, a story written in blood. Miss Hardwick was rinsing out a teacup in the tiny kitchen when Kylie passed by. She made sure to keep her voice calm as she said her good-byes to the elderly librarian. "Thanks, Miss Hardwick," she called. She was already making a to-do list: go to her dorm room, pack a bag, grab her passport, get to Logan Airport. "I appreciate your help," she told the librarian. "I'm off."

"Good night," Miss Hardwick called back as she set the teacup to dry on the counter. "And good luck. Jet said the person who came for the book would need it."

By the time Sally returned with her coat and her keys, Miss Hardwick was headed out the door. The light in the rare books room had been flicked off, the glass cabinets locked.

"Wait a second." Sally glanced around. She felt a chill along her spine. "Where's Kylie?"

The crystal beads of the chandelier above them in the entranceway swayed as a breeze came through the open door.

"Oh, she's gone off with the book," Miss Hardwick responded as they left together.

"Gone off?" Sally asked. "With what book?"

Miss Hardwick was in a hurry to get to the Black Rabbit Inn; five o'clock was looming, and she did like her nightly whiskey. All the same, she paused on the pavement. She'd known Sally ever since she was a child, and had always pretended not to notice when Sally checked out more books than the rules allowed. Sally had been a melancholy girl, but a sweet one, and a major reader. *Little Women*, *The Secret Garden*, all of the Edward Eager books, with *Half Magic* and *Magic by the Lake* withdrawn several times, and then, during the summer when she turned twelve, as much Jane Austen as she could get her hands on, *Persuasion* and *Pride and Prejudice* and *Emma*. She had always watched over her sister, who had been a wild little thing, not a huge reader, but one who had been drawn to books that seemed beyond her years, Mary Shelley's *Frankenstein*, for instance, and Shirley Jackson's *We Have Always Lived in the Castle*.

"The one that Jet put on the shelf, dear," Miss Hardwick explained. "*The Book of the Raven*."

Sally turned terribly pale upon hearing this news. She looked as if she might faint. What book was this?

"Would you like to join me for a drink?" Miss Hardwick suggested. Not only was the whiskey excellent at the Black Rabbit, but the martinis were famous for the punch they packed, and tonight the special was meat loaf, a local favorite.

"Where did that book come from?"

"Jet left it. I thought it was for Franny, but apparently not. It was in the *Do not resuscitate* section." Sally looked even more puzzled. "The magic section. It was a little joke your aunt Jet and I had. If a patron took out a book from that section, they were responsible for what happened next."

"What sort of book was it?"

Sally looked as she had when she was a girl, suspicious and intelligent, her eyes bright with worry.

"It was the sort that burned your hands as a matter of fact," Miss Hardwick said. "Your aunt said it was a Book of Shadows and that I should stay away from it."

Sally had gone stone-cold. A left-handed *Grimoire.*

They went out together and Sally, though preoccupied, returned a wave to Miss Hardwick as she walked toward the lights of the inn. The notion of a book she'd never heard of made her nervous, for she'd believed that she was aware of every volume in their collection. And yet, how much damage could one small book do? How powerful could it be? That was when Sally began to run, because she knew the answer. Words were everything, stories were more powerful than any weapon, books changed lives. She ran along the spotty pavement to Magnolia Street and when she arrived she saw that the gate was open. Gillian's battered black and white Mini had been parked on the road at a curious angle, and Gillian, herself, was out on the porch waiting for her.

"We came when we heard about Gideon," Gillian said. "Kylie left a message for Antonia."

There was Antonia, up on the porch with Franny. Kylie had run off and now must be found, they all agreed that was the logical way to proceed. But Antonia noticed that her mother and aunt Gilly were stealing worried glances and speaking about the curse. *Pure nonsense*, was Antonia's first thought. *Seventeenth-century superstition*. How could they take this seriously, although clearly they did. Antonia recalled that her mother had spoken harshly to the cousin from Maine who'd blurted out something about a curse at Jet's funeral.

Sally had often been a distracted parent, too wrapped up in her own hurt and guilt when she lost her husbands to entirely be there for her daughters, and it had fallen upon Antonia to be the dependable one in the family. She was the serious older sister who made certain Kylie did her homework, who corrected math and science papers, and who'd suggested that Kylie apply to Harvard so they would be together in Cambridge. Antonia was the daughter who never reproached her mother, or asked for the limelight, the clever girl who did as she was told, who went to bed on time and always was at the top of her class. But as practical as Antonia was, she had a story she kept to herself. Until she'd become pregnant, sleep had eluded her, and she'd always had a problem with lucid dreams that often absorbed her wholly, seeming more real than the life she lived. To avoid dreaming she stayed up, buzzed on coffee and schoolwork, reading until all hours. When she'd first started medical school, her circadian rhythms were so off, she'd gone to a sleep clinic but had received no satisfactory answers. Since becoming pregnant, coffee was out of the question, and she'd been dreaming more all the time. If this had been any other day she would have said nothing about the disturbing dream she'd had the night before, but her sister was missing, and it was time for her to speak her mind.

"I dreamed of a death by drowning," Antonia said after a measured pause, uncomfortable when Sally and Gillian turned to study her, both clearly nervous. "It was one of us."

"People in our family can't drown." Gillian was quick to dismiss the dream. Talk of drowning was never a good idea, not in their family.

Witches don't weep or drown or fall in love, Franny thought, *and yet it happened all the time.*

"Well, this one did," Antonia insisted.

In her dream, there had been toads in the shallows, some inky in color, others vermilion, still others a deep opalescent green. A pile of black stones was carefully arranged on the edge of the shore. The dream was a portent of what was to come, and perhaps it was best if Antonia kept its content to herself. Her mother and aunt were so distraught she couldn't bring herself to tell them that the drowned woman in her dream had red hair.

Antonia was asked to phone Kylie and, of course, she agreed. They were as close as sisters could be, speaking every day. If Kylie were to talk to anyone it would most certainly be her sister. Antonia made her way to the farthest section of the huge garden, past the beehives. She stood beneath one of the magnolias brought to Massachusetts long ago by a lovesick man who opened his beloved's heart by planting trees. Dusk had fallen and the sky was streaked an inky blue. The air itself seemed heavy and dark. Antonia could feel her baby moving inside her. She had thought being pregnant would be annoying, but in fact she felt comforted by the baby's presence.

Kylie picked up on the seventh ring. "I can't talk," she said.

"You have to talk." Antonia was pacing in the grass, wet droplets clinging to the hem of a maternity dress that was more of a tent. "I'm so sorry about what happened to Gideon, but I can meet you at the hospital. We can get him the best care."

"That won't help." Kylie already sounded very far away. "It's the curse."

Antonia stopped where she was. The magnolia was blooming, and the leaves were waxy and damp. "There is no curse. Yes, we're different, but they would have told us if there was a curse."

"I stopped in Cambridge for my passport. I'm leaving. If I don't break the curse, Gideon won't come back. This family has ruined our lives. Tell them I blame them for everything that's happened. If they had taught us magic, I might have been able to fight the curse. At least I would have known not to fall in love."

Antonia could usually talk her sister out of anything, convincing her not to dye her hair blue or attend Yale rather than Harvard, but now she wasn't so sure. Perhaps it was best to join in. "Tell me where you're going," she said. "I'll go with you."

"Not this time. This time I'm on my own."

She was gone before Antonia could say another word. It was then that Antonia remembered that it was just last week that Kylie had put a red rinse in her chestnut hair. Her dream came back to her, the red-haired woman drowning. She went back to the porch where Gillian sat on the top step. Sally was pacing. She knew bad signs when she saw them. A cat in the road. A cloud in the shape of a noose. A daughter who felt betrayed by her own mother. The full moon lifting into the sky.

"She said you ruined her life," Antonia informed her mother and aunt. "She's left and she won't say where she's going. All I know is that she has her passport."

Sally sank down on the stairs beside her sister. Here they were, in the place where they'd first learned who and what they could be. There was a ring around the rising moon, a sign of trouble to come. They'd seen it before and now it was back. Gillian might argue that the rainbow manifestation was caused by the reflection of light through ice crystals, but Sally remembered the phrase of Shakespeare's, *Something wicked this way comes*, the title of a book she'd loved as a girl. On this night the sisters held hands, reaching for each other without thinking, just as they had when they first came to Massachusetts, when the world was dark and cruel and they had no idea what might await them.

Franny had slipped inside and returned with a hastily packed bag. It was the one she'd used long ago when she had gone to Paris for Vincent's funeral. Her nieces turned toward her, her dear girls, her last chance to love someone.

"She's gone," Sally said in a small voice, as if the world had ended again, as it had when she and Gillian were little girls who had lost everything before they arrived on Magnolia Street.

"We need the person who can find her." Franny held up Vincent's letter. "Fortunately, we have him."

Boulevard de la Madeleine. The man who could find what was lost.

Fate was what you made of it. You could make the best of it, or it would make the best of you.

The *Grimoire* was stowed in Franny's bag, which made it quite heavy, but she had her trusty umbrella to lean on. Sally packed in under five minutes, then made certain to lock the door. Gillian stopped at home to retrieve her passport and let Ben know she had to leave town. Family business, by now he was used to that. As for Antonia, she was too far along in her pregnancy to travel, and so she was asked to pay a call on the Reverend once a week, for they couldn't deny one of Jet's last wishes. They might be gone for a while. They wouldn't be back until they found what they were looking for.

PART TWO

The Book of Spells

I.

Vincent was waiting in the last of the pale sunlight on the Boulevard de la Madeleine. It was May and he was in the most beautiful city in the world, one he knew quite well, all the same he was anxious and had half a mind to disappear, just veer onto a crowded street and lose himself again. He had been missing for so long that he wondered if he would seem like another person entirely to his sister, if she would walk right past him, or, even worse, if she would face him straight on and be disappointed. *This is who you've turned out to be? After all I did for you and how much I loved you, this is who you are? A lonely old man with a mongrel dog? What happened to the boy who was so brave, the one who would do anything for love?*

The plane from Boston had been delayed, then the car service had made a wrong turn, but finally they were here at last, his family, dressed in black, looking as if they had arrived for a funeral, unloading their battered suitcases from the trunk of an old Peugeot. Two women in their forties, one pale, the other dark, who he assumed were the daughters of Regina, the child he'd had with April Owens, and a very old woman with red hair, waving a black umbrella at him. Could it be his sister? Impossible, he thought. Dodger raced over to greet the new arrivals, barking and wagging his tail. "Oh, hush, you foolish thing," the old woman told the dog. It was then Vincent saw a vision of Franny as she'd been, his beautiful sister, willful as always. "Don't just stand there!" she called to him.

When he went to embrace her, Vincent felt as if no time had passed, but it had and they stared at one another taking in all the transformations age had wrought, then laughed. Vincent was introduced to his granddaughters, which turned out to be an awkward situation; they were related by blood, yet were unknown to one another. Did they shake hands or hug? They did both, and yet there was a distance between them. Poor Sally, Vincent thought as he helped them carry in their bags. She looked shattered, but wasn't that the Owens fate? Vincent knew what it was like to endure the curse; it twisted around you, a snake of despair, and forced you to do whatever was necessary to survive. He hoped they would forgive him for doing his best to escape it, even if it meant abandoning them. No one ever said he wasn't single-minded; he'd been so since he was a boy, perhaps because Franny had always given in to him and protected him. Frankly, she'd babied him, and he hadn't minded having a big sister who believed he was a gift to the world, albeit a troublesome one. Vincent knew that there was always a cost incurred to get what you wanted, and the price he'd paid was steep. He hoped his granddaughters understood there would be a bargain to be made. For whatever you did, and whatever you were yet to do, magic exacted a payment.

Agnes Durant had arranged a cold supper of salmon and asparagus. She welcomed them graciously, and her warm presence made the evening a bit less uncomfortable. Sally and Gillian had never fully understood Vincent's relationship to their grandmother, April Owens, only that they were distant cousins, several times removed. When the sisters were young, their grandmother told them that Vincent was the most difficult man she'd ever met, and the most compelling. *It was before he knew who he was. I always knew, but I wanted him anyway.*

If not for Agnes's charm and her ability to keep a conversation going even among the most dour guests, Sally and Gillian might have simply stared at Vincent, for how could one present a lifetime over a single dinner? *Tell me about yourself. I am brokenhearted, I've lost my daughter, I'm no longer young, I was wild and I paid a price, I'm a woman who is afraid of magic and of the future and of this very moment.* Instead, when asked how they were faring, both Gillian and Sally replied, *Fine.*

Franny and Agnes had last seen each other nearly sixty years earlier, at Vincent's false funeral, but oddly Agnes looked no different. She was as elegant as always, and she seemed years younger than her age, miraculously so. Franny leaned over to whisper to Vincent. Hadn't Madame Durant been in her fifties when Franny came to Paris for Vincent's funeral? Wouldn't that make her over a hundred now?

"It's her bloodline," Vincent confided. "The Durants don't age."

Sally, who was unable to eat dinner, pushed her gold-rimmed plate away. The silverware was intricate and heavy, though it was tarnished, the silver turning black in the hands of a witch. It was all well and good to have polite conversation concerning the architecture of the house and the length of the flight from Boston, but Sally didn't wish for small talk any more than she wished for food. She had more pressing issues on her mind.

"You say you're a finder?" she asked this new grandfather of hers, the edge of suspicion in her tone.

Vincent shrugged, not wanting to praise himself too highly. "I've had the ability on occasion."

"I hope so," Gillian said. "We've come across the ocean to see you for that reason. I hope it wasn't for nothing."

Franny glared at her niece. "Of course it isn't for nothing. It's a talent of his. One of many."

"You have your own talents," Vincent reminded her.

Sally was quick to interrupt their mutual admiration. "Shall we begin the search tonight?"

It was not a question really, but rather a demand. She couldn't quite think of Vincent as family, though he had the gray eyes the Owenses were known for and seemed oddly familiar, perhaps because she'd seen his face in news articles about musicians who had died too young to fulfill their promise. He had that one song their mother, Regina, had played over and over again when she thought her children were asleep.

"We should begin immediately," Vincent agreed. "Night is best."

They would proceed to Amulette for the ingredients that were needed. A light rain was falling and Agnes lent her visitors umbrellas and raincoats. "Don't go over to the other side," she cheerfully warned Sally and Gillian as she bid them good-bye.

"Unlikely," Sally said flatly. The left-handed side of magic and its Crooked Path would never appeal to her. She had avoided magic her whole life long and always proceeded with logic.

But people often did the unexpected and left-handed magic was very tempting, even for those convinced they couldn't be corrupted. It was a way to get what you wanted, and in return all one must do was dispose of both empathy and compassion, bothersome and unnecessary elements when walking the path. Was that really so high a price in exchange for your heart's desire? For those whose own needs and desires came first, the trade could easily seem worth the price. Still, once you had what you wanted, left-handed magic took everything else in return. You didn't even realize that you'd been burned until you looked down to discover you had been turned to ash.

They went on foot, through the gardens of the Tuileries, down the stairs leading to the riverbank. In the dimming light Franny had thrown up a cloak of protection to ensure that no one would notice them. This was a private business, after all. The dog, Dodger, was happy to be unleashed as he bounded down to the river, yipping with joy. Franny, on the other hand, had her troubles. Her knee. Her hip. Her condition had been improved with her own salves, yet she was still unable to keep up with the others, which was quite annoying. She had her umbrella to lean on, all the same she took the stairs slowly and Vincent hated to see that.

"I'm old," Franny reminded him when she noticed his bleak expression. "But it's still me in here. So be careful."

Vincent laughed, then offered his arm so that Franny could link her arm through his. He assisted her while acting as if he was merely walking at a slower pace for his own comfort. He remembered that Franny had never liked to ask for help, and that certainly hadn't changed. They took the staircase back up from the river path near the Île de la Cité, slowly yet again, then crossed to the Left Bank. It was after hours for the other shops on the street, but there were no set hours for what they needed. The sky was still overcast, and if you had the sight it was possible to feel those who had walked through the streets at night, who had lost those they loved during other dark springs.

"What are we willing to do?" Vincent asked as they neared their destination.

"Anything." Franny shrugged. "Everything."

Sally and Gillian were ahead of them and although Gillian was busy raising questions about Vincent's abilities, Sally took note of Amulette right away. The book in the darkened window. The sign above the door written in pale red ink that to her looked gray. She stopped at the threshold, where the ivy with its black edges had to be trimmed back each and every day. Vincent noticed that Sally had the sight and was impressed. Most had to traverse this street several times before spying Amulette.

"Sally has the gift, but she's never wanted it. You'd know that if you knew her." Franny was not about to reprimand him, still she carried a measure of hurt over his disappearance "You missed a lot."

"I had a lot," Vincent responded.

Franny understood. William. She thought of how happy Vincent had been when he'd first fallen in love, how they'd sat in the small garden on Greenwich Avenue for hours discussing William, and his attributes—smart, loyal, no bullshit—all possessed by one beautiful man. "That you did," she agreed.

Amulette was shuttered, but when Vincent pressed the bell beneath the ivy, the door opened, and they were briskly ushered inside. It was the proprietor who greeted them at this hour of the night and he quickly supplied the ingredients Vincent asked for: rosemary for remembrance, elm to connect with the inner voice, red chestnut for guidance, walnut to free them from shadows and trauma, mandrake to open the door to the other side. All these were burned in a brass dish. A block of wax held over the heat and softened into human shape.

"Can I have something that belongs to the girl?" Vincent asked.

For an instant Sally panicked, but Gillian whispered, "You have the ribbons."

In her bag, Sally carried two blue ribbons she had always tied around her daughters' wrists when they were mere babies. She looked through her wallet and found them. "I'm not sure which is Kylie's," she told Vincent.

He closed his eyes and took the first ribbon. "This one." He tied the thread around the wax figure which was placed in the dish with the herbs where it melted. "Do you have an atlas?" he asked the proprietor. A worn leather tome was brought down from an overstuffed shelf.

"This is the book that will tell us where she is," Vincent assured Sally.

Who is lost can be found. Who is found can be repaired. Who is repaired can be lost. Who is lost can be found once more.

He needed an amulet, but nothing in the glass case called out to him. He knew that his granddaughters were watching him with critical expressions. He was good at this, he'd been a finder ever since he made his way to Greenwich Village when he discovered who he was, and yet now he was unsure of himself. He hadn't used any of his skills for years, perhaps he'd lost those talents Franny had spoken of.

Franny knew what he was thinking. "Go on," she said with complete confidence in him.

It was then that he thought of the key Jet had sent. He lifted off the chain on which it had been strung, then opened the atlas and let the book fall open where it may. A map of seventeenth-century Europe was sketched in shades of red and black. When Vincent held the key on its chain over the page, it began to swing back and forth, faster and faster, until it spun in a circle. By the time it stopped on the correct location, the room had grown so cold that beneath the black drapes the windows were frosted with ice.

"London," Vincent said. "That's where she is."

It was said that there were two triangles in the world that contained the strongest magic. The White Triangle that included Lyons, Turin, and Prague, and the Black Triangle, containing San Francisco, Turin, and London. Franny and Vincent looked displeased, for reasons neither Sally nor Gillian understood. But the clerk at Amulette was aware of what the meaning of the finding was. He gave Vincent the card of a professor in London and assured them this fellow, Ian Wright, had been working in the field for decades and was well regarded for his scholarship.

"Working in what field?" Gillian asked, confused.

As the clerk closed the atlas ash speckled his hands, and he quickly took up a small tea towel to wipe off the black residue. The Dark Art left a stain that was wise to quickly clean up. That was when Sally and Gillian knew. It was the Crooked Path. Kylie was being drawn to the left-handed side.

No one spoke as they left the store. Vincent looped the key around his neck once more. He could feel it there, a quickened pulse. For the first time in a long time he felt as if anything could happen. Because they would travel on this night, he insisted they take a taxi back to Boulevard de la Madeleine rather than walk.

Franny gave him a look and said, "I'm quite fit."

"It's for me, dear," Vincent said, so small a lie it didn't even burn his tongue. "I'm exhausted."

"I Walk at Night" was playing on the radio when they got into the taxi. The driver was singing along in muddy English. Vincent was embarrassed to hear himself, but Franny patted her brother's back. "So beautiful," she said proudly. "No wonder they still play it."

Sally had never listened to her grandfather's song before; she hadn't been interested since he clearly had never been interested in them, but now she had little choice.

Isn't that what love makes you do? Go on trying even when you're through.

Sally had grown up convinced that Vincent Owens was a coward who had deserted them all, but now she wondered if there wasn't more to it. He was sitting up front with the taxi driver discussing whether or not the rain was gone for good, and then he suddenly turned to look back at Sally, as if he knew what she was thinking, as if he thought the very same thing.

What wouldn't I do for love?

The taxi waited outside while they went to fetch their luggage. They would leave for London on the night train. Why wait, they all agreed. Agnes packed a bag with supplies they might need to ensure they were safe. Red thread, sage, salt, lavender, red and black ink in iridescent glass jars, a length of rope, thin sheets of red paper bound in red leather, long sharp pins. "It's always best to be prepared," she advised. As the sisters and Vincent carried their suitcases downstairs, Agnes beckoned to Franny. "Come into the pantry for a moment. I have something for you."

"Completely unnecessary," Franny assured her. The others were waiting impatiently in the front hall with their suitcases. They had a train to catch. Yet Agnes insisted. Once they were alone, she handed Franny a small leather pouch. Inside was a charm in the shape of a triangle, made of pure, elemental gold found in river sand. The talisman, which was known to protect its wearer from evil, had been in Agnes's family for hundreds of years, and had belonged to her six-times great-grandmother, Catherine. On one side was an eye, on the other side a crow. The amulet was strung onto a thin length of cord, and Agnes encouraged Franny to slip the talisman over her head. Franny did so, but she wasn't happy about it. "It should go to Sally. It's her daughter who's missing. Her mission."

Agnes smiled faintly and gave a tiny shrug. They were both old, and because of this they likely knew too much. How dark the world could be, how great the losses we all must eventually face were. "It's for you, Franny. When evil comes looking for someone, you'll be ready."

II.

On the flight to London, Kylie had stayed awake all night long, sandwiched in between a large snoring man beside her on her right and a dead-to-the-world eleven-year-old on his way to visit his father in London on her left, doing her best to ignore them both. She'd appropriated a pair of gloves from the library so that *The Book of the Raven* wouldn't burn her hands as she finished reading it. Inside were the principles of the book.

> *Language was everything. Trust was for fools. Love came and went. Words could be stolen.*

The text gave off a faint orange glow and there was the stink of sulfur, but everyone on the flight was asleep and no one paid any attention to the tall young woman with a wash of red in her hair who was so engaged in her book she didn't notice when there was turbulence halfway across the Atlantic. No one knew who Kylie was or what she'd been through. She had left the person she cared about most in the world in a deep coma at Mass General, where the doctors were concerned he might never be roused, and, if he was, whether or not the damage he'd sustained might be irreversible.

Images of Gideon on that afternoon in the Cambridge Common continued to surface, how alive he was, how carefree, other than his worries about an exam he was certain to pass. All Kylie could do was try her best to concentrate on the book. Nothing else mattered other than lifting the curse. The prose was written on thin pages of vellum, bound in black calfskin that had been tied together with knotted black thread. It contained fewer than a hundred pages, but was difficult to read; parts had been written in Italian, and some of the script disappeared as it was being read, vanishing from the page as if washed clean before her eyes. This was literary magic, written by Amelia Bassano, who had studied astrology with a great master, and the conjurations and charms she had known were so powerful they flared in the dark and could be read by the light of their meaning alone. Kylie had taken a class in conversational Italian, but she was far from fluent and so she'd bought a phrase book at the airport bookstore to help her decipher sections of the text, not as helpful as she'd wished, for it appeared an archaic version of that language had been used.

The book advised the practitioner on the practical uses of what the author referred to as *magia nera*, black magic. How to call up maladies to befall one's enemies, how to force a liar to tell the truth, how to conjure demons that would haunt men's daily lives as well as their dreams, how to bring a rain of destruction down from the sky.

Know what you want, and be sure of it, for regret gives birth to more regret and nothing more.

The light that emanated from the writing caused the flight attendant to rush over to see if the flickering was created by a lit cigarette, but Kylie had quickly covered the book with a napkin, and the flight attendant, who then assumed she must have imagined the wavering yellow flare due to her own exhaustion, apologized for disturbing her.

Once she'd arrived in London, Kylie found a small, shabby hotel in Bayswater. The bedsheets were grimy, and the bathroom was down the hall. "We plan on sprucing up," the desk clerk told her, as if she cared. She felt a million miles from home, alone in a world to which she didn't belong. Kylie took a few bites from one of the packaged sandwiches she'd bought in a quick mart at Heathrow, but it was stale and she had no appetite. She had to hurry and she knew it. She didn't take a shower or change her clothes. The longer it took to discover a way to end the curse, the more likely she was to lose Gideon. According to *The Book of the Raven*, her first act should be to create the sign of the pentacle of Solomon to summon the spirit of Hecate, goddess of the crossroads and of sorcery. If she did so, she would discover the direction in which she would find the knowledge she needed.

Kylie lifted the fringed throw rug and used a black felt pen to sketch a pentacle on the scuffed wooden floor. She burned sage and sandalwood in the metal dustbin, herbs her aunts had given to her to smudge her dorm room. "Never be without these," her aunt Jet had advised, but Kylie had stuffed the herbs into a drawer, remembering them only when she stopped at Dunster House on her way to the airport to toss her passport and a change of clothes into her backpack. Now as the pungent smoke arose in the dingy hotel room, she stood in the center of the circle that was intended to unite the four sections of the world and the four elements. She would do whatever she must to follow the instructions set down in *The Book of the Raven*, although she worried about her abilities. She had few skills, other than spying auras and telling what the weather would bring, and no reference for magic—her mother had seen to that. Surprisingly, that had begun to change. Ever since she'd opened the first page of *The Book of the Raven* she could see what was previously unseen; she could feel what she'd never felt before. She could view the edges of the future, which caused a strange double vision. It was the sight, the inherited ability to see what was to come, a skill that had been repressed and rejected by her mother, a talent Kylie now welcomed.

Before the plane had landed at Heathrow, she'd reached the last page of *The Book of the Raven*. Her skin continued to blister as she touched the paper, but that didn't faze her. A practitioner of left-handed magic must not flinch or fear. So said the raven, the writer of the book. *Without courage, you will never find the answer.* The book was divided into six sections. "How to Gain Your Deepest Desire." "How to Make Him Love You." "How to Protect Yourself and Others." "How to Seek Revenge." "How to Curse Those Who Have Wronged You." "How to Break a Curse."

There it was, the last chapter, exactly what Kylie needed, yet despite all attempts, the last two pages were inexorably bound together. Kylie feared she would ruin the book in her attempts to separate the fragile vellum. She must discover a way to convince the book to open to her, to decide that she was worthy, the person the book had been waiting for. Now, in her hotel room in Bayswater, so far from home and from everyone she knew and loved, thinking of Gideon, she stood in the circle and breathed in the scent of sage and sandalwood, hoping the smoke would not set off the fire alarm and bring the desk clerk running. She recited her vow to do what she must, cutting her hand with a corkscrew left atop a tiny, foul-smelling fridge, and adding her own blood to the fire. When thick beads of blood, so dark they appeared black, spilled into the mixture, the smoke billowed a brilliant red. Kylie ran to open the window and waved her arms to disperse the crimson swirls, but the smoke would leave its mark on the ceiling, so the next guest would wonder what on earth had happened, never knowing that in this small room, the door to left-handed magic had been flung open on an ordinary day. It was here that a young woman gave herself over to the darkness, to blood and bones, to black thread and knives and ashes, to the curse that had been growing stronger for three hundred years, once planted in the earth in Salem, Massachusetts, and now blooming here, in London, and inside her heart.

Kylie paid for a two-night stay, informing the clerk that she was a student whose goal was to finish up some research at the British Museum. She then found her way to a store near Covent Garden known for its collection of magical provisions. It was a small, untidy shop, rather seedy, mostly frequented by women in search of herbal remedies for beauty or health. Here one could find infusions that contained yarrow and rue for women's monthly problems, peppermint for ailing stomachs, white willow for headache. The owner was a retired midwife named Helene Jones.

"How did you find us, dear?" Helene asked as Kylie bought a small bundle of herbs, along with a bottle of cologne containing rosewater and a wand made of hazel wood.

She'd looked up a directory of magic stores and this particular shop, Helene's House of Magic, was simply first on the list. "Just lucky," Kylie said, and Helene had given her a discount since she appeared to be a student, newly arrived in the country and new to the Nameless Art. The girl was clearly naive, for she asked

Helene where she might find those who practiced left-handed, an issue that was never discussed, for those who practiced did so in private.

"I'm so sorry," Helene said in a clipped tone, not quite as affable as she'd been previously, her expression revealing her distaste. "I have no idea what you mean."

A clerk named Edward had overheard, a shady young fellow looking after his own interests. When Kylie left the shop, Edward was waiting outside, finishing up a cigarette. "I know where you can find what you're looking for." Edward looked over his shoulder to make certain no one could overhear, before turning back to Kylie. "It'll cost you."

Kylie offered up the locket that her mother had given her on her birthday, which contained a photo of Jet. Edward studied it with a suspicious glance. The color was black, not silver as she said, and that confused him. Kylie witnessed an aura blazing around the clerk. Green, the color of a fool. "Believe me, it's silver and it's worth more than you deserve for some information you should willingly share."

"Keep your jewelry. I'd rather have cash," Edward informed her. "People don't share information about the Crooked Path for nothing," he said scornfully. Americans were so entitled, even in matters of magic.

Kylie took out twenty dollars. "It's the best I can do." Kylie seemed dangerous at that moment, as women often do when they know what they want.

"It won't hex me to have dealings with you, will it?" Edward asked, hesitating, before he took the cash. He'd had some run-ins with left-handed magic when working as a delivery boy for the shop and had a missing tooth to show for it.

"Of course not," Kylie said, even though the clerk would likely have a bad case of hives by morning, with a hex from *The Book of the Raven* that was more sleight-of-hand trickery than real magic, a small reminder that he had done his best to extort her. That's how the left-hand path began, with small resentments and bitterness receiving the first dark responses. "Go on, then," Kylie urged.

Edward proceeded to prattle on about a private library not far from where she was staying, near Lancaster Gate, across from Hyde Park. "They've got everything you could be looking for. Names, faces, places. Only thing is, you've got to be a member to get in. And don't mention me to anyone there. I've made a few deliveries to them. They tend to get pissy about their privacy."

The Invisible Library had existed for hundreds of years, but had been at the same address since the mid-nineteenth century when the neighboring blocks of terraced houses were built in the Georgian style. If you didn't know what you were looking for, you would never see it. If you narrowed your eyes and half spied it, a woman named Mrs. Hempstead, a housekeeper of sorts who lived in the basement apartment, would come out and chase you away, accusing you of disturbing the privacy of nonexistent tenants.

The collection of books of magic had begun in 1565, funded by wealthy men who were interested in magic, but who didn't wish their curiosities and pursuits to be made public. It had occasionally been forced to shut down, during the war, for instance, when bombs were falling in London, and then in the eighties, that egocentric decade, when it had been impossible to find a librarian willing to take on a position that was quite thankless. One had to be on call twenty-four/seven in case of emergencies, and the silence of the job had driven one librarian mad at the turn of the century. In the sixties another librarian, high on pot and willing to expose the library's membership and location, had spoken with a reporter, but thankfully the journalist could never find the address to document the story.

There was a metal box at the top of the steps in which people could leave manuscripts, with a notice on the lid firmly warning that once deposited, a manuscript could not be returned and that there was no assurance a book would be accepted. People brought books they had found in attics and at jumble sales, books their grandmothers or aunts or they themselves had written, books of family lore, personal *Grimoires* whose owners had passed away, books with brown-paper covers that were said to make a reader lose his or her vision, left-handed books that stank of sulfur and fish.

Kylie knocked on the door to the library, not the usual way to gain entrance, for members had keys and let themselves in. If Gideon were with her, she would likely have had more courage; she wished she could conjure him to stand beside her on the step.

When no one answered, Kylie tried the brass door knocker. Nothing happened. She imagined Gideon whispering in her ear, the half Gideon who was there in her imagination. *You can't give up now.*

Kylie took *The Book of the Raven* from her backpack and invoked an entry incantation.

> *What you were, you will no longer be. What has been broken, will be restored. Open to me.*

When Kylie and Antonia were growing up, their mother had told them if they ever were lost it was always best to find their way to a library. The sisters had depended on one another from a young age. *I love you* was always answered by *I love you more*. But if they were alone or separated, if they were in need, or in trouble, if they were in search of knowledge, or a friendly face, or simply a phone to use to call home, all could be found in a library.

Please Kylie added to her entreaty. *Please let me in.*

Her voice was barely audible, yet she heard the lock click. She stumbled on the stair, and the librarian, a man in his seventies, reached for her arm and ushered her inside.

This morning a spoon had fallen while the librarian had made his tea, which predicted company coming, although he hadn't imagined this childlike tall young woman, clearly lost. Yes, the rule was you needed to be a member to be admitted to the library, but rules didn't always apply. It was an extraordinary place, after all, in both form and content. The floor was marble throughout, the hanging lamps were crystal, and the extraordinarily elaborate ceiling moldings had been painted a deep, glossy red. The fabric of the draperies was a rich scarlet velvet that didn't let in the sunlight, for the books must be protected from light and greed and misusage.

The librarian introduced himself as David Ward. He was tall and distinguished looking, his eyes a cloudy blue that revealed nothing of what he felt inside, a man who was calm even in the midst of a storm. He'd had a storm in his life, and it had ruined him, and he'd vowed never to allow his raw emotions to control him again. He had recently passed his seventy-fourth birthday, but despite his vow, he had never been able to escape his past. He often felt too much, as he did now when he saw a girl who was on the edge of taking the Crooked Path.

"I suppose you've come for a book," David said.

"Actually, I already have a book. I just can't open it." Kylie reached into her backpack to bring forth the small black text she now cradled in her hands.

David Ward narrowed his gaze, astonished by what he saw before him. He was well aware of the author of the book and of her reputation as a poet and a courtesan. There were those who believed that Amelia Bassano was the Dark Lady of Shakespeare's sonnets, and others who were convinced she was the true author of his plays. Though she was the woman few had heard of, it was possible she had been the author of the greatest plays ever written.

David hadn't been aware that Amelia Bassano had written this second book, but he understood its purpose after one glance. *The Book of the Raven* was a Book of Shadows, a dark *Grimoire*, one she'd written both for herself and for the benefit of others. "I assume you're here to donate the text." He was actually quite excited about it. There was no doubt that however dark it might be, the book was a treasure.

"Absolutely not." The girl looked fiercely territorial upon hearing his suggestion; she held the book more tightly, refusing to relinquish it. "I need to find information about the author and about my family." It was then that she dropped her brave face. "I'm cursed," she said in a reedy voice.

David felt prickles down his neck. He gazed at his left hand and saw that his fate was changing as the girl spoke.

He brought Kylie to the reference room where there were dozens of oak cabinets set under glass fixtures shining down pools of dull yellow light. The library still made use of the old method of cataloguing, each entry written on a white card, some of them three hundred years old. David had begun to digitize the library's holdings, but some of the material was resistant to technology and there were books that spat at him when he attempted to nudge them into the modern age. He had found references to Amelia Bassano in other *Grimoires* on the library's shelves in the past, for she had moved in both royal and literary circles, and had been a student of Queen Elizabeth I's astrologer, Dr. Simon Forman, but he had never seen a direct reference to *The Book of the Raven*.

When Kylie pointed out that her ancestor Faith Owens's name had been written down in the seventeenth century as the owner of the book, David wondered how it had fallen into her hands. He brought them both cups of tea and set to work beside Kylie, so that they shared an unexpected intimacy. They had a similar style, neither spoke while researching and assessing the information they gleaned, much of it in bits and pieces. After an hour more in which they had little success locating the Owens name, the librarian realized Kylie held her hands over her eyes. Daunted, having discovered nothing of any use, tears had welled up. David wanted to say something reassuring, but he was no good at sympathy. Instead he handed the girl a handkerchief. That was when he saw that the tearstains were black.

"You might have mentioned you were a witch," he said gently. "It will help with our research."

Kylie glanced up at him, her eyes brimming and black, truly bewildered. It was then the librarian understood she was unaware of the truth about her family or herself.

"Should I have said nothing?" he wondered aloud. He had made mistakes such as this before, saying too little, saying too much.

"I'm not a witch," Kylie told the librarian. "My aunts are healers. They have a greenhouse, they grow herbs, and people come to them for remedies. It's nothing more than that."

"Witchery is not a choice. This is not the Unnamed Art, which women have been practicing for hundreds of years, perhaps since the beginning of time, training themselves to use herbs and green magic. It's a bloodline situation." When she still looked blank, he added, "An inheritance."

Kylie mulled this over, thinking of the rules her mother had set out when she and Antonia were young. She felt the shivers, as one did when the truth suddenly became evident. "Fine," she said in an even tone. "Let's look for my family."

They poked around in various genealogy catalogues for the Owens name and found there were many listings of births and weddings and funerals, particularly in Essex. Kylie's eyes burned, but she read on, as if reading could save her from her fate.

"May I ask what the curse is?" David Ward asked.

Kylie peered over at him and was quiet. *Trust was for fools.* Was it rude not to answer?

When the girl hesitated, David thought perhaps he had been too forward. "Of course, you are entitled to your privacy."

What had secrecy done for her in the past? Absolutely nothing. "It ruins whoever loves us," she told him. "And it ruins us, too."

David understood her meaning, for he'd been ruined by magic and love. "I see," he murmured, and went back to the catalogue. "It's likely that you need to go back to the birthplace of the person who set the curse." He had begun to scan witch trials, hoping to find her family's name. Part of the skill of research is the ability to guess what might have been, the glimmering of a sixth sense combined with the doggedness of a detective, along with the precious talent of being able to imagine how another's life might have been lived.

They took a break for tea, heading for the simple kitchen in the rear of the building, where David heated tomato soup and brought out a small platter of crackers and cheese. Kylie was ravenous, she realized, and very grateful to be fed, delighted to know that tea included food. She felt surprisingly comfortable here, even though she had always hated spending time at the Owens Library, perhaps because her mother was in charge.

"You must have talents you don't know about," David Ward suggested.

Kylie shrugged and spooned up soup. "Nothing much. I can forecast weather. I think I may be able to change it. I see colors around people. It always seemed like a game, like knowing what people will say before they speak. I didn't think it was magic."

David threw her a look; there was an awkwardness in not knowing how to respond. To have magic inside of him was what he'd always wanted. Instead, he had settled for second best, being an expert. He certainly was not about to make an admission, but he had walked on the left-hand side when he was younger, in the blundering way of men in need.

Kylie didn't mention the dark aura she saw around the librarian, a dense halo of blue. As for David, he didn't ask what she saw when she studied him. He knew what it was. He felt guilty for every moment he was alive.

After their tea break, they went back to the task of inspecting the Owens family files. The name surfaced in records in East Anglia, where Matthew Hopkins, the self-proclaimed witch-finder general, had begun his search for evil in 1644, resulting in 233 dead, before his own death by drowning, at last ridding the world of the being in which true evil had resided. And there it was, the name Hannah Owens. David eagerly showed Kylie the page of slanted scrawling of the town notary. Hannah Owens had been arrested, tried, and found guilty. It was written that she was a cunning woman who encouraged other women to turn to witchery and that she was too dangerous to be allowed to live. Hannah had come from a village called Thornfield where a man named John Heron had testified against her, saying she had enticed him into her bed and that she had a tail and practiced the Dark Art. Fortunately, the witch trials ended as suddenly as they'd begun, and for just as little reason. In the end, Hannah was let free from jail, fined three shillings that she didn't have, and therefore beaten three times with a whip instead.

"Hopefully this John Heron got his comeuppance," David Ward mused.

It was written that after Hannah was released from jail, she was murdered by a man named Thomas Lockland, who claimed she had turned his wife's affections cold by use of witchery. David soon found a marriage document between a woman named Rebecca and this Lockland, but Rebecca's name had been crossed out. In each generation that followed, the oldest son had carried a curse blamed on a hex called down upon them by Hannah Owens, who had been burned to death in her own garden.

"The Locklands were a grand family once," David revealed. "With a huge land grant from the court. The manor is up in Essex, just outside Thornfield. Somehow, your family and theirs were intertwined. It seems both were cursed, and this Hannah Owens seems to be the connection."

So that was it. To find the curse she had to look not only into *The Book of the Raven*, but into the history of her own family. Kylie thanked the librarian and packed up her bag. Time would not allow her to stay longer. The library had been a haven and she dreaded what came next, for those who wish to understand left-handed magic must embrace it first. The most recent Lockland was listed as still living in Thornfield.

"I'll see what he knows about the curse," Kylie told the librarian before thanking him and saying her good-byes.

David Ward was worried for her, even though it wasn't his place. In truth, he'd spent most of his life fretting over one thing or another. He'd twisted himself to fit into a family and had failed despite his attempts. To this day, he often dreamed of his own daughter, lost when she was not much older than Kylie. In his dreams his girl was often perched in a tree, unreachable, with gravity having no pull on her. "You could stay," he found himself telling Kylie. "There's a room here at the library for overnight guests. We have volume after volume listing curse-breakers."

Kylie shook her head. "Not my curse," she said, and there was little he could do to refute that. It was raining outside, the dark green rain that meant something was about to change. It happened before deaths and discoveries, before people went on journeys that were successful and those from which they would never return. When Kylie asked how she could get to Thornfield, David directed her to Liverpool Street station, then took his wallet from his gray suit jacket and thrust the fifty pounds that he always carried for an emergency into Kylie's hands.

"Oh, I couldn't," Kylie was quick to say. *Trust was for fools*, *The Book of the Raven* had insisted. But then they exchanged a look, for certainly Kylie could use the cash after giving the rude boy at the shop a twenty, so she swallowed her pride and said, "All right, then. Thank you."

David's hands ached when he pressed the money into hers. He might not have magic flowing through him, but after a lifetime of study he knew when the future was uncertain. They walked to the door together, and as he watched Kylie duck into the rain, he thought of his own daughter, whose favorite summer dress was blue, blue for protection and for luck, although she'd had no luck at all, not even when he'd made a bargain for her future using the Dark Art.

David wanted to explain that there were curses that could be broken only with a payment that was far too costly for most people to bear, but he had failed at his attempts to protect the person he loved best in the world, so he kept quiet now. He had second thoughts as Kylie was leaving, and called out to stop her. She had already decided not to go back to her hotel, but to instead take a taxi directly to the train station. Time was everything when it came to bringing Gideon back. Still, she took a moment to turn to face the librarian. He had one bit of advice for the girl from his own experiences in the world of left-handed magic. "Don't trust anyone," he called.

Kylie gazed back at him with a faint smile of gratitude. This was one bit of advice *The Book of the Raven* had already made abundantly clear. "I don't intend to," she assured him.

Perhaps the book would protect her. David certainly hoped so, although he was not a hopeful man. He continued to watch as Kylie dashed down the steps and hailed a taxi, her red-brown hair spattered by raindrops. They had been researching all day and time had vanished as they dove into the records of the past. It was already that blue hour when people had left work and the streets were nearly vacant. Dappled light fell onto treetops and pavement and the city felt haunted. A taxi stopped and Kylie scrambled in. David Ward raised his hand in a gesture of farewell, deeply unsettled by his fears of what might come to be. The girl rolled down her window, but before she could call out her gratitude, the taxi plunged onto the street and rounded a corner and she disappeared, something that the librarian had witnessed once before, only this time the circumstances were different, and hopefully the outcome would be different as well.

III.

Antonia was walking through the mud in her dream. Of course she was alone. She was the one left behind to take care of things, the responsible one who did what she must without anyone's help. In her dream, however, she was much wilder, she was wrecking her dress and as she trod through a bank of reeds she lifted her skirt, for the hem was already soaking. This traipsing about seemed foolhardy in a way she would never be in her waking life. Still, she had no choice but to go forward. How strange, she rarely wore dresses, but this one suited her well. There were crows above her, clouds of cawing birds blocking out the sun, their jeweled blue-black feathers falling to the ground. As she entered the water, there was a woman in the shallows, facedown, her dress floating out like a lily, her arms and legs unmoving. Antonia approached, but before she could stop herself she went under and she went under fast.

She awoke with a gasp, spitting water. She could feel her baby moving inside her, and sat up in bed. Her window had been left open and the rain had come in on gusts of wind and now everything in the room had a damp green sheen. The Charles River had flooded and Storrow Drive was impassable. It was a Sunday and even though she would have preferred to try to track down her mother and Gillian and Franny, she kept her promise to look in on Reverend Willard, driving up in Gillian's car, bringing along some packaged cookies. She unpacked the biscuits in the car, arranging them on the paper plate before going into the retirement home. *There*, she thought, *as good as homemade*.

When she walked in the door, everyone knew who she was, the Owens girl who was a medical student. A woman who was visiting her father stopped Antonia in the hall to ask if she could check in on her dad, for she'd arrived to find him listless and clearly unwell.

"I don't work here," Antonia said.

"Just a look," the woman pleaded. Everyone knew what an Owens woman was capable of and this one was studying to be a doctor as well.

The woman's eyes were brimming with tears, and there Antonia was, the responsible sister once more. "Fine," she allowed. "But I'm only a medical student."

Still the woman insisted; she'd gone to Jet on several occasions, searching for cures for headaches that wouldn't cease, a husband who complained night and day, and a son who couldn't seem to get or hold a job.

Antonia went into a corner room, shared by two elderly patients. The one by the window was the father. He was so close to death a black cloud of ash was already spreading across the ceiling. Antonia tried not to pay attention to such illogical signs, especially when working at the hospital. But some things couldn't be ignored. There were ashes on the old man's bedsheets. Antonia quickly took the father's vitals and listened to his chest. A nurse had come in to watch. "He had the flu and it's just lingered," the nurse said. "He says he's feeling fine."

"I say it because it's true," the old fellow said feebly. He was listless and half asleep, eyes closed.

"Pneumonia," Antonia decided. "He needs IV antibiotics."

The nurse was cautious. "I have to have a doctor's order."

Antonia lowered her voice. "When does the doctor come? If it's tomorrow, this gentleman will likely be dead."

Antonia and the nurse shared a wordless exchange of agreement. The medication was brought in, the door clicked shut, and an IV was inserted. Half an hour later the old man had opened his eyes.

Antonia finally made it to the Reverend's room, still carrying the plate of biscuits, though they were a bit worse for wear, flaking pale crust. "Hey there," she called. "Here at last."

She sounded ill-tempered, even to herself. Half of her morning was already gone and she was eager to get back in the car and head home. Reverend Willard sat in a plastic chair, gazing out the window. He loved the spring, though he was convinced that this dark, bloomless season might be his last one. That was why he was so tearful. He turned to see a pretty young woman who was quite pregnant. The Reverend had no idea who Antonia was, only she wasn't Franny, who was always quite sour and difficult, so it was a relief to have this fresh, young woman appear, though it was clear that the pale crumbly biscuits she offered were store-bought.

"I'm filling in," Antonia informed him, fetching the old man some fresh water and placing the biscuits on his bedside table.

"These aren't Jet's biscuits," the Reverend said. "Hers are homemade."

"Yes, well, I can't bake. I can't cook at all. I'm a disaster at it. These will have to do."

"You can't cook because you don't care," the Reverend said. "It makes all the difference, you know. Jet cared."

"Of course, I care," Antonia hotly replied. "I'm just busy. Actually, I'm overwhelmed."

The Reverend nodded knowingly. "You're nervous about being a parent."

"I didn't say that!" The old man seemed to think he knew everything when he didn't know the first thing about her.

"It will all change." The Reverend gestured to her extended belly. "You'll feel differently once he arrives."

"She," Antonia corrected him. "And cooking doesn't make you a good parent." She tried one of the store-bought biscuits and found that the Reverend was right; it was wretched. After the first bite she pitched it into the trash. "Anyway, how do you know if you'll be any good at it or not?" She'd had pangs of worry about this very issue. She had the impression that she had closed off her heart long ago; from the time she and Kylie were children their mother warned them that love was trouble and trouble was love. Since then there had always been a fierce distance between Antonia and other people, excluding her old, beloved friends and her family. Why shouldn't there be? She'd been avoiding matters of the heart at all costs.

"You don't know," the Reverend went on to explain. "That's the point. You'll love your child more deeply than you can imagine. It will happen to you and your husband."

"Lesbian," Antonia informed him.

"Wife?" the Reverend guessed. "Girlfriend?"

"This is not an interview. It's a social call," Antonia said briskly. Still, as long as she was there she took his pulse, which she found to be elevated.

"Well, who do you love?" he asked. "Who will love you in return?"

"You're very personal, aren't you?" Antonia said. "I'm fine on my own."

"You're afraid of the curse." The old man sympathized. "I don't blame you. It killed my boy Levi."

"There is no curse," Antonia apprised the Reverend. "Bad things happen for no reason."

Reverend Willard lowered his voice. "You don't know the half of it. Bring me something chocolate next time and I'll tell you all about it."

"You can't have chocolate." She would stop by the nurses' desk and recommend an EKG to the nurse who was open to suggestions. Just to be safe. Courage was fine and good, but when it came to medicine, caution was often more useful.

"I can have it if you bring it," the Reverend said. "Who's to know?"

Antonia had begun to find the old man a source of amusement. And something more. She took his hand in parting. He still had a strong grip. "Maybe. As long as you don't turn me in to the nurses."

"Don't forget the cake," he called after her as she left. He was certainly stubborn, and Antonia admired that. He wanted what he wanted at this point in his life, that much was clear. "The one your aunts make," Antonia heard as she let the door close behind her, suddenly craving chocolate herself.

When Antonia stopped to check on the house on Magnolia Street, she found the Merrill brothers at work in the garden, which was already wildly overgrown with plumy weeds and a dense tangle of thorny vines that could leave a gash if the person weeding wasn't careful. The brothers softly cursed the thorns as they piled up bundles of branches that would later be tossed on a bonfire, but when they caught sight of Antonia their dispositions changed. She was a beauty and her youth cheered them and made them feel young again. "All's well," they shouted optimistically, though it was clearly not the case. Why, just look at the shingles on the porch, ragged and ready to blow away in the next storm. Examine the height of the overgrown phlox. The place was a vision of neglect, as if Franny and Jet's presence had held the house together. All the same, Antonia appreciated the jolly sentiments. She waved and called out a hello, then found the hidden house key behind the twisted wisteria.

Several Post-it notes had been attached to the front door by disappointed clients in search of Franny, whom they planned to make do with now that lovely Jet was gone. *When will you be back? I need you. My son. My husband. My daughter. My life. How can I find what I'm looking for?* Children were ill or disappointing, husbands strayed or lost interest, love was wished for or wanted extinguished. Antonia collected the notes, shaking her head as she did so. People were always looking for magic. She'd sat on the back stairs and listened to the nonsense of local women who visited the aunts. They wanted to blink away their tears and stretch out their hands to receive a pardon or a cure or the key to love and fortune. *Good luck*, she thought. *You're on your own now. Try going to a therapist or a doctor or a pharmacy because no one can help you here.*

Antonia had decided to become a physician because she wanted a life buoyed by facts rather than an ancient art that left one rooting around in the darkness of *could-bes* and *maybes,* untested possibilities that might easily lead to disaster. This was the price of being the older sister. She was vigilant and always looked before she leapt. She was the one Kylie depended on when their mother was preoccupied. Should they walk into the dim woods? Absolutely not. Should they leap from the flat ledges above Leech

Lake? Not on your life. There were bees and poison ivy to watch out for, broken limbs and concussions. This is the way a doctor is often formed, an individual aware of possibilities others chose to ignore.

Gillian, who often spoke about topics that Sally kept off limits, always argued that science and magic were twin arts aiming for the same results. "But one is proven!" Antonia would insist, to which Aunt Gillian would defiantly fling back, "And one has no need to be!"

Now as Antonia entered the darkened hallway of the old house, exhausted by dragging her extra baby weight around, she wondered what the Reverend knew about the curse. He was aware of much of what had transpired in this town, both within his family and theirs. When Antonia first heard about the curse at Jet's funeral, she'd imagined it was little more than a joke, another odd bit of history that had come down through the generations, a story twisted over time, with details that had always been sketchy. There was no law against believing in magic; she'd come upon ingredients that her aunts used for enchantments in the greenhouse, and it did no real damage, or so she'd thought until her sister went missing. Everything was now topsy-turvey, even her own usually calm psyche. She was exhausted and wished she could stretch out on the window seat on the stair landing to nap. She both wanted sleep and feared it. Who was the drowning woman in her dream and what was she trying to tell Antonia?

In the front hall, Antonia stumbled over the mail that had come in through the brass letter slot to collect in a messy pile on the rug. Most of it was from Hardy and Hardy, the law firm that handled the Owens estate, all addressed to Frances Owens. Since Franny was unreachable, Antonia sat in the parlor and tore open the most recent envelope.

Dear Miss Frances Owens,

We have tried to reach you via phone and mail to no effect. Your sister's will is here with us and it must be reviewed by someone in the family so that her wishes can be seen to properly.

Yours respectfully,
A. S. Hardy, Esquire.

Antonia folded the letter into her pocket. She might have ignored it completely, but she was the practical sister, the dutiful daughter, the niece who looked after the family obligations. She toured the house to make sure there were no leaks, no mice, no lights left on, no faucets dripping, no birds trapped in the parlor, no fluttering moths behind the curtains, no racoons in the attic, no teenagers sneaking into the greenhouse to look for herbs or have fumbling sex, then she took the time to write out the monthly check for the brothers for their groundskeeper fees, even though they always made a fuss and said that Miss Frances Owens never needed to pay for their services.

She hoped the stop at the attorneys' office on Beacon Street would be brief. Traffic was bad in Boston, as always, but she managed to fit Gillian's Mini into a tiny space. The law firm had been at the same address since the late seventeenth century when there were cow paths rather than roads. There had been at least one attorney in every generation. Antonia remembered the old man, Arthur Smith Hardy, from the time she was a child. He'd been Isabelle Owens's lawyer, a rather intimidating gentleman who wore a gray pinstriped suit and a black tie, clothes appropriate for both legal work and funerals. Antonia felt the sting of anxiety as she was ushered into his office. To her surprise the only one in sight was a young woman with shining pale hair, who was sorting through files spread out on the floor. The woman, not quite thirty and extremely attractive, looked up, somewhat indignant at having been interrupted, pushing her hair out of her large expressive eyes.

"I'm here to see my lawyer," Antonia informed her. "A. S. Hardy."

"I'm A. S. Hardy." The woman on the floor had the darkest eyes imaginable, nearly black. You could fall into them if you weren't careful. She had a reputation among other attorneys for her fierce presence both in a courtroom and in her practice. It was said that any client who looked at her directly would be unable to tell a lie. She arose from the carpet and reached out her hand. "Ariel," she introduced herself. "Ariel Samantha Hardy."

"I thought I would be seeing the old man." Antonia was so matter-of-fact she was often perceived as rude, as her aunt Franny was. Be a forthright woman and all hell could break loose. Still, she assumed that lawyers were used to blunt conversation, and, in fact, her tone didn't seem to faze Ariel Hardy in the least.

"My grandfather," Ariel said. "He passed away five years ago. This is my father's office. Mine is down the hall, but it's a mess. When I heard you had set up an appointment, I thought you'd be more comfortable here."

Ariel gestured for her to take a seat in one of the worn leather chairs. Antonia, who'd been sleepy for months and had been impatient about getting home so that she could take a long nap, bad dreams or not, was suddenly wide awake.

"I'm sorry to hear about your grandfather." She wasn't really, she barely knew him, but Antonia knew well enough to be polite.

There were twenty-three overstuffed files on the desk and even more in the basement; that was how long the families had been doing business. "Grandpop was ninety-seven and he passed in his sleep. Not a bad way to go. Now I'm following in his footsteps." Ariel handed over the most recent folder. "Your aunts owned all the real property jointly, therefore Miss Frances owns everything now. The house is in a trust that pays for itself, regarding taxes and expenses. Once Miss Frances is deceased the property can never go outside of the family. If no one chooses to live there, it is to remain empty."

Antonia was stunned by the mention of her aunt Franny's eventual demise. She certainly wouldn't think about that now.

Ariel Hardy dropped her voice. "I hear the house is haunted."

"Not at all. That's the local people's nonsense." Antonia found that she was dying of thirst. "Do you have any water?"

Ariel fetched a glass of tepid, cloudy water. "If you don't mind, this is supposed to be a reading of the will, so I'll just get on with it."

Since Antonia was the only member of the family available, she would have to do, and of course she agreed. "Read away."

"There's a trust for the house, as I said, and another trust will continue to support the library. As for Bridget Owens's personal belongings, your aunt wanted everything to go to your mother and your aunt Gillian, except for her personal library, which is to be sent to Rafael Correa. She also left him a packet of letters that can be found in her night-table drawer. If you deliver them to me, I'll have them sent on."

Antonia was baffled. "Who is Rafael Correa?"

"Apparently someone she was quite close to. I suspect they were separated by the curse."

"There is no curse," Antonia was quick to say. She wondered if this Rafael Correa was the handsome older man she and Kylie had spotted lingering around the edges of the funeral and the luncheon afterward, leaving with the little lost dog Jet had brought home.

"I'm just repeating what my grandfather told me." Ariel clearly meant no offense, but when she had information, she felt it only right to share it with a client. "Maria was said to be a witch."

"There are no witches," Antonia said. "Only people who want to burn them."

Ariel grinned and handed over a small tarnished key. "Although you might want to see Maria Owens's papers. They're in a locked box in the basement. As far as I know no one's gone through them, but you're welcome to take a look."

"Maybe another time." As in never. Antonia's entire life had been based on science and logic and the notion of a curse was preposterous. Yes, she knew her aunts made remedies and teas, and that her aunt Gillian believed in amulets and enchantments, but they certainly didn't call down curses and deal with the Black Art. Antonia slipped the key into her purse, where it fell among other items she would likely never use: throat lozenges, paper clips, pens that no longer worked. Her hand still felt oddly hot and she found she was quite dizzy, which anyone in her condition might be. At this hour of the day she often had a snack to keep her energy up. "Do you have any fruit?" she asked.

"Of course." There were some plums and bananas in a ceramic bowl, which the attorney offered Antonia. "I'm sure the curse is just a story." Ariel laughed. "I mean, do you feel cursed?" Their eyes met then. Big mistake.

Antonia devoured a plum, but she was still starving. She was shaking as a matter of fact.

"Do you want me to order sandwiches?" Ariel asked. "There's a place around the corner."

"Yes." Antonia no longer had the urge to leave. "Cheese is fine. No mayonnaise. No mustard. Lettuce, but make sure they wash it and double the tomatoes. Pickles would be great."

"Perfect," Ariel Hardy said, although she didn't move to make the call.

The baby kicked Antonia without warning, swiftly bringing her back to the here and now. The Reverend was right. You didn't know if you had the ability for some things until they happened to you. You could surprise yourself with what emerged from inside yourself. It now occurred to Antonia that perhaps she herself was the woman in her dreams who was drowning, the figure with red hair, her white blouse floating out all around her, going under fast. Antonia sat back in the leather chair, her head swimming, her carefully planned future utterly disrupted. She made certain to bite her tongue. She was usually too quick to give her opinions and now it seemed as if it might be best for her to be quiet for once in her life. Everything was the same and everything was different. It was then she knew what her current situation was. This is what happened when you fell in love.

IV.

The professor's office was in Notting Hill, just off Westbourne Grove, at the end of Rosehart Mews. It was easy enough to miss, and meant to be so, as Ian Wright didn't wish to be disturbed when he was writing, and he was always writing.

There was an indistinct pentagram formed of gray bricks set into the cobblestone, but the image was faded and the stones were old. Anyone who didn't take careful notice could easily miss the address, for there was no number marking it, only the faint star that disappeared on those rare occasions when snow drifted down, but which stood out in the rain, for it was darker when wet, gleaming and nearly black. Sally spotted the sign in the window right away, but of course she was looking for it. *Control and removal of black magic.*

The front door, painted black, opened from left to right. There were bells above the threshold, but they were rusted and the jangle they made was more of a cough than a chime. It was just Sally's luck to be the one who must beg for assistance, exposing her broken heart to a stranger. They'd begun the afternoon in London at the pub at the crossroads, a cozy place called the

White Bull. Franny had insisted they draw straws to decide who would approach the professor. The Owenses were no good at asking for help, it was not in their nature, and no one wanted the task of seeking it out. Sally had won the draw, which, in her opinion, meant she had lost. She was frustrated, but it was fate that she should be the chosen one. Her daughter was missing and it was her responsibility to find Kylie. She had no choice and set off for the mews, despite her anxiety about approaching an alleged expert on left-handed magic.

"You made that happen," Vincent declared to his sister once Sally had gone.

Gillian had gone up to the bar to order sandwiches and drinks and was out of earshot. The pouring rain outside had stopped, but everything was damp, the streets flooding with murky puddles. The usually busy neighborhood was all but deserted as it was just past the lunch hour. People had taken shelter and stayed where they were in case another round of rain struck, as was predicted. So much the better in order to pick up one another's thoughts. Vincent grinned. He had distinctly sensed a silent incantation for luck emanating from Franny's direction when it had been Sally's turn to pluck a straw. He'd seen his sister's lips move as she whispered, and he'd known Sally would choose the short stick.

"I don't know what makes you say that." Franny took her brother's hand, feeling fortunate to have him near. How had they managed to get so old? And yet, some things remained the same. She flicked her gaze over a man at the bar who was staring at Vincent, nearly swooning, though he was more than twenty years younger. It still happened, just as it had when they were young. People fell head over heels for Vincent and he didn't even notice. How had he managed to remain so handsome? Franny supposed that wasn't due to magic. It was simply who he was.

"I know you," Vincent scolded Franny. "Nothing's done by accident."

"Do you think I can control a damned thing in this world?"

"I believe you can. Every now and then." Vincent felt his deep love for his sister. She'd always been the one to rescue him when they were young. "I've always believed in you."

Franny lowered her gaze so that he wouldn't see the sting of tears in her eyes, as if she could trick him. She, who was known for her cool demeanor, had somehow become a person at the mercy of her emotions, which was not like her at all. Or at least it hadn't been. The transformation had begun with Jet's passing, and now she blamed Vincent for her complete undoing. Ever since spying him on the Boulevard de la Madeleine, her love for him had opened her heart. All the same, she rapped his hand as if he was still the wild, fearless boy who had never adhered to any rules. Still, it was no mistake that Sally would be the one to leave them behind. Franny knew that something awaited Sally if she went to seek out the professor. Something unexpected and rare. Something that happened only if a person followed her fate.

"Hush," Franny told her brother. "It's my last good deed."

"You!" Vincent laughed. "Doing good? That's rich."

Gillian finally returned with three glasses of port and some chicken salad and tomato sandwiches. She'd enchanted the bartender without trying, having inherited a fair share of Vincent's magnetism. "On me," the bartender had told her, but she knew what he meant. *I've fallen for you in an instant, I don't know what's happened to me, but I'll leave my wife, my job, my home.* It was the Owens charm. Some of them had it in overabundance, while others, such as Sally, hid their inner light. Gillian had always been a firefly, drawing men to her when she was young, and trouble along with it. By now she was used to rejecting men's overtures. She grinned and said, "Taken."

"Lucky bastard," the bartender said gloomily about whoever had her hand.

Gillian wasn't so certain of that. Ben expended considerable energy trying to make her happy, hiding their marriage, living apart, but it was a thankless task when only one thing could make her happy, the arrival of a child, and there seemed no magic strong enough for that.

"Don't ever fall for a woman like me," she'd advised the bartender.

She still had the urge to ruin things, and some inner neurosis made her consider gesturing for the bartender to follow her into the ladies' room for some hot, insane, and ultimately disappointing sex for which she would hate herself afterward, but she had changed. Now she merely considered it and walked away. However, if she thought she was trouble, her great-aunt and grandfather were far worse. They didn't just find trouble, they conjured it. Now as she observed them sitting near one another, she understood they were a closed circle. "What are you two plotting?"

"We don't plot," Vincent told his granddaughter. "We conspire."

Franny threw back her head and laughed.

They ate their lunch of slightly stale sandwiches and chips, and soon half an hour had passed. Gillian turned to gaze through the window, unsettled. There was a violet sky now that the storm had passed, and yellow light pooled as it shone through the window. The world seemed incandescent to Gillian; she could see layers of time and space and possibilities that hadn't been there before. As a girl Gillian couldn't escape the petty jealousies she felt when it came to her sister's talents. She'd wondered why she had nothing other than her beauty, which, frankly, she found boring and would have traded away in exchange for Sally's abilities in a flash. The situation wasn't helped by Sally's pathetic longing to be normal. When they were young, Gillian would often stand alone in the wavering heat of summer, naked, deep in the woods where no one could find her; she would close her eyes and try her best to make magic, standing still as flickering dragonflies alit on her shoulders and arms. There was a shadow world, but she seemed the only one in her family who was refused entrance and she feared that beneath her fragile beauty, she was ordinary. She had tried and tried, appealing to the other world until she had throbbing headaches, all to no effect. In the end, Gillian would tread back to the house on muddy paths, her face hot with disappointment, unable to cast even the smallest enchantment.

It was only now, in a worn leather booth of this pub, that the edges of everything softened and she could see a glimmer of the souls of those seated around the tables and the bar. This world was framed by the other world, the one that could only be accessed by those who possessed the sight. She had a vision of her sister walking down an alleyway with water rising on either side of her, and glittering silver fish swimming over the cement, and bells ringing. There was no mistaking a prediction of love. She looked into her teacup and an image of Sally flared as she knocked upon a door, her heart in her hand.

What was happening to Gillian here in London, and what on earth was taking Sally so long? Gillian had a sinking feeling when she thought of Sally navigating the world of left-handed magic. Despite her cool exterior, Sally was more vulnerable than she'd ever admit, and far more caring. On the night their parents had died, Sally had told Gillian to go to bed, then she had gotten out from beneath the covers and tiptoed through the inky darkness of the near-empty house to the living room. The world had altered. They had no parents and the night had been filled with shadows, so Gillian had scrambled out of bed to follow her sister. There was Sally in the dark, sobbing.

Thinking of that moment, Gillian now interrupted Franny and Vincent. "I'm afraid Sally's not safe."

They turned to her, unhappy to be drawn away from their conversation, but softening when they saw the worry in Gillian's face.

"Don't be silly," Franny said. "We're in London. What on earth could go wrong?"

Professor Ian Wright had taught at Oxford and at the University of St. Andrews, and although he'd been a great favorite with his students, he'd been let go from both positions because of his unorthodox teachings. He was now within days of finishing his life's work, *The History of Magic*. He was actually at the point of copyediting, a time-consuming endeavor he had little choice but to accomplish, for the book was scheduled to be published by an American press in Illinois the following year.

Initially, he'd been wildly excited about coming to the end of this huge project, but that pride had evaporated into a strange sort of despair. He had spent his thirties and forties on the manuscript and the years had gone past much too quickly. As he reached the end of two decades of working on his book, which had grown to over a thousand pages, a monster he had no wish to slay, he felt the unique sadness of completing a task that had been set out when he was young, when time had seemed endless. He was still handsome at fifty, exceedingly so, with dark hair and dark, liquid eyes, and an obvious sexual power, but despite his good looks, he had no vanity, and even as a younger man, he'd barely glanced in a mirror. You never knew what you might find gazing back at you from the glass, especially in his line of work.

There were those who insisted that there were no demons in the world, but Ian knew otherwise. Take a turn to the left and you'd find darkness everywhere, in corners of rooms you'd walked through every day, on the streets late at night, in the hearts of men you thought you knew, and in your own heart as well. Then you had to choose. You were on the Crooked Path or you weren't, or, if you dared, as he did, you walked the line between left and right, hoping you wouldn't fall to your knees.

At present, Ian wore his hair long because he never had time to get a haircut and it nearly reached his shoulders, though he wore it pulled back with a leather band. He usually threw on a black jacket, a white shirt and black jeans, except for the times when he took to the street at five a.m. to run through the first gray light of morning. His work was risky, and he took chances; his daily runs provided a block of time when he was thinking of nothing but racing through a sleeping city. He'd started running not for health, but because he'd had a life of crime and knew what it was like to be trapped inside a cell. All that was long ago. He was still ashamed of his behavior, but not of what it had taught him. Some things stayed with you, the joy of throwing yourself into the world after you'd been caged, of going as fast as you could and not stopping for anything, not even red lights. Running still made the world seem like a dream, as it had back when he was fifteen and too alive to take heed of danger.

His office on the mews was composed of two small rooms, one more cluttered than the other. The first chamber held his desk, which he sometimes used as a dining table, along with a hot plate, a small refrigerator and a closet that had been made into a pantry, which mostly stocked whiskey, rice, and tinned food. In the second, smaller room there was a single bed. His mother, Margaret, who had always doted on him, had made the coverlet, hemming the cotton sheets with blue thread. Ian was fairly certain she'd folded some lavender and sage inside the blanket's batting that caused him to dream of home. When it came to magic, his mother was always elusive, unwilling to share her secrets regarding the Nameless Art. *What you learn yourself will suit you best,* she had told him. *Be a man who knows how important books are.*

In fact, he'd become a collector and there were books in a jumble everywhere, crammed onto shelves and stacked wherever there was space, a table, a chair, a bureau. A person could hardly see the good Persian carpet anymore. Some of the books were quite valuable. He'd had several break-ins lately, and he'd taken to padlocking his door when he went out for the evening.

It was Ian's goal to one day wrestle his library into proper order, arranged and shelved by author and subject, but that day had yet to come and he relied on his memory when looking for a reference. He had books so dangerous they needed to be kept under lock and key in a dusty cabinet, including a rare copy of *The Key to Hell* by Cyprianus, composed at a school for the Dark Art in Germany in the eighteenth century, and Agrippa's *Third Book of Occult Philosophy*, written in 1510, and the famous Icelandic book *Rauðskinna*, or *Red Skin*, which contained some of the darkest magic imaginable, the name taken from the color of the cover.

Many people believed black to be the color of magic, in fact it was red. A red moon, a red mark on the skin, red boots, a red heart, red love, all added up to red magic, the strongest there was. It was said that when *Red Skin*'s author, Gottskálk, died in 1520, his book was buried with him, but if that was true, then there had been grave robbers, or perhaps the book itself refused to be destroyed and crawled out from the earth. Ian had gotten hold of the book on a trip to Reykjavík, exchanging an immense amount of cash, his savings as a matter of fact, to a man who refused to speak except to tell him *Eg vorkenni þér*. I pity you. That pronouncement didn't frighten Ian one bit. It was better for him to lay claim to the text than to let it serve the purposes of someone who wished to do evil in the world. That was why he was on this wavering line that had become his life. He walked the left to protect others from it, all the while knowing that when you walk a path for too long it can easily become the direction you have taken. He worried about that, but didn't every man occasionally have dark thoughts? Weren't all souls finely calibrated mysteries?

Sometimes the cupboard holding the most lethal of the texts rattled, the books inside raging against being locked up and kept in the dark, though it was for their own good and the good of others. Ian hushed them, and when he was exhausted and had been working and drinking too hard, he called out for them to shut the hell up or be shredded, not that he'd ever do such a thing. Books were everything to him. They had saved his life. And yes, he supposed his mother had something to do with that as well, for she'd been the one who had opened that world to him. *Don't think you know everything, when you know so little. Stop wasting your time and read this.*

Fortunately, most of the volumes in his collection were more well behaved then the ones in the dark cabinet. *Little Albert*, which contained homey spells that would catch fish and rabbits, along with healing charms and ways to render oneself invisible. *The Dragon Rouge*, a French *Grimoire* that listed enchantments and ways to keep evil at bay. And of course, *The Magus*, written by the British occultist Francis Barrett, which at the time of its publication in 1801 was a comprehensive compilation of magic of all kinds, the copies coveted, covered with black cloths in bookshops, the very text Vincent Owens had found when he was a boy who broke his mother's rule that he must never go downtown.

Control and removal of black magic was Ian's day job; he was quite good at it and was often called in to old estates, haunted houses, homes in which hexes were prevalent. On a high shelf, he kept a collection of small glass bottles that glowed green and blue and inky black, all containing the evil he had collected on these outings. He'd been in the department of religion and philosophy once upon a time, but hadn't much cared when he was released from both prestigious universities where he'd taught. There had been too many department meetings, too much responsibility, and too many reprimands—he needed to make a living beyond the occasional lecture given in drafty halls.

The notice in the window was difficult to see because the glass needed washing and there was ivy growing up from a patch of dirt beside the door, but for those who were in need of help, the desperate and the distraught, the placard was perfectly evident. Ian had grown up with magic, not that he'd been happy about it at the time. His mother had always been a practitioner of the Nameless Art, and all the while Ian was growing up he'd wanted nothing to do with the masses of herbs drying in the rafters and the tinctures his mother had concocted in their kitchen or the people in town who seemed to both fear and revere her. Needless to say, none of his schoolmates were allowed to come play at their house, and, anyway, his mum, Margaret Wright, had thought play to be a ridiculous waste of time. They were outcasts, and Margaret couldn't care less. Ian, on the other hand, spent his early days in a fever of resentment, morphing from an unruly child into an uncontrollable teenager. Their neighbors made the sign of the fox when he lurched past, a gesture meant to protect them from evil and black magic. *Go fuck yourself*, Ian would shout at them when he was all of eleven years old. He held up two other fingers in response, the ones that would have been chopped off had he been a robber long ago so that he could not use his bow hand. Everyone knew his meaning. *I've still got mine, whether or not you like it.* People continued to tell him to piss off even when he had grown to be as tall as a man. By the age of fifteen he was handsome enough so that his neighbors' daughters stared at him with longing, all the more interested when their parents threatened to lock them in their rooms if they dared to have anything to do with Ian. Although these girls promised to avoid him, many were quick to break their vows to stay away, their hearts shattered in return for their defiance.

Growing up in Essex, Ian had felt perched at the end of the world, a landscape of marshy fens and forests and fields. He'd longed for a different life. He wanted a father, brothers, the comradery of other men. At the very least, he wanted a kitchen with an electric stove and room of his own, for their cottage was small and he'd slept on the couch. He left home at sixteen, abruptly storming out after an argument with his mother about some trivial matter, some chore he'd neglected, and it had taken years before he got back on track. He was nearly thirty by the time he went to university, and it was a miracle he made it there. As soon as he was on his own, he joined up with petty criminals, becoming a thief early on. Perhaps it would have been better if someone had chopped off two of his fingers; it might have turned him away from larceny. As it was, he was good at crime, almost unnatural in his abilities as a robber. He thought he recalled his grandmother mention they had a distant ancestor, someone in the far-flung past, who'd been an outlaw and a horse thief who had thrown in his lot with a player from the London theater with a bad reputation, so perhaps robbery was in Ian's blood. Sometimes he'd take the money and return the wallet to a pocket or purse before it had been noticed missing purely for his own amusement. He was cocky and full of himself and he'd enjoyed his risky, wild life until he'd been arrested.

It had happened in his own hometown when he'd come for a visit to see his mum out of guilt. A good deed had changed his life, for better and for worse. An old policeman named Harold Jenner, who'd caught him shoplifting from the market when he was a boy, and had been fool enough to let Ian off with nothing more than a stern talking-to, now nabbed him once more, this time for lifting a wallet.

"I'm doing this for your own good," the officer had told him when he apprehended Ian.

He'd wound up doing eighteen months in prison. Much like a crow, he'd stupidly held on to bits and pieces of what he'd stolen, a collector not of books back then, but of incriminating evidence: purses and backpacks, wallets and jewelry, all of it in a messy pile in a rented room on a bad street in London, there for the cops to see when they came to cart him off. Three weeks after he was released, he was back again. He felt like an addict, out of control, unable to stop himself from taking what he imagined he was entitled to, not yet understanding that no one is entitled to anything other than his freedom and the choices he makes.

It was in prison that he found his way to magic. For one thing, his mother visited, bringing books for him to read, and what had previously seemed like far-fetched nonsense now was quite fascinating. The first time Ian's mother had come to see him he'd glared at her defiantly when she handed him the first book of magic. She'd meant for her gift to both console him and educate him. That first text she brought him was de Laurence's *Oracle Mystery of Life and Destiny*. Lauron William de Laurence, who'd lived between 1868 and 1936, was a book pirate and a plagiarist, a rogue and a thief, but also a magician. It was beginning reading, but Margaret thought her son would appreciate the author's character. Ian had snorted a laugh as he looked through the chapters. "Hidden Treasures." "Recovering Stolen Goods." "Lucky Numbers."

"This is pure shit," Ian had said to his mother. More than ever he found himself at the mercy of his rages, which grew worse in the gloom of his cell.

Margaret didn't intend to give up on her son. As a boy he had loved to catch eels in the fens, but he'd always let them go. Margaret had known there was hope for him then, for he'd always freed anything he'd trapped, watching the eels whirl away into the deep water as if he were contemplating the clouds in the sky.

"When you're ready for real magic, let me know," Margaret had told him, resolute when it came to matching a cure to the person in need, leaving the book behind despite his complaints.

He was ready by the time the following visit came around. "I could read a bit more," he told her.

She next brought *The Magus*.

"Looks like crap," he'd said, scowling.

"Maybe it's too complicated for you," Margaret had said to get a reaction. Ian had accepted the challenge and had been reading ever since.

"Do your time and learn what you can," Margaret had told her boy and for once in his life he'd listened. That was the good luck. That was what saved him, those books. He celebrated each text he completed by getting a tattoo from a pal who used ink from broken pens and straight pins held over a match to sanitize them, more or less. Luckily, the fellow was a true artist who did quite good work. At the end of his time served, Ian was covered with ink, nineteen tattoos in all, and every one told a story. His chest was inked with a series of images, and his arms were sleeves of magic. On his left forearm there was a lion, there for courage, and on the other forearm was a serpent biting its own tail, the symbol of the universe. On his right arm a glass bottle had been inked, so delicate and shimmering it seemed real enough to break. Inside the glass, a man and a woman wrapped around one another, the marriage of opposites, love eternal, love of my life. The sleeve of tattoos on his left arm began with the hand of alchemy; above each finger floated a sun, a star, a key, a crown, and a bell. In the palm of the hand there was a fish. On his torso, a dragon, a magic circle from *The Book of Solomon*, the triangle of elemental fire, a demon trap with a scorpion in the center with Hebrew letters surrounding it, skulls and pentacles, intricate images that twisted around each other in a single shade of blue. On his back, between his shoulder blades, there was a crow with its wings spread, each feather carefully wrought, each taking an hour of pain to perfect. Ian sometimes imagined the crow to be his other self, the person he'd become in his cell, the creature who flew above the building when he closed his eyes. He wanted freedom so badly he couldn't even feel the sensation of a hot needle pricking through his skin. There were times when he thought of himself as a book that was being written with blue ink printed on his flesh. The images could not be removed or reversed, and he was glad of that. They heralded who he was, a tribute to the books he'd read that had set out the path for the rest of his life.

Since that time, he had stayed on the right-handed path, straying occasionally when his work demanded it, and paying a penance when he did. He was single-minded and he knew what he wanted. At university he wasn't daunted by the fact that he'd started ten years later than everyone else and was often the oldest person in his class. He'd gotten his degree in history at Oxford, then did his doctoral work in Eastern religions, failing to mention on his applications that he'd never completed secondary school. Perhaps a bit of forgery was involved, but who could blame him for wanting to make up for his past misdeeds? That was so long ago anyway, a life that had belonged to a boy who would have gone to the left side if the old policeman hadn't stopped him, the reason why Ian always visited Harold Jenner's grave when he went home to Essex and why he'd never called the police when his place was robbed. Whoever it was had only taken books, and it would have been unbearable for Ian to be the cause for someone to spend time in prison.

In recent years, he'd become the sort of man who phoned home every Sunday and visited at least once a month. He liked to sit in the kitchen when his mother's clients came to see her, and he felt a rising pride over the fact that the family's business had been magic for more than three hundred years. They were what was called cunning people, healers above all else. Perhaps because of his troubled early days, Ian remained interested in left-handed magic, not as a practitioner, but as an investigator of the Dark Art. His academic work had led him to do strange and improbable things and he had loved every minute of it. He'd had trysts with secret societies and with sorcerers, searched bookshops and barns for magical volumes, paid off informants in third-rate cafés, encountered sources who were either too talkative or strangely reticent, considering they'd agreed to tell all. All is not everything, he'd discovered, and the left was a path of secrets. There were huge gaps in his knowledge. Those who walked to the left kept their own counsel and trusted few, not unlike himself.

Last night he had been at The Café in the Crypt beneath St. Martin-in-the-Fields Church in Trafalgar Square, one of the hidden meeting places beneath the crowded first floor for those who practiced left-handed magic and were on the prowl. He'd stayed for nearly an hour, making himself scarce in a discreet corner, eavesdropping until he felt as though he might have been noticed as an outsider. He spied ashes on the floor, there to trap anyone who wasn't on the path. The ashes could put you in a foul mood so that you'd pick a fight and you'd find yourself tossed out on the street having been beaten and bruised at your own expense for a laugh. Fool that he was he'd stepped right in the ash and as soon as he did he could feel his strength draining. He'd had too much to drink, as well, enough to become woozy, which was a drastic mistake when walking the Crooked Path. In his younger days he'd known weeks of debauchery, but now he rarely drank and three whiskeys did him in completely. He did his best to slip out unseen and unmolested, making sure to keep his mouth shut. Ian still had his robber's ways and usually went unnoticed, dressed in black, his hair pulled back, yet all the same he'd had the sense he'd been followed when he departed the Crypt. He looked into the sky to see a cloud of crows, well aware that such birds never flew at night unless there was an emergency. He heeded the warning and took a taxi rather than the tube. His heart was pounding, the way it used to when he was attempting a robbery, but back then it had been a thrill to outsmart everyone, and he always thought he'd be the victor. On this particular night, however, he felt he might not win.

"Can you dodge around a bit?" he asked the driver once they'd headed away from Trafalgar Square.

"Wife following you?" the taxi driver guessed.

"I'm a bad boy," Ian admitted, failing to mention there was no wife and likely would never be one given his inability to commit or emotionally connect with anything other than a book. He liked women, it was true, he simply botched up romance. *You keep your-*

self hidden, his mother had told him. *As do you*, he'd shot back. He was still angry at not having known his father. *And I'm alone*, Margaret Wright responded. *And don't mind being so.* The implication was, he was not.

"I don't mind helping out a bad boy once in a while," the driver said.

They'd rode around aimlessly for twenty minutes, then Ian had directed the driver to Westbourne Grove. He got let out at the corner by the pub. On most nights he would have gone in for a nightcap, but he still felt a shadow behind him, a pool of darkness spreading over the cement as if ink had spilled. Indecipherable rustlings came from the alley where dustbins were stored. Ian was over six feet tall and didn't scare easily but he'd had a sick feeling in the pit of his stomach, the same feeling he'd had when old Harold caught him and sent him off to prison. Fear was fear and it came on its own like a fox.

Ian went down the lane whistling, for it was no use to hide himself and perhaps best to simply appear casual, an ordinary man not worth noticing. He let himself into the house and stood with his back to the door, clammy all over. He should have felt secure, surrounded by amulets, talismans, good-luck charms, blue beads, sacred thread, pentacles, books of great power, yet he didn't feel in the least bit safe. Ian went to get himself a drink, and as soon as he turned to the cupboard for a glass he heard the bells above his door, that wrinkly metallic cough. After that he remembered nothing. A pool of darkness, a groan, a flutter behind his eyelids.

When he woke today in his own bed, it was already past noon, and he knew he had been hexed. Despite his expertise in the field of magic, he was frozen, unable to take even a shallow breath, suffocating in his own bed, and there was no one to call out for help.

Sally carried lavender and sage in her coat pockets and before leaving the pub, she'd taken a shaker from the table and sprinkled salt on the soles of her shoes. She was purposeful and yet despite all of her intended protection, including a dress hemmed with blue thread, she grew unmoored by the time she reached the door on Rosehart Mews. As it turned out, puddles had washed the salt from the soles of her shoes and the lavender and sage had mostly fallen out to sprinkle the road when she darted across. As for the thread she had used, it was poorly dyed and already unraveling. She wasn't quite as protected as she'd hoped to be.

There was no answer when she knocked, but when she leaned against the door it slipped open, and she was surprised to find it unlatched. The bells made a small rough sound that announced her presence. Sally called hello and received no answer. She could feel that something had gone wrong. The atmosphere seemed to be shrinking inward, as it does during a storm, and a charge of something resembling sheer, blue electricity raced through her. She passed the piles of books stacked on the carpet, the small refrigerator and hot plate, a sink, a teacup washed and set out to dry on a wooden rack, a glass of whiskey, seemingly untouched. She opened a door into a second smaller space that functioned as a bedroom. The room was dark, but she could see a handsome man lying prone on the bed, naked, although at first glance he didn't appear to be so; due to his blue tattoos he seemed a painting as much as a man. His eyes met hers, and held her stare, but he failed to object or tell her to get the hell out, though he appeared to be trying to move his mouth.

In a moment, Sally realized that in fact he was gasping for air. It was as if he were drowning, and he spat out water, nearly choking as he did. He could not move or speak and was clearly panicked, both by his sudden malady and by the fact that he was making a fool of himself, uttering gargling noises when he meant only to speak. The palms of his hands were covered with red powder. The glare of that shade of red was so intense it forced Sally to take several steps back. She marveled at her sudden ability to see that color again when for so long it had registered in shades of gray. Red was all she could see now. The ceiling was streaked with the same dye that was on the man's hands and feet, so that it appeared as if a profusion of blood-hued flowers had bloomed on the plaster, then fallen down upon him. On the floor, beside the bed, bird bones that had been dyed scarlet were tied into a bundle with red string. It was as if only one color in the world existed here. Red heart, red hands, red magic.

The room was steamy, so hot and damp it was impossible to see through the windows for the cold glass was covered with a damp film. Sally shrugged off her raincoat, overwhelmed by the heat and sweating through her clothes. She would have liked to take everything off, but instead only unbuttoned the top buttons of her shirt. On the cluttered bedside table there was a poppet, a hand-stitched doll dressed in a white shirt and black pants, its hair long and dark, its face featureless, clearly meant to represent the man in question. The entire chest of the doll had been marked with spots of ink, then cut open with a sharp knife. Beside it was a small, bloody bird's heart. Blood blistered down onto the floor, forming into pools that scorched the wood. Sally had the urge to run from whatever masses of dark magic had been released here, but perhaps it had been no accident that she had been the one to choose the shortest straw. It seemed clear to her now, as clear as the branch-like blotches of red all around her, that she was meant to be here. *Save a life and a life will be saved in return*, Maria Owens had written in the family *Grimoire*. This was the bargain that would bring Kylie back. This was the person she was meant to rescue, a man made of flesh and blood and ink who stared at her with wild eyes. She found herself thinking, *This is the one*.

Not only was Ian unable to speak or move, but his chest was burning as if he were having a heart attack. He likely was; the pain ached deeply and spread out along his torso to the base of his abdomen. He needed an ambulance, clearly, he should be in a hospital, still he was rapt, unable to look away from the woman before him, as if he had fallen under her spell. Her dense black hair was loose, and she smelled like lavender, a calming scent that evoked his childhood, for in his home the sheets had always been pressed with the oil of that flower.

Sally tore down the threadbare curtains to let in some light, which flickered over the half-dazed victim. She spoke a healing spell in Latin, which eased the throbbing pain in his chest. The blur of the red world around him came into focus and his thoughts were less scattered. He gasped and took a breath. Ian knew a witch when he saw one, though he'd never expected such a person to arrive in a sopping black raincoat, her dark hair mussed from the wind, her eyes the color of silver. This most likely would not end well. He tried his best to rouse himself from bed, to no avail, and he wondered if he'd had a stroke.

"Don't move," Sally reproached him. It was evident that he was the sort of man who thought himself invulnerable, and it likely stung deeply to be in need of help. But a curse was a curse, and this one was strong. "The more you struggle, the more of a hold it has on you."

The sight was coming back to her in a rush and Sally willingly accepted her gift. She would need it to find Kylie, so she might as well use it here and now. As she stood at the bedside she was flooded with images. She could see this man's history. There it was, as if she'd opened a book, the sullen childhood, the fights, the day he went to jail, the dim path, his mother watching over him while he slept, worrying over what he would become.

"You've been bad, haven't you," she said. It was a statement not a question, not that it was any of her business. Still, she wondered what might have justified this attack. She thought he glared at her in response, but it didn't matter. There was no time to lose. Luckily there was a space unmarked by ink in the middle of his chest. When she laid a hand upon his skin he was burning hot, and so was she. The heat traveled up her arm into her heart before she could withdraw from him. Quickly, she seized a pen from the desk and wrote out the charm for banishing evil and removing unknown fever and illnesses.

A B R A C A D A B R A
A B R A C A D A B R
A B R A C A D A B
A B R A C A D A
A B R A C A D
A B R A C A
A B R A C
A B R A
A B R
A B
A

When she was done, the professor was still paralyzed; that was when she understood she needed help. "Stay exactly where you are, until I come back."

An American, Ian thought. *Telling me what to do*.

His gaze fell on her as if he were spellbound. For all Sally knew he'd lost his hearing, so she leaned in close and told him what she wanted. He wasn't deaf and could hear perfectly well; all of his senses were working, perhaps too well. Heat streamed through his body, and he was abashed to be so thoroughly seen, and what's more, to be so completely aroused by a woman who was nothing more than a stranger and a witch telling him what to do in his own house.

"Once I help you, you'll owe me your loyalty." This was the bargain, about to be sealed. She seized a small pair of scissors on the night table and cut herself, then took his hand and made a similar slash across his palm. Their blood spilled onto the sheets and he saw that hers was black, and he congratulated himself on being right about her. "You'll return the favor to me," Sally said.

For once, Ian was willing to oblige. *Get me out of this and I'm yours,* he found himself thinking. His heart was burning and he'd never known such pain, but his left arm was fine so perhaps it wasn't a stroke after all, but something else entirely.

Oh, shit, Ian thought as he realized what it was. *This cannot be the way it happens.*

PART THREE

The Book of Wonder

I.

To remove the malediction afflicting Ian, *Dracaena draco* must be obtained, a cure composed from the bark of the Draco tree, which only grew in the Canary Islands and in Morocco and was said to sprout from the scarlet blood of a dragon. The red resin it produced could generate miraculous results, affecting the cortex cells, so that if one was paralyzed, either in the body or mind, the resin poured onto cold washcloths could cure the afflicted person in a matter of hours. Vincent had rummaged through the professor's desk to find a directory of local herbal shops, then he and Gillian had gone off to the nearest one, which fortunately was just around the corner on Needham Road. The costly *Dracaena draco,* which was stored in a metal cannister at the shop, was kept safe under the watchful eye of the clerk.

"It's expensive," the clerk warned. He took a moment to observe the old fellow who looked strangely familiar. "Do I know you?" he asked.

Vincent shrugged, evading the truth. *You know the song, but you don't know me.* "We'll take as much of the herb as you have. Quickly, please."

They also purchased a sheaf of the Draco's leaves, to be used as a stimulant when boiled with water. The afflicted was to gargle, then, when he could open his mouth, spit out the red residue, never swallowing the mixture. Once a person's mouth and tongue were coated, the potent chemicals of the tree would be incorporated into his bloodstream.

Franny was waiting for them at the threshold of the flat when Vincent and Gillian arrived with the proper ingredients.

"How's the historian?" Vincent asked.

"He'll live whether he wants to or not," Franny answered. "We'll see to that."

While Vincent and Gillian continued to search through the office for any references that might be helpful, Franny returned to the bedchamber, where Sally quickly set to applying washcloths soaked with Draco, assessing Ian Wright as she did. He had a long, dark knot of hair, and handsome angular features. She tried not to focus on his face, that was too personal. Ankles, legs, torso, chest, most of it covered with ink. Sally quickly became familiar with him. The cage of his ribs, his well-muscled arms. He was lanky and tall; she could tell he was a runner, as her daughter was. She would not think of Kylie for those thoughts were unbearable and fraught with dread. Instead she concentrated on the man before her, whose glance caught hers. Black eyes flecked with gold that gave nothing away, even when he was in the throes of pain.

A wild card, she thought. *A man who will always do as he pleases.* She then found herself thinking, *Let's just see about that.*

The historian flinched when the resin burned, but Sally said, "Stop that," and he complied. Very odd, since he never did as he was told. Ian closed his eyes and let the cure sink in. He groaned, which was clearly a good sign; sensation in his body was coming back to him and as it did he began to feel pain and then elation.

As Sally rinsed the washcloths in a pan of warm water, she blinked in the shimmer of all the red that she saw. One thing that had not been affected by the poison was Ian's male member, over which Franny had thrown a hand towel for modesty's sake. "He's certainly not shy," Franny said, clearly amused.

What sort of professor was he anyway? The illustrated man, a revelation of pain and beauty, his soul laid bare. Sally wondered if his students and clients who came to him for help had any idea what could be found beneath his clothes. When he took women to bed did he leave the lights off or blindfold them, did he wear his clothes to keep himself hidden so that he didn't reveal the story of who he was? Sally had blundered upon him naked and unhidden and therefore knew the answer to who he was from the start. Magic was everything to him.

Sally was deeply unsettled as she considered the afflicted man, wondering if they could bring him back. Franny herself had been unmoored in much the same manner when she walked into Haylin's hospital room thinking perhaps she had lost him, to illness or to another woman. "If this is upsetting you, I can take care of him," Franny offered, interested in what her niece's response might be.

Sally shook her head and continued the treatment. Ian made a gurgling sound every time she spooned tiny portions of the Draco mixture into his mouth. Too much of the elixir and the cure would do more damage than the hex it was meant to correct. Franny had already soaked the dark materials that had been left to seal the curse—a poppet and a bird's heart and bones—using rubbing alcohol to lessen their effectiveness. Someone wished to be rid of Ian, that much was clear, or, at the very least, damage him. Franny tore the soaking-wet poppet apart with a darning needle she carried in her purse. In no time the foul doll was nothing more than string and batting, its power dissolving in a small pile of ash. Franny felt that whoever had set this hex had done so by the book, rather than by the strength of their own magic. All the same, just to make certain, she untied the bundle of bird bones and tossed them out the window, and finally she burned the red thread that had tied them together over a candle while reciting the incantation that would send the intended malediction back to its original owner.

Contere bracchia iniqui rei. Et linguia maligna subvertetur.

Franny left a folded piece of red paper in each of the four corners of the room. On all four she had written the incantation to cast away evil.

Omnis spiritus laudet dominum. Habent Moses et prophetas.
Exurgat deus et dissipentur inimici ejus.

When they had done all they could, Sally pulled up two spindly chairs so they might continue to observe Ian. The intensity of their combined gaze was daunting. Ian closed his eyes and wished he could disappear, which unfortunately was not within his abilities. Nothing seemed to be in his command, not even his damn prick, which always knew his mind before he did.

"He's an interesting man," Franny mused. "Certainly not average. But who wants average?"

Sally shot her aunt a curdled look. Franny knew full well that Sally had been trying to be average her whole life long. As always, Franny derided her wish. "Why on earth would you want to be normal?" she always asked. "As if there was such a thing." Still, as a girl, Sally had chosen the most ordinary pastimes, she had even joined the Girl Scouts and gone hiking, contracting poison ivy and cursing the rocks in her shoes, miserable from the start. All the same, she had sold cookies for the Scouts with a ferociousness that surprised everyone in her troop, and was mortified when Jet bought every box, so that they had Thin Mint cookies for breakfast for nearly a year.

"You're looking at him quite closely," Franny noted.

"He's supposed to help us find Kylie. I'm watching for signs of life."

"Oh, he's alive," Franny said with a chuckle. "That's certain."

Franny had been the one to send Sally here, after all. She'd seen something in the palm of her niece's hand in the shape of a crow. Flight and freedom in a language that some women were able to decipher. Sally, herself, had a particular affinity for birds, and could call them to her from the treetops with a whistle. As for Franny, she'd had a beloved familiar when she was young, a crow named Lewis that rarely left her side. What this cursed man had to do with crows, Franny didn't yet understand. She recognized the meaning of several of his tattoos—the magic circle from *The Book of Solomon*, the triangle of elemental fire. "I'll bet he's gone over to the left every now and then. I wouldn't put it past him."

Sally threw her aunt a look. "He's hearing every word."

"Let him. I'm just saying he's not an angel." Franny assessed Ian with a gaze so direct it made most people squirm, Ian included.

"It doesn't matter what he is. All that matters is that he'll help us." Sally noticed that Ian could now move his fingers and toes. She felt disoriented as she watched the afflicted man fight off the hex. As for Ian, he experienced the effects of the Draco resin, the blood returning to his limbs, his heart no longer seared with pain, his thoughts no longer fractured. He might soon be able to speak, but he was not quick to do so. Even in his weakened state, he was shrewd enough to know it was best if he bit his tongue. The old woman was a witch as well, and a clever one.

"We should question him while he's still in this state," Franny suggested. While he was vulnerable and might tell the truth.

"Give him a minute," Sally suggested. "Let him catch his breath."

He did exactly that, inhaling so deeply that he shuddered, stunned to discover how good it felt to have air fill his lungs. Breath was life and this woman Sally had returned that to him, and now he was in her debt, and they both knew it. She fixed him chamomile tea, always healing to the mind. Ian was now able to drink on his own, taking sips, and slowly he was restored. He was vain enough to be beset by real embarrassment when a tawny blond woman and a handsome older man were called in by the two witches, and more of his shabby chairs were brought into the bedroom, so that he was soon surrounded by a semicircle of strangers.

The older man was well dressed and sounded vaguely French as he explained that a girl had disappeared, the dark-haired woman's daughter, and they feared what she might do on her own. They needed an expert in left-handed magic, and Ian had come highly recommended. The facts of Kylie's disappearance drifted down and he did his best to comprehend, though his head was throbbing. Ian was suspicious and grateful in equal measure, which meant he kept his own counsel and didn't reveal that most of his senses had returned to him, and could now speak if he wished to. The older man introduced each of them, but all Ian heard was the name Sally, the luminous, perpetually distressed dark-haired woman who had saved him. As Ian listened, he was reminded of a dream he was often plagued by on nights before he had to lecture in public. There he would be, calmly discussing the dichotomy between the paths of magic, white and black, right and left, only to look down and discover he was naked, with the ink on his body dissolving into blue pools, leaving him without the printed armor that protected him from evil.

"If you don't mind, might I have some clothes?" he asked in a raw voice. His heart was still wildly pumping, fueled by his embarrassment. He and Sally regarded each other, then both quickly glanced away. Usually, he was not so modest. He went out running every day, and in hot weather often stripped off his shirt as he dodged through the streets in lightweight running shorts. Once, on a hot summer morning, when the sky was still dark, he'd pulled off his shorts as well to run naked through Hyde Park.

Sally proceeded to the closet where there were white shirts on hangers, along with a few black jackets and black jeans folded haphazardly on a shelf. Ian had so many books that even here there were piles precariously stacked. Sally took a clean shirt and a pair of jeans to leave on the bed, then they all left Ian so that he might have his privacy. Sally was already joining Vincent and Gillian in the front room, and so it was Franny who turned to close the door. Ian stood beside the bed, facing away from her, still naked. Franny paused in the threshold and looked back. A crow was inked across Ian's wide back as if spanning the sky. It was then Franny understood the lines of Sally's left hand. Here was the fate she would make for herself.

After a while Ian managed to join them in his parlor. His inhalations were still shallow, he was sleep-deprived and he limped, his feet burning, as if they'd been held to the fire. He continued to feel caught up in a trance, but his cloudy mind had begun to clear. Sally was distracted, checking her phone, but when he said, "Thank you, Sally. I'm fairly certain I'd be dead without you,"

her eyes met his for an instant before she quickly averted her gaze. Why was it only then that he noticed the color red was everywhere? A sheen of it still smudged his hands and feet, and there were large clumsy footsteps on the carpet, as if whoever had hexed him had stepped into his own poison.

"I'll grab the vacuum," Gillian decided. Poison was poison and they best be rid of it.

Franny held her back. "That kind of stain won't come out unless you use bleach. And not without gloves."

Ian's research among those who practiced left-handed magic caused many people to dislike him and think of him as a traitor, writing about mysteries that were best not divulged, but what had happened here went beyond that mild emotion. Whoever was behind this brutal attack had been eager to be rid of him. Ian recognized some of the materials—the figure, the bones, the madder root—as those used in an ancient curse he'd written about in *The History of Magic*, having found the original spell in *The Voynich Manuscripts* at Yale University on a research trip to New England. It was unbreakable in most cases, for the poison paralyzed the lungs and the heart as well as the mind. Someone was seriously pissed or they wanted something he had badly. Ian thought perhaps it was whoever had been breaking in, stealing his books and his notes. He hadn't paid enough attention to that, feeling an immediate sympathy for anyone who was a thief. Now he tossed Vincent a heavy set of keys. "The cabinet is on the right. Do me a favor and check for a red book."

As it turned out, no key was needed; the lock had already been split open, and there, on the carpet, was the rock used to do so. The cabinet was brimming with magic texts, books that carried a bitter scent most mortals loathed. Vinegar, blood, the almond scent of cyanide. As Vincent rummaged through, he came upon several books he'd never seen before, rare editions he wished he had time to study.

"Look for *Rauðskinna*," Ian urged. "In ancient Icelandic. But don't touch it."

Vincent and Franny exchanged a look. Neither was the least bit surprised when *Rauðskinna* was nowhere to be found.

"Oh, fuck." Ian got to his feet in order to take a look for himself. The text of red magic was indeed missing. "That's what they came here for. It's a book of curses I paid a fortune for in Iceland. Fortunately, you need a password to open it." His notebook was still in the desk drawer with coded passwords listed. Some books refused to open without a key of some sort, a word, an element, a touch of the hand.

Sally cut him off before there was further conversation about the importance of his collection. "My daughter has gotten hold of a dangerous book. *The Book of the Raven*. Have you heard of it?"

Franny observed the historian. He was staring at Sally unblinking, his heart hammering against his chest. Franny could see the crow beneath his shirt when his back was turned to her. She nudged Vincent, leaning toward him to murmur, "Do you see what I see?" she asked.

"I don't see that sort of thing anymore," Vincent said, though it was plain as day, the emotion that must be avoided, the height of red magic, the impulse and the curse, what broke you in pieces, what you couldn't give up even if you tried.

"I've heard rumors concerning a book by that name," Ian claimed, forcing his scholarly self to take charge. "The author was a poet." He frowned, clearly not wishing to say any more. The rumor was that Amelia Bassano had been betrayed by William Shakespeare, and that she'd had her revenge in the darkest way possible. Fortunately, her Book of Shadows was said to have been burned upon her death, as was the tradition with personal *Grimoires*, but perhaps the book had survived.

Annoyed, Gillian approached the historian directly. She was astonished to find she could spy his aura, when she hadn't been capable of such magic before. His aura, however, was quite confusing; it continually changed color, first gray, then violet, then ink blue. "You have to help my sister. She saved you."

Ian might have said many things, he might have answered as a fool, as he'd done often enough when he was young. *Make me, see if you can, my life is my own, this curse has nothing to do with me, the book is only a rumor, and if it does exist, it is likely dark and unmanageable, I need time to recover, I am limping, can't you see, there's red powder on my hands and on my ceiling and my floor.* He was a rebel and a loner and he had several important lecture dates to prepare for at which he was to discuss his book, soon to be published, twenty years of his life spent looking for magic, and now it was here, unbidden and refusing to leave.

"I intend to repay you," he said, just as Franny would have predicted, for she had seen inside him when she spied the crow on his back and she knew his story. He stalked away, to call his lecture agent and cancel his speaking engagements. His back was to Franny again, and again she saw through him. She glanced over at Sally and wondered if she knew that crows were more intelligent than most men, and more loyal, and that you could not choose them, they must choose you, they must come to you and once they did they would never leave you, at least not of their own accord.

II.

On her next visit to the Reverend, Antonia decided to surprise him with a Chocolate Tipsy Cake. She would show him that, indeed, she could make something with care. Although she'd never baked before, she knew the recipe for the cake by heart, so last night she'd given it a try in her small kitchen, traipsing out to the nearby market to purchase dark chocolate, a sack of sugar, some fine cake flour. Antonia did her reading for her neurology class while the layers baked in battered tins, hoping for the best but not truly expecting it, glancing at the oven every once in a while just to make certain there was no smoke. She'd made the frosting out of butter and powdered sugar, cocoa, and vanilla. She knew that Jet waited for the cake to cool before frosting and waved at the tins with a dishtowel to help the process along. In the end, the layers were tilted and the frosting was too thick; she'd left out the rum, with only a splash for tradition's sake, but it was a perfectly serviceable cake and she was rather proud of herself. She'd set the finished product on a plate jammed into the back seat of Gillian's car, where it nearly fell onto the floor mat as she rounded a corner too quickly. At the retirement home, the admitting clerk, about to complain about the cake, was stared down by Antonia's cool glance and no one stopped her when she made a detour into the lunchroom for a knife and two plates and forks. The Reverend was at his favorite spot by the window when Antonia arrived in his room. He was currently remembering fragments from the past he'd forgotten yesterday. How he'd loved to cut daffodils with Jet and deliver them to the cemetery, how they would sit there in lawn chairs that Jet kept for just such occasions in the trunk of her car, how they were so in sync they would not even have to talk, how they would walk past the new saplings and the old sturdy trees on the path back to the parking lot, where they would often have a lunch of egg salad sandwiches and pickles while sitting in the car before Jet brought him home. Today was one of his good days, when he could see and hear and remember. It became even better when the Owens girl came in with a cake and closed the door behind her. "I had the feeling you'd be back today," Reverend Willard said.

"Did you?" Antonia set the cake on top of his dresser and cut two slices. "It's my first Chocolate Tipsy Cake, so don't judge me too harshly."

"Who am I to judge?" The Reverend tried his best to keep an open mind, especially when it came to the Owens women.

Antonia handed him a slice of cake, then perched on the edge of the bed with her own plate and hesitantly took a bite. It might not look perfect, but it was utterly delicious.

"Yum," they said in unison.

Antonia hadn't stopped thinking about Ariel Hardy, and yet when Ariel's number had flickered up on her phone, she hadn't answered, but had instead stepped into the shower and let the water run for nearly half an hour, a surefire cure for thinking too much. "How do you know if you're in love?" she found herself saying now as they ate their cake. Antonia felt comfortable confiding in the Reverend; she had the distinct impression that her secrets were safe with him.

"Love does as it pleases. It can't be controlled." The Reverend took another bite of the cake. "Almost as good as your aunt Jet's."

Antonia was pleased by the compliment, and perhaps that was why she confessed more than she otherwise might have. "I've never been in love."

"You should try it. And don't worry, Jet will end the curse."

Antonia took his plate, for as it turned out Reverend Willard could only eat a few bites. She patted his arm. If he'd forgotten Jet was gone, who was she to remind him otherwise? Antonia would leave the rest of the cake for the nurses; it was always prudent to be on their good side. She had only come to visit because she was obligated and she'd been told it was a family tradition to look after the Reverend, but before she left she paused to hug him good-bye.

"I'll see you next week," he reminded her. "Unless I'm dead."

With his dry humor, the old man was one of the few people who could make Antonia smile. "You'll be alive, and I'll be here."

"I dream about Jet." He knew she was gone, only he didn't like to think about that.

"I do, too," Antonia admitted. She now realized that in her drowning dreams, Jet was on the other side of the lake. Jet had always told Antonia and Kylie to never be afraid to be who they were. *Everything you give to the world will come back to you threefold.*

"I ruined her life and she forgave me." Reverend Willard had written Jet many letters of apology and she wrote back forgiving him over and over again, notes he kept stuffed into his night-table drawer. After all this time, and scores of letters, he still hadn't quite managed to forgive himself.

May in Boston was mild and beautiful, the good weather finally returning after that dreadful spring. The streets were emptier once the students had departed for other homes and other states, and the professors had disappeared to summer houses, but Gideon was still in his hospital room, with little change in his condition. His mother had rented an apartment on Beacon Hill in order to be at her son's bedside every day, with his stepfather working at his law firm in New York and driving up on weekends. Gideon's parents rarely spoke to each other, afraid of what they might say. The doctors had told them his recovery was a matter of time, but they could tell it was a matter of fate. People mended despite all odds, Antonia Owens told Mrs. Barnes when she visited. Antonia came every day, hoping that Kylie would phone Gideon's room. In the presence of Mrs. Barnes, she was very positive and hopeful, a manner she had been practicing and perfecting in medical school. *Be rational, but don't think the truth is always the correct answer.*

There was something called the Glasgow Coma Scale and Gideon had scored well, suggesting there was no permanent damage to his brain. When his hand was squeezed, he exerted pressure in return. He was in there, Antonia was sure of it. Today she came to the hospital directly from the retirement home up in Essex, still smelling of chocolate. She knew that Mrs. Barnes needed some respite from standing guard, and Antonia preferred to spend time with Gideon alone, when she didn't have to keep a pleasant expression on her face to ensure that her fears about his condition wouldn't be evident and upset his mother any further. Mrs. Barnes was already wrapped up in fear, and who could blame her?

"Go out for coffee," Antonia told her. "Take a walk. Make sure you have some time for yourself." But all Gideon's mother could do was go back to her rented apartment and cry.

What filled the mind of a person in a coma was a mystery. The networks of the brain shut down, but some of these patterns might be rerouted to places most minds didn't use. It was not sleep that befell such a patient, but a state much like being anesthetized. Parts of the brain went dark, but people in comas had dreams, memories, visions, and some had vivid nightmares. Recordings of sounds at all pitches had been played in an attempt to stimulate Gideon's brain and his responses had been charted. He was reacting to certain noise, according to his EEG, especially when music was played, with Yo-Yo Ma's recordings affecting him more than any other. Gideon was in there. He was. His mother thought she'd seen her boy's eyes brim with tears as he listened to Bach's Cello Suite No. 1 in G Major, but when she spoke to the doctors they were evasive. *Wait and see*, was all they said.

During Antonia's visit, she noticed that Gideon was moving his hand without any stimulus. She went to see the doctor in charge and was told it was an uncontrolled tremor, nothing more, but she didn't think so. Gideon's movements were specific, and actually quite odd. He appeared to be trying to fit a key into a lock.

Antonia lightly ran a finger over his wrist. "Tell me where you are."

He couldn't answer, though he tried. He was in a labyrinth. The walls were constructed of hedges with black leaves. He had a key in his hand. It had once been silver, but now was black. There was the door, but he couldn't quite reach it. He was used to being in charge of his body, he was so tall and strong, a runner who could go for miles, who had run the last Boston Marathon, cheered on by Kylie at Heartbreak Hill. But now he was in a different place where none of those attributes mattered. It was like walking through water, every step took supreme effort and led nowhere. He simply could not reach the door. He was so frustrated he shook his head, but in his hospital bed he merely winced.

"Talk to me," Antonia said, leaning in. If only Kylie could speak to him, perhaps she could reach him. Antonia dialed her sister's number but all she got was a fast beeping and no answer. "Oh, Gideon," Antonia said. "If you could only hear me."

In his in-between world, Gideon recognized the voice as belonging to Kylie's sister and he wished he could tell her where he was. He wished there was a way to get back. He couldn't get to the door and he couldn't use the damn key. He groaned and Antonia took his hand. She could feel that he was captured, as surely as if he'd been bound with rope. Gideon grasped her hand for a moment; it was no tremor, she was sure of it, then he let go. He had no choice but to return to the darkness and search for the door that would open the world to him once more.

Antonia had agreed to meet Ariel for a late lunch, to discuss the papers in the Owens family trust. When she arrived, forty minutes late, Ariel was waiting for her outside the restaurant on Beacon Hill, her back fitted against a brick wall, reading a mystery that had an Emily Dickinson line as its title, *Started Early, Took My Dog.* The hour technically made it a dinner date.

"Sorry. Time got away from me." Antonia was exhausted as usual, but for some reason she felt utterly awake in Ariel Hardy's presence.

"How's the boy?" Ariel asked.

"Not good."

Antonia was still puzzling out her drowning dream. There had been crows in the trees and the water in the pond was tinged green. She had taken note of a glass jar deposited on the ground; inside was a thin slip of paper, twisted around like a snake, printed with pale red ink. The weeds were tall and she didn't realize they were stinging nettle until it was too late; she'd already reached for the jar. As she read the note, the palms of her hands were on fire. She fumbled with the note and let it fall; in a wild attempt to escape the ill effects of the nettle, she ran into the water in the hopes of soothing the flame she now felt. After she woke she couldn't remember the message she'd read in her dream.

"You'll love this place," Ariel told her as they went inside a restaurant called Incanto. "I used to come here with my grandfather every Friday." There was no sign on the door, but the courthouse was nearby and Incanto was a great favorite with attorneys and judges.

As she followed Ariel inside the tiny restaurant, the idea of being cursed in matters of love struck Antonia as something she should take seriously. They were immediately seated at a table by the window and it was clear that Ariel was a regular, as the maître d' knew her by name. By now, Antonia's head was pounding. As the bread was served, a plate of salted butter that was left for them began to melt. Antonia pushed it away. That old wives' tale about butter melting when someone was in love was utter nonsense. It simply couldn't be. Exhausted, Antonia closed her eyes while Ariel ordered white wine. "Just water for my date," she heard Ariel say.

Antonia was remembering more of the dream she'd had the night before. There had been dragonflies darting through the air and the day was so brutally hot steam was rising from the surface of the water. Her hands had stopped smarting from the nettle as she went deeper, even though she knew it was dangerous. She thought she heard a voice calling her back to shore. She thought the sky was filling with clouds as a shadow was cast, but the shadow was formed by the crows winging above her, gathering in masses, as they did when trying to protect one of their own. She didn't look back, she didn't care anymore, she went deeper, and cursed or not, warned or not, she reached for Ariel right there in a restaurant on Charles Street and kissed her as if she had never kissed anyone before, because the truth was, she was already drowning.

III.

There was a train from the station on Liverpool Street that ran from London to Witham in Essex in under an hour. The view out the window was a blur, first urban and gray, and then the deep flickering green of the lush countryside splotched with sunlight that faded as the hour grew later. Once off the train, Kylie was directed down the street by a ticket taker, and there she found a local bus that made so many stops in a string of little towns that it took nearly another hour to reach Thornfield. It was a small village, with most houses dating to the seventeenth century, many with mossy slate or tiled roofs and gardens set behind stonewalls. The area was famous for its roses, many of which had already begun to bud in bursts of salmon and crimson along with a pitch-black variety that was known as the Thornfield Rose.

The village was considered picturesque and had been featured in many guidebooks about the region, most of them showcasing the forest on the edge of town, where some of the most ancient trees in the county could be found, huge oaks, hundreds of years old, which were said to sing on gusty days. Children in the village stood out on the street or in their gardens to listen for the trees when the wind came up. Magic had been here longer than the school or the library or the firehouse and had become part of everyday life. Elderly women were respected, and a little feared, for many had retained the old knowledge and held on to that bit of power; they could protect themselves, leaving salt outside their doors and planting lavender for luck. On All Soul's night most everyone stayed home. People held house parties and insisted it was too chilly to venture out, but the truth was people frequently became lost in the fens on the occasion of that night. Now, on the verge of summer, with the unfolding roses incandescent in the fading light, people still kept the windows in their children's bedrooms closed at night. Doing so protected against the damp, the children were told, but the mist doesn't need double locks and drawn curtains. It was magic lurking out there, rising from the fens and shadowing the lanes. People walked with torches in the fluttering twilight, and usually avoided trekking alone in remote places. But when they needed a cure, when their children couldn't sleep, when their lovers left them for another, they knew where to go.

Kylie stopped at a shop called Marian and Jason's Teahouse. There was a Thornfield Rose bush outside the door of the shop, with one black flower already blooming. Bees were gathering, droning in the falling dusk, drawn to the scent of the blooms. Kylie had lost her appetite; each time she thought of Gideon in his hospital bed, she felt sick to her stomach, but once inside the shop she ordered a scone to keep up her energy, along with a cup of tea, to which she added three sugar cubes. The scone arrived with a curious dollop of heavy cream on the plate and a small pot of shimmering black jam. Marian Dodd, the owner and cook, looked at Kylie, unblinking, when asked if she might know a resident called Thomas Lockland.

"What's your interest in him?" Mrs. Dodd asked. She wasn't a woman who was easily fazed, but she had a peculiar, chilly expression when Lockland's name came up. Mrs. Dodd's daughter, Mary, had dated Tom for a while. He was handsome and charming and they'd all felt sorry for his rough upbringing. They thought the notion that he was a self-centered rogue was mere gossip, then he'd gone ahead and broken Mary Dodd's heart, dumping her for no apparent reason, which caused her to move to London and never return, not even for a weekend. Mrs. Dodd hoped to never set eyes on Tom again.

"I think our families knew each other long ago," Kylie explained.

"Oh, I see." Mrs. Dodd seemed to flinch as she nodded out the window, saying she believed he was currently at number 23 on the far end of the High Street, the main thoroughfare in town. "He comes and goes," Mrs. Dodd told Kylie.

When Kylie thanked Mrs. Dodd for her help, the proprietor responded by saying, "Good luck to you." Kylie couldn't tell if her comment was sincere, for as she went out she noticed that Mrs. Dodd held up her index and pinkie fingers, making the sign of the fox, traditionally used as a counter-charm against hexes to send left-handed magic back to its originator.

The High Street wasn't especially long, a mile at most, and it was easy enough to locate number 23, a small one-bedroom cottage in need of repair. Once she'd arrived, Kylie hesitated, thinking of Gideon. She made her way into a grove of linden trees across the road and took out her phone to call the hospital. When she was put through to his room the phone rang and rang, then suddenly was picked up.

"Gideon?" Kylie was standing in clover in a damp, muddy dip beside the road. There were cows in a nearby field, all black and white, resting in the shadows. Kylie had to blink back tears. "Talk to me," she said.

"Kylie, it's me."

Antonia, her dear sister, to whom she didn't wish to speak.

"Put him on," Kylie demanded.

"Kylie." Antonia sighed.

"I want to talk to him," Kylie insisted.

"There's no point. He can't speak. We're all so worried about you. Just tell me where you are."

Kylie laughed, but the sharp burst of laugher turned into a sob. "I'm not crying," she said, embarrassed by her raw emotions.

"You should be here with Gideon," Antonia urged. "Wherever you are we'll come get you. You know I'll do anything to help you."

"Then hold the phone to his ear."

"Kylie, he's in a coma."

"Are you trying to help me or not!"

The phone was held up and Kylie could hear Gideon's breathing, a shallow, watery sound, as though he were drowning. "Come back," she said to him. She wiped her black tears away with the back of her hand. "I'm getting you out of there," she promised. "You just have to wait for me. Wait right there."

When she hung up, she collapsed in the clover and wept, then wiped her face with the tail end of her shirt. She felt different, as if nothing could stop her. She had no choice in the matter if she intended to bring him back. She made her way out of the grove of trees. *The Book of the Raven* advised that only a person who has been cursed will understand the meaning of carrying the burden of being exiled from her own life. You cannot do as you please, only as the curse commands you to do. That would end, no matter the price. Kylie took in the last few breaths of the life she'd led before arriving at number 23. Out here in the country the air was perfumed with the scent of ferns and juniper. Kylie had wrapped *The Book of the Raven* in newspaper, then again in a scarf, which was carefully tucked into her backpack. There was a tremor in her hands as they rested on the iron gate. She recalled the librarian's last words. *Don't trust anyone.*

When she lifted her gaze and looked through the window, Kylie spied a handsome man in his twenties at his desk, his attention riveted on the book he was reading. The vine at the window scraped against the glass as Kylie leaned upon the sill, a slight sound, but one that caused Tom Lockland to turn from his studies. He was the seventh generation in his family to have that name and he carried the weight of those who'd come before him. He closed his book and turned off the light before rising from the desk.

It was only natural for Tom to be wary as he opened the door to Kylie, for he was a man who'd been bred to be cautious. His shaven head only served to bring out his sharp, intelligent features. Although he had been studying the Dark Art since he was a boy, the magic he practiced was a thin, weak strain, and the best he could accomplish were parlor tricks, sleight of hand, small incantations that called up desire in the women he met, and impressed drunken patrons in pubs when he held fire in his hand. Any real witch would laugh at his attempts, but not at his expertise in poison. That was one art in which he excelled, bringing people to the brink of death, using the herbs in an old poison garden that grew wild in Devotion Field where he foraged for *Amanita virosa*, a local variety of mushroom known as the Destroying Angel.

His life's work was revenge and he was more than willing to use left-handed magic to do so. Like called to like, and to destroy something you often had to become it yourself. Tom had claimed the Crooked Path and took to walking at Lockland Manor, once his family's sprawling estate, now belonging to the National Trust, visited by scores of hikers and vacationers when there was fine weather. The house itself had been built in the 1300s, but it was mostly a shell, topped by a tall spire, for it had been consumed in flame, and for those who dared to venture inside it was possible to look through the damaged ceilings to the sky above. It should have all been his—the parkland, the manor house, the family wealth—but the Locklands' circumstances had grown worse with each generation and people in the village had calmly watched them come to ruin. There was drink involved, and bad luck; marriages were wrecked, lives were cut short, poverty haunted them, jail terms led to disaster. It was a tradition for women married to the Locklands to disappear and leave their men, and there were few who could blame them. Tom's own mother had vanished on his fifth birthday and his father had neglected him, leaving him to sit outside the pubs he frequented where Tom would wait till all hours, having been reminded not to call his father *Dad* in front of any of the ladies, beaten when he talked back, sleeping in a shed whenever one of these ladies was brought home for the night. Tom had learned that women were heartache from the moment you encountered them and that men were not to be trusted. The first Thomas Lockland swore he'd married a witch; he'd taken their son away from his wife to be raised by his sisters, but in the end his wife had ruined him. When she ran away, he tracked her to the house of a woman who practiced the Nameless Art and after his downfall at the hands of this woman, Hannah Owens, his wife had run off with another man and the child they'd had during her marriage to Lockland.

The family curse had been initiated when his seventh great-grandfather was poisoned only half an hour's walk from the village, in a place called Devotion Field, where an apothecary garden had once grown, rife with dangerous plants including yarrow and black nightshade, wolfsbane and foxglove and lords and ladies with its toxic black berries. All this bad fortune had been conjured by a cunning woman who had long ago been burned. Festivals were held on what had once been her land on the old holidays of May Eve, All Hallows' Eve, Candlemas, and Lammas, with women gathering as the wheel of the year moved forward. On these occasions, white paper bags lit by candles arose into the violet sky so that stars seemed to be both falling and rising.

People in the village were fools for the old folkways and they always had been, leaving out saucers of goat's milk for witches on overcast nights, allowing crows to fly through their windows rather than chase them away, drinking herbal teas they thought would strengthen their constitutions. It was the village council that had voted to remove the Locklands from their property nearly three hundred years earlier and Tom intended to pay them back threefold. Let them sit in their houses and hide, let them lock their doors and leave the streets of the village empty. When he had the power to do so, he would make them understand what it was like to be in exile in your own home.

Tom fixed his gaze on Kylie upon encountering her, immediately interested. It wasn't her beauty that drew him in, but the aura of magic around her. Even someone with as little talent as he could tell she had power. "Did you want something?" Tom asked, for in his experience people always did.

Kylie took a breath. The next step was about to begin. "Tom Lockland?"

"That would be me." Tom took in the measure of the girl and decided that she was far more than a spoiled American.

Kylie introduced herself and said, "I thought you might help me. I've heard that you know something about curses."

"A bit." Intrigued, he beckoned for her to come inside. He'd spent the best part of ten years searching for a way to break the curse that had afflicted his family for more than three hundred years, to no avail. The older a curse was, the more difficult it was to disperse, for it took root and grew, twisting through a person's psyche and heart with punishing strength. Some people said that removing it could cause more damage than the curse itself.

"I need to know how to end it and I don't have much time," Kylie admitted.

Lockland had gray eyes, a rare pale color not unlike her own. It was not every day that a cursed American came to your door. It might be a bit of luck. Kylie was too tall, a good five inches taller than he, slender, with coltish arms and legs, and was wearing a dreadfully large raincoat and rumpled clothes in which she'd slept. She was a reluctant beauty, and that always appealed to Tom, who considered such women to be a code to crack. Convince her she was more than she'd ever imagined and she might just be yours.

Once escorted into the house, Kylie paced rather than taking a seat. She kept her backpack hooked over her shoulders as if ready to flee at any moment.

"Would you mind telling me what you're doing here?" Tom asked.

"My boyfriend is in a coma," Kylie told him. "It's very serious."

"I'm not a physician if you're looking for medical help."

"I'm not in need of a doctor. Gideon has plenty of those." She stared at him then. "I'm in search of magic."

Another man might have laughed at this announcement, but not Tom. He nodded, even more interested; after all, he was looking for the very same thing. It was after five and ordinarily he would have poured himself a whiskey. Instead he fetched them both cups of tea. To Kylie's, he added a sliver of a wood mushroom that would cause even the most vigilant and wary individuals to reveal themselves.

"Anyone who falls in love with us is ruined," Kylie said between sips of tea. The taste was refreshing, and she drank one cup and then was poured another. "My boyfriend Gideon was struck by a car. That's why I have to end the curse. There's no other way to bring him back."

Kylie was talking too much and she knew it; she was about to tell Lockland about *The Book of the Rav*en, it was on the tip of her tongue, but she stopped herself, recalling the librarian's warning.

"Do you have any idea of how this might be accomplished?" Tom cocked an eyebrow and waited for her response. He wasn't particularly educated, and had never gone to university, but he'd had to be shrewd in order to survive his childhood. When he smiled, he was disarming, and even more handsome than she'd first noticed, with movie-star looks from a bygone era.

"That's why I'm here. My family was from this village, and I assume the curse must have begun here."

"And your family is fine with what you're doing?"

"That doesn't matter," Kylie said.

Lockland could spot an insincere person, he was one himself, and this girl was honest. He'd had to be canny to get through life in this dreadful village where people held gatherings to celebrate magic and were proud of their heritage. The library had been a witch's house and it was said that writers often came all the way from London in search of inspiration when they were blocked. Many of the former inhabitants of Thornfield had been devotees of green magic, known for their use of the Nameless Art, particularly in matters of health and well-being. Healing, however, was not Tom's interest.

When and if Tom finally broke his family's curse, he would turn it back upon the townspeople who had stood by to watch his family's ruination. He would open up doors that had been closed for centuries; he'd paint all the mirrors black and burn down the library with its foolish collection of *Grimoires*, women's magic, green magic, earth magic, red magic. Devotion Field would disappear in a blaze, children would be lost in the fens, people would take to their beds, unable to be cured of an illness that rained down upon them. *Let them be cursed*, he thought. *Let them know what it's like.*

"Whatever you can teach me, I want to learn," Kylie told him. She had a sweet, innocent voice that affected Tom in a way he wouldn't have expected. He almost felt his heart go out to her, but he stopped the sudden haze of compassion, easy to do when you've had enough practice. By now, Kylie had finished the tea. She had the urge to tell all, to confide in someone who would understand her.

"Place your hands flat on the table," Tom suggested. He did the same. When their knees touched they both felt a jolt. "Let it rise up," Tom said in a quiet tone that almost sounded hopeful.

The table shuddered and rose off the floor, floating between them. Kylie gasped; without thinking, she lifted her hands and when she did the table fell with a clatter. Tom smiled broadly, sweat on his brow. This girl not only had power, she released something in him as well.

"We did that," he said proudly.

Kylie's cheeks flushed. She could feel her blood turn hot. "I'm willing to do anything to break the curse."

Tom Lockland considered her. "Are you sure?" These days you didn't want to take advantage of anyone. You had to convince them they wanted what you wanted.

When Kylie nodded, Tom seized a knife from the table and quickly slashed his arm. He grinned and handed it over. Being with this girl would give him the power he needed and had always lacked. The knife was cold in her hand but when Kylie cut herself she was burning. Her breathing quickened, as drops of black blood fell to the floor, burning as magic ran through her.

"Who were your ancestors?" he asked.

"Maria Owens," Kylie answered. "She was raised by a woman named Hannah who was tried as a witch. It happened here in Thornfield. There was another woman named Rebecca involved with the family. I think we may both be related to her."

Tom realized who she was. The seven-times great-granddaughter of a witch who had been married to his six-times great-grandfather. They were, indeed, distant cousins, for long ago Rebecca had given birth to both his ancestor and hers, born two years apart. Lockland's sixth great-grandfather had been removed from a woman considered to be wicked, while Kylie's ancestor, Maria Owens, had been born in a snowy field, then given over to a woman who raised her with kindness and dedication and magic.

This is what Tom had been waiting for. A conduit to magic, a witch in his control.

"We can break the curse," he promised this cousin of his. "But only if you trust me."

Tom brought Kylie to the local pub at the only inn in the village, the Three Hedges, established more than four hundred years earlier. He had little to offer in his own kitchen, having been living on cheese, toast, and beer, and Kylie hadn't had a decent meal since she'd left Boston, only the snack the librarian had offered her in London. They had a fifteen-minute walk through the falling darkness. There was a green smell in the air, a mixture of clover and grass, and the air was cooler under the gleaming sky. When Kylie stumbled over the pavement, Tom took her hand, looping his fingers through hers. “Steady,” he said. “You don’t want to come all this way and break a leg.”

Kylie laughed, but she didn’t pull away. He was what she needed, a partner in magic. They had made the table rise and she wondered what else they could do. She had felt so vulnerable ever since Gideon’s injury, it was a relief to have someone to help her sort everything out and, truthfully, the weight of Tom’s hand was a comfort.

“The town’s provincial,” Tom warned as he opened the door for Kylie and escorted her inside. There was a wave of smoke and the burnt smell of fried food. “You never know what the citizens of Thornfield will say or do. They don’t know what to think about people like us.” Kylie presumed he meant people who dealt in magic.

The pub was crowded, it was the only place to go for a drink, after all. Kylie kept her eyes downcast as she made her way past a group of local men near the dartboard. They then sat at the end of the bar, undisturbed, as Tom always was when he came into town. People avoided him; there were rumors that if you crossed him you’d regret it and even men who didn’t mind a good fight every now and then out in the parking lot had nothing to do with him.

It all seemed fine enough, a cozy dinner for two, unmolested, but when Kylie went to the ladies’ room, a waitress followed and swiftly locked the door behind her. Kylie was so taken aback she lurched forward, not noticing that her locket had become unclasped, her mother’s lovely birthday gift to her, and now fell into a shadowy corner.

“Are you mad?” the waitress, a young woman called Jesse Wilkie, asked. "What are you thinking?" Jesse had gone to school with Tom Lockland, until he'd dropped out. He'd been good-looking and surly, a type Jesse was often attracted to, Lord help her, but she'd known to stay away from Tom. Her grandmother had made her promise never to have anything to do with the Locklands, and under her beloved grandmother's tutelage, Jesse had learned to have concern for the fate of other young women. She'd seen him hurt one after the other, discarding them with ease. "What are you doing here with Bad Tom?" she asked.

"That's not a very nice thing to call him." Kylie felt stung to be upbraided by a stranger.

"Well, he's not very nice, so there you have it. It's a name he deserves. You're from America, and maybe you don't know about our history here in Essex, but my advice is go home. I'm telling you woman to woman." Perhaps Jesse had a fondness for foolish girls because she'd been one herself and dated a few fellows who were utter mistakes. Kylie, though tall, seemed girlish in her oversized clothes, with no makeup, her glossy red-tinted hair pulled back in a sloppy ponytail. Still, in Jesse's opinion, no one was too young to be warned about a man such as Tom. "He's a miserable character from a miserable family. All they do is cause trouble. It's black magic. You might not believe in it, but around here it's a fact. We all know to stay away from it. You wouldn't catch me walking on the grounds of Lockland Manor. Not for any price."

"He told me about his family," Kylie said, surprised to hear how haughty her tone was, as if she'd been the one who'd been insulted. Outsiders tended to band together, and if anything Jesse's blunt distaste for Tom made Kylie more contrary in her response. It was in her nature to come to the defense of an underdog. "I know they've been treated terribly in this town. He wants to restore their standing."

"Good luck with that, because it's never going to happen. The Locklands were a bunch of robbers." When Kylie moved to unlock the door it became clear to Jesse that she was getting nowhere with this girl. "Don't say I didn't warn you."

Kylie went back to the bar. There were two bowls of vegetable stew set out and some rolls and butter. Tom had ordered her a whiskey, but Kylie stuck to water. "I've been warned," she told him. "You're bad."

Tom frowned and cursed softly. "People in Thornfield like to provoke me with their moronic opinions. And you wonder why I hate this place."

People were staring at him and talking among themselves. Kylie overheard a few comments, mostly centering on what a bastard her companion was. Despite the gossip and the veiled insults, Lockland maintained a wary stillness. He repelled some people, but others were wildly attracted to him, drawn to him as though he were a beacon. There was a light inside him, one that flamed and lured Kylie to him. She noticed that the waitress who'd ambushed her was staring and that there were spots of red on her cheeks. Perhaps she was a vengeful ex-girlfriend of Tom's, for he'd admitted there were many of his past wrong choices in town and because of his failed romantic history, Kylie might hear awful rumors about him.

"Mind your own business," Kylie remarked to Jesse as she passed the waitress on her way to the door when their supper was done.

"What goes on here is my business," Jesse responded. "I'm the manager. Stay clear of Tom Lockland if you know what's good for you."

As they set off down the High Street, a wind had come up and the birds stirred in the bushes. What fools some people were. Kylie agreed with Tom on that. They walked along the fens, where water rimmed the side of the road. Already the night was pitch dark and pools that had collected at the change in the tide were difficult to avoid. Kylie stumbled into a puddle that nearly reached her knees. Tom seized her arm so that he might pull her back to the road. "Stay here by me," he said, and she did so, for she had a fear of water, instilled by her mother with all her talk of drownings and sea monsters. If there were to be a monster anywhere, Kylie found herself thinking, it would likely be here on the outskirts of Thornfield. The twisted forms of old trees emerged out of the dark and there were tall hedges of bramble on either side of the road that shifted in the gusts of wind, throwing up a peppery smell that made Kylie's eyes itch.

"I usually stay away from water," she admitted.

"Let me guess. You were warned away by your family."

Kylie was surprised that he'd guessed correctly. "My mother. We were never allowed to go swimming."

"What people don't understand they fear." Tom seemed more relaxed then he'd been at the pub. "I'm sure they'd all warn you away from me."

She saw the way he was looking at her, even in the falling dark.

He took a step closer. "Or maybe they already have."

There was something there between them that made Kylie uncomfortable, a flicker of heat. "I'm in love with someone," she reminded him. "Gideon."

"Glad to hear it," Tom said with a laugh. "Can't say I've ever experienced it. I don't think it runs in my part of the family."

It was now so dark that when a sheep in the meadow they were passing suddenly appeared at a fence, looming in the night like a ghost, a scrim of panic overcame Kylie, head to toe. Everyone was so far away. She'd only been in Essex for a few hours, yet she felt understood by Tom Lockland. As they'd walked along, he slipped an amulet into the pocket of her raincoat, an unbreakable knot that would keep her close to him, a binding spell, what the Greeks called *katadesmos*.

Once at the house, they said good night and Kylie went up the narrow stairs to the bedroom. She could hear Tom downstairs, making up the couch, and she considered all that magic had done to them. Gideon, who was so good at heart, would never understand what had ruined them but Tom Lockland knew what it meant to be cursed. Kylie turned off the light. There was a candle on the bedside table, which she lit before opening her bag. In the flickering yellow light, she slipped out *The Book of the Raven*, turning to the last two pages that were stuck together. *What are you willing to sacrifice? How much are you willing to pay?*

"I need to read you," she commanded, but the pages would not open. Magic was thwarting her and time was spinning away. She recalled Jet's warning that whoever ended the curse would face danger, but that everything worthwhile was dangerous.

Kylie made her way downstairs in the dark and found Tom sprawled on the couch, a book in hand, one he planned to toss onto the flame of his small fireplace when he was done. Worthless, he thought, as most books were in his opinion. He was pleased when Kylie appeared, but not surprised. He'd concocted a *Need You* spell, made of wax and pins and a small straw poppet, hidden beneath her pillow.

Who one dared to love was complicated, but who to trust was even more confounding. Kylie thought of the warnings from the waitress at the inn, and of the librarian in London, and from her aunt Jet. She felt such shame each time she thought of her beloved Gideon, whose life she had all but destroyed. Perhaps it was best if she stopped considering every option and simply acted on instinct. It was dark in the parlor, but there was the glow of bright moon shining through the window and they could see each other quite clearly.

"I don't know how to do this by myself," Kylie admitted to Tom. She had *The Book of the Raven* in hand, but Tom pretended not to notice the text and gestured for her to come sit beside him. He felt pins and needles. Right away, he sensed this was the book he'd been searching for.

Tom ran a hand over Kylie's. "Let me help you," he said.

A partnership such as the one they were forging was a dark agreement in which one person was certain to win and the other was fated to lose, a contract bound in desperation with red thread that grew tighter every time you tried to break what tied you together. *Don't think, don't wait, you are here and they are far away. It is dangerous, it's a risk, trust no one or trust the person beside you.* In a daze, Kylie offered him the book that had been waiting for three hundred years for the right person to find it, only to be given over to the wrong man.

IV.

While the others slept, Vincent let himself out of the flat so that he might walk alone, something he'd done as a young man, an old habit that had been renewed ever since William's passing. He walked blindly around the island where they lived, and then in Paris, a city he knew well. Here in London he took his time on unfamiliar streets. Before he knew it, morning had approached, and the black skies were turning to pearl along the horizon. It was the most difficult hour for Vincent, when he felt most alone. For more than fifty years he'd woken with William in his bed, and now sleep eluded him; he couldn't bear to wake without the man he'd loved for so long. After a year, it still had not quite sunk in that William was gone; perhaps it never would.

Walking through London made Vincent's heart impossibly heavy. He had become accustomed to having the company of the stray dog, Dodger, who was now enjoying the guest room at Agnes's house. Still, Vincent had a purpose for this walk. He'd always been a finder, able to locate places, whether they were on the map or off the grid. He had come upon a reference book in the historian's office marked with an unusual stamp formed with pale red ink and as usual he had been able to locate the address without a map or any guide, though it was a place that most people walked past without seeing. The Invisible Library. Bayswater. Vincent took his time crossing Hyde Park, happy for the solitude he found there. The only noise that could be heard were birds stirring in the bushes, and then, as Vincent approached the Serpentine, there was a sudden wild squawking from a group of ring-necked parakeets perched in the wavering branches of the lime trees. The birds were said to be descendants of two parakeets Jimi Hendrix had set free from their cage in Mayfair years ago. It was so early that Vincent spotted several foxes outside their hidden dens and a shadowy vixen at the edge of the lake. The streetlights were flickering out as dawn approached and the city looked ashy, a vista in black and white.

When he reached the street, he spied the outline of a building shrouded in protective spells, set off from prying eyes. It contained more magic literature than all of the museums and bookstores in London combined, much of it under lock and key, with access to its private members and occasionally available to serious scholars. Vincent stood outside the building and breathed in the chilly morning air. When the library came into focus, it looked like any other house on the street, a tall milk-white Georgian-style building, but there was no actual address, only the numbers 17608415 on the door, healing numbers that are meant to repel black magic. He went up the steps and did his best to open the door, but it wouldn't budge. *When they find the lock, you'll have the key,* Jet had told him in his dream, but he had no way to unlock this particular door, for it was forged out of iron, then encased in hazel wood and painted a slick black so that it looked like any other on the street. Quite suddenly Vincent felt a fool when he thought of his dream. Perhaps he'd misunderstood Jet entirely. A lock needn't be made of metal. A key was not necessarily something you held in your hand. He swore softly at his own stupidity. By now Vincent knew, nothing was what it seemed.

He returned to the park, where he sat on a bench facing the library waiting for someone to arrive. Vincent had never been terribly good at being patient; he'd been a rebel, too wild to listen to reason, he'd wanted what he'd wanted, but the years had taught him something. William's harrowing illness at the end of his life had revealed what real patience was. *Wait and see*, William always said. *Tonight might be better, tomorrow might be pain free.* As William's health plummeted from a cancer that was untreatable, he had appeared luminous, resolved to have as many days as he could with Vincent. They stayed in bed, the windows open, light reflecting from the sea. *Love of my life, the one loss I will never survive.* Yet he had survived, but barely, often wondering why he was still here.

"Do you ever regret running away?" Vincent had asked William during his final day, for it was in this way they had escaped the curse; they had started new lives and never looked back. It was their last night together, but they didn't know it. The lines on their hands were blurred, their futures unsure.

"I didn't run away. I ran to you," William told him.

It was the perfect answer, the one that broke Vincent's heart. He should have been more patient, he shouldn't have rushed through his life, for now he had arrived here, alone, in a city he didn't know, in the early morning light, filled with an absurd desire for the past. If only he could close his eyes and be transported to Greenwich Village on his birthday when they first met, when their lives were ahead of them, when he had no patience and plunged into love.

Now he was a man who could wait when he had to. Less than

forty minutes later, the librarian arrived. *Now it begins*, Vincent thought. And then he had the oddest thought. *Here is the key.*

David Ward noticed the man on the bench who was observing him. He recognized Vincent immediately, the same handsome profile that had been in magazines and newspapers after his sudden death. David had been a fan of Vincent's back when he was young, and had listened rapt to "I Walk at Night" over and over again, wishing he'd had the courage to announce who he was, as Vincent had. This was in the days when people more often hid their sexual nature. It was easy to do, if you didn't mind breaking your own heart. David had been married and he'd kept his most authentic self a secret even from those to whom he was closest. He'd forsaken his true self to be a family man. He'd thought there were no other choices.

He remembered the day he first heard Vincent's song on the radio. He was still working at the British Museum back then, specializing in artifacts from Persia and Mesopotamia; he hadn't yet been contacted by his current employers, a board of magic practitioners who understood that David Ward was good at keeping a secret. Too good, perhaps.

Before he became the keeper of the magic stored here, he'd been to the left side and had been in a state of spiritual agony ever since. Working here was a penance of sorts; he would now do good in the world where before he had been willing to do evil. His daughter, Eve, had come down with meningitis; it had occurred suddenly, on an ordinary day. Eve was ten, the light of his life, and the reason David had stayed married. He'd furtively begun a separate life on nights he was away from home, fearing that if he made an admission regarding his sexuality, his wife would be granted full custody. When Evie became ill he knew where to go for help, a practitioner of the Dark Art who often visited the museum. David went to a mansion in South Kensington knowing that in exchange for his daughter's life, he would be required to complete a task. He knew the city was in the triangle of black magic, and that it could be found on streets and alleyways for those willing to look for such things.

David was to commit a murder on behalf of another of the magician's clients. He didn't even argue. That's what desire mixed with desperation could do. He sat at a bar and poisoned a stranger's drink. In the mayhem of waiters doing their best to help the young man having a heart attack at the bar, David had found his way out, continuing on to the hospital where his daughter had miraculously recovered. It was a misdiagnosis, the doctors said, but David knew the truth, he had traded one life for another. He had chosen the Crooked Path and he would pay for it for the rest of his life.

It was never the same with Evie. That was the price. When she'd found love letters he'd written to a man he was involved with, she called him a liar and a hypocrite and his wife told him to leave and he'd gotten into a taxi and fled in shame, without putting up a fight. He shouldered his guilt and there was no room for anything but self-recrimination. He accepted the job at the Invisible Library, and one day a black-edged note was slipped under the door and he knew that Evie was gone. She and her boyfriend had been in a motorcycle accident, skidding on wet pavement late at night. He knew it was his fault. His daughter's original fate had caught up with her because he hadn't been able to bring himself to slip the full dose of poison in his target's drink. The stranger he was meant to do away with had a heart attack, but he had survived.

Even then, Vincent's song had spoken to him in a deep, fierce way; he played it constantly for several years and could recite it word for word even now. And here was the musician himself, a man who was supposed to be dead for nearly sixty years. Instead of unlocking the library door, David crossed the street and entered the park. A message was a message, a sign was a sign, and it appeared that Vincent Owens had returned from the grave. For years, David had sought out a spell that would bring back the dead, even though he knew that what came back from the other side would be dark and unnatural. The sheer permanence of the loss of his daughter undid him in a thousand ways. But now here he was, about to meet a man who had risen. The trees in Hyde Park were leafy and green, but at this hour they appeared black. Funny, he had worn a black suit and a black tie today, as if he would be attending a funeral.

"Have you returned from the dead?" David Ward said. Necromancy was referred to as *The Knowledge* and human history was littered with those who had chased after a cure for death. "Is it possible?"

"I'm not back from anything. I've always been here." When David shot him a puzzled look, Vincent added, "In hiding."

"Too bad," David said. "I thought you had *The Knowledge.*" It was a joke, a play on taxi drivers' crash course in knowing the city, only the left-handed version had to do with raising the dead. David tried such a spell once and no good had come of it. Afterward, he'd been sick for weeks, vomiting up strange items: beads, feathers, earrings, cigarette butts. All of it, he'd come to realize, were items that had belonged to his daughter. He ceased fooling around with necromancy then, and was wise to have done so.

"Actually, I thought you might be able to help me." Vincent handed the librarian his great-granddaughter's photograph, a lovely girl Vincent had yet to meet, cursed in love, but blessed in all other things, for whose safety, he believed, only he held the key. "She's gone missing."

"Kylie," David Ward said, wondering if he would remember this day as unlucky or if he would be grateful for it forever more. "I know where she is."

Ian went running early, out the door before six. He did this every day and he wasn't about to stop due to the attack that had, frankly, left him a bit weak even after his cure. He certainly wasn't about to allow the presence of his uninvited guests to interrupt his schedule, even though Sally was among them. Sally, who wouldn't speak to him, who gazed away if she caught him observing her and had once said, "Stop it right now!" Well, of course, she was right. He had no business getting involved with her, or with anyone else for that matter. As for Sally, she'd be gone before he knew it. All the same, he was affected by her presence and needed a run more than ever to clear his head.

The Americans had taken over Ian's flat, leaving him to sleep on a blanket on the floor of the front room beside the bookcases, where he couldn't get any rest. He still ached and his pulse was ragged. Ian hoped exercise would help to restore him. He had first considered that running might be his salvation when he was in jail, and as soon as he got out, he began to run in earnest. Each time he hit the streets, he remembered what it had been like to be locked up, as this morning he remembered being trapped inside a frozen body, spellbound and incapable of moving.

He would have to pay back Sally Owens for saving his life. Last night they'd had a quick supper of soup Franny Owens had made, using all the ingredients in his pantry it seemed. "What are you staring at?" Franny had asked him. He'd been fumbling around in a drawer, searching for spoons, then had suddenly stopped and looked up, riveted.

"Nothing," he said, as if he were a guilty boy caught stealing.

"You're staring at my niece," Franny declared. "Do you think I'm a fool?"

"Actually, no. I think you're a witch."

"Then you're not so stupid after all."

"Did you think I was?" Ian found he was both hurt and offended by the notion that she'd formed a bad opinion of him.

Franny had laughed then, a lovely surprising sound. "I think you're *too* smart for your own good."

They'd exchanged a look, and at that moment he was able to see Franny as a young woman. He felt both drawn to her and afraid of her, and more than anything he felt that even at this stage, he had a lot to learn.

"I fell in love when I was fifteen," Franny said, wistful.

"Did you?" They had lowered their voices conspiratorially. Somehow they'd leapt forward to become allies.

"I still am, even though he's gone. Not everyone's that lucky."

"I suppose not," Ian agreed.

"You could be."

"Unlikely," he told her. "No heart."

Franny laughed again and he grinned, pleased to have amused her. He was an excellent liar, but apparently she saw right through him. "To find out where my great-niece is, we have to find out who we are," Franny went on. "You're the historian. You're the one we need."

Ian was grateful that Frances Owens would have such faith in him, but he felt a stab of uncertainty all the same. He gazed at the others, Sally setting the table, Gillian curled up in his leather chair talking to Ben on the phone, Vincent paging through *The Magus*, the volume that had changed his life when he first broke the rule not to read magic books.

"The question is, are you willing?" Franny asked, sounding as if she were his therapist. He'd been to one of those and he knew they always threw everything back at you so that you would answer your own questions.

"Willing to?" he asked.

"You know exactly what I mean."

All at once Ian understood the discussion they were having was about Sally. "I don't know what to think," he admitted.

"That's your problem," Franny said. "You should be sure."

He mulled her comment over in silence as they finished dinner. It was true that the one image he couldn't dispel was of Sally leaning over him, telling him to do as he was told if he wanted to live. He could not forget the way she looked at him with her cool gray, disapproving eyes.

"Cat got your tongue?" Gillian asked Ian when he hadn't spoken a word through the meal.

The two sisters regarded one another and laughed. Could it be? It could not, and yet the butter was melting in its dish on the table, a sure sign that someone had fallen in love.

"What do you want from the poor man? He's just escaped death," Franny said on Ian's behalf. "He's in recovery."

Ian understood how true this was. He'd been in recovery for more years than he could count, distancing himself from people. Somehow, plummeting into that strange red paralysis had woken him. He could now see people as they truly were, despite their age. Franny as a red-haired girl who would do anything for those she loved, Vincent as a wild, free spirit walking down a city street with a wolflike dog at his heels, Gillian as a child spinning with her arms out, hoping not to fall, but not really caring if she did, and Sally, Sally was right there before him, a dark, serious girl who wished she would never fall in love, so afraid her heart would break that she had never unmasked it and had thereby broken it herself.

"Are you all right?" Sally asked Ian as she ladled out more soup.

He nodded, unable to take his eyes off her. They laughed at him when he didn't speak and asked what sort of answer was that? Ian didn't blame them for being entertained by his lack of speech, an unusual state for him; he was a talker, a man who could lecture for three hours straight, barely stopping long enough to take a breath. His mother had always said that his arrogance alienated people on the spot. This time he kept quiet, knowing how obnoxious he would sound if he spoke the truth. *You need me more than you know.*

He left the sleeping Americans and headed directly to Lancaster Gate so that he might dig around for references to *The Book of the Raven* unhindered by his guests. He was a member of the Invisible Library and had his key with him. When he reached his destination, he pulled on his jersey, then took the steps two at a time up to the door. He knew he was setting out on the Crooked Path, magic that had no beginning and no end and instead circled like a snake, its tail in its mouth, so that you could not venture off the route you set out upon. He had a dark side, and, he feared, a deeply emotional side as well. Ian felt the stirrings of his other self inside of him, the one who'd been a thief, locked up long ago then discarded, but there all the same, the flinty part of him that made him fearless when a wiser man would have been alarmed enough to turn away.

Sally had heard him in the front room before he left, brewing a quick cup of tea before he headed out the door. She had no reason to trust Ian, and every reason to need him. She'd thrown on some clothes, slipped on her boots, and followed him onto Westbourne Grove, where she caught a taxi in order to keep up.

"We can't follow a runner," the driver warned when Ian turned into the park. "He'll be on paths." It was a warm morning and Ian had stripped off his shirt, clearly not one to follow the rules of decorum. Just as the driver began to warn Sally that this fellow she wanted followed would likely run across the grass, Ian took off over the dewy grass and they could no longer closely follow him.

"Just do your best," Sally suggested.

They lost him for a while, but then she caught sight of Ian crossing Bayswater, headed toward Lancaster Gate. She felt her heart pound; it was as if she were tracking a wild creature, one that preferred to disappear. Sally quickly paid the driver, thanked him for being so persistent, then got out and crossed the street. She had borrowed one of Ian's white shirts without asking, not that it mattered. He had plenty more. He turned as if she'd called his name even before she darted up the steps to join him. "I assumed you might run away," she said.

"Run away from my own flat?" Ian opened the door, gesturing for Sally to enter.

"I thought we might have scared you."

"You don't scare me." *You're still a good liar*, he thought to himself. *You'll help them as you're bound to do, and it will all be over soon. It's nothing anyway. It's your imagination.*

"What is this place?" Sally asked.

"A library. For people like us."

"What sort of people is that?" She had narrowed her eyes, clearly expecting an answer she wouldn't like.

"People who like books," Ian said, proud of his dodgy answer.

"I like books," Sally said. "I'm a librarian."

"Are you?" Of course she would be. Ian found women who were librarians exceedingly sexy. It was a combination of their love of books, which always increased their beauty, along with the fact that they usually knew more than he did, which he found oddly arousing.

Sally eyed the ornate moldings, extraordinary in detail, but, in her estimation, spoiled when painted a deep, glossy red. "Awful color," she noted.

"It's the color of magic. That's probably why you don't like it." Ian gave her a sidelong glance and when she stared back at him he felt a sort of panic. *Fuck*, he thought. *It can't be this.*

Sally disapproved of the library. It wasn't just the color that glazed the woodwork that disturbed her, it was the content on the shelves. "Magic ruins people, why would I like it?"

"I used to believe that, but then I grew up." Ian gave her a look he intended to be mocking, but it turned out to be something else entirely, some raw emotion that embarrassed him. Why was he debating her? He knew who he was, a self-centered man, not terribly interested in other people's issues, always the thoughtless boyfriend who didn't blink when a woman decided she'd had enough of his cool, selfish ways and left him, since that was what he wanted all along. No entanglements or complications. His work was more than enough for him. He'd seen what love could do, how it drove so many to practice left-handed magic; he'd been happy enough to wake alone in his bed.

"So you found your salvation in magic," Sally said in a scornful tone. "And you think it's fine if you occasionally go to the left to get what you want."

He heaved a sigh. What made her think she knew him, and worse, what if she did?

"It's written all over you. You don't just believe in magic, you're consumed by it."

Now he was provoked. There were a thousand other things he could be doing this morning. "If you so disapprove, maybe you should go your way and I'll go mine."

Whenever Sally was vulnerable she was unpleasant and she knew it. Could it be they were alike in this? "I shouldn't have said those things," she admitted. "I'm desperate."

"We can find her." So now it was we, was it? Ian felt ploddingly stupid. He was overthinking. What they were forging was a business transaction, the oldest one of all. A life for a life.

He went to speak to the librarian, who had helped in his research before. When he began asking questions about *The Book of the Raven*, the librarian nodded, and led them down a long corridor to the reading room. Ian glanced over at Sally, who seemed folded in on herself. Magic hung in the air, thick moody gasps of it in every breath.

Vincent had been at work for well over an hour. He'd been given a pair of black cotton gloves to use as he looked through stacks of *Grimoires*, some donated, others stolen or found by accident, still others having narrowly managed to escape being burned, their pages singed, the paper emitting the acrid green scent of smoke. So far, he'd unearthed several references to Amelia Bassano, who knew astrologers and royals and theater people, but no mention of *The Book of the Raven*.

Sally wasn't surprised to find that her grandfather had beaten them to the library. Her aunt Franny had confided that long-ago Vincent had practiced on the left-hand side, and that he'd been born with the temperament for magic, always curious, able to see what others could not.

"Your girl was here," Vincent told Sally. "Yesterday. She has the book, but it refuses to open."

Stunned, Sally turned to the librarian. "Did you help her?"

David Ward explained he'd found little concerning *The Book of the Raven,* only a mention of Amelia Bassano's practice of magic. The librarian seemed to be more interested in references to the Owens family history.

"Our history?" Sally said, wary.

He thought it wise to pursue that avenue of research, for every curse began in the past.

Sally quickly scanned the entries which recorded that a woman named Hannah Owens had been tried as a witch then set free when the witch mania temporarily passed and those imprisoned were released for no reason, just as they were arrested without cause.

"That's my home," Ian told them. They waited for him to say more, but he remained silent, confused by the turn of events. He had not believed in the concept of fate, and yet here they were, with ties to the same county. He thought of himself as a boy of ten, standing at the edge of the fens, certain that if he only waited long enough he would know why he'd been fated to grow up in a place he despised.

Ian asked to look at the book, a genealogical record of his own hometown, Thornfield. He had a bone-rattling chill of recognition when he saw the name Lockland.

"Hannah Owens was involved with the Locklands in the mid-seventeenth century," David Ward said. "As far as I can tell, the original ancestor saw to it that she was burned as a witch."

Sally felt a shiver run through her. "Did you mention this to my daughter?"

"I suggested the Locklands might have retained documents. There was a reference to the last remaining member of the family, Tom Lockland."

Bad Tom, Ian thought. *That piece of shit.* He'd heard Tom Lockland was stealing magic books from practitioners and historians in an attempt to access magic. A few months earlier, Tom had come slinking around Ian's office, with the nerve to ask if Ian wanted to hire him as an assistant. The answer had been no, and ever since Ian had wondered what Tom had really wanted. Now he wondered if Tom Lockland was responsible for the disappearance of *Rauðskinna* and if the hex might have been an act of revenge for Ian dismissing him out of hand.

Ian had known Tom since Lockland had been a boy lurking around the town where they'd both grown up, seeking vengeance in whatever small way he could. Tom was twenty-five years younger than Ian, but he had a reputation in town by the time he was twelve. It was a bad age, set between being a child and being a man, and people often were lost during that year. Tom had been tossed out of school time and again, known as a fellow who set fires in the thickets in the forest and it was thought he might have a hand in a fire begun in the bins behind the local library, which thankfully was put out before the flames could leap to the building. After prison, Ian was trying to make amends, he'd imagined Tom was a kindred spirit who could use help in steadying himself. Ian's wild youth had not defined him and he wanted to share that knowledge. He knew the rumors about the Locklands; the family that had gone downhill, from great wealth and near royal standing to ruin. Ian had imagined they had something in common, and had been arrogant to think of himself as a potential mentor, but Tom sneered at the friendship he'd offered, stalking away and telling Ian to piss off.

In the years that followed, he'd heard gossip that Tom often camped out at Lockland Manor, once for an entire year, flinging up a tent inside one of the derelict rooms, living there through a brutal winter, stealing boots and a coat from an old couple who phoned the police when they saw a teenager break into a run in the field, but who, when a detective came to question them, found they couldn't speak to lay blame on Tom. There was madder root on their hands and feet and dusting their front hallway and they never did press charges. Tom knew about poison even then, Ian realized.

He remembered how Tom had set out glass around the perimeter of his tent, arranged in the shape of a pentagram to reverse any ill will. Tom was headed toward the left even then, happy to use the Crooked Path to get back at anyone and everyone. He didn't care that the manor house was in shambles, too expensive for the county to keep up, little more than a relic, he thought of the estate as his even then. Magic didn't come naturally to him, but he had some learned skill. Once when Ian was visiting his mother, taking a walk with her Labrador retriever, Jinx, the dog had rushed over to a barn on the Lockland estate, barking like mad. Because of the dog's racket Ian had stopped to peer into the house. Tom was naked in front of a bonfire that spat out flame and smoke, fed by the fuel of books he'd found in the manor house. The act of burning a book was such a brutal and meaningless act Ian had shouted out, but Tom turned to him and jeered. "I'll do whatever I want. You can't stop me. Nobody can."

Ian had told his mother what he'd seen, and Margaret Wright had shaken her head, though she hadn't been surprised. She practiced the Nameless Art and therefore saw through people to their core. "If you knew the whole story, you'd know the reason. The past can take over if you let it. This town is not the reason he's cursed, yet he blames each and every one of us. It's what's inside him that's the problem. The neglect he suffered, that's what ruined him. If you think you're nothing, that's what you become."

Ian thought it would be faster if he ran home, considering London traffic at this hour, but Vincent insisted on getting them a taxi. The librarian had given Vincent his phone number, in case more research was necessary, something he'd never offered to Ian despite all the time the historian spent at the library. Vincent noticed he'd been given Ward's personal number. "You could call to let me know how the girl is," David said. "If you don't mind."

The rain that had previously eased had returned, pelting down upon the streets. The world was dim, and they were fortunate to get a taxi, or maybe it wasn't luck. Maybe it was Vincent out there on the pavement beneath a streetlamp that flickered gray and then bright once more.

"Are you ready for this?" Vincent asked Sally as he opened the taxi door for her.

Sally had always avoided her talent, but now, she could feel herself opening to that side of herself. She could already see the inside stories of those around her, a trait of those who have the sight, whether they want it or not. There was the taxi driver's remorse over an argument with his son, and the librarian's suffering over the loss of a child, and the man beside her, leaning forward to give the driver his address, who believed he was immune to love. For twenty years he had thought of nothing but his book. Without it, he feared he could become his old self, drawn to the left for his own selfish reasons, forsaking love. His mother had always insisted that no one was immune to love. It was impossible, she vowed. On his last visit home, she'd grabbed his hands to see what his fate might be. As she read him, she breathed out an audible sigh of regret as she scrutinized the lines on his right hand, the fate he had been given, but then she'd stunned him by laughing out loud when she looked at his left hand. "Won't you be surprised," she had said.

"You can't keep it from me if you know what's to be," Ian had insisted.

"Fate will make the best of you," Margaret Wright scolded, using an old adage that many mothers told their children in their village. "If you don't make the best of it. That's what the witches say."

Now in the taxi, he thought his mother would be amused to see how baffled he was whenever he was in Sally's presence. He could barely bring himself to look at her. His first instinct was to leap out of the taxi at the next red light and run in the other direction, but he stayed where he was, already reproaching himself for being a fool.

"We'll pick up the others, then take the train to Essex," he told Sally. "We should get there as soon as possible. All right?"

She knew she would say yes even before Ian asked the question. Her world had already begun to change. If magic was what was needed, magic it would be. And so she said yes to the man who would lead her to the first Essex County, where the land was so marshy unwitting people sank into the fens if they weren't careful, where the crows protected each other and Devotion Field was often the setting used to celebrate weddings, where it was possible to find what you'd lost, where there had been ashes rising on a day when a woman burned, when Maria Owens first decided that love was not a blessing but a curse.

PART FOUR

The Book of Love

I.

As the train hurtled through the darkening evening, Gillian hunched back in her seat to observe the rising pink moon from the window. When she was young, people said she could bewitch men with a single glance, but the truth was she'd never had the power to do so. She'd veered onto the Crooked Path when she got involved with a man who was nothing but trouble, and she'd learned her lesson. *Never love someone who cannot love you back*, Jet had told her. *That is the way to heartbreak and nothing more.*

Gillian had been glad to sit by herself on the train so that she might have her own private thoughts uninterrupted. They were passing near the village of Canewdon, once called the village of witches, and Gillian gazed out, assuming she would spy only the sky and the countryside, but there was more. She leaned forward, rapt, as she did her best to make out the shape on the other side of the glass. No one else looked out. No one else noticed anything unusual.

Franny and Vincent were in seats next to one another, their heads close, chuckling as they spoke about the past. Sally and Ian had wound up together accidentally. As soon as Ian sat beside her Sally called out, "Oh, Gilly, come sit with me." Ian had immediately risen to his feet, assuring them he would be happy to move, but Gillian had begged off, explaining that she was drained from the time change and wanted to sleep. Ian and Sally then exchanged glassy looks. "I don't talk while traveling," Sally had warned him, sounding haughtier than she meant to. Ian understood completely. What she'd meant was simply *Leave me alone.*

"Fine," Ian had assured her as he'd retaken the seat beside her. He wished she didn't have a heart-shaped face. He hadn't even known there was such a thing, but there it was, scowling at him. "Don't say a word. That will be a pleasure for me as well," he said flatly. Distance, he told himself. And yet he couldn't heed his own advice and edged closer to her. "We can never speak if that's the way you'd like it to be." Good lord, he thought, what was wrong with him?

Sally had started, indignant. "Are you trying to be rude?"

"I don't have to try." Why not be blunt? That had always been his method of navigating the world. "I was born that way, and I'm sure my mother, who you'll meet before long, would agree." When Ian saw the curious look on Sally's face, he added, "If you don't want me here, that's your choice." He sounded like a besotted lunatic, even to himself. "I can go sit in the loo."

Sally laughed, charmed despite herself by the way he held forth, for at heart he was his mother's son. You could judge a man by whether or not he got along with his mother, and beneath his bad-mannered façade, Ian was devoted to his. "Of course, I want you here. You owe me that. But you have my solemn promise, I will ignore you," Sally assured him "It should be easy to do."

Whatever was inside him flared, and he looked hurt.

"Now I've insulted you." Sally was surprised, not expecting

him to be so thin-skinned. Perhaps that was the reason for all of the ink. Beneath his clothes, his tattoos were his armor.

"I owe you and I'm here." Ian was doing his best to sort it out. "Shall we leave it at that?" He was bringing her home to his mother, who had never met a woman he was involved with, since none lasted, not that he was involved with Sally, but mothers will think as they please and his would get a good laugh out of this.

"Yes," Sally said, chastened. "I'm sorry. I'm the rude one." She turned away, overcome. For a moment, she stared out at the darkening light. Bats flickered over the trees. There was a false story that had passed through generations claiming witches couldn't cry. Perhaps that made it easier to burn them; perhaps you could drown a woman if you convinced yourself she had no feelings at all.

"Your girl will be found." Ian sounded sure of himself. He knew Essex as well as anyone, having spent hours out in the fens and the bogs, despite his mother's warnings that he would drown if he wasn't careful. There was an old abandoned house past where they lived, nearly surrounded by water when the tide was high. He'd spent a good deal of time out there, watching the herons and egrets and spoonbills perching in the trees and wading through the water. In his opinion, that was magic.

Gillian looked out the window and wondered if she was too greedy. She had a perfectly good life and yet she wanted more. As she gazed out she saw something, an unexpected shadow. It was a figure out in the fens, what people called a shade, not a ghost exactly, but rather a memory, as if a person was caught in an unending cycle of time they couldn't break, unable or unwilling to move on to the world beyond. Gillian had heard about such sightings in Salem and Boston, layers of regret set in between the brittle history of the past which caught a soul and kept it there to repeat a moment or a deed. It was said you could walk down Beacon Street at dusk and glimpse half a dozen of these shades. Though witches were born with the ability to see spirits, Gillian had never come upon one herself, and now she craned her neck to see, moving so near the window her nose touched the glass.

In the distance a girl of eleven was plodding through the water weeds, carrying her possessions above her head so they would not be soaked. A crow soared across the sky, black against the violet twilight, difficult to see, but clear enough when Gillian narrowed her eyes. The bird had been circling above the trees for three hundred years, following a girl who had left the mortal world long ago. On some nights the machinery of time was rewound as the past leaked into the present. It was as if the back of a watch had been slid open to see its workings. Even for those with the sight it was a marvel to behold time in all its beauty and confusion: *What has been, what is, what will be.*

The girl in the fens turned as if she could hear the train that wouldn't exist until hundreds of years later, cocking her head, so that strands of her long dark hair nearly covered her face, for she seemed to catch a glimmer of Gillian, who had cupped her hands against the glass so that she could stare out without any flickering reflections to obscure her view. The girl walking through the water-logged landscape was carrying a black book. It all seemed familiar, as if it were an image Gillian had seen in a dream.

Do you see me as I see you? Do you wish me to know what you know?

The train moved on and soon enough there was nothing beyond the glass, only the dark settling over reeds and water, fish and fox and crows. Gillian leaned forward to talk to Sally through the split in the seats. "Are you okay?" she asked her sister.

The historian was reading; he was never without a book, and this small volume was a *Grimoire* written by a girl in Manningtree, whose mother and sisters had been put to death during the witch mania. His gaze shifted; he saw Gillian take her sister's hand and found himself moved by their tenderness.

"Of course," Sally said. "I'm fine."

Exactly what she would say, not that Gillian believed it for a minute.

"I saw a shade out there," Gillian murmured.

"A shadow," Sally was quick to correct her sister, denying magic as always. "Likely a tree."

Gillian shook her head. "It was a girl. I think it's good luck. There was a crow with her."

In their family, crows signified good fortune. Sally squeezed her sister's hand, wanting to believe. They really weren't so different anymore. When Gillian shifted back in her seat, Sally noticed Ian's gaze. "Did you want something?"

"I always want something. Right now, I want to go to sleep." He was a good liar, but Sally didn't believe him for a minute. She felt his gaze on her still.

They were quiet for a while, then Sally said, "Are there ghosts out there?"

"Time is out there. Everything that ever happened is still happening. For instance, if I took your hand in mine." Which he did as he was speaking. "It would be happening for hundreds of years."

"Would it?" Sally said.

"That's what people say."

She slipped her hand from his. His touch had burned. This was not going to happen. It most certainly was not what she was looking for.

"It doesn't matter," he said when she withdrew from him. "It's still happening." When she frowned, Ian shrugged. "I'm only repeating local lore."

"Magic," Sally said disdainfully.

"It's not the thing that ruins you," Ian assured her.

"Isn't it?" She looked at him deeply. Despite her cool demeanor, she found him curious and intriguing.

"I know from experience. People ruin themselves."

At last they came to the town where Ian had grown up, called Thornfield, the place he had found so intolerable that he'd spent his entire youth plotting his escape. The village had arisen around a grand manor house, which was now derelict, having been abandoned when the family who owned it fled in shame.

When they arrived, Ian whistled for the taxi, driven by a fellow named Matthew Poole, with whom Ian had gone to school. Matt Poole helped fit their luggage into his large blue van, clearly in need of repair, but the only taxi based in Thornfield.

"Looks like you've brought a crowd to see your mum," Matt said as he dealt with the suitcases, tossing them into the rear of the van. "How will they all fit into her house?"

It was well known that Margaret Wright did not care for comforts, let alone luxuries. She believed in a simple way of life, one that didn't differ very much from the lives of her grandmother and great grandmother, and she still used a pump for her water and an outbuilding for her toilet. These were among the reasons Ian had despised his home when he was young. Back then, he thought what he wanted most in the world was a fast car and a flat in London.

"They'll be at the Hedges," Ian told Matt. "I called ahead." He turned to Sally then. "I'll come by for you in the morning and we'll find her."

"You're not staying there with us?"

Ian looked at her. His pulse was too fast. *This cannot be it.* A man such as himself should have as little to do with a witch as possible.

"Is there something you need him for?" Franny asked, amused when she overheard Sally's question. The historian was such a good-looking man, after all, and they'd seen every bit of him.

"We all need him to look for Kylie," Sally replied. She turned to Ian then, though she did her best not to look at him directly. "I thought we would start the search as early in the morning as possible. That was the only reason I thought you would be staying at the inn."

"If I didn't go visit my mother, she'd have my head," Ian explained to Sally. *And I wouldn't trust myself being under the same roof as you, and I have no idea what I'm doing here in the dark in the town that I couldn't wait to leave, nor do I understand why I don't want to move on from the place where I'm standing right now.*

"Of course," Sally deferred. "You must go."

Ian said his good nights and headed off down the High Street, turning onto Littlefields Road, which led toward the fens. His mother lived on the far side of town, down a rutted dirt lane. She'd never had a car and preferred her bicycle. When she'd gone to see Ian in prison, she'd taken the bus, and she hadn't traveled since. Anyway, it would do him good to walk and clear his head, although once he'd set off he realized it was the season of the toads, and there they were, littering the road, calling to one another in the green heat of their mating season, the males puffed up and glowing faintly, paying no heed to the fact that they were sending out their mating call on the road, so that if a car passed by many of them would be squashed.

"Go on," he said to the toads as he made his way.

They continued to ignore him, and in the end he was the

one who had to watch where he walked, stepping carefully over them, for it was bad luck to kill a toad. Ian decided it was easier to walk through the woods where the worst he would tread on were ivy and weeds. If there was anyone in this town who knew magic, it was his mother. He could study all his life, he could write the definitive *History of Magic*, but Margaret Wright knew the Nameless Art inside out, and that was why he needed to see her.

Gillian heard the calling of the toads, an urgent chirping sound. Here, in the first Essex County, she felt as though she were an entirely different person, or maybe it was simply that after all this time, she finally knew who she was.

"Do you ever see anything strange when you're walking in the marsh?" Gillian asked their driver, Matt, as he loaded their luggage into the taxi.

"We call it the fens. You'll find water, miss, there among the weeds. It's a place where you need to be careful, otherwise you may drown and join the others who have. You'll find toads out there as well, especially at this time of the year. That's what you're hearing now. They used to be hunted by those wishing to protect themselves from evil. They say there's a witchbone in every toad. Folks called the Toadmen delved into magic, and my great-grandfather was one of them." Matt took out a tin cough-drop box and shook it. Gillian could hear something inside rattling around. The taxi driver lowered his voice.

"I've got my own witchbone. You cut it out of a toad and dry it in the sun and you make sure to keep it close to your heart for protection and courage. I wouldn't walk through the woods without it. It protects against evil and gives you power, especially over horses and women."

Gillian glared at him. When she spoke her tone was dark. "You think women and horses are in the same category?"

"Not at all. Don't get me wrong. I'm just saying that men are fools who need all the help they can get no matter what or who they're dealing with. Every traveler used to carry a toad bone if they were lucky enough to be given one. Even ladies such as yourself."

Matt continued to talk, but Gillian was no longer listening to him. Perhaps the girl in the fens had been holding up a white sliver of a toad bone, one used to keep a person safe from all the evils of the world. Perhaps it was a message for Gillian. *Be who you can be, not who others think you are.*

Gillian was the last to get in the taxi. She took her time and breathed in the cool, fresh air. Ever since she'd spied the girl in the fens she could see spirits drifting through the canopy of the trees. The scent all around was the green perfume of the watery fens where a woman could get lost, where she might drown if she wasn't careful, if her bloodline didn't protect her so that she was too buoyant to go underwater. Gillian had no need of any charms such as boiled milk thistle that would allow her to see shades. She glimpsed one right now. A woman walking down the street who'd been let out of jail to find her home ransacked by those who thought her to be a witch. The woman stopped and turned to stare at Gillian, a slaughtered tabby cat in her arms. The rustic cottage she had left abandoned when she fled into the woods was currently the town library, called Cat's Library, for reasons no one in Thornfield could recall, and this shade had walked down this lane every night for three hundred years in a loop of time Gillian had stumbled across. Gillian wanted to go closer, but how could she justify running into the street? Instead, she held one hand over her heart as a greeting, and in return the woman nodded before she disappeared.

Gillian scrambled into the back seat beside Sally. She'd always thought that Sally was the sister with power, but perhaps she'd been wrong. It appeared Gillian had skills she hadn't imagined, and being here had woken what was inside of her. Everything that had been done could not be undone, but what was to come was unknown. Fate could make the best of you or you could make the best of fate, that was what Jet always said. "We'll find Kylie," Gillian told her sister.

"We will," Sally said, her voice shaky.

The sisters held hands as the van headed toward the Three Hedges Inn. It was a ramshackle place thought to be charming by Londoners who came for the weekend to look for antiques or hike in the forest where masses of wildflowers could be seen each spring. There were tales of how forbidding these woods once were, there had been robbers and horse thieves and men who thought of murder as sport, but people tended to laugh at such stories now, even the ones about women who were drowned and burned and who had cursed those who had done them wrong. All the same, it was a tradition for hikers to take a black stone and leave a white one in its place, to appease any magical forces, just in case danger still existed, perhaps in the form of a root one might trip over, or a child separated from a class on a school trip, or a woman stung by a bee.

The road was a bumpy, single lane that was dark and overgrown, but by the light of the fat pink moon, they soon saw the inn before them, a squat whitewashed building with a thatched roof. There was a pub and a function room where the town council had monthly meetings and wedding and engagement parties were held. The inn itself had six rooms to let, and three of those were said to be haunted and weren't usually rented out. Tonight, however, they would be, for Americans would likely not notice the tapping in the walls or the chill in the corners of the rooms. Visitors from the States tended to keep their headphones on and ignore what was going on around them, and frankly they made the best guests as French and German tourists were inclined to complain about the shabbiness of the decor. Furniture was frayed and rugs were threadbare, but wasn't that all part of the lure of the place? Sally and Gillian and Franny were given the haunted rooms. They happened to be the biggest and most well furnished, even if most people refused to stay the night.

"If you see any figures, throw salt in their direction," said Jesse Wilkie, the manager of the pub who had taken a break from her duties as a waitress in order to help them with their luggage. She was in her mid-twenties and the youngest of the staff, except for a boy called George who came to help on weekends, putting out the trash and carrying in the boxes of groceries. "If the salt doesn't work, then say *Begone* three times. My granny told me so when I was a girl. That should do the trick."

Franny rolled her eyes. The advice was total nonsense, although it might work if a bat managed to get inside, after you threw a blanket over it, pulled on a pair of leather gloves, and brought it out to the garden.

"Do you have ghosts out in the fens?" Gillian wanted to know.

"Oh, we have them everywhere," Jesse said cheerfully. "My granny said there was once a lady she knew in town who had relations with one. Or maybe she just said that so no one would ask who the father of her child was."

"I'm happy to take one of the haunted rooms," Vincent said. "I don't believe in ghosts."

"We're fine," Franny told Jesse. "Don't worry about us."

Vincent wished he did believe. He'd waited for William to return to him in some form for weeks after his death. He had avoided sleep. *Come back to me*, he'd whispered. *Love of my life. Love eternal.* One night, he'd heard a scratching and had run outside, only to find that the vines had twisted around the window ledge. Vincent had collapsed in the sandy earth, exhausted, remembering what their aunt Isabelle had told them, what comes back from the dead comes back as dark and unnatural if forced to return, brought back by necromancy and spells. All the same, Vincent was made to use magic and when he'd arrived in Paris to stay at Agnes's, he'd brought along a pure white candle to William's grave when he went to the cemetery at night. He would light it and wait till it burned down to a pool of wax, the dog Dodger at his side. And still, the night remained empty and dark. He could not call up the dead; he didn't even think it was possible.

"See you in the morning," he told his granddaughters now that they were parting for the night, giving them a peck of a kiss, which to his joy, they didn't reject. "If you need me, holler," he told Franny.

"And the same to you," Franny, his childhood protector, teased him. "I'll come running and beat them off with my umbrella."

"He's a handsome old man," Jesse said as she led the others down the corridor to their rooms. "I'll bet he was quite the romancer in his day."

"He was a musician," Gillian informed her.

"That explains it," Jesse said brightly. "Always beware of a man who can make music. He'll steal your heart." She noticed all three women wore boots, though there was fine weather, with the old woman donning a surprising pair in red leather that Jesse thought very trendy for someone her age. "I adore those," she said.

"You should get yourself a pair," Franny suggested to the young woman who was helping them get settled in.

"I might just do that," Jesse said, already sensing that once she slipped on a pair of red shoes, she would be certain to go a bit wild.

Jesse first led Sally and Gillian to their rooms and stood back as they embraced and said good night; the old woman kissed both of the younger ones, though it was clear she was a bit fierce and something of a cold fish if she didn't care for you. Jesse felt honored to find the old woman appeared to enjoy her company.

Jesse opened the door to Franny's room. It really was the nicest one, overlooking the front garden. She thought if anyone would complain it would be this lady, so it made sense to give her what they called the Harpwell Room—since two or three guests had sworn they had heard a harp being played in the middle of the night, complete balderdash in Jesse's opinion. It was more likely the jukebox down in the pub, a fixture there since the fifties; perhaps rock and roll sounded angelic when it came up through the floorboards. "There's been a glut of Americans in our village," Jesse told Franny. "I can't imagine what they think when our pub closes at eleven."

Franny felt her heart hit against her rib cage when she heard about other Americans in town. "You've had other Americans recently?"

"We always do. They come from as far away as California," Jesse said dreamily.

"But this week? Any Americans?"

"A girl." Jesse shrugged. "Wouldn't listen to a word I said." Jesse had carried Franny's bag into her room and set it on the rickety baggage stand. When she turned Franny was right behind her. "You scared me now." Jesse laughed. "People say there used to be witches here and they could do with you as they pleased."

"What did you tell her?" Franny wanted to know. When Jesse looked blank, Franny clicked her tongue against the roof of her mouth, sounding like the clack of a crow. "The American girl!"

"To stay away from the fellow she was with. He's a bad sort, and she seemed innocent."

Franny instantly softened to Jesse Wilkie. "That was good of you," she said. "We should all watch out for other women."

"I try," Jesse responded proudly before she left Franny to get her rest.

They would do more than that, Franny thought as she sat on the bed, which, with its old saggy mattress, would do her no good at all when it came to a night of sleep. They would bring Kylie back home, and quickly, for the longer she was lost, the more the left would claim her. In the morning they would go after her, but tonight Franny would stay awake and read through the *Grimoire*, paying special attention to everything that had been written by Maria Owens, first in her childish scrawl, then later in her small, well-formed script. There were enchantments jotted down in red ink composed of hibiscus and the brown ink of hazelnuts and gall-nuts, in which a wasp lays its eggs, used before the larva could burrow out, with deep crimson blood, with the black bark of haw-thorn branches or the soot of lamps, some of these inks indelible, others invisible, some laced with vinegar or rainwater, written in English and Latin and runic.

She thought about the house on Magnolia Street, and how Aunt Isabelle had called to her on the day before her death. She had chosen Franny, whom she'd seen as the strongest, to carry on as the caretaker of the book. "If it isn't written down, it will likely be forgotten," Isabelle had told her. That was why women had been illiterate for so long; reading and writing gave power, and power was what had been so often denied to women. Franny had always been conflicted about who to leave the book to when it was time to do so. Sally was the stronger of the sisters, but she had no interest in magic. And Gillian, would she even want the responsibility? Perhaps it would be best to leave the book to whoever lived in the house and was willing to take it on. That individual would likely leave the light on the porch turned on and open the door to any woman in need. The book was a burden and a blessing. Franny thought it was likely it would choose its own caretaker.

She unpacked, setting the *Grimoire* on an old walnut desk. Franny handled it with affection, and with respect. She hoped to find a reference to *The Book of the Raven* and perhaps a method for finding daughters who went astray. She knew that each hour that a woman was missing equaled a day in which all could go wrong, and every day was as good as a year. There was no time to waste, for daughters might disappear for one reason, and remain unaccounted for for completely different reasons. A misstep, an accident, an error, a man.

Franny went to the window to take in the measure of this land of her ancestors, where women were both drowned and saved. What had been inside those women was inside of her now, blood and bones, courage and fear. She wished Jet was beside her, for Franny had the distinct impression that she had come home and she would have loved to share this moment with her sister. There were glowworms in the trees and the world was a marvelous thing to behold. How must it have been to gaze out over this village three hundred years ago when the stars shone so much more brightly and a book was worth a woman's life? There was the pink moon and a familiar scent that was puzzling to Franny. For some reason she felt a surge of hope. They were not going to lose another woman here in Essex. She opened the window and breathed more of the fragrance, then realized what it was. The lilacs in the garden down below were in their last bloom, a pale purple gleaming in the dark. Franny was reminded of something Jet had told her every year as they worked in the garden together.

Where there were lilacs there would be luck.

Margaret Wright had grown up in Essex, and like many here, it was the only home she'd ever known. She might have left for a bigger town after having her son, one where everyone didn't know her story, but she had no desire to be anywhere else in the world. She was born into the Nameless Art, with her mother and grandmother raising her in the tradition of green magic in the very house in which she still lived. By the time she was thirteen she was well versed in all that grew in the woods, able to discern which could harm or heal. It was her obligation to follow her path, and it was clear from the start that she would be a healer. She was a cunning woman, not a bloodline witch, although she'd known one such individual in her time, a very old woman named Cora Wilkie, who said that in an earlier time local people had nailed the feet of women suspected of witchery to the ground so they couldn't run away. Cora had lived out on the fens. It was a muddy trek to see her, and few people bothered, but those who did were grateful to her, for her cures were a revelation. A book she had handwritten, *My Life as a Witch*, was in the local library, carefully stored in plastic. For hundreds of years women who were suspect had their houses burned down, their animals were killed, their children taken away, and yet they were still here. If you knew where to look, it was possible to find witches in villages and towns throughout this county. They'd outlasted their enemies.

Margaret Wright's sixth great-grandmother had passed down a story about a fire in the woods nearby that had burned alive a woman who practiced the Nameless Art. It was a cautionary tale recounted throughout the generations. A woman with knowledge, one who could read and write, and who spoke her own mind had always been considered dangerous. Hannah Owens hadn't been forgotten, though she had become as nameless as the art she had practiced. All the same, on Midsummer's Eve, when light triumphs over darkness, women came together in Devotion Field and danced until midnight. They no longer recalled the meaning of the dance, called the Witch's Reel, but they remembered the steps and taught them to their daughters and granddaughters, all of whom were happy to come together to celebrate. It was the longest day of the year, after all, and people in neighboring towns could hear the gathering from a great distance for there was joyous music and a bonfire was set with sparks filling the inky sky.

Margaret knew quite a bit about love and its dangers, but that hadn't stopped her from falling for the wrong man. Such things happen even to the wisest women, especially when they're young. Ian's father was a man named Jimmy Poole, a distant cousin of the fellow who ran the taxi service. Jimmy Poole traded in horses and belonged to the Society of the Horseman's Grip and Word, a secret society, whose members had to walk an actual crooked path, made of stones and bricks and sometimes, for a laugh, horse manure, in imitation and appreciation of left-handed magic, undergoing an initiation that included being beaten and made to drink horse urine, before being hanged with a rope from a hayloft that was meant to break at the last moment. All of this was done to test a man's courage; if he passed and didn't beg to be let free of his initiation, he was taken into a brotherhood in which he was granted the secrets that allowed him to speak to horses so that they would bend to his command. There was magic in this, the real stuff, knowledge that had filtered down from the bloodline witches who lived in the fens when this was a hideaway for ragged outliers, some of whom lived in the trees with the herons.

Jimmy Poole was a handsome man, too handsome, and Ian resembled him, in form and in temperament, perhaps too much so, at least in his youth. Ian's father had never meant to stay in Essex or continue on with Margaret Wright. He asked her to make certain no baby would come of the nights they spent together. He was very clear about that, ready to walk away if she protested, for though he wanted her, there were plenty of other women in town, many of them more attractive. Margaret promised no child of his would come of their nights, but her mouth was scalded when she told this lie. She wanted a child more than anything, more than truth, more than any man. She mixed the cure she'd seen her grandmother give to women who wanted a baby and could have none, a secret recipe begun by Cora Wilkie long ago, one used only in their county, made of myrrh, juniper berries, licorice, pennyroyal, hemlock, and black and white hellebore. Some of the ingredients were so poisonous, a person must wear gloves simply to handle them, but Margaret was well trained, and she wasn't afraid to partake of the potion that would bring her heart's desire. Nine months later she took one look at Ian and knew that he was trouble and that she would love him more than anyone else on earth. And now here he was at her door at such an ungodly hour, a man of fifty, but still her child, the one person for whom she would have given up her life. She'd made him supper; all the dishes he liked best were waiting, covered by dishcloths, still warm.

Margaret opened the door and said, "You're late," as a greeting, and Ian laughed and bent to kiss her cheek.

"I've brought some chaos with me," he said, which surprised neither of them. On the train, he'd silently recited an ancient incantation that scholars in Alexandria had relied upon when they wished to concentrate on their studies, blocking out the outside world. But it hadn't worked. "Ma, I think I might be in love."

"That would serve you right," Margaret said, delighted despite her son's look of worry. The news didn't stop them from sitting down together at the old pine table. Ian had been so deep in thought walking home, that he'd become lost in the woods for the best part of an hour, even though he knew the place as well as he knew the back of his hand, and he was indeed late, and there was supper to attend to.

Gillian sat perched on the edge of her lumpy mattress in her room at the inn. Most people were asleep by now, but her internal clock was off, and besides, she felt she wasn't alone in the small chamber at the top of the stairs. The wallpaper was decorated with large purple flowers, and the rugs had been hand stitched by village women years ago when a sewing circle met in the lobby on Thursday nights. Gillian wore a flimsy blue nightgown, her tawny hair pulled back; for some reason, she felt young again, ready to take a risk. If the room was haunted, so be it. Perhaps she had something to learn from the other world. She was the selfish sister, the one who couldn't pass a mirror without stopping to gaze at herself, the one who'd dated men who were nothing but trouble. Long ago, a man had nearly destroyed her. She'd thought his sort of love could withstand the curse and now, whenever she heard about women who were caught up in a relationship that was tied to violence, women who stayed for years, sometimes for a lifetime, she understood. Gillian had been that woman, unable to walk out the door, reduced to nothing. She'd changed her life, but the wild girl she'd once been still lived inside her heart.

"I'm not afraid of you," she said to any shade that might be nearby. She breathed deeply and evenly. "Maybe I can help you," she offered. "Or," more honestly now, "you can help me."

She had lit a white candle she'd found in the desk drawer and it flickered, casting shadows on the wall. She thought perhaps there was a girl in the corner, made out of ash and dust. There was a knock at the door, which startled her. "Don't go anywhere," she told the shade. She went to the door and opened it a crack. Sally was in the hall.

"What are you doing here?" Gillian asked.

Sally had been down in the pub until closing, questioning people about Tom Lockland. "What do you want to talk about him for?" was the response she most often received. Jesse Wilkie overheard the conversations, and had approached to let Sally know she had seen him with Kylie. "She seemed under his spell," Jesse had told her.

"What do you mean?" All Sally could think of was that horrible man her sister had been involved with years ago. Gillian had been possessed, until at last she understood she had to break free.

"He has that effect on some girls. Mostly ones who are lost. He has a way of drawing them in, convincing them they can trust him or that he can help them in some way."

Sally's heart was racing. The wicked enchantment that had befallen Gillian could not be happening again. She went into the restroom to throw cold water on her face and do her best to calm down, which frankly was impossible. It was then she saw something metal glinting on the floor, but before she could see what it was, a little shadow scooted out the door into the bar, the silvery bit in its grasp. She followed the shadow, a cat as it turned out, as it skittered upstairs, where it managed to slip under a door. Her sister's room. "Gilly," Sally had called. "Open up."

Gillian had cracked the door. "I'm being haunted," she announced. Gillian had been having unwanted memories of her old boyfriend Jimmy, the one who'd nearly ruined her life. She felt shivery and threatened, as if the darkness of that time might happen all over again, as if there were certain family legacies that repeated themselves despite how hard you tried to avoid them.

"Is there a cat in here?" Sally asked.

Gillian opened the door wider, allowing her sister inside, relieved to see her. "I think it's Maria Owens. I saw her in the fens." Without thinking, they had slipped into whispers. They sat on the bed together, knees touching.

"She's been gone for over three hundred years," Sally said.

Gillian shrugged. "In some ways. Things don't necessary vanish completely." There was the cursc, after all. That had lasted.

"I should be out there looking for Kylie right now," Sally said in a hushed voice. "Before anything happens. I shouldn't have agreed to wait till morning."

"Looking for her in the middle of the night makes no sense." Gillian didn't add what she was thinking. *Something's already happened. It's happening still.* She elbowed Sally and nodded toward a corner. There it was, a huge tabby cat, playing with a strand of silvery thread. "Come here, baby," Gillian called.

The cat looked up, then disappeared through a crack in the wall.

Sally went to the corner where the cat had crouched. The air was especially cold. She knelt down, cold herself now, for she had discovered the necklace she'd given to Kylie on her birthday. She flicked open the locket and there was the photo of Jet. No matter what darkness awaited them, Jet was still with them, in loving spirit and in memory.

II.

Things that are begun in the dark are never meant to be, that is why they are so often initiated in places where no one can see the business at hand. Close your eyes and believe. Let desire take you, blood and bones, no matter who you might harm. The Crooked Path always begins in darkness; it always has and it always will. Do not reach to turn on the light, do not consider options, do not think twice. This is the left side, the zone not of the heart but of need and desire, what you must have, what you're greedy for, what you will take no matter the cost.

Tom Lockland ran a finger across the base of Kylie's wrist; there was a tiny black moon-shaped speck there, a witch's mark Kylie had never noticed before. She had been blind to everything, herself, her history, the dangers in the world. Kylie thought now of the rasp of Gideon's breathing. She called his room every day and begged the nurse to hold the phone to his ear. *Pointless*, she was told. Still she pleaded, until a kindhearted nurse relented, positioning the phone so that Kylie could hear Gideon breathing. She almost contacted Antonia then to ask if she could arrange more phone calls, but was afraid of what her sister would say. *Come home, get out quick, don't trust anyone you don't really know. I'm your sister, I'm not some stranger who has desires all his own. You are asking for trouble and trouble is what you'll get.*

Kylie had power, more than she'd ever suspected. People could say what they wanted to about Tom Lockland but he had been more truthful about magic than her family had. He held his thumb on her witch's mark and she felt her pulse racing. She was stronger than she had ever imagined. She could understand the birds' chattering, she could start a fire with her breath. Surely she could figure out how to open the last two pages that revealed how to reverse a curse. "This is what magic is for," Tom said. "To destroy the thing that was meant to destroy you."

In the weedy ash-filled garden behind the house, Kylie opened *The Book of the Raven* to a page written in red ink, made of madder roots or berries or blood. *Let the wrong man into your life and you have set out on the path before you know it. A step at a time, until you are turning left.* It was a warning, but she didn't take it to heart. Tom was merely a distant cousin, nothing more, an ally who could help her save Gideon. For that, it was worth taking the Crooked Path.

As for Tom, he had been looking for a curse-breaker in every magic book he could get his hands on. He'd recently acquired the scarlet-covered *Rauðskinna*, the feared book of ancient magic, from Ian Wright, who had turned him away when he came to Notting Hill for assistance, with Ian saying he couldn't help him work black magic. Tom had broken in, then set out madder root mixed with poison, bound with his own hair and fingernails and with the bones of birds and a sympathetic wax figure of Ian. But the book had turned out to be worthless, turning ice cold in Tom's hands, refusing to give up any of its magic. There were plenty of curses in its pages, violent and blood-tinged, all were binding and irreversible, made of such dark magic they could not be dismantled, but apparently a code was needed to open the book, and Tom hadn't thought of that possibility. He wound up tossing *Rauðskinna* onto a fire in the back yard, fairly certain he had heard the book scream, as mandrake is said to do when it's pulled from the ground. The smoke was so thick his eyes teared, and even though he was covered with soot, he had stayed until the book was a pile of gleaming ash, the words rising like glowworms into the air, as if each one had become a living creature. Now, with Kylie's book, he had another chance.

As Tom made a fire in a metal bin while the sky grew dark, Kylie found herself wondering what her life would have been if she had lived here in Thornfield three hundred years earlier. It was likely she would have already had a husband, children, hands blistered by heavy work; she would have sought out omens in the stars, counted the silvery fish in the fens to see how many years she would live, gone to a woman who was skilled in the Unnamed Art when she needed an elixir or a cure or perhaps help with a man who could not be trusted.

Holly, thorn apple, hawthorn, rowan, oak, ash, all were tossed onto the flame.

"Will you do anything to get what you want?" Tom asked her.

What she wanted was Gideon, here in this world. Kylie nodded, afraid she would be unable to speak.

The wind was up and sparks flickered into the air. It was possible to do anything with magic, Tom told her. Curse the living, bring back the dead, create love, or extinguish its fire. A great fall would bring great success. Kylie turned her back to him as they stripped off their clothes. By now the sky was black.

"Face me and face your fear," he said.

Her fear was that she would lose the one person she loved

most in this world, and that was a fear she didn't think she could live with if she didn't act now.

"You said you would do anything," Tom reminded her.

She turned to him then. She could see the left-handed path and she understood how lonely it was. What would you do for the one you loved? Would you place yourself in exile, see wrong as right, forsake all others, do what you must?

"Anything," Kylie said.

In the morning she stared at herself in the mirror over the bathroom sink. It had happened, she had changed. Her hair was black. The reddish chestnut color was gone and now seemed to have belonged to another girl entirely, a naive person who had walked another path. A bargain was a bargain, and you always paid a price. Impossible for her hair to turn pitch black, and yet it had happened in a single night, just as the vines had grown to cover the entire house while they slept in the grass. She woke up covered with ashes, her skin burned by sparks. When they left, Tom didn't bother to lock the door. The landlord would eventually arrive to find the place deserted and in shambles. Tom had half a mind to start a fire in the parlor, for he'd learned Lockland Manor had been burned from the inside out, with flaming arrows flying through the windows to meet their mark, but he hadn't the patience for such things when he was so close to getting what he wanted.

The vines were growing so fast the chimney could no longer be seen. There were thorns on all the trees and the grass was singed in a circle. They had done that. Solomon's circle, Solomon's Key, the oldest magic on earth, and the darkest. Kylie pulled on a clean black T-shirt and jeans borrowed from Tom, then threw on

Gideon's raincoat, which had also turned black, perhaps from the ashes rising from the bonfire.

Kylie had her backpack and Tom carried two sleeping bags strapped to his back along with his own rucksack filled with whatever dark materials he might need. It was early and the air was fresh. They had to hack through vines to get through the yard. A thorn pierced the palm of Tom's hand and a vine tore his shirt. "Careful," he told Kylie. As she ducked down Tom ran a hand over her newly dark hair, pleased by her appearance. This was the work of the left hand and his handiwork as well. He'd changed her. "Beautiful," he said with a tinge of pride.

It wasn't yet light, still the birds were singing.

"That's the nightingale's song," Tom said.

Kylie stopped in the road to listen. The song was so beautiful she nearly cried, but what was done was done. They were headed to the forest. As they walked, the ferns Kylie passed turned black. She belonged to the darkness inside her. That is how curses began. A desire that cannot be held back. A wish that must be granted. Beneath Kylie's feet, the grass turned to ash. The gash on her hand still bled and black drops fell onto the path. She could almost hear Gideon. He was in a room that had no key. He was calling her name.

The trees were so old in the forest they were protected by the government; they had stood by in times of magic, plagues, love, betrayal. It was an ancient woodland, untouched for centuries, still home to plants that could no longer be found anywhere else. Most of the old forests had been destroyed as roads were built and villages clustered in places where the trees were once as tall as the sky. There were wild bluebells beneath the hazel trees and hundred-year-old pollarded beeches. All around there was ash and oak, hornbeam and field maple, many so old they had been listed in the *Domesday Book*, written in 1086 as a survey of all that grew in England and Wales. The trees had been protected by brutal dictates. Anyone caught stealing from the royal forests during Richard the Lionheart's reign would face a punishment that included the removal of the thief's eyes and private parts. The forests were thought to be living creatures, with breath and fire and water and air, revered as the owners of the earth, while men were shadows that walked through the trees for the brief period of a lifetime. Wild mistletoe, clover, sorrel, bee orchids, St.-John's-wort, all grew wild on the forest floor. Fields were covered with buttercups and yellow archangel flowers and the bark of trees was covered by gray-green lichens. There were several thousand-year-old oaks but perhaps the oldest tree was a two-thousand-year-old lime tree.

Beside the manor house was an orchard of apple trees, a variety the locals called Witchery, that Rebecca Lockland had planted from the seeds in an amulet given to her by Hannah Owens when she tried to break the love spell she'd set upon her husband. Soon the trees would bloom with pink and white flowers; only a few remained, for Tom had been chopping them down, using the fragrant logs as firewood that fueled the massive fireplace in the great room. It was here he stored his axe and some cookery items. It was his house, after all, abandoned or not; no one was taking it from him. Vines twisted through the windows that no longer held glass, and the once gray stone was black with smoke and ash from the time when the house was burned. Every now and then a visitor stumbled upon a forgotten treasure. Some hikers had come exploring and discovered an ancient pair of leather gloves, used for riding, and a velvet cape, riddled with moth holes.

Kylie made her way inside carefully. There were pools of rain left by passing storms, for little of the roof was left and it was possible to see most of the sky.

"Hello!" Tom called into the emptiness. His voice came echoing back and they both laughed. He took Kylie's hand and spun her around. She could feel the power that she had inside. Skin and bones. Heart and soul. The black-haired girl who was not afraid of the left-hand, who would bring back the one she loved, who could do more than she had ever imagined.

It was nearly summer, and the heat of the day had been a delight, especially when traipsing through the green woods, but when they entered the house they found it to be chilly. Tom lifted boards from a pile of broken-down furniture into the huge fireplace, then set a fire. He had been sneaking off to the manor ever since he was a boy. In his dreams, this is where he resided, and there was no one to tell him what he could and could not do.

Kylie sat in front of the fire, her black hair falling down her back. She concentrated and closed her eyes and the flames leapt up and burned a hot red.

"See what you can do," Tom said proudly.

He meant revenge and she meant salvation but either way they were in it together.

A group of hikers had reached the house and approached the threshold. They saw smoke billowing from the huge brick chimney and stood back. There were those who said only bad luck could be found here and the hikers had the shivers, all the same they laughed as they ran off, making sure to break off twigs from the apple trees that were said to be enchanted, which indeed later bloomed in their hands when at last they reached the road.

Kylie turned to watch the hikers flee. It was clear that there was darkness nesting here, and they wanted no part of it. There were three couples, all of them young, chattering as they dashed back into the woods. How innocent they seemed, how free to do as they pleased. They did not turn fires red, or cut their arms to drip blood onto the earth, or stare in the mirror, uncertain of who they'd become. Oh, how Kylie wished she could go back in time, before she'd come here, before she'd heard about left-handed magic, when she was sprawled out on the Cambridge Common, and the sky was blue, and Gideon was squinting through the bright sunlight in order to see her, when the world seemed brand-new.

III.

Antonia had assumed she wouldn't dream, for there was hardly any room in her bed, not with two bodies stretched out, for she had always believed that dreams were propelled by solitary space, but in fact dreams were born of heart and soul and experience. Now, Ariel's jasmine oil scented the sheets, and her clothes were scattered on the floor. Antonia knew it was a mistake to lead people on and allow them to believe she was emotionally available, when she wasn't. That was the great thing about Scott; he understood her, which was why he was the perfect father for their child. But the last time they'd gotten together for a meal in Harvard Square, he'd studied her, then said, "You used to be less shut down."

"I was always shut down. That's one of the things you admire about me. Never overly emotional."

Scott had shaken his head, disagreeing. He was her oldest friend, after all, and felt he knew her best. "It's still inside of you, you're just hiding it."

"You're saying I'm vulnerable and sensitive?" Antonia had laughed, but she had become uncomfortable with the conversation. "That will never be me. Should we share dessert?" Ever since she'd made the Chocolate Tipsy Cake she'd acquired a sweet tooth.

"I'm being serious," Scott scolded.

"The tiramisu?" Antonia said evasively.

They had dated for some time, before they'd come out to each other, trusting one another more than anyone else. "You are who you are."

"I know. I may be a terrible mother."

"You'll be great! But that's not what I'm talking about." Scott leaned forward. "Let yourself love someone. This isn't high school, kiddo. You don't have to hide who you are. You're beautiful inside," he said bluntly, for they both knew that although she was striking, she was not a great beauty like her sister. "Where it counts."

Antonia averted her eyes. She was ridiculously emotional and hormonal. "But what if I am a terrible mother?"

Scott came around the table to sit beside her. "You won't be. All you have to do is be you."

"Are you sure about that?" Antonia asked her dear friend, the father of her child, who had always been honest to a fault.

"I'm sure," Scott told her before he called the waiter over.

Antonia waited for the stinger, a funny one liner that added the punch line *Not really, definitely don't be you,* but there was none. Scott was sure of her, and sometimes that sort of faith was all a person needed. Looking back on it, she blamed Scott for her night with Ariel. Or perhaps it was the wretched day she'd had. She'd visited Gideon, then had joined her neurology class to observe a girl who had been struck by a car while riding her bicycle. Antonia had nearly been provoked to tears, totally inappropriate for a medical student and utterly out of character for someone as stoic as she. Afterward she'd phoned Ariel without thinking it out. She must have sounded desperate, for when she arrived home Ariel was sitting on the floor beside her door reading *The Borrowers*. "What can I say?" Ariel was sheepish, her glossy hair falling into her eyes. "I like kids' books."

"That's convenient because I happen to be pregnant." Embarrassingly huge, actually, and not feeling the least bit attractive.

"I noticed. Maybe that's why you're so beautiful."

The rest had just happened, and the truth was, Antonia had wanted it to. They were entwined before she had unlocked the front door. With every kiss she forgot the despair of her afternoon, the sound of the ventilator, the whiteness of the girl's eyes, the chart the doctor on call had passed around to the students. Antonia was logical above all else, but now her insistence on rational thoughts and action seemed absurd. The girl in the hospital had been struck out of the blue, if she had left her house ten minutes later or ten minutes earlier the accident wouldn't have happened. Walking through the corridors of the hospital, Antonia had been overwhelmed with what she thought was anger, but what she was actually experiencing was an intense desire to be alive. She had been alive with Ariel Hardy. There was no way to deny it.

In her dream, she had been walking through tall grass with Aunt Jet, who was young, no older than Antonia herself. Antonia looked down and realized she was wearing a white dress trimmed with lace. Jet was in a white slip, wearing red boots.

How do we find Kylie? Antonia asked her aunt.

The same way we lost her. With the book, Jet said.

Jet signaled for her to approach, intending to tell her niece a secret that most young people weren't privy to until it was too late. *What you wind up regretting aren't the things you do, it's what you don't do that you will never forgive yourself for.*

"Bad dream?" Ariel asked when Antonia awoke with a start, having slept till nearly nine. As it turned out, Ariel had a habit of waking at five thirty a.m., a practice begun in her law school days when there was never enough time to study, but she'd stayed in bed so as not to wake Antonia. She still wasn't wearing a stitch.

"Not exactly," Antonia said. "I was talking to my aunt Jet." And then she blurted, "I was wearing a wedding dress."

Ariel tossed her head back and laughed. "Well, I guess last night *was* good."

Ariel reminded Antonia of a lily as she stepped out of bed. There were dozens of water lilies in Leech Lake and Antonia had always wanted to leap in and swim among them, but she was forbidden. Evidently, there had been a near drowning sometime in the past in that very lake, and strange stories about a sea serpent. Antonia had gone so far as to concoct an experiment of her own, leaving out bread crumbs on the shore and setting up her camera so that it would take a photo if anything pecked at the bread and set off the string attached to the camera's shutter button. All she'd come up with were a few blurry images of sparrows.

"Can you swim?" she asked Ariel.

"I most certainly can. I was on the swim team in high school and college. My best stroke was the butterfly."

Antonia felt her heart flip over in a way she didn't recognize, a fish in a lake, a woman in thrall. In retrospect, she should have never called Ariel Hardy, or gone to the law firm, or opened mail that had been addressed to Aunt Franny. "We're probably a mistake."

"I believe in making mistakes," Ariel said. She took a vial of the soothing jasmine oil that she always wore out of her purse and dabbed some on her wrists and her throat after she'd dressed. She found that the scent flustered other attorneys when they were opponents. It made them misjudge her and overlook just how resolved she could be. *You're a terrier*, her grandfather had always said to her, and it took a while before she realized he meant it as a compliment, and that not letting things go was a plus when practicing law. As for her love life, he'd told her that she would know when she'd found the right person, and it was likely that she also wouldn't let go in matters of the heart.

"What if I'm cursed?" Antonia said.

They were two rational, practical women who were flushed with emotion, and in Antonia's opinion, emotion obscured truth.

Ariel sat on the edge of the bed. "I already know about the curse. I've read the files. Almost all. Don't forget you have the key."

"The key won't help," Antonia said. "You know we can't fall in love."

"Shouldn't, not can't."

"Look at what happened to Gideon."

"He was struck by a car. It was a horrible accident and it could have happened to anyone. Anyway, the curse probably didn't include lesbians," Ariel teased. "We probably didn't exist."

"We always existed and it's always been dangerous to fall in love with us."

Ariel leaned to kiss Antonia. "Everything is dangerous. That is the human condition. In any case, who said anything about love?" Antonia felt her heart sink until Ariel whispered, "I thought I'd wait till tonight to say it."

Was this what love did? Make you so grateful for a word or two that you'd practically beg for such things to be said? *Don't go, cancel everything, stay here with me, I can't wait until tonight.*

"This is a bad idea," Antonia said. "It's definitely bad timing. With my sister missing, I can't think straight."

Ariel seemed disappointed as she headed for the door. She thought Antonia would have known better. "This is not about thinking," she said.

Perhaps it was guilt that compelled Antonia to visit the Reverend later that afternoon, or perhaps she simply wanted someone to talk to. She called Kylie several times a day, but her sister never answered and now there were so many pleading messages on Kylie's phone that there was no longer room to leave another. Reverend Willard was out on the patio behind the retirement home in his wheelchair, his face tilted to the sun. His skin was so fine his veins could be seen clearly. When Antonia pulled up a chair next to his, he opened his eyes.

"Annie!" he said. When startled his voice was a dry rasp, and he blinked several times, for it was becoming more difficult for him to tell the difference between his dreams and his waking life.

Had this been a week earlier Antonia would have reminded him that was not her name. Now, she let it go. If Annie was what he wanted, then Annie it would be.

"I'm getting used to you," the Reverend said cheerfully.

"Don't," Antonia advised. "My aunt Franny and my mother and Gillian will be back soon and they'll take over. You'll be rid of me then."

"What about your sister? The tall one?" The Reverend had on a white shirt, a black tie, and black trousers. Many of the other men his age were in bathrobes and pajamas, but he didn't like to be seen in public that way. He missed his dog, but there was some man who had driven up from New York the other day, bringing Daisy for a visit, and she'd sat in the Reverend's lap as if she'd never been gone.

"Everyone went to look for my sister," Antonia said, thinking it was too complicated to say much more, only adding, "She's missing."

"Then you should make apple pie," Reverend Willard suggested. When Antonia seemed baffled, he went on to explain, "Jet said that was how you found a lost daughter. You baked an apple pie."

"She told you that?"

"Apple pie is one of my favorites."

When the Reverend fell asleep, Antonia walked the few blocks to Magnolia Street and unlocked the door, after collecting the new stack of Post-it notes left by their neighbors. *My son is unmanageable. My migraines have grown worse. I'm afflicted with sorrow that I cannot shake. Just yesterday, I was betrayed.* Antonia crumpled up the messages, then went inside and fetched the mail that had been slipped through the slot—an electricity bill and the local paper—before going on into the kitchen. The house was so empty it echoed, and the woodwork looked dusty. Two baby field mice had somehow gotten in, and Antonia scooped them up in a pot and let them go free in the garden. The mice stood still in between rows of lettuce, frozen in fear, until Antonia shouted "Run." She'd waited there for a while, prepared to wave away any hawks that might go after the poor baby mice while they skittered off through the clusters of lettuce leaves.

At last Antonia went to the kitchen to look through cookbooks, some of them so old their pages were taped to stop the paper from crumbling, two from the seventeenth century, although one of those was not quite a book, but rather a handwritten journal belonging to Maria Owens, featuring dishes like hedgehog pudding, Indian pudding, plum pudding, and something that was called Birds' Nest Pudding, made with cored apples and custard. This was the book that appealed to Antonia. She thumbed through the pages and indeed came to a recipe called *Lost Daughter's Pie.* In small flowing script were the instructions for the crust, made with butter and water and fine flour, and the filling, apples, cinnamon, and lemon if available, and pats of butter. *Bake, place on a windowsill, and she will come back to you.*

Antonia rummaged through the kitchen and found what items were available. Yes, there were apples, last year's winter apples stored in the cabinet, wrinkled and small, but apples all the same, and a lemon, and a block of yellow butter in the fridge. Apples were said to be the food of love, as well as the food of the dead, of shades and spirits that went unseen; it was the fruit that could call to those who couldn't hear any other sound. Antonia hadn't time to fix a crust, but luckily there were some packets of saltine crackers in the back of the pantry cabinet, and she used them to line the pie plate, then made the filling, going a little too heavy on the cinnamon, she feared. She did the baking in the newer oven rather than the old woodstove, turned on the timer, then took the opportunity to have a nap on the window seat on the staircase, which had always been a cherished spot to curl up and read. When she woke, the scent of apples and spice filled the air, and she blinked back tears. Kylie used to follow Antonia everywhere when they came to visit the aunts; they slept up in the attic, as their mother and Gillian had done when they were girls. When they first moved in, Antonia was furious about leaving her school and Scott Morrison. She and Kylie would spend hours in the greenhouse plotting their escape. *We'll be our own people,* they'd vowed to one another. *We'll do whatever we please. We'll talk every day on the phone no matter how far apart we are.*

Antonia slipped on some oven mitts and took out the wretched-looking pie. But despite the fact that it was tilted, with a crust that was salty and pale, the pie smelled delicious. Antonia set it on the windowsill as the recipe instructed. A single wasp was drawn to the sweet smell, and she batted it away with the mitt. "*Begone,*" she said as if she had invoked a spell she didn't wish to have interrupted. She laughed at herself then, as she opened the window for the wasp to fly out before closing it and making certain all of the windows were locked. It was totally illogical to think that a pie made on one side of the Atlantic would call to a person on the other side, still you never knew the effects that might be caused by one small action halfway across the world.

She took the pie and walked back to the Reverend's. By now the staff knew her; she was privately referred to as *the pregnant Owens medical student* or *the red-headed one* and they waved her on, thinking she might take after her aunt Franny, and no one wished to defy *her. Do what you want to, do what you will, none of us will stop you if you bring no harm to others*. Antonia went directly to the dining room, emptied now after a very early dinner hour. It was only half-past four and still bright outside, but here it was later than anyone might think. Antonia grabbed a plate, along with a knife and a fork.

The Reverend was already in bed, mortified to be seen in his robe. "I thought you'd disappeared, Annie," he said accusingly.

"I went home and made the pie." Antonia cut him a small slice. "How does this bring my sister home?"

"She'll know it was made with love and she'll find you."

"Jet told you this? You're sure?"

"She said love was the most important ingredient."

The pie had been made with love, that much was true. Antonia, terrible cook and levelheaded medical student, would do anything she could to locate her sister. She tried the pie, and found it wasn't half bad. In her ninth month she was hungry all the time.

"Are you ready for your life to change?" Reverend Willard asked.

"No." The baby kicked her, and Antonia knew she had better be ready. "Maybe," she said.

"Greatest thing you'll ever do," the Reverend informed her. Antonia thought about how he had lost his beloved son; he had never gotten over it, because no one can get over such a loss, and yet here he was, being kind to her. If he kept this up, she would be on the brink of tears. Then he ruined it by saying, "If you get married, I'll officiate. So you'd better hurry up. I don't have that much longer."

"There is no wedding in the future," Antonia told him, thinking about her strange dream in which she wore a white dress. "I'm not involved with anyone," she said in a firm tone, and yet her tongue burned, as if she were telling a lie.

"Fine," the Reverend said. "Have it your way."

The pats of butter inside the pie had melted and were running over the rim of the plate. When she first came to visit him, all those years ago, Jet had told him that butter melted in a house when someone was in love. He'd been a grouch in those days, but he always liked to hear Jet's stories. He hadn't believed in love. He'd lost his wife young, and had ruined his son's life by refusing to accept Jet Owens. Now he was open to everything and anything. He wasn't even the same person anymore and when he thought of the man he'd been, locked alone in his house, filled with so much regret he could barely speak, he pitied that fellow, and was grateful for the day when Jet Owens came to knock at his door.

"I think I'm exhausted," he told Antonia.

She straightened out his blanket. "Just remember you're not dying while I'm watching over you," she told him. "Don't even think about it." She sat beside him and took his hand. She had decided to stay until he fell asleep. Sitting there quietly, not rushing around as she usually did, she could feel the baby settle inside her. *Heart of my heart. My darling one.*

She began to hum a song, one that came to her unexpectedly while she sat there beside the Reverend in the fading dusk, the scent of apple pie perfuming the air.

The water is wide. I cannot get o'er it.

"Jet used to sing that," the Reverend murmured.

It was in equal parts a love song and a lullaby, a tune so old no one knew when it had first been written. Jet had sung it to Sally and Gillian when they were young, and then to Antonia and Kylie. It was a traditional folk song, handed down through the generations, one Maria Owens first heard in a field in England three hundred years earlier. Antonia sang it in the hush of the retirement home, for by now the hallways were dark, and everyone was asleep, but that didn't mean people didn't dream of ships and of dark water and of someone they loved too dearly to lose.

On the drive home, Antonia kept the car windows open. The pie sat on the passenger seat, in danger of falling each time she stepped on the brakes. She only had a week or two to go until the baby arrived. No wonder she was exhausted. If Kylie were here, they would meet up at Antonia's apartment to watch an old movie and order a pizza and make each other laugh with imitations of members of their family. Kylie did a great Gillian, becoming a bombshell who was smarter than anyone in the room. Oh, how Antonia missed her sister. How she worried that she would be lost to her forever. She breathed deeply, remembering when they would pluck apples from the trees in their aunts' garden where there was an orchard of a variety called Look No Further. Home, Antonia thought, and for all her logic, she nearly cried right then. That was when her phone rang.

IV.

Tom had sent Kylie to the shop on the outskirts of the park to pick up something for supper, which would give him time alone to more fully inspect the book. "Let me try to figure it out," he suggested. He held out a hand to collect the book, a smile on his handsome face. "A second pair of eyes never hurt," he urged, and, when she hesitated, he added, "You don't have all the time in thc world."

Kylie thought of Gideon in his hospital bed. Still, she felt a twinge of anxiety as she handed over the book.

"There you go," Tom said, once the book was his. He seemed pleased with Kylie, as if she were a student who had passed a test. It hadn't been easy to claim the book, which she always kept with her. He'd had better luck with her phone, which he'd fished out of her backpack and tossed into a ditch while out by the orchard of twisted black apple trees behind the house. "Have a nice walk. It will take your mind off your troubles."

Kylie did feel her spirits lift once she was in the forest. A fern, a leaf, a tree, a path, all of it was comforting and reminded her of home. She had been thinking of the house on Magnolia Street all day, missing it terribly, remembering the times she and Antonia had sneaked into the garden at dusk to look for rabbits. There were often dandelions turned to fluff in the grass that Antonia would hold up to Kylie's face. "Make a wish," Antonia would command. "Wish and never tell!"

Tom's desire for revenge, intriguing at first, had become exhausting. The store was close by and Kylie cut through the forest onto the road that merged with the High Street if you went east and led to the motorway if you went west. The roadside market was small, with bins of fruits and vegetables out front. There was a single parked car in the lot, there with all the windows open and the radio playing. The group of young American hikers who had turned away from the manor when they felt the darkness within were here, exhausted from their days in the forest, now stopping for drinks and crisps. Kylie's heart leapt; somehow she had managed to misplace her phone and she had a desperate urge to call her sister.

"Hey there," one of the young women called out. "I thought I saw you before." She sounded like a New Yorker. "American, right? You look a little lost."

"I've misplaced my phone," Kylie explained. "Could I borrow yours? My sister's having a baby in Massachusetts. I just want to see if she's all right."

The young woman handed her phone to Kylie through the window. The hikers were all seniors in college, and this was their big end-of-the-term vacation, the sort of trip Kylie and Gideon had meant to take together. "My sister's having a baby, too. We'll both be aunties."

Kylie returned the young woman's smile, then turned and called Antonia. She was shivering even though the night was warm. She didn't know what time it was in the States, afternoon she supposed. The phone rang and rang, and just when it seemed as if no one would answer, her sister answered with a clipped, "I'm driving." Logical, wonderful Antonia. Kylie had never missed her more. "Who is this?" Antonia added, not recognizing the number.

"It's me. I'm in England."

"Kylie! Why don't you answer the phone? They're all over there looking for you."

"They shouldn't be." Kylie thought of how angry she'd been at her mother, how she'd stalked away without a word. "I don't need them."

"Don't you? What the hell do you think you're doing?" Antonia wanted to know.

"I came to break the curse," Kylie told her sister.

"If I wasn't so pregnant I'd fly over and kick your ass. Forget that stupid fairy tale. You need to come home."

"It's not a fairy tale. Jet left a note about how to end the curse. I know I can bring Gideon back."

Antonia had been driving in heavy traffic, and she now pulled over to the side of the road. Cars whizzed past her. She closed the windows to drown out the sound of the highway. "How do you plan to do that?" she asked.

"She left a note that she had hid an old book in the library. It has instructions for ending a curse. I just haven't managed to find them yet."

"If Jetty left a note it was probably for Aunt Franny, not for you. I'm sure she never meant for you to go wandering through England. Where are you exactly?"

Kylie gazed around. The sky was shadowy and dark, with bats flickering in the trees. "In Essex. The first one."

"Well, come back to your own Essex County." Antonia thought of her dreams, of a lake and a drowning, of a girl with red hair and their dear Jet, young once again. "You're going to get into trouble there."

"How is he?" Kylie was still wearing Gideon's raincoat; it was the only thing that helped when she was shivering. She pushed her black hair out of her face and kept her back to the parked car, avoiding eye contact with the young American woman who was signaling for her phone to be returned.

"He moved his hand," Antonia said. "He's still in there."

A sob escaped from Kylie.

"Come home now," Antonia told her.

Kylie made the mistake of shifting her stance. The woman inside the car caught her eye and waved.

"I'd like my phone," the young woman called. "We've got to go."

"I'm kind of with someone here," Kylie said.

"What do you mean with someone? Like a guide?"

"A man."

Agitated, Antonia got out of the car. The baby was so low, standing still was uncomfortable, and she began to pace on the grass. She hated driving home to Cambridge at this hour of the day; there was too much traffic and the sun was in her eyes. Maybe that was why she felt like crying. What was left of the apple pie was in the car. Could it be that was why Kylie had phoned?

"What man?" Antonia wanted to know.

"He said he could help me. He's cursed, too. I thought he could at first. Now I'm not sure." Kylie felt humiliated and degraded by throwing in her lot with a stranger who wanted such dark results for those who had cursed him.

"Do you even know who he is?" Antonia asked.

"He's somehow related to us. He's taught himself left-handed magic."

"Are you listening to yourself?" Antonia said to her little sister. "Even I know that means the Dark Art."

"He understands me," Kylie said stubbornly. She had left the book with him and it was dawning on her that her sister might be right. Trust was something a person earned.

"You've only just met him. He can't understand you," Antonia said. "He doesn't even know you."

"He's told me things we were never told about our bloodline."

"Oh, for God's sake, Kylie, stop all this nonsense and listen to me. You need to let Mom know where you are and let Franny handle this."

Her sister was always the same, even when she was three thousand miles away. The dependable sister, the one who believed in proof, logic, and rational thought. "You don't know who I am anymore," Kylie said sadly.

"Of course I do. I know you better than anyone. Certainly better than whoever that man is."

If her sister wanted proof, proof is what she would get. Kylie snapped a photo of herself on the stranger's phone. She looked sulky, a tall, awkward young woman with long black hair standing in a parking lot.

"Hey," the woman called to her, pissed off now. "Seriously. I was doing you a favor. We've got to go."

"You'll see," Kylie told her sister. "You won't even recognize me."

"I love you," Antonia said, but Kylie didn't answer with *I love you more*. Instead, she sent the photo, then ended the call while Antonia was still talking, saying she would know Kylie anywhere and anytime. The hikers had started their car, which was roughly idling.

"That took long enough," the phone's owner said, a bit huffy, when Kylie returned it to her.

"Thanks, I really appreciate it," Kylie said as she went on into the store to pick up some groceries before it closed. But maybe it had been a mistake to call. She missed her sister and she missed Gideon. She missed who she used to be, but Kylie was someone different now. She felt an attraction to Tom, to the story he told. She picked up a few bottles of beer, some local cheese, pickles, and a loaf of bread then walked out without paying. All she had to do was whisper a spell of protection and hide behind her long black hair, and before she knew it she was invisible to most people's eyes. She felt a rush of emotion breaking this simple rule.

Do not steal, do not lie, do not trust a man you can never really know.

On the side of the road, as the traffic on Highway 93 hurtled by, Antonia clicked on the photo she'd been sent. There was a tall young woman in a parking lot. Kylie's inky black hair had blown across her face when a gust of wind picked up, but she could be seen quite plainly. It was her sister, the person Antonia knew better than anyone. Yes, she looked different, but it didn't matter if her hair was black or brown, if she looked frightened and desperate and alone, it didn't matter if she was in the first Essex County or the second, in Cambridge or halfway around the world. Antonia knew her sister better than Kylie knew herself. She got back inside the car and called her mother.

The room was stuffy, and Sally had gone to open the window. There were lilacs outside in the softening air. She had been thinking about her conversation with Ian on the train. The way he leaned toward her when he agreed with her and leaned away when he disagreed, as though he'd been burned. She had wanted him to come closer, but then she happened to see the palm of his left hand, the fortune he had made. The lines matched hers exactly.

As soon as she answered her phone, all such thoughts fell away when she heard Antonia's voice.

"Are you all right? Is the baby all right?"

"My baby's fine. Your baby is the problem. Some man seems to have gotten a hold on her and he's leading her over to the left-handed side."

Sally felt a knot of panic inside of her, near her heart, something bitter, something cold. "Bad Tom."

"Well, whoever he is, get her away from him. He's the one filling her head with dark magic."

Everyone in the family had heard stories concerning Maria Owens's daughter, Faith. She was said to have practiced left-handed, and had then forfeited her magical abilities until her seventieth birthday when the sight revisited her after she'd lived a life of helping others. On the day her powers returned, she went out and found a little girl who had been missing, held against her will so that her parents would pay a ransom. She went on to do so time and time again and this way she became a finder. There were those in the Owens family who were finders and she was one, rescuing scores of missing daughters. People said she baked an apple pie every week, set out on her windowsill to cool, and that those children she hadn't managed to locate found their own way home, often in the middle of the night, knocking at their own doors and crying out for their mothers. In the second Essex County, in the town where she'd lived, one out of every ten girls who were born was still called Faith.

"Kylie is confused." Antonia gazed at the photograph of her sister as cars raced past on the highway. The baby was moving inside of her and she felt so comforted whenever that happened. "Let her know where you are so she can find you," Antonia told her mother. "Bake an apple pie and put it in the window."

"Here? We're at an inn. Why a pie?"

"It's Jet's advice. The Reverend told me. I made one myself, and she phoned me less than an hour later."

"You're seeing the Reverend?"

It was ridiculous for Antonia to have such affection for the old man who had caused so much trouble for Jet long ago. Why, she'd heard that long before Jet and Franny and Vincent ever came to the house on Magnolia Street, the Reverend had started a petition to keep members of the Owens family out of town. That didn't at all seem like the benevolent geezer she visited, but then again, Antonia barely knew him. All the same, she hoped his pulse rate had gone down. "Jet told him about a *Lost Daughter* spell. Make the pie."

When they hung up, Sally went down the hall and told her sister they had to bake a pie. Gillian slipped on her shoes and said, "What are we waiting for?"

No questions were asked. That was one of the many things Sally had come to appreciate about her sister, she didn't have to know every detail before she jumped in to help. They went down to the kitchen in their nightgowns. There was a bin of apples, and a canister of flour in the cabinet, and pie plates in the bureau. Sally could make quite a good crust, she liked to add rosemary, and although the pub's kitchen was basic, she found a good amount of that fragrant herb in a tin on the counter, along with cinnamon and nutmeg. When they cut up the apples, the flesh of the fruit turned from white to red, just as some roses do, with pale buds turning scarlet once fully opened. It was not an ordinary pie. It was baked with love to call a daughter home. They had tea while the pie baked, Courage, which Franny had brought along. When the cook came at daybreak, a fellow named Lester, he would be surprised to find them sitting there in their nightgowns, sharing a plate of buttered toast, with the pie already cooling on the windowsill so that people in the village awoke thinking they were young again, and many came outside in their nightclothes to stand in their gardens and watch the morning sky lighten, for it was a beautiful day, without a sign of the rain to come.

PART FIVE

The Book of Dreams

I.

Ian found an account of Hannah Owens's trial in a cardboard box stored in Cat's Library, a dismissive report sentencing her to jail for witchery. It was not yet six a.m. when he made his discovery, for he hadn't waited for the library to officially open. He might have broken in, he knew it was easy enough to go through the bathroom window, accomplished as a teenaged thief when he snatched cash from the drawer beneath the circulation desk. Fortunately, there was no need to break in. The librarian, Mrs. Philips, a longtime acquaintance of his mother, had been phoned and politely asked if Ian could do a bit of research. Everyone in town knew he was constantly working on his book, not that anyone thought he would finish it, and it had come as quite a surprise to one and all when Margaret Wright announced that his book was to be published the following spring by Bradbury Press, a small American publisher in a town called Waukegan, Illinois, a place no one had ever heard of and that some people guessed was a figment of Margaret's imagination, since she'd been through so much with that son of hers, who had turned out perfectly fine after all.

Since the librarian usually awoke at four a.m. anyway, to read in bed, she met Ian at the library with a coat thrown over her nightgown, unlocked the door, patted him on the shoulder and went back to bed with a pile of books, as per usual, allowing him to have the stacks to himself. In the town records, stored in the attic, Ian found what he wanted. Hannah Owens had been accused of all manner of evildoings by a witness who had testified that she spoke with Satan and had a tail like a common beast. She was a healer, unmarried, with no issue, all marks against her from the start. Her crimes were imaginary, but her punishment was not. And there was one aspect about Hannah that was quite unusual. Ian brought this information to the inn later in the morning for the Owens family to see. The air smelled sweet and reminded him of picking apples when he was a boy, the sweet-tasting variety called Witchery, a fruit that only grew out by Lockland Manor.

When Ian arrived at the inn with the files, Vincent was the only one present in the lobby, holding a cup-to-go filled with lukewarm tea.

"Take a look," Ian said, handing over a copy of the records. "This Owens woman clearly wasn't your average village resident." In a world where more than ninety percent of the women were illiterate, Hannah had signed her name, and not with an X, but with a lovely flourish of letters, all well formed and quite readable. Those women who could read were usually members of the court where they might have access to tutors and libraries, but Hannah was clearly living in poverty. Before the time of her trial, she had resided in the cottage where the library now stood, but it had been taken from her by the town council to repay her victims for the witchery they had allegedly suffered at her hands.

Ian had been ridiculously eager to show off his findings to Sally, and felt disappointment rising within him. "Aren't we missing some people?" He meant Sally of course, but he didn't want to show his hand, although in all likelihood the old man had the sight and was one of those individuals who could always recognize a lie.

"Oh, they're already gone. I've been left to meet you and let you know we don't need you."

Flustered, Ian blurted, "I'm here because Sally needs me."

"Apparently not. It turns out Kylie is with that Lockland fellow. They've gone in search of her. They've got the address of a house he's been renting on the High Street, number twenty-three."

"Fuck." Ian stormed out of the inn, with Vincent following. "They should have waited. I know that little prick, and he's more dangerous than you'd think."

"You try stopping my sister. And just so you know, he doesn't stand a chance up against her," Vincent responded, but Ian was no longer listening. He'd noticed Matt Poole parked in the lot, dozing in his van.

"I've got to have this, Matt." Ian was already opening the driver's door so that Matt awoke with a start.

"Have what?" For a moment Matt thought he was being robbed, and fortunately he recognized Ian before he reached for the hammer he kept under the seat just in case some drunken tourist got the idea to skip out before paying his fare. Ian's mother, Margaret, had brought Matt's sister, Lisa, back to health after things had gone wrong with her first pregnancy. Nowadays, Matt's sister had two grown boys, and on the first of May, the day she might have lost her child if not for Margaret, she always brought Margaret Wright a Sticky Fingers Cake, made of fudge and rose truffle.

"Hand over your keys. There's nobody in need of a cab now anyway. Come on," Ian urged when Matt stared, wide-eyed. "It's important."

"This cab's my bread and butter," Matt complained. "You were always a wild driver."

"That was years ago, Matt. Come on."

"I don't know why I do these things," Matt grumbled as he gave over the keys. But the truth was there were no customers, and Matt could now sit out on the porch of the inn and take a nap, hoping Ian was a better driver than he was when he was young and there had been several accidents that had involved drink and trees.

Ian was still a fast driver, and Vincent twice suggested slowing down. They pulled over once they reached the dodgy end of the High Street, where the houses were in ill repair. The thickets were so deep around the house, with thorny vines climbing over the porch and the roof, that it took a moment before Sally and Gillian could be seen at the door. There had been no answer to their knocking, and Sally was doing her best to open the lock with a hairpin, to no avail. Franny had made her way into the tiny, neglected yard, where a single lilac bush grew. She was peering through the window into the parlor, her hands up to the dusty windowpanes as she attempted to look inside. The glass was too cloudy to see through, but she could sense the ill will within the house, the darkly flickering remnants of left-handed magic. Vincent came up beside her. "This doesn't look good." He took note of two dead little house sparrows in the grass wrapped in twine.

When he was young, Vincent had wandered through Lower Manhattan to places where left-handed magic could be found. He'd tried most of it, sympathetic magic in which wax figures were used along with blood magic in order to get what he wanted, which mostly was his freedom. He'd made his way downtown on dark streets at a time when he didn't truly know who he was, only that he wasn't the person his parents expected him to be. Whatever rules their mother laid down, he balked at; he went the other way, into the darkness, staying out all night at his favorite bar, called the Jester, drinking himself into a stupor, performing silly magic tricks, lighting fires with a snap of his fingers, turning off the lights with a puff of breath, hoping to impress people. Franny had been there with the cure for drunkenness, a mixture of cayenne, caffeine, St.-John's-wort, and tomato juice, which she dispensed along with a tirade on his irresponsible acts. If Franny hadn't pulled him back, anything might have happened. Back then, only she had known the truth about his sexuality; she knew without him saying a word, before he admitted it to himself. Young people were easily lost, they took chances, certainly he had, and he had compassion for those who fumbled around on the left side.

"She's just a girl," he said of Kylie. "She doesn't know what she's doing."

"You make your choices and you pay for them unless someone with a clear head stops you," Franny said grimly.

"She thinks she can end the curse and save that fellow of hers," Vincent said. "She's got the book, so maybe she will. Our generation certainly didn't manage to remedy anything."

It was only now, in this far-off place, that Franny remembered something Jet had said on the seventh night, after she'd come home from the library. The wind had picked up and the leaves had shuddered. It was their last night together, the time to say anything and everything.

If anyone can do it, it's you, Jet had told her. *You've always been stronger.*

At the time, Franny had thought Jet meant she was strong enough to survive her sister's death. Franny had responded, *No, I'm not,* for she had no idea how she would live without her sister. Jet had embraced Franny and said, *Everything worthwhile is dangerous,* then she'd gone inside, leaving Franny in tears. It was only now that she understood what her sister meant. Franny had been the one meant to end the curse all along.

Ian took the path to the front door, then hacked through the vines. If you didn't know there was a house standing here, you'd think there was nothing but an overgrown wood. The stink of left-handed magic hung in the air, bitter, yet somehow enticing. "You were supposed to wait for me," he told Sally.

She blinked looking up at him and found herself thinking the most curious thing. *Hadn't she done that all of her life?*

"You're supposed to be helping us," Gillian chimed in. "Where were you?"

"At the library. Doing research that concerns your family." Ian handed Sally the information.

Franny came over to see what he'd discovered. "A few sentences," she said, shaking her head. So little had been written about Hannah Owens it was as if she had never existed.

"Most didn't even get that," Ian responded. "If a woman doesn't write her own history, there are very few who will."

Sally leaned toward her sister. "What did he just say?"

"He's talking about himself," Gillian said. "His life's work."

"No. He's talking about us."

Since there was only one copy of *My Life as a Witch* in the library, Ian had photocopied the text. "You might want to take a look. Cora Wilkie lived here in the fifties and sixties when my mum was growing up. She's still got a load of cousins in town. She lived out at the far point that's more water than land."

"I doubt I'll have time for it," Franny responded briskly. All the same, she was developing a soft spot for Ian. He was tall and lanky, with broad shoulders, as her Haylin had been and he liked to talk, a trait she'd always appreciated in a man. Why, Haylin wouldn't stop talking for a minute; when they walked through town he would stop and speak to all of the neighbors they met, even the ones who were terrified of Franny. "You should write about those women who were never written about," she told Ian.

Once again, he could see Franny as she'd been as a young woman. The long red hair, the freckles on her milky skin, the wide mouth set in a line when she was certain she knew the right thing to do. He'd felt quite empty now that he'd finished his book, adrift about what to do next.

"The lives of the witches in Essex," he said, considering.

"Now you're thinking," Franny said. "Start with Cora. I'm sure she'll manage to pay you back if you do."

Ian leaned over and kissed Franny.

Gillian elbowed her sister, in shock. "Is he insane?"

"Possibly." Sally waited for her aunt's reaction.

To their surprise, Franny laughed. "It had better be good," she told him.

"It will be. I'll dedicate it to you."

"Lord, no."

Still, they could all see she was flattered. As for Franny, she noticed that Sally was staring, wide-eyed. *Wake up, girl! Look at what is right in front of you. Is your heart beating too fast? Are you shaky when you see him and when you walk away? Well, that's love all right, and it will still be there, even if you want to pretend it's not.*

Franny leaned in and kissed Ian's cheek, then he was the one to laugh, and he bowed to her, as if she were a queen. Franny looked across the grass and nodded to Sally. You could live a little or you could live a lot.

Vincent walked around the house. No birds sang here, always a sign. He found the back door that was now all but covered with hedges, and made his way inside. He had often looked for sympathetic magic on the Lower East Side, the strong stuff that could intensify an enchantment. He recognized the wicked ingredients on the small kitchen table: black wax, pins, black thread, madder root, belladonna, the berries of lords and ladies, the heart of a dove, a strange white bone, ashes, a black candle. Vincent sat down and placed his hands on the table. *Down paths, down roads, through the woods, through the village.* And then nothing. The path he could see when he closed his eyes stopped in the woods.

Franny came looking for her brother. She sat across from him, her hands on the table, her fingers touching his, adding her power to his own. *Take me wherever she might be, across the land or the water or out at sea.* The table seemed to shudder, then it rose off the floor, faster than they expected, as if grateful for the release. They couldn't hold on and could only watch as it hit the ceiling, sending bits of plaster fluttering down. Vincent stood to protect his sister, then brushed the dust from his coat. They'd been blocked by left-handed magic and the path turned to ash, making it clear Kylie could not be found this way.

When they went outside the thornbushes closed over the back door.

Sally and Gillian were waiting beside the lilac tree that had never flowered.

"I'd say she was here until this morning," Vincent said. There was still a scrim of ash over the grass, and when he'd held his hand on the door it was still warm.

"Can you find her?" Sally asked her grandfather.

"When I left for France, no one could find me. The same thing is happening now. You can't find someone who refuses to be found."

"We can hope she seeks us out," Franny added.

"That's not enough." Sally was firm. What if Kylie never looked for them?

"I know where he is," Ian said. "Out at the manor house. He's been camping out there on and off for years."

"We should go there now," Sally said.

"Of course," Ian answered, ready to do anything she requested. Is this what it felt like? To say yes before he'd even thought it out? To want to please her so? "Let me go on my own. I know him."

"No." Franny stopped him. "It has to be someone with bloodline skills." She patted Ian's arm. "I'm afraid that's not you." She turned to Sally. "If she's on the left-handed path, she has to come to us. If we go after her, we'll just chase her further away. Give her a little time."

"Not more than a few hours," Sally said. It was Ian she spoke to now. "Then we'll go."

Margaret guessed the visiting Americans her son was bringing by would not have the stomach for many of their local dishes, with recipes hundreds of years old, stewed eels, for instance, considered a delicacy, with ingredients that could be caught in a wire basket in the fens and flavored with parsley grown in the kitchen garden, might be an acquired taste. Pigeon casserole, two plucked gamey birds baked into a coffin of crust, might not be their usual fare. Instead she baked a faux blackbird pie, so they might have a bit of the flavor of their county, replacing the main ingredient with magenta-colored eggplant. She had fixed her ploughman's pasties, which had vegetable filling stuffed into the crust at one end and jam spooned in at the other, so that it was both a main course and a sweet. She'd made sure to cook Ian's favorite ginger pudding as well, for that was a dish that brought good fortune to whoever took a bite. It was quite a crowd once everyone arrived, still a bit dazed from Matt Poole's driving on the rutted, muddy road. The house was small, so they would dine outside.

After everyone was introduced, Sally politely excused herself. "Just a breath of air," she assured them, but everyone knew when a mother was grieving over her child. Margaret set down the pale blue plates she kept in the cabinet and gave Ian a look. *Go to her now or there'll be no going to her later.*

Even though Sally was already out the door and his mother hadn't said a word, Ian grabbed a pair of high boots from the entryway and went off without another word to anyone, all of whom were tactful enough not to discuss the two who'd gone missing.

"Tea?" Margaret asked Franny. The women were busy sizing one another up, intrigued by what they saw. One had practiced the Nameless Art all her life, the other had been born with magic.

Franny took a muslin sack of tea out of her purse. It was what they all needed most of all. "I've brought my own."

"May I?" When Margaret was given the go-ahead, she sniffed the tea. Currants, vanilla, green tea, thyme. "Lovely." She knew courage when it was right there in front of her.

"There are no blackbirds in this pie, are there?" Vincent asked, amused as he peered into the wood-heated oven. "My sister has a penchant for crows."

"Goodness, no," Margaret responded. "You're not locals yet."

Gillian eyed the purple-black vegetables in the old sink where some unused eggplants soaked in a briny salt mixture. There was no running water and jugs had to be carried in from the well house.

Margaret asked Vincent and Franny to bring their tea out to a table set up in a splash of sun near the garden. As Gillian began to follow, Margaret caught her by the sleeve to ask if she might help fix the plates. "I can tell you're a good cook."

"Oh, no, I'm dreadful," Gillian assured her.

Margaret reached for her box of recipes. She'd seen the copy of *My Life as a Witch* in Gillian's purse and remembered when she herself had gone to see Cora.

"Seriously, I can't cook," Gillian told her. "Any recipes would be wasted on me."

All the same, Margaret handed her a card. It was a very simple recipe that had been used for generations. The ink was red, likely blood. Margaret hadn't been born with the sight, but she'd been at the Art long enough to decipher what a woman wanted most in the world. "It was given to me by Cora at a time when I was in desperate need."

"I'm not desperate," Gillian was quick to correct her.

"Just take a look," Margaret suggested.

Take two lettuce roots and pour your urine upon them.

If the root shrivels, throw it out. If it germinates, plant it in a pot on your windowsill. Boil garlic each night and eat the entire bulb.

Bake the following cake and feed to the man involved, using eggs, flour, milk, your blood, and honey. Be on top and he will be hungry for more.

"What is this?" Gillian said, gazing up at the cunning woman before her.

"Recite the incantation each night."

Gillian turned the card over, tears rimming her eyes.

Goddess of the Night, Hecate, honored above all, you are the beginning, you are the end. From you are all things, and in you, eternal one, all things end.

"This is the recipe that worked for me when I wanted a child," Margaret Wright told her. "I've been grateful ever since."

Sally couldn't bring herself to have lunch with the others under her family's watchful eye. She was falling apart and didn't want their pity. What was worth living and dying for? How did one go on in the trembling darkness of what might happen next? Women who lost daughters or husbands, women who were skin and bones, who were filled with sorrow, women who couldn't find their way home, who denied who they were or what they might be willing to do. Instead of joining the others at the table, Sally walked to the marsh. She'd left her boots behind and held up her skirts. The sun beat down on her narrow shoulders. She stopped to watch a cloud of crows soar overhead. With one hand across her eyes she still searched for them vainly even after they'd scattered to perch on the banks, where they couldn't be seen in the tall grass. She wanted a sign. A voice, a song, an omen. Clouds that turned pink, a vision of another place and time. This was a remote area, one where you rarely saw a person, perhaps the occasional fisherman on a long boat. Sally's heart lifted when she saw a figure in the reeds. Perhaps it was her daughter, it surely must be, but as she waded forward she observed a dark-haired girl she didn't recognize treading through the land that was half earth and half water, a leather bag held above her head for safety's sake. Everything was blue, her dress, the water, the sky.

"Wait," Sally called. "It's too deep," she scolded.

The girl turned and their eyes met across the marsh and then Sally knew it was a shade out there; Maria had steadfastly been repeating her steps for three hundred years, unable to rest while the curse was at work. Sally stood there spellbound as the girl vanished between the bands of shadow and light. Once she had, the crow gave a shrill cry and lifted back into the sky.

"Are you all right?" Ian had come up behind Sally, breathing hard. He wasn't entirely sure what had happened until Sally turned and he saw the wonder looming in her eyes. "You witnessed the appearance of a shade."

"It was a girl." Sally's palms had grown clammy and panic overtook her. She started off into the water. "I won't let her drown."

Ian didn't wait to hear any more of her explanation. He was vain about his knowledge of the marshes and fens. People drowned by accident all the time and Sally wasn't going to be among them. "Stop right where you are, Sally. That was not your daughter. It was a ghost if it was anything at all. Something that was mortal and is no longer. I've seen her, too." He'd been high on LSD at the time, but there was no need to mention that. He had seen a shade with black hair, a young girl who vanished as he approached.

Sally continued on until she was waist deep in the water.

"Damn it, stop!"

The urgent sound of his voice made her do so. Despite his knowledge of the hazards of the terrain Ian stepped blindly forward into the water to follow. When he caught up to her he was overcome with inexpressible longing and couldn't speak. Instead he bent to kiss her.

Sally leaned in, then leaned away. "There's someone drowning." She could barely breathe.

Ian laughed and said, "Yes, I know. It's me."

There was no girl now, there was only this man who'd come after her without bothering to take off his boots. He was cruel to remind her that she had a heart. And perhaps he felt a fool, for he backed away.

"We call that the Witch's House," he said of the abandoned house by an inlet of the shore.

By now, Sally knew the history of Thornfield, how witches were tried here, drowned with no evidence other than rumor and gossip and fears spoken aloud. Even when Ian was a boy, people would stare when his mother rode through town on her bicycle late at night whenever someone fell ill, though most people agreed that she was more reliable than the doctor, who lived forty minutes away and had a temperamental vintage MGB that often didn't start in rainy weather, of which there was a great deal in this county.

"You'd never live in a place like this," Ian said, his gaze falling on Sally's beautiful worried face. She worried a good deal, and he wished he could put an end to that.

"I come from a place like this," Sally told him. "Have you never been to Massachusetts?"

"New Haven was as far as I got, to do a bit of research at Yale. And New York, of course. I was lost in the public library for days."

"But you prefer Cat's Library."

She'd seen the truth. He was a country boy who happened to live in London. "I do." Some places got ahold of you, and this one was a landscape he couldn't go without.

Sally laughed at how seriously he'd said *I do*. "Do you think I proposed to you?"

Ian was immediately ill at ease. He had kissed her and wanted to do so again. He was burning up, really, though he was standing in the cold, green water. *This could not be it.* In his mind, his story ended with him alone in his flat in London. Likely, his body wouldn't be discovered for days. He'd pictured his funeral. His mother, the Poole family, maybe an old girlfriend or two, maybe not. "Do you want a proposal?" he asked, then felt like an idiot.

Before Sally could answer he pointed to the shell of an abandoned cottage across the fens. "That's where I used to hide out. Me and the herons. I did some bad things out there." Drugs and drink and girls he vowed to love while he knew he'd never phone them up again. All the same it had been so beautiful in the fens, to sit there on the porch that was falling to pieces as he watched the moon rise had saved him in some way.

They went a bit farther, moving slowly. Sally realized how deep the mud was; it could pull you down if you didn't keep moving. "Are we now trapped here for life?"

Ian wanted to say, *I wish*, but since they were not stuck and since that would likely offend Sally he turned toward higher ground and a path that he knew would be more earth than mud. When he gestured for Sally she stood there unmoving. "Are you coming or would you prefer to drown?" Ian asked pointedly. He was known to sulk when he didn't get what he wanted and what he wanted was Sally, and to drop the pretense that there was nothing between them.

"My people can't drown." Was she so helpless that she couldn't find her daughter? She knew this had happened to Maria. Her daughter had disappeared for years, and the loss had nearly ruined her. "We have to find her," she said.

"We will, Sally. But come with me now out of the water."

When Ian reached out his hand, she took it, and they were both discreet enough not to exchange a glance.

Look ahead into the trees where a crow has settled, such a wild and beautiful creature. Look up, look away, and if you still see him then you will know. This is the way it happens, on an ordinary day, this is the way the future is revealed.

They were a mess when they reached solid ground and Sally's breathing was shallow in her chest. She was disoriented and the sun on her shoulders seemed to be burning her; her hand in his was aflame as well, but when she turned back, there was the shade once more. She kept thinking about that kiss. She kept feeling it as if it were happening all over again in a loop of time that failed to stop.

The dark-haired girl had been out in the marshes, in a coil of time in which she made her escape before Hannah Owens's house was set on fire by the first Thomas Lockland. Perhaps Sally could spy the shade because she was stunned by grief, raw and open to the world in a way she'd never been before. She, who believed her heart to be cold, who had been married twice but had feared committing to anyone, who expected the worst and got it, who'd made a vow when she was not more than ten years old that she would never fall in love, was standing in a muddy dress, barefoot and burning, who instead of walking away did something rash, kissing Ian so deeply they might have vanished into the bog where many had disappeared in the past, but fortunately fate had seen to it that they had reached dry land.

II.

From a distance, Kylie could detect smoke from the fireplace as it spiraled through the trees. Her sister's voice echoed in her head and, indeed, she considered turning around. Antonia was so often right, turning to logic when other people might panic. Kylie could run back to the village and grab the taxi she'd seen idling outside the inn, but she'd left the book behind, and the curse was still unbroken. She went on, through the ivy and the ferns, thc scent of clover filling her head. She was dizzy, she was all alone, she had already made one mistake after another. Everything seemed spun from a dream, and she was a sleepwalker wanting one thing, to undo time and go back to the afternoon on the Cambridge Common before the storm struck. For all she knew, Gideon might be having the very same dream. He wanted to reach her but he couldn't get to the door. In his dream he saw a shadow just as Kylie observed the very same thing; it was Tom Lockland standing there outside the manor house, waiting, frustrated that Kylie had taken so very long just to go to the market and back.

"About time," he said.

She saw something inside him then, what he'd been hiding, a dark line, the sort that appears when there is a crack in a china plate.

"I got lost," Kylie said simply.

"Well, follow me then."

They went along a path behind the house down to a stream, where they shared their picnic, eating from the packages Kylie had picked up at the shop, cheese and bread and pickles. She found she could eat only a bite or two. Her stomach was a nest of nerves. There was so much power in the curse and it had lasted so long, she feared what disaster a single mistake might cause. There was always a price to pay, although what the price might be was unclear.

"There's got to be a way to open this damn thing," Tom muttered.

He leafed through *The Book of the Raven* as he drank one of the beers, the other bottles kept cooling in the stream. He'd been studying the text while Kylie was off on her errand and had realized that its purpose was to grant the reader their deepest wish, the one desire at the core of someone's being, worth the price to be paid. He wasn't interested in ending a curse. It was creating one that was his fervent desire. It was payback to everyone who had ignored him and belittled him. A curse for a curse. He'd brought along the ingredients most often needed to invoke dark magic, and before Kylie had returned, he'd found what he wanted under the section "How to Seek Revenge." It was possible to summon the Red Death, a plague set upon the town. He wasn't strong enough to call down so great a curse. This was why he'd brought Kylie over to the dark side. He had a witch with real power. So much the better that she had no real sense of her own capabilities, for he intended to use her skill for his own purposes.

There had been a great deal of rain that spring and the rushing water was high. The banks were slick with heaps of last autumn's falling leaves, as they dissolved into mulch. It was a warm, still evening and when Tom was done with his beer he pitched the empty bottle into the ferns, then stood and ambled down to the bank, where he stripped off his clothes. He had brought the book with him and tossed it into the tall grass. It was said that whoever carried a fern seed could become invisible as promised by the villain in *Henry IV, Part I* when a highwayman assures his accomplice, *We have the receipt of the fern-seed; we walk invisible.* But ferns could also allow a practitioner to find answers, understand birds and animals, discover a treasure. If you have the sight, you can see more clearly wherever there are ferns.

"Afraid?" Tom called to Kylie, teasing her about her inability to swim.

There was, indeed, a twist of fear in her chest. It was the way he threw the book down so carelessly, as if it belonged to him. Still, she couldn't be waylaid by her fears. Kylie stripped off her jeans and shirt, leaving on her undergarments and shivering despite the warm air. She had a stab of panic. How had she gotten here, so far from home, a black-haired girl in the woods with a man she barely knew?

Tom had plunged into the water and when he arose he shook the drops from his hair. "See what you've been missing?" he called. "Nothing to fear."

She made her way through the reeds into the water, which streamed around her legs, cold as ice. Water calls to water, like calls to like. Kylie went deeper, but when she tried to dive it was impossible, it was as if the surface of the water was a solid wall, and she could only float. This was the proof Tom wanted. This was the reason her mother had never allowed her to swim.

Witches couldn't drown, that was the test that was always used against them, their strength turned into weakness.

Tom was watching her, and she thought she saw a flicker of resentment in his eyes.

"It's too cold," she told him, making her way back to the muddy bank, more confused than ever. Who had she been before? Certainly not the person she was now. Or was it only that her true self had always been hidden? As she stepped out, shivering and panicked, she slipped on the wet leaves, and as she lurched to steady herself, *The Book of the Raven* tumbled into the shallows. She dodged after it, and grabbed it as it floated there. Tom came racing toward her. "What have you done?" He tried to seize the book from her, but she grasped it even more tightly. Before her eyes the paste Jet had used on the last two pages dissolved. All she had needed was water, the element they were drawn to and was most dangerous to them. The last page opened and "How to Break a Curse" was revealed. Tom came to the bank and pulled his clothes on over his wet body as Kylie read the last page. It was what she suspected, a terrible bargain, but the only way to break the curse once her beloved had been afflicted. Someone had to die, and if it wasn't to be him, the only way to change fate was to take his place.

Tom grabbed the book away, a wary look in his eyes. "Get dressed," he said, for Kylie was in her sopping underclothes, her black hair streaming water. "You'll freeze to death before we get anything accomplished."

Kylie dressed quickly, but while her back was turned, Tom stalked up toward the manor with the book. Kylie ran after him, her heart pounding. *Who you trust is everything. Who you trust can save you or ruin your life. Never give your words away.* She tracked him to the manor house, following his wet footprints. He had already begun to set out a circle of red madder root around them, mixing in the poison he had used in the robbery in London.

"I want the book," Kylie said. "It's mine."

"It was," Tom said. "And now it's mine."

He used a match to spark the flame and as the first billows of smoke flooded the room, there was the sound of fluttering, birds' wingbeats, perhaps, or bats that had taken up residence in the chimney now flickering through the treetops as they fled the smoke and fire. Bees flew out from behind the mantel, where the walls were thick with honey. Kylie had heard that bees driven from their hive portend disaster. The smoke drew upward and the fire flamed orange and blue until Tom threw on a handful of russet madder root, which turned the blaze red. Red for magic and for love and for a curse returned. Revenge had taken the place where his heart used to be, coiling and uncoiling, turning darker with every breath.

He couldn't care less that the first rule of magic was to do no harm. The curse of Red Death would blanket the village of Thornfield, affecting residents before they knew it was upon them. It would slip under doors and find its way through windows and hop from person to person; the more you loved the more you would spread it with a touch or a kiss. Breathe in and it had you, breathe out and you passed it on. Tom Lockland liked the irony of the curse. The closer you were to people, the more likely you were to become ill.

He opened *The Book of the Raven* to the page upon which the Red Death had been written in blood and ink and spoke the first words of the malediction.

The rain will rise and fall. It will undo you and all who you love. Their souls, their hearts, their livers, their lungs.

Use with caution and with care, use only in the most dire circumstances.

There were field mice living in the house, but they had all fled. Nothing living dared to be near. The bats in the rafters were gone as well, out into the darkening net of the sky. Tom brought out a handful of grass poppets bound with black thread meant to represent the people in town. He took a knife and slit his skin so that he might sketch a map with his own blood on the floorboards. There was the church, there was the inn, and the library and the school, the market and the dress shop, and the teahouse. And there were the people, those who had dismissed him, defied him, ignored him. They would get what they deserved, each and every one. Mud and earth, belladonna, lords and ladies, straw and grass, and black thread and horse nettle, so poisonous a user had to wear gloves when handling the herb to make a tincture that would produce the hex. He tore his clothes, then threw the poppets into the fire. It should rage, it should bloom as if it were blood, causing the clouds above to fill with illness.

Kylie stood by in shock at all he was willing to do to hurt others. She had been enchanted, she had been a fool; it had happened to other young women, and would happen again. "You said you would help me break the curse!"

Tom had read the last page, and now understood how a curse could be broken. A life for a life. "Are you willing to die?" he said mockingly. Kylie lifted her chin, defiant, and he saw that she was. He lost his temper then. He'd never had patience for fools.

"When my curse is set, yours will be unbroken, and you won't have to die, you fool. The people in the town fulfill the curse's bargain. Let them take your place."

He had revealed himself to her. There was nothing but darkness looming inside him.

"I'm not willing to have them take my place," Kylie told him.

"But I am. That's what matters."

He'd guessed she might resist him, that was why he'd stowed a pair of handcuffs in his bag. He seized them now, shoving one of the bracelets over Kylie's wrist, and clasping the second cuff around his own. Iron stole a witch's powers, but these cuffs were made of brass, unbreakable even with the use of magic.

"Take them off," Kylie demanded, as if she would be the one to command him.

If she kept her power from him, he had little choice but to take it from her. The ritual would last all night, into the next day. But as far as Tom was concerned, he had all the time in the world.

They sat there through the night, with Kylie thinking of every way in which she might flee.

"It won't work," Tom told her. The hours had passed in the gloomy dark. It was already morning, though no birds sang. "The time is here."

The fire flamed higher as sparks rose into the air, red glowworms of light. The cuff was digging into Kylie's wrist as Tom dragged her closer to the fire. He chanted the invocation to call forth the plague, and as he spoke the smoke turned from gray to red and rose up through the chimney to become clouds dispatched by the wind. The Red Death spun through the air, carried toward the village. Already, there was a net of mist that was turning to rain. Tom was intent on stoking the fire, and he took no notice of the shade on the staircase. The dark girl with pitch-black hair and gray eyes. People say a ghost cannot look at you, for if it does it will reexperience the pains of being mortal, but this one did, it looked directly at Kylie and held her gaze as it began to disappear. Kylie understood the shade's meaning even though it wasn't spoken aloud. It was then Kylie thrust her wrist forward, and Tom's was pulled along, for their arms were now locked together as one. In an instant, their flesh was in the flames, the handcuffs burning red hot.

"You idiot," Tom shouted. He wrenched away from the fire, nearly breaking Kylie's arm in the process. By then the handcuffs were searing into their flesh, and sparks flew. They both had burned their flesh above their left hands. Tom fumbled with the key in his pocket and unlocked the cuffs as quickly as he could, cursing as he did. As soon as he did, Kylie grabbed the book and ran. She stayed clear of the poison he had set out for any intruders; she all but flew. She didn't care about the burning circle coiled around her wrist. She didn't care that she was far away from home. All she had to do was follow the rules of magic.

She heard Tom Lockland call for her to stop, but she was a runner and she always had been. She was barefoot, but that didn't matter. She'd run barefoot in the summers all around Leech Lake and now she was glad she had. The farther she ran, the clearer her head was. She had the one thing she needed, the book that would end the Owenses' curse. The sky was blooming with red clouds; the air was on fire and the red rain fell on her as she left the forest and found her way to the road. She went past the old trees as their leaves dropped into red, muddy puddles. She breathed in the red droplets, knowing what the bargain was. A life for a life, that was the cost. She'd lost her way, but now she was herself again, and for this she thanked the ghost of the girl in the manor who had told her with a single look, *Run.*

III.

Jesse was the first to see the rain. She hadn't expected anything unusual; she'd taken for granted it would be another ordinary day and had dressed accordingly, in jeans and a blouse she especially liked, gray with a frilly white collar, to be worn under her apron in the pub. They were serving meat pies and macaroni and spinach salad for those who wanted lighter fare for an early lunch. She'd been busy all morning because Rose, the woman who usually came to help clean up, had called in sick. Really, she'd had a fight with her husband, she'd admitted to Jesse, and had been up all night and now there was horrid weather moving in from the west.

"Don't come in," Jesse had told her. "Catch up on your sleep."

Jesse tried to be supportive of her coworkers, although it was annoying to have the work of two laid upon her. She was taking out the trash when a black dog ran past. She thought it might be Matt Poole's sister's retriever, but then it disappeared like a shadow. When she looked up she saw that the sky had turned red. There was a mist in the air, and it seemed to be moving through town. And then all at once the rain came down in sheets, a rain as red as blood. Jesse tossed down the dustbin and fled back to the kitchen door, but the eerie fog that accompanied the rain followed and she rushed inside and locked the door behind her, and even still the red mist did its best to get under the door, which thankfully had been caulked only a few weeks earlier.

The bar was crowded as it always was at the lunch hour, and people were staring as Jesse came in, then doubled over coughing. The bartender, a fellow named Hal, went to look out the window. He saw the clouds, their red tendrils dipping into the treetops and a rain spattering down so hard it shook the leaves from the trees. He called for everyone to remain calm and stay inside; they should phone their loved ones and tell them to do the same. Perhaps there'd been an accident at the power plant three towns over. The windows were hastily closed, but the mist had stuck to the soles of Jesse's shoes and had dusted the folds of her clothes; it was there in every cough and already spreading.

Two men in their eighties, who'd taken refuge in the bar, now collapsed and Gillian, who'd come down for some lunch, was ministering to them, demanding the kitchen staff bring her lemons and ginger and salt and hot water. She knew a curse when she saw one. She grabbed the bar of black soap she carried in her purse, then washed her hands and insisted everyone do the same. All through town people had succumbed to the illness and those who listened carefully could hear crying. Matt Poole had climbed into his van and locked all the doors when he saw people running into their houses, screaming for their children to leave their toys and hurry inside. He started driving at top speed, barely able to see through the mist, skidding as he went, hoping to outrace the haze. He could swear that he saw his sister's dog, but it was only the shadow of a cloud. When he reached the town limits he noticed that the red sky went no farther, but rather hung above the fens where it thundered down. The curse was Thornfield's alone.

Matt drove to the mud-splattered lane beyond the village limits where the Wrights had always lived and kept on until his van got stuck. He damned the road and the van and himself, then got out and ran the rest of the way, right through the brambles which stuck to his trousers and his jacket, ignoring the sodden earth that was flung up as he went, so that his face was smeared with mud. There was stinging nettle he did his best to avoid. Though he was breathing hard, he noticed that no birds were singing, not a one.

"What's this now?" Ian narrowed his eyes as his gaze focused on the long view he could spy from the kitchen window. Something strange had happened to the sky. Ian had just embarrassed himself by questioning his mother about love, which was foreign territory to him. He had planned to be offhand and casual, but the minute he said Sally's name his mother laughed, and then he understood she already knew and that she was amused to see him torn up the way he was.

"I never thought I'd see the day," she told him.

"Fine," he'd said. "I'm through discussing it." As the figure outside grew closer Ian was surprised to see who it was. "Matt Poole's arriving."

"Ian," Matt shouted from the front yard. "Something's gone wrong."

Ian cast a fleeting look at his mother, whose eyes were closed. She had picked up the scent of death. She often was called to deathbeds, to ease the transition of the dying, and she recognized the bittersweet tinge in the air. She threw open the door and Matt came racing in, shaking, his clothes soaked through with sweat.

"Somethings happened in the village," he said. "A red cloud of illness has settled over the roofs."

He didn't need to say more. Ian had read about such things, diseases called down in Egypt and Persia, rains of death, of toads and frogs, of snakes and illness, a rain of revenge. Summon a red rain and you never knew who might be sacrificed. Margaret had heard of the Red Death as well, and was already paging through her *Grimoire*, that her mother and her grandmother and her great-gran had used. *To purify, to end illness, to battle maledictions.* Rosemary, lavender, basil, mint, and woodbine for purification. Garlic, ginger, golden seal, clove, all antibacterial elements, along with an elixir of honey and boiled nettle.

"We'll go to town now," she told Ian, who nodded, quickly going to the entryway for his coat on the peg and pulling on the old boots he wore to trek through the fens. "Get my bag," Margaret called to him. He knew what she meant, the one she took around to houses when she was called upon to heal the sick; it, too, had belonged to her great-gran and had been handsewn by a bootmaker in Thornfield a hundred years earlier.

"Don't let your mum go," Matt told Ian. "It's not safe out there."

"She won't let people sicken without helping," Ian said. "You should know that."

Ian picked up the keys to Matt's van. No matter how defiant he'd been as a boy, he'd been well aware that his mother put others first. He'd been cross about her generosity to strangers and neighbors alike back then, for she seemed to ignore his most basic desires and concentrated on those who came to her for help. All he'd wanted was a room of his own and a normal house like everyone else. Now he felt a good deal of pride as his mother packed up her bag of elixirs. "Ready," she said. She turned to Matt and told him to remain in the cottage and stay out of the rain. He'd had asthma as a boy, and she'd been called in many times when his mother feared he wouldn't be able to draw another breath.

"The van's stuck," Matt informed them.

"I've got wooden slats to put under the tires," Margaret told him. "When you live here you assume there will be mud."

"I could drive you," Matt said, though he was utterly shaken.

"Don't worry," Ian assured him. "I know how to drive."

When they reached the Three Hedges, Ian pulled over to let his mother out. Margaret was wearing a plastic raincoat and boots and had a mask over her mouth and nose. She went around to his window. "You're not coming with me," she guessed.

"I'll be back as soon as I can. I have to do this for Sally."

"They told you this was for family members to see to. And besides, the girl has to return on her own accord. She has to want to leave the left side."

Ian nodded, his face grim. "I think I know the cause of the plague," he said, meaning Lockland.

Margaret knew that her son was still called to trouble, no matter the cost to himself.

"Be careful," she told him as they said their good-byes.

After he'd let off his mother, Ian drove west on the High Street, which by now was deserted. No birds, no cats, and not a soul. Everyone had locked themselves in their houses, windows shuttered as they hunkered down behind bureaus and in bathtubs. The rain fell harder as he turned in to the road that led through the forest. He didn't park in the lot, but instead drove as close to the manor as possible, leaving the van in a thicket, hidden by currant bushes and saplings. Not far from this spot there was a glassy blue pond where children skated in winter. Ian had gone skinny-dipping there when he was a teenager, so high on psychedelics he was fairly certain he should have drowned. A groundskeeper had come upon him, an old friend of his mother's who'd shouted for him to get the hell off the property, which, after some banter —*Make me. I will if I have to*—Ian wound up doing as he was told, for he was chilled and the area was spooky. It had taken him hours, and a curative tea his mother insisted he drink, before he regained his senses.

The red rain hadn't fallen on these grounds, Lockland had made sure of that. While the village suffered, the parkland remained intact. Ian made his way to the house so distracted with his thoughts of Sally that he walked through a trail of red powder scattered in the front hallway before he noticed it had been set out for anyone who dared to enter the manor. The house had been burned from the inside out, but the black and white marble tile floor was still there and Ian staggered over the patchwork tiles. He managed to get to the huge parlor but at that point the world was a haze to him as it had been when he ingested mushrooms at the pond. He should have beaten Bad Tom senseless years ago when he caught him throwing stones at his mum's Labrador retriever, Jinx, but he'd thought he understood Tom, another boy without a father who had never been taught how to be a man. Ian was usually so cautious, but he'd stepped into the poison that had brought him down before. There was no one as easy to fool as an expert, and Ian collapsed in a room where all he could see was the woodwork that had been stripped by the rain and a fire burning red.

On all of the High Street there wasn't a living creature, not a dog or a cat, not a bird or a bee, but for anyone who squinted and looked carefully, it was possible to see a young woman making her way unsteadily, through gusts of wind and rain. She was barefoot and her clothes were scarlet, her black hair streaked red by the rain. Gillian noticed her when she happened to pass a window, and she quickly called for Sally. Both wondered if the figure might be a shade from long ago, trapped in a bubble of time, for the figure was ghastly pale, with freckles scattered across her parchment white skin, her black hair in knots. When at last the stranger stopped at the inn and gazed in at them, they were stunned to see who she was.

Sally gasped and went to fling open the door, but was stopped when Hal, the bartender, stood in her way, his arms crossed over his chest.

"No one in or out," he admonished her. That's what Margaret Wright had told him, for safety's sake. More than half the people in the pub had been afflicted. Young men who usually wolfed down their food at the bar were now resigned to sprawling out on the floor, as weak as babies from the effects of the red rain. "This door doesn't open," Hal said crossly.

Rather than argue, Sally raced through the kitchen, hoping to find another exit. She made her way into an attached shed used for storage and found what had once been the milkmaid's door for the daily delivery of butter and cream. When the door swung open, she called out to her daughter, who staggered toward the building. Kylie's eyes were rimmed with black tears, and she likely would have been unrecognizable to most who knew her, but she was Sally's darling girl, who Sally pulled out of the gusts of wind so they could take refuge in the shed. There was hay on the floor and the old metal pails hung on rungs, unused and rusty. Sally embraced Kylie, her life, her heart, her girl returned.

"He's cursed everyone," Kylie managed to say. Including her, for by now her fever was so high she couldn't think straight, and by the time Sally and Gillian managed to bring her upstairs to bed, she was burning up.

Outside, the roads were flooding with blood-colored puddles. Franny had been tending to the ill, using the black soap that had first been made with antibacterial ingredients by Hannah Owens during the Black Death. Franny now brought the soap and a basin up to the small room under the eaves where the children of the innkeeper had slept in the seventeenth century.

"You can cure her," Sally said to her aunt, for what was done could be undone, and Franny was the person most able to fight this cursed disease.

The girl had all the symptoms. A pox was rising on her fair skin with patches of angry red-stained marks, and her every breath rattled in her chest. She seemed delirious, and recognized no one.

Gillian drew the curtains. She didn't like the expression on their aunt's face.

"Let's get her comfortable," Franny said. As Gillian and Sally eased off the raincoat, *The Book of the Raven* fell to the floor.

"That damn book," Sally said. She intended to go after it and toss it away, but Franny was quicker.

"I'll see to it," Franny assured her.

Gillian and Sally removed Kylie's muddy, sopping wet clothes and washed her body with warm water and black soap, the washcloths turning red. Her teeth were chattering as if she were still in the stream behind Lockland Manor. Franny opened the desk drawer, withdrawing the sewing kit. Fortunately, there was blue thread, which she strung around Kylie's ankles and wrists, taking note of the burn on her wrist. In the palm of the right hand is the future you are born with, but the left hand holds the future you have made yourself, and the lines on Kylie's left palm had stopped. Franny felt a chill up her spine. Soap and thread would not help. She slipped off the amulet Agnes Durant had given to her to wear for protection. "Make certain she wears this at all times," she told

Sally as she looped the cord over Kylie's head. "I'll do my best to stop the rain."

The *Grimoire* was in Franny's suitcase, but instead she turned to *The Book of the Raven*, which had been used to call down the red rain. She turned to the page Tom Lockland had studied so intently he'd left blotchy fingerprints on the page.

"Don't use that book," Sally warned.

"What started it will end it," Franny said.

Franny lit a fire in a brass dish. She used red magic, cutting her palm with a letter opener and adding her blood to the mixture, then she tore off a piece of the curtain at the window and wrapped a figure formed of melted soap in a bit of the blue fabric for protection and good health. She paged through *The Book of the Raven* until she came upon an ancient Aramaic incantation Amelia Bassano had discovered long ago. Franny began to recite the verse that would cause the red rain to cease.

Gone are the evil spells and the ones that send it.
Protect the people in this house and in this village, not only now
but for all generations, now and forever and ever.

Franny threw open the windows and repeated the spell without ceasing. The lethal red rain became a spattering, and then a haze, halted by the incantation, leaving the High Street a scarlet river. There still were no birds in the sky, but after a moment Franny could hear them stirring in the thicket beneath her window.

Margaret was seeing to the ill who had gathered in the pub, providing glasses of water mixed with mint and vervain to cool fevers. She heated water with honey and lemon and ginger for those afflicted by coughs, and quickly fixed poultices of rue and lavender to bring down the swellings of the pox and boils. There was a thick mixture of rowan berries, cooked nearly to a liquid in a kettle, slippery when skimmed over the skin, that brought down fever. With the end of the rain, people were coming out of their houses, looking for help and Vincent had persuaded Hal to open the door. “All for one and one for all,” he said. When Hal had continued to look blank, Vincent admonished him. “These are your neighbors, man.”

Jesse Wilkie, who was still quite unwell, managed to call over to the next village where there was a proper police department and a hospital, asking for ambulances and immediate care to be sent for close to a dozen of those stricken, the oldest and youngest being the most affected, their hands and feet burning red.

Poultices were needed for Kylie as well, and when Sally and Franny went to fetch them, Sally looked around the crowded room and she realized that Ian was nowhere to be seen.

“Where would he be?” she asked Margaret.

“I’m afraid I couldn’t stop him. He’s never been one you can tell what to do,” Margaret said apologetically “He went to find Tom Lockland. In all honesty, he did it for you.”

“For me?” Sally said.

“Of course,” Margaret said. She gazed at Sally, a bit puzzled. “I thought you understood. It’s all for you.”

“You go,” Franny told her. “We’ll see to Kylie.”

Franny then did the oddest thing, she embraced Sally and held her near, which was not at all like her, then she backed away and gave her the slip of paper on which she’d written out one of Maria’s spells. She handed over a pair of scissors from the sewing kit and a straight razor from the shared bathroom on their floor. For every act of love there was always a sacrifice.

"Thank you for everything you did for us," Sally said to Franny. "You saved us."

In Franny's opinion, it had been the other way around. Before Sally and Gillian arrived in Massachusetts, Franny had been sure she could never love anyone again. She'd been in mourning for her beloved Haylin and the girls had been in mourning for their parents. They had expected to dislike one another, but it hadn't turned out that way. Franny saw how alike she and Sally were, fated to make many of the same mistakes. If she could wish anything for Sally, it would be that she could fall in love completely, holding nothing back. That was why Franny had her choose the short straw in the pub in Notting Hill.

Both were now somewhat mortified by their show of emotion, all the same, the protectiveness Franny long ago felt for Sally and Gillian when they'd arrived at Logan Airport had never dissipated. They were her little girls, born to her or not, and they always would be.

"That's enough of that," Franny said, backing away.

"It certainly is," Sally agreed, blowing her nose on a napkin.

Gillian had come up wearing her jacket, ready to go. She shook the car keys Jesse had lent her. Like most people in town, Jesse believed in the power of the Unnamed Art. She'd taken three strands of yarn, and as her grandmother had instructed, twined them together into a bracelet while speaking a charm, and given it to Gillian, promising the band of thread would help to keep both Gillian and her sister from harm.

Sisters, hand in hand,
Poster over sea and land,
Thus do go about, about.
Thrice to thine,

And thrice to mine,
And thrice again to make up nine.

"You don't have to go," Sally told her sister.

"Of course I'm going."

There was no time to waste and, as Franny always said, everything worthwhile was dangerous. They walked out into the muddy, crimson street. Jesse's old Vauxhall was parked under the tall hedges, and Gillian quickly got behind the wheel. Sally was about to slip into the passenger seat, when she saw Vincent approach. He'd been out walking, checking to see if any neighbors were in need of assistance. Walking was something he needed to do to clear his head and he had been thinking about the dread he'd had about Jet on the night of her death. It had taken this long, but he finally understood, and he gestured wildly for Sally. A key could be many things, but so could a lock. This one was Lockland, and Vincent was indeed the key. He knew what you had to give up to open the lock.

"You're off to find him," Vincent said knowingly, for it seemed Sally was a finder, just as he was. "He's the lock, and you need to know what the key is to be rid of him. You must give up the one thing he wants."

Sally listened, then embraced Vincent before quickly getting into the passenger seat. "Can you drive on the wrong side?" Sally asked her sister, nervous, especially when they took off at top speed.

"I can do everything on the wrong side," Gillian assured her. "Where to?"

Jesse had told Sally the way to the manor. "Go west and keep driving."

Theirs was the only car on the road, and they soon enough reached the forest. The red rain had gone to the east and inflicted little damage here, with only a drop or two destroying patches of ivy and ferns. Gillian parked in the lot for visitors; through the trees they could spy the ruin before them. There were buzzards and kestrels and sparrow hawks, all on alert, for skylarks and starlings and nuthatches nested here in great abundance. The birds made a racket when the car pulled in and fluttered around Sally when she stepped out of the car.

"It doesn't look like much," Gillian said of the ruined manor.

Sally had the spell Franny had given her. In every hex-breaker there were sacrifices, and most began with what was most dear, a gem, an amulet, and in this case, locks of hair, a gift you thought would always be yours.

Sally and Gillian had left the car to walk into the forest, stopping in a shadowy glade carpeted with ferns, lady's fern, maidenhair, spleenwort, hart's-tongue, bracken.

"You're sure?" Gillian asked, for they had discussed what came next, and she knew what her sister intended.

Sally nodded, then sat cross-legged on the ground. Gillian draped her scarf on Sally's lap so that the hair she was about to cut could be collected. Sally closed her eyes and imagined Ian as he'd been on the day she had found him. Once he'd begun to recover, they'd left him to dress. Franny wasn't the only one to see him fully unclothed, Sally had as well. She'd turned back at the last moment; she'd spied the crow on his back and that was when she'd known he was the one. She'd fought it all this while, but her fate had written the future on both palms of her hands, the left and the right, the one that was made for her and the one she'd made for herself.

Save a man once, and you have a heart. Save him twice and he has yours.

When all of Sally's hair had been clipped off, the birds came to gather strands for their nests. Her beautiful dark hair gone, her one vanity, her night to Gillian's day, was now wound into the trees. This small sacrifice was given with humility and devotion, an offering from the age of Achilles, a practice of warrior women from the beginning of time so they could not be dragged away by their hair. Sally took the razor and cut her arm, dripping blood into the spell before they set a small pile of her hair on fire. When it burned, the smoke wasn't red as she expected, but milky white. There was the scent of lilacs, and where there are lilacs, there will be luck.

When Sally arose, Gillian assumed she would accompany her, but Sally shook her head.

"I know you want to help me, but just your being here is help enough."

Sally had dark pools under her eyes; with her shaven head and narrow frame she seemed little more than a girl. But she was a woman in her forties, with grown daughters of her own, and she refused to hear any arguments, no matter how persuasive her sister might be.

"Two against one would be safer," Gillian told her sister. "How can I let you go?"

Sally shook her head, defiant, and said, "You know it has to be me."

My daughter, my sacrifice, my magic.

Wild blackberries grew here, the fruit and bark used as ingredients in many of the oldest spells, often called the bramble. Sally felt her bloodline inside of her, everything she had ignored and avoided and despised when she was young, the power she had denied, the magic she had believed would ruin her could save her now. Gillian watched her sister, still beautiful without her hair. Up in an arched window there was a shadow reflecting in the only glass left in the house. It was the dark girl Gillian had seen in the fens, trapped in time. The shade lifted her hand and Gillian raised hers in return. Her frantic heart was in her throat. *You live in the past. But if you are here, help us.*

As Sally went forward she thought about the women before her who had fought to protect those they loved, those who had been erased from history, who never had a chance to tell their own stories. Vincent had told her that like follows like, what you take away you also must give. She reached the front door, the same door that their ancestor, Maria's mother, Rebecca, had fled from so many years ago. It opened to her touch, the wood hot, the air all around her buzzing with energy. The air was hotter inside than out. The floor was stone, dug from quarries in the north by men who were little more than slaves. Long ago, the hanging lamp would have held five hundred candles, all white and aflame, the stone walls would have been covered by French tapestries, the chairs made of leather and walnut, the large tables hewn from a single oak, the bowls made of brass.

Tom Lockland was in the great room, there before the fire. He was the avenging angel, hunched over, lost in his dreams of revenge. Whatever small magic that was in his blood had surfaced and bloomed. When he heard footsteps, he turned to face Sally. He knew her right away, the silver eyes, the delicate features that resembled Kylie's. With their shaven heads, Tom and Sally looked alike, but that just went to show one couldn't tell much from appearances. They had nothing in common except the past.

"I tried to help your daughter. None of this would have happened if you hadn't kept her away from magic."

"I was wrong then," Sally said. "And you're wrong now."

"I wonder if Professor Wright would agree with you. I've been stealing from him for years. If he'd been as smart as he thought he was, he would have remained a thief. At least he was good at that."

Sally looked beyond Tom to see Ian prone on the floor, afflicted in the same way he'd been when she first found him, paralyzed from the herbs taken from the old apothecary garden in Devotion Field. He'd been sure of himself; he'd thought he could take Tom in a fight, for he was six inches taller and two stone heavier, but he was no match for poison.

"You don't care who you hurt," Sally said.

"Certainly not Wright. He's a sorry example of what magic can do to a person." Tom saw the shock on Sally's face and grinned. "Are you sure you still want him?"

"I do, cousin," Sally answered.

Tom's gaze grew darker. "Don't call me that."

In truth they were barely related, and if he'd ever been part of their family, it no longer mattered. His past had made him ruthless beyond measure. He still carried the scars of being an exile in the village and in his own household, and Sally might have pitied him once, but not anymore. She took out a mirror and held it up so that anything he sent out to her would return to him threefold and then she saw him for who he was. She began the incantation from her family's *Grimoire*, one Maria Owens had written down for a desperate time. The sacrifice was to come, not the loss of her hair, which would grow back in a few months' time. Maria's spell would take away abilities Tom might possess, few as they were, but it would take Sally's as well. That was the price to pay. That was the key. She would no longer have magic.

I renounce all that I have to be rid of you. You will walk away and never return.

Tom lifted his arm in the air, his index and middle finger raised, a gesture of defiance since the thirteenth century. He wanted Sally to know he was undefeated.

They say people don't change, not at their core, not unless they face great trauma, but fate can change, and the lines on Tom Lockland's left hand were already disappearing despite his challenge to her. Sally heard a whispering and when she looked there was a girl with black hair on the stairs. She was repeating the enchantment that Sally had spoken, her lips moving, her intention clear and pure. It was not magic that had caused the curse, but mortal foolishness. Betrayal, abandonment, scorn, suffering, revenge, love. What felt right in the moment, what caused disaster, what you wished you could call back, for what was done could be undone. Sally repeated the incantation along with the girl on the stairs, even though she knew what it meant and what it would cost her to be rid of Tom. It was a revelation to feel a stab of grief now that she was losing the one thing she'd always wished to rid herself of. She was already losing her magic.

"Cousin," Tom Lockland said, pleading now that he was losing the power *The Book of the Raven* had given him. "If you do this to me, the same result will come back to you threefold."

"I don't mind," Sally told him. "I relinquish it all."

Tom shook his head, amazed by Sally's folly.

There were crows above them now in the spaces where the ceiling had crashed through, so many the sky was turning black. A world without magic was an impossible thought. Cures, remedies, stories, books, ink, paper, talismans, protection, hope, conjurations, oaths, blessings. *I have saved with this charm, many thousand score of men and women,* a magician vowed in 1391, one of the first written mentions of the Nameless Art. Human history is the history of magic, in Egypt and Greece, in the tombs of red-haired women buried with amulets and herbs on the steppes of Russia, here, in the fens, where women were found a thousand years after they'd been drowned with black stones in their mouths.

Sally's last act of magic was the one that meant the most. Ian opened his eyes and watched the crows above him through the timbers of the ruined ceiling. A beautiful woman crouched down beside him. Sally placed her hands on his face and used all she had left inside to draw out the poison. He had been dreaming he was a crow and that he was high above the manor house and could see everything, acres of land and clouds, fields and trees so old they had lived longer than anyone on earth. Ian's chest had been burning and his blood had been so hot and he'd had to rise above himself. He thought he could not survive another poisoning, but he had, although he was still burning when he looked at Sally. He didn't notice that she had shorn her hair, he didn't care if she had lost her magic; all he could see was her heart. She had saved him twice, and they both knew what that meant.

Out in the woods, Gillian began to recite a *Begone* incantation. It never hurt to have some assistance from a sister, and this was a simple spell that had been used by women since the beginning of time, with words that resembled the wild clacking of birds when they were spoken aloud. Once said, the intended would fly away, and as gusts of wind came up Tom began to run from the house, through the brambles and the branches, a grim look on his narrow face.

Tom knew the police would come looking for him if he stayed. Had he kidnapped Kylie? Not at all, despite the mark on her wrist, for he had the same burn circled around his own wrist. Had he assaulted people? Only if you could prove he could turn hatred into a red cloud. All the same, he kept on running until he reached the motorway, where someone stopped and he told them his story, how he was a good man who'd been betrayed by one and all, treated unfairly in a cruel world.

On the day Tom Lockland left Essex, Sally had no hair and no magic and Ian couldn't have cared less. He could only think how lucky he was to be alive. How lucky to be staring into her eyes.

When Sally cried, so relieved that Ian had come back to her, her tears were no longer black, but instead were clear, like anyone else's. It was what she had always wanted, from the time she was a girl, to have no bond with magic, only now her loss was breaking her heart. She held her hands over her swollen eyes. "I'm normal," she wept.

"You'll be fine," Ian said. "Look at me—I'm supposedly normal."

Sally laughed through her tears. It was true, he was far from normal, but magic was all he cared about, all he wrote about, all he wanted in this world. What was she worth to him without it? "Why would you want me? I'm nothing now."

If she wanted an argument he'd give her one. He was always ready for that. "We still have magic together." And because they did, she kissed him rather than argue with him, at least this time.

Gillian watched them walking back through the field, slowly, for Ian was still reeling from the illness, and their arms were around one another's waist. Even from a distance it was possible to see that Sally was what she'd always wished to be, an ordinary woman with no ties to the other world. Her gray eyes, the ones the Owens were known for, had turned pale blue, but she looked young again, at least from a distance, as if her life was starting anew.

Already, people were forgetting that Tom Lockland had ever

been among them, although every May there would be a town gathering to remember this day so that no one would forget how easily everyday life could be suddenly disrupted, for disaster was always a moment away, in the wind, in a red rain, in the illness that had spread through the village on a beautiful spring day.

IV.

Antonia dreamed that a toad had stopped in front of her on a grassy path. She was barefoot, frantically searching for her sister, but the toad was in her way. "Go on," she told it. "Move." In response it burped up a silver key. *Don't you understand anything?* someone said to her, and when she looked toward the lake she saw Jet, young again and a bit disappointed by how dense Antonia was. *You already have everything you need.*

Antonia scrambled out of bed, waking Ariel, who was confused. They'd gone to bed early and had barely slept an hour.

"Is it the baby?" Ariel asked, but Antonia didn't answer. She had already gone to the living room to search through her purse. Ariel had followed her, a sheet wrapped around her body.

"We have to go now." Antonia did feel a strange pressure inside of her, but that wasn't what caused her to hurry.

"Where are we going?" Ariel asked as they went into the bedroom and pulled on their clothes.

Antonia leaned on the bed. The pressure was deep, a tight band around her middle. A few breaths and it was gone. "The law office." She held up the silver key that would open the box of Maria's papers.

"Right now?" Ariel asked.

"It should have been yesterday," Antonia answered. "It should have been three hundred years ago."

The metal box was stored in the subbasement, at the bottom of an old filing cabinet that contained the Owenses' documents, the deed to the property on Magnolia Street, along with an accounting of bills from the carpenters, birth and death certificates, wills, records from the Owens School for Girls, letters written in Portuguese tied in blue ribbon, and a faded envelope on which *Do not read unless you have the book* had been scrawled in pale ink. Antonia had asked to be alone, and Ariel, though concerned that Antonia's pains seemed to be sharper and closer together, went up to her office to brew coffee that turned out to be too bitter to drink.

The paper was so thin Antonia could see through it, the ink fading as she read, worrying her as it disappeared, word by word.

The Book of the Raven nearly ruined my daughter Faith's life. I could have destroyed it, but it was written by a woman of knowledge who wrote it in order to grant the reader her heart's desire, whether it be revenge or love. It will instruct you on the way to end our affliction, then you must pass it on to the next woman who needs the raven's knowledge.

I thought a curse would protect us, but curses come back to you threefold. There is only one way to put an end to it. Courage. My letter is written for the bravest among us. To save a life, a life must be given.

To end the curse, the book in which it was originally written must be destroyed. The Grimoire which was mine must be no more.

The future rises from the ashes of the past,
Begin at the beginning and end at the end.
To have a blessed future, dispose of a cursed past.
Return it to its element, no matter how deep.

Antonia sat back on her heels and took a breath, feeling a wave within her that she had no power to fight or resist, nor would she want to. She panted until the burst of pain diminished, then scrambled over to her purse on her hands and knees to search for her phone. As she punched in the number she looked up to see Ariel perched on the stair, her face drawn with worry.

"I don't know if you realize this, but you're having a baby," Ariel said.

"Not yet," Antonia insisted. She knew who to call, the bravest among them, the bravest of the brave.

Ariel had already contacted Scott and Joel to meet them at Mass General, which thankfully wasn't very far. An ambulance had pulled up on Beacon Street. Antonia had dreamed she was walking into a lake, and now she was surrounded by a puddle. Her water had broken and the phone was ringing. "Pick up," Antonia muttered.

"It's time," Ariel said, refusing to be put off.

At last the phone was answered, which was a huge relief. There was a baby to be born, after all. "You'll never believe this," Antonia told her aunt Franny, even though she was the most practical person among them. "I know how to end the curse."

Now that the red rain had passed, stopped, as it had begun, by *The Book of the Raven*, the inn had fallen so quiet the mice felt free to wander the pantries and the hallways. Kylie was upstairs in a small bed in the smallest room. They had tried every cure in the *Grimoire* to break Kylie's fever and bring her back, and none of it had worked. Margaret was sitting with her now, with a steam vaporizer filled with rosemary and lemon water to help her breathe.

"Go have a rest," Margaret suggested to Sally, who had not left the room. It was long past midnight. "It will do no good to make yourself ill."

Sally nodded. "For an hour or so."

Ian was stretched out in the hallway, asleep on the wool carpet. She had saved him twice, there really was no fighting it, he belonged to her now. Sally leaned down and told him he needed a proper bed, rather than the floor. Ian thought he was dreaming, but as it turned out, he was not. He remembered that he must not speak, so for once in his life Ian said nothing, knowing, as he followed her down to her room, only a fool would question what was meant to be.

Down in the bar, Jesse had recovered. Craving a bath and a good night's sleep, she was locking up for the night, leaving Vincent the keys to the liquor cabinet.

"Have whatever you like," she'd told him. Vincent took a good bottle of scotch whiskey up to Franny's room, where she was studying *The Book of the Raven*.

They were both in rotten moods, all the same they toasted and drank down the whiskey in gulps. "I hate to bring it up," Vincent murmured as he poured them a second drink, "but our girl Sally has lost her magic."

Vincent had briefly lost his magic, years ago, but that hadn't been a permanent situation. Franny had known the moment she glimpsed Sally with her hair shorn down to her scalp and her eyes turned pale blue. What had happened to Faith Owens when she used the book had now happened to Sally. Sally had her wish come true. She was finally like everyone else, without the Owens-inherited protections. "If she's not careful, she'll fall in love," Franny said.

"You know she will. You sent her to his house."

"Still in light of all this chaos around us it's highly unusual, wouldn't you say?"

"It happens all the time," Vincent assured her.

"Not to people like us."

"More than anyone, to people like us. Just look at us, Franny, we lived for love."

"Well, no one said we were very smart."

Vincent laughed. "No one did."

"Would you have changed things?" Franny asked.

"Never. I had what I wanted. Once upon a time."

"You still have time, Vincent." He would always be young to Franny, her little brother, always trouble, always loved.

"Live a little?" It was an old joke between them.

"Darling boy." Franny put her hand to his heart. He most certainly wasn't done yet. "Live a lot."

When the telephone rang, Franny looked and saw something black dart by. It was most definitely not a mouse, and although she said nothing, her pulse had begun to race. There was Antonia on the other line, in the throes of early childbirth, on her way to Mass General, revealing Maria's instructions on how to break the curse. "You'll never believe this," she said, but Franny did. She believed every word.

"What was that all about?" Vincent asked when the call was over. Franny drank her scotch in one gulp. "Bad news?"

"Good news," Franny said. "Antonia is having her baby and I'm going to bed."

She embraced Vincent, then kissed his cheek. That was when he understood. They could always read each other, from the very start.

"I can tell when you're lying," Vincent said.

"You were always good at that. We can't have another generation suffer as we did."

Vincent looked like a boy standing there and Franny could not have loved him more. How lucky she'd been to have seen him again after all this time. How she wished Jet was here with them.

"Is there no other way?" Vincent urged.

"There's only one way to break the curse."

"Then that's what we'll do. Together."

"*We* will not." It was always going to be her and her alone.

"I can't stop you?" he said.

"When could you ever?"

"You were always difficult," Vincent said, his eyes brimming with tears.

"You were worse," Franny told him. "But you know the truth as well as I do," she said, and he did. Love was a sacrifice. It was all things and everything. It was the way they had lived their lives.

The Book of the Raven was open on the desk. It was late, but not too late for what she must achieve. Franny understood that the book itself was magic. Words were everything, they built worlds and destroyed them. Alone in her room, Franny knew what she must do. Before she made the sacrifice and destroyed the part of their past that held them back, she would make certain to keep their history. She copied everything in their family *Grimoire* into a red journal found in a desk drawer that was stamped with the logo of the inn, three hedges in whose branches perched three blackbirds. She began and didn't stop until every spell and cure had been copied down. Wood avens to cure toothache, black hore-hound for nausea and monthly cramps, salted leaves to heal the bite of a dog, elderberry and cherry bark for coughs, dill seeds for hiccoughs, hawthorn to calm a frantic heart, and nettle, which made a fine soup, ladled out to treat burns, infections, and inflammations. Apple for love, holly for dreams, ferns to call for rain, feverfew to ward off colds. List after list of all that mattered, silver coins, pure water, willow, birch, rowan, string, mirrors, glass, blood, ink, paper, pen.

As she wrote, the ink on the pages of the original *Grimoire* rubbed off onto her fingertips and sank into her flesh and bones, so that her veins turned dark blue and then black, threading up her arms, straight to her heart. She could feel the years unwinding. She could feel the magic inside of her. She had always wanted time to move backwards, and now it did. As she wrote she was a young woman with long red hair in love with Haylin Walker, she was a girl quarreling with her mother over the strict rules she'd set forth to keep her children away from magic, she watched over Vincent when he was a boy looking for love. Franny wrote out the enchantments of the women who came before her, going back through the generations until she reached Maria, who stood on the gallows and cursed a man who had betrayed a sacred trust.

At last, Franny had transferred everything from their *Grimoire*. When the new book was completed, Franny heard something in the wall beside her bed. She recognized the clacking. She had finished just in time, for the deathwatch beetle was waiting for her.

That was the black shadow she had seen slipping by. It had begun to follow her as soon as she took the call from Antonia. Now it emerged from the wall. In a short while the sun would begin to rise, the sky would lighten and then turn red. Red for blood, for magic, for love.

As she prepared to go, Franny noticed her reflection in the silvered mirror above the bureau. She looked so young she laughed to see herself. What a life she had, most of it unexpected. She would not have it any other way, not even the losses. This life was hers and hers alone.

The deathwatch beetle was beside her as she pulled on her red boots, it was dark as ink, curious and devoted to its mission. "Stop being so bossy," Franny told it. "I know where I'm going."

Give a life, save a life. That was the way to break the curse. Kylie would wake in the morning as if she had never been ill and the curse would be broken after three hundred years. Franny didn't need to drink tea for courage; it was something she'd been born with. She looked down to spy her fate in the palms of both her left and right hands, the future she'd been given and the one she had made for herself crossing over each other to become one. This last day, this final deed of love. A life for a life. And even now she knew the truth, how lucky they'd been. Franny scrawled two notes, one to leave on her pillow beside *The Book of the Raven*, the other to slip under Vincent's door.

You did everything right, my dear brother. Live a lot.

On her way along the corridor, she paused at Sally's room and fit the red book under the door. It was not as large as the first book, for Franny's script was small and not as elegant as the writers of the past. There were no striking illustrations of plants and symbols, she hadn't time for that; the pages were plain, but they would do. It was a book of practical magic, containing their history, past, present, and future, with plenty of blank pages for the future, Franny had made sure of that. *Write what you must, write what you will leave behind, write magic.*

It was still dark when Franny took the carpeted stairs to the lobby, holding on to the oak banister to take some of the weight off her knee, stopping to grab a coat from the rack. A maid who came in early to sort the laundry would later swear she'd spied a young woman with red hair go out the door. She was carrying a large book and she didn't look back. There were bees swarming the chimney of the Three Hedges Inn and swirls of pollen in the air, dusting rooftops and windowpanes as the bees' hum entered into people's dreams so that everyone in town slept more deeply, with many not waking until noon had come and gone.

Franny proceeded down the High Street, then turned and found her way on the small lanes where the hedges were twelve feet tall and the birds were still sleeping in their nests. It was a beautiful morning, perhaps the most beautiful day there had ever been. She'd had everything. A breath, a blink, a kiss, who needed more? Like any witch, Franny could smell water. She crossed Devotion Field where there were oxeye daisies, and poppies, and wild chamomile, and, in the shadows, enchanter's nightshade, named for Circe, who changed men into animals with her curse. Franny did not blame Maria, who swore her oath with a rope threaded around her throat. For those few instants, Maria Owens had forgotten that love was more important than life itself, even if it was a riddle no woman could solve.

Love was inside every story. Love lost and love found, red love that stained your heart, the darkest love that twisted into despair or revenge, love everlasting, love that was true. You carried love with you wherever you went. The sky had cracked open with fragile blades of light; greenfinches flew over the tall grass and magpies chattered with their arrogant calls. Crows soared above the treetops as Franny tread through the grass. For a moment the sky was black, then when the crows passed by the world was ablaze. Franny stood there for a moment to take it in. She understood why her sister had felt lucky even when she knew the end had come. Oh, beautiful world; most glorious day. Franny paused in the place where Hannah Owens's cottage had been. Perhaps she knew, or perhaps the past called out to her. It was possible to spy scraps of charred wood in the weedy grass. The earth was still marked by the fire, black and ashy in spots where only nettle and bindweed would grow. There were shoots from the poison garden Hannah had kept, stalks of yarrow and black nightshade, wolfsbane with its magenta hooded flowers, foxglove that could slow a heart, a mysterious plant named lords and ladies laden with berries that should not be touched, that could be used as a poison or as a cure depending on who gathered them.

Franny heard the clacking that was meant for her, and so she walked faster. She had no need of a cane or an umbrella to lean on. She had business to attend to. She walked just as quickly as she had when she was a girl, when it was all her brother and sister could do to keep up with her. There was the pond, so reedy and green. When she reached the shore, she knelt for a moment to catch her breath. A dozen toads sat in the grass. She could hear the song she and Jet had always turned to when Sally and Gillian were young, frightened by storms. *The water is wide. I cannot get o'er it, and neither have I wings to fly.*

Darling girls, Franny thought, *who came to show us how to love again.*

By now the sky was a vivid blue. All the same, Franny was

glad she'd taken a raincoat from the rack in the hall. It was Gideon's old coat that she'd grabbed, left on a peg to dry out, huge and ill-fitting on Franny's form. In the quiet of the morning, she could hear Gideon's heartbeat. He would be the last victim of the curse and the only one to survive it. To be young and alive was a glorious thing. When you possessed it, you were likely unable to fully comprehend that it was a marvel and a gift, no matter your circumstances.

The glade was overgrown, smelling sweetly of grass. Franny realized just how heavy the book was and placed the *Grimoire* beside her in the grass, then grabbed off her boots and her stockings. Here she was, where she was meant to be, no protection, no blue thread, no beloved, no brother, no sister, only herself on her last day.

Franny gathered flat black stones from the ground. Their weight was comforting and cold when she filled the oversized pockets of the coat. The stones here were nothing like the craggy gray shards of granite at Leech Lake. Franny and Jet and Vincent would lie out on the cliffs on hot August days until their bare shoulders and backs were sunburned. Everything was delicious back then, even their sweat was sweet. No wonder that bees had buzzed around them. No wonder they could spend all day being so lazy and happy. Time lasted forever, with each hour so thick and slow the minutes were honey pouring from a jar. Franny remembered the day Vincent leapt from the highest rock. She remembered Jet floating in the water, as beautiful as a lily. There were lilies here as well, cream-colored buds attached to thick, waxy green leaves. Franny was reminded of the blooms on the magnolia trees all around their house, a genus so old it had existed before there were bees, the leaves tough as leather so that it might protect itself from harm, the flowers glorious and wild.

Once upon a time she was a girl with red hair who could communicate with birds, who watched over her brother and sister, who fell in love even though she tried desperately not to do so, who lost her beloved and believed there was nothing left for her until she took in two little girls who reminded her of what love was. She had thought it was hard to love, but it had turned out to be easy, all you had to do was have the courage to open your heart. The future was what mattered most, whether or not it continued without her. Let there be courage. Let there be love. Franny had overloaded her pockets, just to make certain she would sink.

You sacrifice yourself and the past and let them start anew had been written in *The Book of the Raven*.

Jet had returned the book to the shelf in the library in case Franny decided that the cure was too much for her, as if she ever would. She recalled the first time they'd gone to the old house on Magnolia Street, sent there after Franny had turned seventeen, a family tradition. The neighbors had watched their arrival with suspicion. Franny had been out front, as always, with Jet tagging along and Vincent waving his arms to scare off prying eyes. Her life had opened like a flower. Her story had begun on that very day, when she took the bus from Port Authority on Forty-Second Street to Massachusetts and discovered who she was.

Like calls to like, love calls to love, courage calls to courage. Franny carried the book in her hands as she walked into the water, heavy as it was. The sodden Owens family *Grimoire* was heavier all the time, the thick paper handmade three hundred years earlier, each sheaf so expensive Hannah Owens had saved for months so that she might afford the material necessary to construct a proper book for Maria. There were toads in the marshy shore that edged the water, their skins gleaning green, shimmering as the light fell over them. A few followed Franny as she walked through the ankle-deep mud. She loved the squishy feel of mud between her toes. She always had. She wanted nothing more than sunlight and grass and the sound of calling birds.

Life, she thought, *this one was mine.*

She had loved all of it, even the terrible times when Vincent had run away to start a new life, when Haylin was injured and then when he had cancer, when Jet told her she had seven days to live. All of it. Every minute.

Franny thought she saw someone on the other shore, out in the distance, beyond the water and the snaky heat waves flickering over the surface, turning the air to mist. There was a girl with choppy black hair, the one who'd spent her last seven days with the people she loved, who had never left Franny, and who never would. When you have a sister, someone knows the story of who you were and who you would always be. They waved at each other across the water.

The Book of the Raven had warned that to break a curse you must love someone enough to pay the price and Franny did. She was willing to drown; it was her time anyway. She thought of the day when her nieces arrived in their black coats, holding hands, certain they were alone in the world. She thought of her brother, whom she'd felt responsible for since the day he was stolen from the hospital nursery, convinced he would never manage to watch out for himself. But he had. They had all managed. Franny was always going to be the one to break the curse. Here was her secret: she loved so deeply the depth could never be charted. She was in a boat out in the ocean; she was ready to do what she must. The water was waist high by now. It was cold but that didn't matter. How strange to feel weighted down by the stones in her pockets. She held the *Grimoire* against her chest. It was already waterlogged and as she went deeper the pages disintegrated and ink pooled in black circles. Words floated everywhere, shimmering on the water. Words made up the world. The book was in Franny's hands, but it was the past, over and done with. There was no point holding on, and so she did what she was supposed to. She let it go.

The skin of the toad became itself again, more green than black, restored and made whole. That was magic; that was how they had lived their lives. How lucky they had been. Oh, beautiful world. Oh, love that never ended. They had been through it all together, and now they were together once more. Franny saw Jet floating in front of her, young again. *My darling girl who knew me better than anyone.* The curse was dissolving. The toad Hannah Owens had found floating long ago, dead in the shallows, the one she had used to fashion the *Grimoire,* was alive after all this time. It was a natterjack, most unusual of creatures, one that appeared in a beloved book, *The Time Garden*, which Franny had read to Sally and Gillian when they were children. She watched as it swam away. This was what was meant to be, this was the path she had taken, this was how much she loved them and how well loved she felt in return.

People in the village wondered why the crows were putting up such a racket so early in the morning. What on earth could make them so agitated? Sally's dreams had been filled with the clicking of the deathwatch beetle. When she opened her eyes she thought she was still dreaming, but, no, she was in the Three Hedges Inn, with a man in her bed, his broad back and torso taking up much of the space, the inked crow wings the first thing she saw when she opened her eyes. Ian's breathing was even and deep, he was alive, and Sally was relieved. Last night they had stripped off their clothes and gotten into bed and the only thing he said to her was "I don't care how we end up." His mouth was close to her ear and his breath was hot. "As long as we're together," she heard him say, but she didn't answer. They were walking a very thin line; the curse was still out there, and yet they couldn't keep their hands off each other. Ian had told himself this couldn't be it, but he knew this would come to be when he first saw her standing in his room; he imagined he would have laughed to think fate could happen this way, but there was nothing funny about it. How was it possible to want someone so much? He didn't say another word until they were done, as if they would ever be done with one another. "This is it," he told Sally. "You know it is."

Now, in the first light of day, Sally spotted the red book that had been slipped beneath her door. She knelt on the carpet and turned the first page and there were the rules of magic.

Harm no one.
Know that what you give to the world will come back to you threefold.
Fall in love whenever you can.

The Owens family *Grimoire* had been copied into this slim journal, and although Sally recognized Franny's handwriting she couldn't for the life of her fathom why that would be. She grabbed on her clothes in a terror, leaving Ian to sleep and noticing that now, with her gone, he had sprawled out to take over the entire bed, one more sign she should stay away. She went to Franny's room to find the bed unslept in. There was also a small black book left behind on the pillow. A white sheet of paper had been left beside it, marked by Franny's familiar scrawl.

The curse is broken. Live your lives as you please.

Sally ran up to Kylie's attic room where Gillian had taken over the vigil from Margaret and had fallen into a restless sleep while keeping watch in a chair. Sally went directly to the bed, and as she did, Kylie opened her eyes. Sally felt relief deep in her bones. She touched her hand to Kylie's head. No fever. No blistered marks on her flesh. No sign of the Red Death.

"Mama," Kylie said, sitting up, completely recovered. "What's happened?"

Gillian had awoken when she heard Kylie's voice and she quickly came to perch on the edge of the bed. "I feel it, too," she told Sally. "Something has changed."

The walls in the room were patterned with paper decorated with lilies and leaves. If Sally wasn't mistaken, the walls were damp, with drops of water falling down. The clicking began again out in the hall.

Gillian and Sally stared at each other, both cold as ice. They both knew what that dreadful sound meant. "No," Gillian said. "It can't be. Kylie's fine." Sally threw open the door and she saw the beetle climbing into the wall to its nest in the rotted rafters, for its work had been completed.

That was when the phone rang. They expected bad news, but it was a gleeful Ariel Hardy calling to say that Antonia's baby had arrived and all was well. There was even more news. Ariel had stopped by Gideon's room at Mass General and he was now sitting up in bed, talking to his mother, with a group of doctors surrounding him, amazed by his sudden recovery.

Kylie wept to hear that Gideon was recovered, but she didn't understand. "How is it possible? It's a life for a life. For the curse to end, someone has to give up her life."

That was when Sally knew who the deathwatch beetle had come for.

Sally left them to race out of the inn without a word. Bees swarmed around the chimney and crows were circling in the distance. She knew what had been was no longer. What was done had been undone. Her beloved Franny who never showed her heart, unless you looked carefully, unless you understood what she was willing to do for you. Sally was barefoot as she made her way through the inn's parking lot, waves of panic driving her to race down the street, her pulse beating fast. It was always water that they feared and water to which they were drawn. It was quiet as she reached the far end of the High Street. No birds sang here, no bees gathered in the blooms. Sally met a man walking his dog, who was startled when he spied her running down the road without shoes, her hair shorn. Even the dog, an old spaniel, was too surprised to bark.

"Is there a pond nearby?" Sally asked in a ragged voice. Every word was glass, each one cut her throat.

The gentleman nodded, concerned, and gestured down the High Street past Littlefields Road. "Go to the end of the street and there'll be a dirt road round the bend. There's a huge old oak we call the Pondman's Oak standing there. You have to head toward the fens."

Sally went off, surprised that she could no longer pick up the scent of water as witches always could. There was always a price to pay, she knew that. You didn't have to be cursed in love to know that when you loved someone you were open to great loss. The path became grass and the scent rising reminded her of the house where she and Gillian had grown up in California, before their parents died, victims of love and fire and of the curse. She remembered arriving at the airport in Boston, holding Gillian's hand, afraid of the two old ladies who had come to meet them, especially the tall one with red hair. But Franny was the one who knew that Sally secretly cried over the loss of her parents. She was the one who said, *You'll be safe here.*

Sally spied a red boot on the shore. She ran into the water, not stopping until she was shoulder deep. Without magic, Sally now had the ability to dive underwater, but she wasn't a strong enough swimmer to retrieve the body and could only paddle above it. When Ian awoke to find the bed empty he'd immediately come looking for her, questioning the man with his dog, and running as fast as he ever had. He didn't bother to take off his coat or his shoes when he saw her. Instead, he ran straight away into the green water where he'd gone swimming so often as a boy. He'd nearly lost his life here one bleak night when he was drunk out of his mind—one minute he was floating and the next he was passed out, facedown, breathing in water rather than air, until he snapped out of it. He'd counted himself lucky that he was a strong swimmer.

"Stay where you are!" Sally called to him. The water weeds could drown a man, but Ian was heedless and reckless and didn't listen to a word she said, and the truth was she couldn't stop what was to be. Look what could happen. Look at all there was to lose. Everything worthwhile was dangerous, her aunts had told her and they were usually right.

When Ian reached Sally, he grabbed for her and insisted she swim for shore. Sally had been out there so long her teeth were chattering with cold. "Go to the inn and have them call for an ambulance."

Sally did as he said and swam to the shallows. But by the time she was out of the water, she realized why he'd demanded that she go back to the inn. He didn't wish for her to catch sight of

Franny as she now was, but Sally turned to see him carry the body to the shore, limp and heavy with water. There was no need for an ambulance. Sally stayed where she was on the shore. Franny was an old woman, but she looked so young, little more than a girl, her red hair wringing wet, leaving scarlet drops of madder root tint on the grass.

Ian delivered Franny to the bank of reeds. Sally knelt beside her, inconsolable, her face streaked with tears. She leaned down to place her ear to her aunt's chest. No heartbeat. There was no sound at all. It was so quiet here, even the toads were silent, and the beetle had stopped its dreadful clatter. Sally's weeping was the only sound. She had called Franny on the telephone when she was four years old, when tragedy struck and her parents died in a house fire, and she and Gillian were left alone. *We're coming to live with you*, Sally had said, and they had, and everything their lives had become had been due to the loving care of their aunts. It was funny how you could come to love people who began as strangers, how they could change your fate, how surprised you could be by how grateful you were.

"I can't give her up yet," Sally told Ian and he understood and sat in silence while she sobbed in the grass. This is what love was, you stayed when you wanted to run away. You held on when you knew you had no choice but to let go.

Later, after the ambulance had come and the family had been asked to sit down in the parlor of the Three Hedges Inn to be told what had occurred, after Vincent had openly wept, and Kylie had been told none of this had been her fault, Ian finally went up to Sally's room and stripped off his sopping wet clothes. He was still shaking from the cold when Sally followed with an armful of borrowed clothing the bartender kept in a bureau. Black trousers, a white shirt, a black tie. She clasped them to her chest, shy and reserved, but burning all the same. She wondered what it would feel like to be in love without holding anything back, to give everything you were to another person and expect everything in return. The story of Ian's life was written all over him, but the one place he had never covered with ink was his heart. That was hers if she wanted it. She didn't have to read his mind to know that, he told her out loud. He had dedicated himself to being alone, no matter how many women he was with, always concealing who he was. No one had ever read his story before. No one knew him. He was well aware that he talked too much, but he didn't speak now. They wondered if they dared to do this, and then they stopped thinking. Thinking was good for some things, but not for others. They felt the sting of what was to be before it happened, a siren they would answer, gratefully and desperately. Ian went to Sally and unbuttoned her soaking-wet dress. She was slow to kiss him back, and then she wasn't. His hands were hot even though the rest of him would be chilled for days to come. It was mortal love they had, but love all the same, deeper than the water beyond the fens, as deep as could be. This day had changed them. For this, and for a hundred other things, Sally would always be grateful to Franny, for on the day her aunt died, she was lucky enough to fall in love.

PART SIX

The Book of Life

Franny's funeral had been small, with only the immediate family gathered at the Owens cemetery, a woodsy plot of land surrounded by a black iron fence no one outside the family dared to cross. Two weeping willows grew in the center of the graveyard and yellow-green moss covered many of the old stones. There was a time when people in their family were banned from the town cemetery, and even though that time was over, this small burying ground was still preferable to most of the Owens relations. Franny's husband had been buried here, and now she had come to be beside him. A hundred white candles had been lit to celebrate her life and the end of the curse. *What begins can end. What is done can be undone. What is sent in the world comes back to you three times over.* They all wore white, a tradition among the family. White for funerals, black for every other day.

Vincent had returned to the States for the first time since he was a young man, and oddly enough, Massachusetts looked as familiar as a recurring dream. The oak trees with their enormous star-shaped leaves, the huge drooping hemlocks and pines, the magnolias with their waxy black-green leaves. The pond in the center of town where the swans nested, the houses with their gables and wide front porches, the weeping beeches in the town cemetery, the landscape of Vincent's past. He wished his sisters were with him as he made his way along the narrow roads, with Franny complaining about the damp weather, and Jet pointing out the fireflies in the trees. He regretted the many years they'd spent apart, and now, just when he'd found his way to Franny again, he'd lost her. From the time they were small, he could always hear Franny's thoughts, and she his, and he knew she was not the ferocious individual she presented herself to be. They had called her the Maid of Thorns when she was young, for she hid her true emotions. Stone-heart, cold-heart, no-heart, biggest heart he had ever known. The red-haired girl who saved him time and time again, who knew him when no one else did. Her love was the fiercest part about her.

On the morning of Franny's funeral, Antonia found Vincent in the second-floor bedroom he'd occupied when he'd first come to Magnolia Street, sitting on the edge of the bed, weeping. She sat beside him and let him cry, black tears falling on the white quilt and the hand-knotted rug. Antonia's bedside manner had improved after her visits with the Reverend. She patted Vincent's hand and nearly wept herself, then shc handed him a tissue from the bedside table and watched as he wiped his eyes. "All better," Antonia said calmly. It was a statement not a question, reminding Vincent of his beloved no-nonsense sister. "All you have to do is get through today."

Now, a year had passed since that day, and the world had changed. The dark spring had taken its toll, but this season the lilacs had surged with masses of blooms. Sally's wedding took place on the first of June, the ceremony held beneath the tree that had been brought to town three hundred years earlier by a man who believed in love. Women still whispered his name, as if the words *Samuel Dias* were a prayer that could bring them the sort of love Maria Owens had found with him. They were buried together in the Owens family cemetery, sharing a single headstone decorated with an etching of a magnolia tree, the oldest tree on earth, here long before men and women lived and died, before there were bees. Men still got down on one knee and declared their love beneath the magnolia's branches; women said their vows here and meant every word.

Reverend Willard, now the oldest man in the county, officiated at the wedding and was proud to do so. He was carried across the lawn in his hospital bed by the Merrill brothers, George and Billy, now close to seventy themselves, and he was clearly overjoyed to still be alive on this glorious day. The Reverend had agreed to perform the service if it took under five minutes and Chocolate Tipsy Cake was served afterward, a bargain that was quickly agreed to.

The cake for Sally's wedding took three full days to bake and was the size needed to feed fifty people. It was the largest of its kind ever made, with so much rum involved that half the town was drunk merely because they breathed the air. Bees found their way into the kitchen, their wings dusted with powdered sugar, but they didn't linger on the day of this joyous occasion, and strays were chased away with dish towels, for no one wished to be stung on a day of celebration.

The sky was cloudless and blue and most people believed that the Owens sisters ensured it would be so. Rain on a wedding day is said to be good luck, but it's also quite messy when the festivities are to be held outside; no one wanted that gorgeous Tipsy Cake to dissolve into a pool of melting chocolate. Blue ribbons were laced through the tablecloths, and everyone in the wedding party had their jacket or dress hemmed with blue thread. The Owens family from Maine was there, told in no uncertain terms to keep family secrets to themselves, and the New York Owenses were all staying at the Black Rabbit Inn, while the members of the Dias-Owens contingent from California had arrived, speaking Portuguese among one another, all of them dark and good-looking.

The weeklong celebration began with a pre-wedding lunch in a nearby field, where the bride and groom-to-be were toasted. Long wooden tables were propped up in the grass. Ice-cold beer and rosé wine were served at lunch, along with oysters that out-of-towners wolfed down, and then, for anyone who still had room, rich slices of Honesty Cake, which made for several interesting speeches in which declarations of love and buried desires were blurted out and later retracted. An older gentleman had arrived from France, very elegant, wearing a black linen suit, and speaking French whenever he wanted to avoid a question. It was said he was Franny and Jet's baby brother, Vincent, beloved and missed for many years. He liked to walk through town at night and the neighborhood dogs took to following him on his route. Everyone in town fell in love with him and people came outside to wave when he passed by. After the first two days of his visit, they all knew his name, and many local people decided to sign up for the conversational French course at the library on Monday evenings.

On the third day of his visit, Vincent was no longer alone. An English gentleman had joined him, arriving in time for the weekend, and he and Vincent were soon ensconced in the bridal suite at the Black Rabbit Inn. A year earlier, before leaving England for Franny's funeral, Vincent had phoned David Ward, asking him if they might meet on his way to the airport. Vincent remembered what William had told him on the last day of his life. *Be in love. It won't take anything away from us.* And it hadn't. Vincent and David now lived together in the village of La Flotte, and had brought Dodger with them to run along the beach and take up space in their bed. It had all happened because Vincent had known it was what William would have wanted for him.

When he'd gone to meet David in London, Vincent had waited on the bench in Hyde Park, surprised by how nervous he was.

"I didn't know if I'd ever see you again," David told him when he arrived.

Vincent laughed. "I think you knew."

"Hoping isn't knowing."

"Isn't it?" Vincent had said.

There was a great deal of excitement now that Sally Owens had arrived back home after a year away, bringing an Englishman of her own with her. Ian Wright was carefully observed by one and all, and had been asked several times if he had known any of the Beatles. Indeed, he had not, he was sorry to say, which was a disappointment. People exchanged glances when they noticed he was covered with tattoos; they had assumed so much ink meant he had ties to the music business, but obviously that was a wrong guess. Several of the Maine cousins began to wonder if perhaps this fellow of Sally's was a criminal, but it was soon discovered that he was a professor and a writer, which would explain why he sat at home at his desk all day and had never met any of the Beatles. But Sally would be returning to England after the wedding, and you never knew who *she* might meet.

It was a surprise that Sally had left town, but it was impossible to know where fate would lead you, and it seemed she had made the best of it. The fiancé she'd brought home was exceptionally friendly, chatting with everyone, even the cousins from Maine; he could hold his drink extremely well and he seemed bemused by the family. Maybe this was why Sally seemed changed, and many people vowed that her silver-gray eyes had turned a pale blue. She had always been so reserved, ice-cold some might say, but now that she'd returned after a year away she actually remembered local people's names, something that had never occurred when she'd worked at the library. Back then she would stare at you, point a finger at the middle of your chest, and announce the last book you'd withdrawn. You were forever known to her as *Fahrenheit 451* or *Olive Kittredge* or *Beloved*.

The taproom at the inn had been rented out for Friday night, and Sally's daughters had decorated with black crepe paper and black balloons. Vincent's guest, David Ward, had taught the bartender how to make a really good martini, and although they were invited to attend, the two decided they would take the opportunity to make a quick trip to Manhattan so that Vincent could show David the house at 44 Greenwich Avenue where he'd lived when he was young, when the world began to open up to him, when he fell in love for the first time, but, as it turned out, not the last.

Kylie and Antonia had planned the bachelorette party for over a month, with Sally putting in her two cents via telephone. *No macaroni and cheese! No embarrassing speeches!* They bickered over the menu and the guest list, but all agreed on one thing. Now that the curse was gone, they could all love someone without fear of reprisal.

Since her return from England, Kylie's hair had remained densely black, worn in a waist-length braid. She left it that way to remind herself of the first Essex County, where enchantments occurred and people went missing. It happened all the time. A woman would be found wandering in a desperate search for her beloved, a man would drink himself to death beneath a holly tree, a girl defied her parents and set off to have an adventure never to be heard from again, all were said to have been *toad*, placed under a spell. Kylie had been *toad.* She had overheard Margaret Wright assure her worried, bleary-eyed family that she would recover. She'd been on the wrong path, but had returned to them, damaged, it was true, but returned all the same. Still, they must remember that those who had been *toad* were altered in some deep way that was irreversible, and their futures could be precarious if those around them weren't vigilant. No snakes, no stones, no nights spent alone for a good long while, no narcotics, no needles, no knives, no razors, no mirrors. Such individuals must be treated with kindness even when they sulked and looked at the world with dread through unenchanted eyes. It was best not to mention the changes that might have occurred, the black hair, for instance, the vacant stares. Best to wrap your arms around the person who'd been missing, for an enchantment is a step out of ordinary life, and when that person returns nothing is the same, not her image in the mirror, not the lines across her palm.

Kylie had, indeed, been changed, but the one constant was her love for Gideon. She and Gideon had moved into the house on Magnolia Street as soon as his physical therapy ended. Gideon didn't often speak about the time when he was between worlds.

"I am so sorry," Kylie said when she first got to the hospital to see him.

"*I'm* sorry," Gideon said. "I was the idiot who stepped in front of a car."

He had changed as well and was a much more serious person

now, planning on applying to medical school. He drove down to Cambridge every Tuesday and Thursday to attend classes, dropping Kylie on the other side of the Charles River. She had left Harvard and now attended Simmons University, where she was studying library science. As it turned out, she had a passion for books. On weekends, Kylie worked with Miss Hardwick at the Owens Library, and the after-school story hour she led was beloved by mothers and children alike. Currently, she was reading *Half Magic*, in which only half of wishes that were made came true, prompting all sorts of unexpected adventures. Many of the children who came on Tuesday afternoons arrived half an hour early, desperate to hear what happened next to Jane and Katharine and Mark and Martha, who was very, very difficult indeed. It seemed that half magic was often quite enough.

Whenever she walked home from the library and turned onto Magnolia Street, Kylie had no desire to be anywhere else. In every generation there was someone who stayed, who planted the garden early in the spring, and kept the bees, and switched on the porch light at twilight so the neighbors knew they were welcome to come for cures and elixirs. As it turned out, Kylie was quite good at magic. She took good care of the red *Grimoire* Franny had left for them, kept under lock and key in the greenhouse. All they had ever known and all they would need to know had been written down in it, and not a single line had been lost. Kylie was in residence on Magnolia Street, and by rights the book belonged to her now.

There was rarely a night when neighbors didn't come to the door for help, which was always given freely, although often there would be payment left on the porch, a hand-knitted sweater, a pot of chrysanthemums, a silver serving spoon, an envelope of cash, and once, quite recently, a black kitten Kylie had named Raven, a great mouser who stretched out on the porch on warm days as if he owned the place.

On weekends there was often a full house on Magnolia Street. Gillian and Ben came to visit nearly every weekend, glad to be out of the city. Margaret's remedy had worked and Gillian had the daughter she'd always wanted, a little girl named Francesca Bridget after the aunts, but called Birdie by one and all. Birdie had been born at Mount Auburn Hospital in Cambridge on March 21, a date that was no longer considered unlucky. Oh, beautiful day. Oh, March 21. People who were born on this day had a unique brand of courage and what more could a woman wish for her daughter? Ben Frye had handed out chocolate cigars to anyone he could stop in the corridor. He and Gillian were both deliriously happy to step blindly into whatever was to happen next. Birdie had a tuft of red hair and her features resembled Franny's; she was stubborn and serious and could call birds to the window with a wave of her hand, sparrows and hawks alike.

"Something tells me she's not like all the other little girls," Ben said of his daughter. He had never understood the Owens curse, but now that it was over he had moved downstairs and was happy to forget whatever it was that had kept them apart. Frankly, nothing could have kept him from his daughter. The baby had silver eyes and she never cried and her father was over the moon every time he saw her.

"She's *not* like the other girls," Gillian said proudly. "She's extraordinary."

The baby girl Antonia had expected, however, had turned out to be a boy named Leo, now nearly a year old, adored by his four parents, adored by one and all. Scott Morrison, Leo's biological father and his husband, Joel, loved to come up to the house on Magnolia Street whenever they could, and Antonia, busy as ever, still came for dinner with Ariel and their son every Sunday evening.

Leo was pure trouble, delightful from the start, and when Antonia saw baby pictures of Vincent she was amazed by how much her son resembled him. In public places, where he might easily be lost, Antonia kept Leo on a baby leash, but he was already close to figuring out how to unsnap the harness, and once that happened Antonia was grateful that he had four people to run after him. Often, when she was over at Mount Auburn Hospital on rounds with the attending physician, she bumped into Scott and they would sneak a look at photos of their little boy and mull over what their high school selves would think of their current lives, in which their utmost concerns were day care and consumption of apple juice.

"We would think our lives were perfect," Antonia told her dear friend. "We would think we were the luckiest people on earth."

Sally still had the keys to the library, which she used to enter the building on the night before her wedding, even though it was after hours and meant she would be late to her own bachelorette party, an Owens tradition the night before the wedding, since weddings had been so rare. She flicked on the lights, delighted to see the library was exactly as she remembered it. She went to the rare-books section and found the shelf she'd always ignored, the one Franny and Jet had insisted they keep for magic books. There was a *Grimoire* written by Agnes Durant's sixth great-grandmother, Catherine, along with a brand-new copy of Ian's book, *The History of Magic.*

She'd gone back for *The Book of the Raven* after Franny's drowning, and had kept it ever since, knowing it should be returned to the library. It was such a small volume that it nearly disappeared when Sally fitted it in between two larger, more imposing-looking volumes of English magic. Some people vow that a book contains the soul of the writer, and often the best ones are written by those who have no voice, yet still have a story to tell. Amelia Bassano knew there would be women who would do anything to fulfill a wish or break a curse or fall in love.

Make one wish and pay the price. Make one mistake and it can haunt you. All the same, love who you will. Know that language is everything. Never give your words away.

The Book of the Raven was meant to go to the next woman who needed it. It might sit on the shelf for another three hundred years or it might be discovered the very next day, either way it would continue to live, for people often find the books they need.

Sally locked up the library for the last time, then ran all the way to the inn. She was the last to arrive and threw up her hands, flustered by the size of the crowd at the Black Rabbit and all the fuss that was made when she walked in and everyone shouted, *Congratulations,* and applauded like mad. She wasn't used to being the center of attention, but after her first cocktail a feeling of recklessness came over her and after her third, a signature drink that Gillian had concocted, called the Toad, which included crushed mint, vodka, grapefruit juice, and rosemary with a splash of rum, Sally got up on the bar of the taproom with Gillian for a hilarious chorus of Lady Gaga's "Bad Romance."

Sally Owens, who had always been so somber and had often held forth about the rules of silence and decorum when she'd run the library, had cast away her dreary black clothes and instead wore a vintage sixties Biba minidress patterned in yellow and magenta, bought in a thrift shop on Westbourne Grove. The Black Rabbit was so crowded there was a line out the door. Many of the clients who'd come to the Owenses for cures over the years were in attendance, along with the board of the library, and the mothers of the children who steadfastly brought their children to story hour, and who, if the truth be told, hung around the edges of the room to hear what happened next. Miss Hardwick gave a speech dressed as Emily Dickinson, all in white. She would remain to oversee the library until Kylie finished her degree and officially took over. The truth of it was, Miss Hardwick would stay until the morning she died, in bed, reading, which was not to happen for quite a long time.

People were well aware that this was Sally's third marriage, but the curse was over, and love was love, and everyone could see the way Sally gazed into the Englishman's liquid black eyes when he arrived with Vincent and his guest. Some folks in town swore they had heard Sally let out a burst of laughter when she was in the arms of her husband-to-be, not some hasty sarcastic hoot, but real joy that lingered, as if she were truly happy, and if that was the case, why, then, anything was possible.

Sally's girls had given her their blessings when she first told them she would be returning to England after Franny's funeral, and Gillian had held her close and whispered, *Live a lot.* Ian had already given up his place on Rosehart Mews, and they had begun to renovate a ramshackle place known as the Witch's House at the edge of the fens, bought cheaply and with the approval of the town council. As for Sally, she had taken a position at Cat's Library, and in the afternoons, Ian went off to join her at the library to work on his new book, *The Uses of Magic.* He had taken Franny's advice and had begun researching local women who had written *Grimoires,* which, at the rate he was going, would likely take him another twenty years. During the cleanup of Lockland Manor, a desk had been found among the trash, and had been brought over to the library where it was now known as the professor's desk. Local people, especially those who had been affected by the Red Death, left pens as tokens of their pride that one of their own had published his first book, which was over eleven hundred pages long, though Ian had been more concise with a simple dedication on the very first page.

To my mother who introduced me to magic, and to Sally Owens who introduced me to love.

Not long after Sally had returned to Thornfield after Franny's funeral, on a day when Ian was at work plastering what would be a guest bedroom, Margaret Wright had arrived and had discreetly taken Sally aside.

"I can teach you the Unnamed Art," she'd told Sally. "It has its failures and disappointments, but you'll be quick to pick it up. Perhaps we should start now, before I forget all that I know."

The Unnamed Art was an acquired skill and Sally was an excellent student. She quickly learned which local herbs were useful and which were so dangerous that plucking them was often a drastic error, with results that could cause spiritual distress and physical agony. Once, when she'd failed to heed Margaret's directions, she'd picked stinging nettle, an error she never made again, and she was thankful that she knew to use jewelweed to cure nettle's agony. She had learned how to make elixirs for fevers and rashes and potions for love, and as it turned out, magic came back to her, not the bloodline magic she'd been born with, but the magic she made for herself. This was the fate she had chosen.

Sally was happy to live at the edge of the world with the herons who fished in the shallow water. When the light was thin and pale, she held a hand over her eyes and looked out over the fens, searching for the dark-haired girl she had seen across the distance of three hundred years. She saw her only once, going knee-deep in water to try to reach her, one hand held over her eyes.

"It all worked out," Sally called to her. "We fell in love and we paid the price, but it's finally over and you don't have to worry about us."

One afternoon, in the chilly blue month of March, on the day when Franny was born and Jet had left the world, Sally was walking through one of her favorite fields, where daisies grew wild and she thought she spied a black heart in the grass. It was a young crow fallen from its nest in the wet gusts of the previous evening, who came to her of its own accord. She named the bird Houdini, after the great magician. She brought it home and nursed it, and when Ian saw it he grinned and said, "Be prepared. He'll never leave."

Much to Sally's delight, he hadn't. She'd left Houdini with Jesse Wilkie at the Three Hedges Inn to be cared for during their wedding trip to Massachusetts. He was meant to stay in the large iron cage the inn kept in the old milking room, but Jesse had a big heart, however, and couldn't keep the crow caged, allowing Houdini to sit at the bar, where he often behaved badly, stealing cherries and orange slices and crossly refusing to accept any pats from those who'd had a drink too many. Occasionally he'd swoop across the barroom so he could stare out the window, lovelorn. The crow made a clattering sound that was quite heartbreaking. "Sally will come back to you," Jesse told him. "Wait and see."

Unable are the Loved to die, for love is immortality, the Reverend quoted at the end of the marriage service, a blessing not only for the happy couple exchanging vows, but also in remembrance of Jet, whose favorite poet was Emily Dickinson, and of Franny, who had sacrificed so much for those she loved. The entire ceremony took under four minutes. Sally wore the black dress Franny had worn at her wedding, and her red boots. The color red had come back to her slowly, first in Ian's flat on the day she met him, in flashes of rose and scarlet, until one day she was cutting an apple for them to share and the color was so brilliant that she burst into tears. Red, after all, was the color of love.

Sally wore Maria Owens's sapphire pendant, as was customary at an Owens wedding. When Sally and Ian kissed they couldn't seem to stop, and a sigh went up among the crowd as people remembered what true love was like, and how lucky those who found it were. The babies in attendance were surprisingly well behaved during the ceremony. Birdie, only two months old, was utterly silent, in awe of the magnolia trees with their huge saucer-sized flowers. Antonia had let Leo run around beforehand so he could tire himself out and yet he still had enough energy to hide under the table where the wedding cake was being plated, refusing to come when called. "He's your spitting image," everyone declared when Vincent came to claim his great-grandson, and even the Owenses from Maine, who were notoriously argumentative, had to agree. Antonia laughed and told Ariel that if that was true they were in for some big-time trouble. Vincent had never adhered to the rules.

Sally adored the little boy, and didn't mention to Antonia that when she and Vincent had taken him into the parlor, Leo had made the books in the study jump off the shelves simply by waving his hands. They'd looked at each other and laughed. Antonia had no idea what she was in for.

"I had to practice for ages to do that," Vincent confided.

When Antonia came looking for Leo, and asked what had happened to the books, Vincent shrugged and said there were known to be little earthquakes in this part of the commonwealth. Sally had then unclasped the necklace she had worn during the ceremony so that she could give Maria's sapphire to Antonia. "To wear at the next wedding," she said to her darling daughter. "How lucky to be able to fall in love."

Vincent sat in the sunlight, where he removed his tie and his jacket and grinned at David, who was so enamored of America he was wearing a Red Sox cap. Oh, how Vincent wished he could tell his sisters how unexpected everything was. He wished they could sit down at the table, today, in the sunlight, so that he could tell them everything. *Once, a long time ago, before we knew who we were, we thought we wanted to be like everyone else. How lucky to be exactly who we were.*

The guests had a lavish wedding supper of lobster and scallops baked into a rosemary crust, with salads of every sort of lettuce, all fresh from the garden, and at last there was Tipsy Cake with cream, served while they all admired Leo and how precocious he was. Why, if you weren't watching him like a hawk, he'd climb into the lilacs and disappear. He might have shaken down the cake table that he ducked beneath, had his great-grandfather not coaxed him out with the promise of a biscuit.

Margaret Wright, who was visiting America for the very first time, made a rum punch that people couldn't get enough of, a drink that cheered up even the most contrary people. The porch was festooned with paper lanterns, and candles set into sand-filled white sacks marked the bluestone path to their door and would be lit when twilight fell. Margaret was delighted when Vincent invited her along on the tour of the greenhouse with David. "This is marvelous," she declared, deciding then and there that Ian must build one for her so that she could grow herbs all winter long.

Women here in Massachusetts had been drowned and beaten and hanged, especially if they were found to have access to books other than the Bible, for the Puritans had been convinced that they alone had the ear of God. On the morning of the wedding day, when several women in the family were sleeping off their hangovers, Margaret decided that she wished to see the spot where the witches here had been hanged. No one knew, she was told. The bodies had been buried secretly, in remote places, for they were not allowed into hallowed ground, although a few were dug up and reinterred in the town cemetery when the witch mania passed. All the same, that morning, before anyone else was awake, Sally had driven Margaret out to the hill where the gallows were thought to have been. There'd been a mist over the ground and the world was beautiful, as if it were brand new. Margaret Wright was a tough individual, but she cried on the hillside as the crows all rose from the trees.

"You'll take care of him, won't you?" Margaret had said to Sally.

"Ian can take care of himself." Sally held Margaret's hand in her own. They'd become quite close during Sally's studies of the Unnamed Art. "You taught him that."

It was likely true, but once you started worrying about someone it wasn't easy to stop.

"Now, he'll take care of you," Sally told Margaret, and perhaps she was right. Just after the wedding service, while everyone was drinking rum punch, Ian had offered to go make his mother a cup of tea, for she'd always abstained from alcohol. True, he'd never returned to the garden with the promised tea, and Margaret had been forced to go in search of him, finding him reading at the kitchen table, ignoring the chaos around him. He had indeed put the kettle on, but then he'd been distracted by an old copy of *The Magus* that had belonged to Vincent.

"The kettle's whistling," Margaret said. She had never seen her son look happier. He was a handsome man, even with all that ink, and of course she saw that for what it was—his pain rising up, his story and his vow to look for magic.

"So it is." Ian hugged her on the way to the stove and Margaret flung her arms around her son, for a moment not wishing to let him go. Such a display was very unusual for both, for they were not ones to easily show their emotions for one another. They stepped back after their embrace, a bit stunned. Love had done this to Ian Wright. He'd never quite understood it before, why it was written about with such fervor, why people did such profoundly stupid things because of it, sacrificing their futures and their lives, making foolish mistakes they'd live to regret. He knew scores of spells and incantations, in Hebrew and ancient Persian, in runic and Italian, but they'd meant nothing to him. Now he had stepped forward blindly into love, a madman and a fool and proud to be so.

"Where's our Sally?" Margaret asked.

"Paying her respects to the dead." When Ian saw worry arise on his mother's face, knowing she thought it might mean bad luck if they were apart on their wedding day, he added, "I'll have her for the rest of her life."

When he was young and in jail, Ian had been told that the one tattoo a man should never get was his woman's name. People would lie to you and betray you; they would cheat on you and make you wish you'd never met them, and there you'd be, marked by their name. Only fools made a pledge announcing a love that lasted forever, but he had done exactly that before they set out for Massachusetts. Across the wrist of his left hand, there was the fate he'd made for himself, a direct line to his heart, the last story he wanted to tell, Sally's name, the most important bit of magic, the end and the beginning of his story.

While the guests gathered in the garden, Sally and Gillian exchanged a look, then left through the gate unnoticed. Birdie was in her stroller, already dozing when they took off, headed toward the end of Main Street, past the magnolia that grew on the library lawn. It was said that Maria herself had planted it there when she was a very old woman, helped by her daughter Faith and by her grandchildren, who were descendants of Thomas Brattle, who had written so eloquently against the witch trials and had secretly loved Faith.

The aunts were divided in death, buried in opposite sides of town. Jet's plot was beside that of her first love's, Levi Willard, and Franny was interred in the Owens Cemetery, beside her husband, Haylin Walker. It was a tradition to bring the recently deceased a slice of cake after a wedding; Gillian and Sally went to the town cemetery first, with Gillian pushing Birdie's stroller along the gravel path. Sally held the plates of cake, along with a bunch of daffodils, Jet's favorite flower. As they neared the gravesite, they saw that a canvas folding chair had been set up. An older man was there, with a sandwich and a thermos of coffee, a little white dog beside him. There were already daffodils on the grave.

The dog began to bark as Sally and Gillian approached.

"Daisy, stop," the man commanded the dog, who ignored him and continued to yap. "So sorry," he apologized. "She's my watchdog."

It was then the sisters recognized the stranger.

"We're Jet's nieces," Sally said. "We remember you from her funeral."

"I'm here every Sunday." Rafael noticed the flowers Sally held. "Her favorites." He watched as Sally placed the daffodils beside those he had brought, then added the plate of cake.

"We always bring a slice of wedding cake to those we love who are gone," Gillian explained. "My sister Sally was married today."

"You should come to the house," Sally urged. "Dinner is being served right now."

"What about the curse?"

"We're rid of it," Gillian assured him. The sisters exchanged a look. They knew how lucky they were. "Franny and Jet did it for us."

Franny's stone had been installed a year after her death. It was simple granite, taken from the cliffs towering above Leech Lake. The town council had voted to pass a special dispensation which allowed the removal of the granite from town land, which made sense, for long ago the Owens family had donated the outlying woods for community use. Sally and Gillian had both been terrified of Franny at first, and they laughed about it now, recalling her long black coat, her red boots, her pale as the moon skin, the way she narrowed her eyes when you were about to speak, as if she knew you were going to tell a fib before you yourself had even thought to do so. Jet was ready to love you, but you had to work to get into Franny's good graces, although once you did, it was worth the effort.

When they reached her gravesite in the Owens Cemetery, Sally positioned the plate of Tipsy Cake on the earth. In a year the grass had grown tall and trout lilies and bloodroot had taken root in the dark soil. Sally and Gillian both lay on their backs, hands thrown over their eyes to shield them from the bright sunlight. Gillian had always had an open heart, but Sally had been convinced that she was born to love no one, and that no one would love her. Then she had come to the house on Magnolia Street and she'd taken her mean aunt's hand and her heart had cracked open, just a little, but a little was enough.

"It's a beautiful day," she told Franny through the dark soil. "It's my wedding day."

"My little girl is named for you and Aunt Jet," Gillian whispered.

They would be eternally grateful for their aunt's love and sacrifice.

Dear, darling Franny, a thousand thank-yous.

Birdie was still napping in her stroller when they left the cemetery, a blanket over her to protect her freckled skin from the sun. She usually fell asleep without the least bit of fuss. Maybe she'd be trouble later, but she was perfect now. The sisters had a plan, one they'd kept to themselves, and there was just so long they could be missing from the wedding, so they hurried into the woods. There was no one at Leech Lake when they got there, except for a few dragonflies hovering over the calm surface. It was early in the season and the water was ice cold.

"This is crazy," Sally said.

"Exactly," Gillian replied. When would they be here together again? When would they have the chance?

They pulled off their clothes and dared each other to get into the water first, then they both counted to three and took off running. Birdie slept in the shade, not in the least bothered when the sisters splashed through the shallows, shrieking before immersing their entire bodies. As they swam out to deeper water, they both were thinking of Franny and Jet and of their summers here when they were young. Sometimes you don't know how lucky you are until the time has passed you by. Sally had the urge to sit her daughters down and say, *Don't waste a minute*, but it would do no good. A person had to live through her life in order to make sense of it.

"Do you think there's really a sea monster?" Gillian asked, her voice lazy. They'd heard such stories ever since they'd first come to town.

"Anything's possible."

"But would it still be alive if it had been sighted in the 1600s?"

"Time is relative. There's probably a loop of us sitting on the porch in our pajamas having chocolate cake for breakfast."

They laughed and held hands, and then Sally surprised Gillian by diving into the blue depths. She could do that now that she had lost her powers, and, as it turned out, she was quite a show-off in the water.

"Unfair!" Gillian cried when Sally reappeared, bursting through the dark green weeds, spitting water and laughing. "You get to dive."

"You get to float," Sally shot back, paddling up beside her sister.

Oh, day they never wanted to end.

"We got what we wanted," Gillian said in a soft tone. "Both of us."

Sally felt a wash of love for her sister. Things didn't last. They both knew that. "Will we have to pay a price for being happy?"

"Everyone does. That's what it means to be alive."

The water was so deep it was said there was no bottom, it reached all the way to the end of the earth. They were drifting among the lilies, abloom with their cream-colored flowers, their long, tangled roots dangling. They were shivery with the cold when they climbed out onto the banks. They waited until they were mostly dry, then pulled on their clothes, which they'd hung on the low boughs of evergreens. Birdie was still asleep. There were crows in the branches of the trees, peering down at them. Toads gathered in the shallows, calling softly.

"What do you think it all means?" Gillian asked.

"It means that no matter what, we will never be normal," Sally said cheerfully. "With or without magic."

"Never," Gillian agreed.

They walked home along the dirt path that was called Faith's Way by the locals. The last of the day's hazy sunlight beat down on them and the air was still. There was the song of crickets, a trilling that filled their heads. It was still officially spring, but it felt like a summer afternoon.

"Will you miss being here?" Gillian asked.

"I'll miss you."

"We'll spend every summer together at Vincent's house in France." Neither of them could bring themselves to call him grandfather; though they had come to love him dearly, Vincent just seemed too young for that title.

"We won't wear bathing suits, even when we're very old."

"And no shoes. All summer long."

Once upon a time they were as different as night and day, but that had changed. Each had what they'd wished for most. How lucky they'd been to be raised by women who taught them what was most important in this world. Read as many books as you can. Choose courage over caution. Take time to visit libraries. Look for light in the darkness. Have faith in yourself. Know that love is what matters most.

All the way home they held hands, exactly as they had when

they were little girls who had taken a plane through a storm to reach Massachusetts. It wasn't so long ago. It felt like only yesterday. They had worn black coats and patent leather shoes as they walked up the bluestone path to the house on Magnolia Street, with no idea of what might come next.

Then and there, their lives had begun.

HISTORICAL NOTE

Amelia Bassano

In my novels, Amelia Bassano is the author of the imaginary *Grimoire, The Book of the Raven*, a text containing a collection of left-handed magic, what has been called the Dark Art. But she was also a very real woman, known as Emilia Bassano Lanier, whose life spanned the years 1569 to 1645, and who was the first woman in England to publish a volume of poems, *Salve Deus Rex Judaeorum*. She was a feminist who wrote a defense of Eve, blamed as the originator of sin, a crime for which all women were then accused. Bassano lived through the plague years in London and the riots that followed, and although fate made the best of her, she did what she could to make the best of fate.

There are those who believe Amelia Bassano was the Dark Lady of Shakespeare's poems, and still others who are convinced that she was much more. It was well known that Shakespeare stole or "borrowed" his plots, and perhaps he did so from Bassano, for she was well versed in issues and ideas arising in Shakespeare's work, subjects it seems unlikely he would have known about from personal experience or from readings. Her depth of knowledge covered themes and issues Shakespeare wrote about, ranging from falconry (she was mistress to the royal falconer), to Italian geography that would likely be known only to native Italians, to Jewish history and references to the Kabbalah and the Talmud, including a surprisingly compassionate attitude toward Jews in general (*If you prick us, do we not bleed?*) in a time when Jews had been exiled from England from 1290 until 1656, and, even upon their readmittance, often lived hidden lives. Bassano was familiar with the Italian stories that were referenced in the plays, and had traveled to Elsinore, where *Hamlet* takes place, and knew the castle intimately.

There are some who believe that she wrote the plays, and never received credit for doing so due to her gender.

Bassano was born into a family of Jewish Italian musicians from a town near Venice who came to be in the court of Elizabeth I. At the age of thirteen she became the mistress of Henry Carey, Lord Hunsdon, aged fifty-six, said to be the son of Henry VIII and Anne Boleyn, and first cousin of Elizabeth I, who was the royal patron of all theater, including theaters producing Shakespeare's plays. Bassano also was said to have had an affair with Christopher (Kit) Marlowe, who perhaps was her teacher in the world of writing for the theater. Bassano's cousin wrote songs for Shakespeare's plays, and another family member was said to design sets and also create music for the plays. As a girl, she was taken up as a ward of Susan Bertie, countess of Kent, and in this way the royal world opened to her. She was also involved with magic and with the court astrologer, Dr. Simon Forman, well known as an occultist and herbalist.

Amelia Bassano struggled for her voice to be heard at a time when women's voices were silenced, no matter how brilliant they might be. In the world of the Owens family, her imagined *Grimoire, The Book of the Raven*, and her clear belief that words are the most powerful magic, have affected every generation.

For further reading about the life of Amelia Bassano:

Grossman, Marshall, ed. *Aemilia Lanyer: Gender, Genre, and the Canon*. Lexington: University Press of Kentucky, 1998. A collection of essays concerned with Bassano's life and work.

Hudson, John. *Shakespeare's Dark Lady*. Gloucestershire, UK: Amberley Publishing, 2014, 2016. A fascinating book which gives a very convincing argument that Bassano was, indeed, the playwright.

LIST OF BOOKS

This novel begins and ends in a library, and you may have noticed that within these pages I mention many book titles. These are some of my favorite books, and I wanted to share the full list with you here. If you look carefully, you may find other references to the books I love within the text and many magic reference books. Thank you to the authors of these beautiful books that changed my life every time I walked into a library.

The Poems of Emily Dickinson
Wuthering Heights, Emily Brontë
Jane Eyre, Charlotte Brontë
Wide Sargasso Sea, Jean Rhys
Little Women, Louisa May Alcott
The Secret Garden, Frances Hodgson Burnett
The Borrowers, Mary Norton
Half Magic, Edward Eager
Magic by the Lake, Edward Eager
The Time Garden, Edward Eager
Emma, Jane Austen
Persuasion, Jane Austen
Pride and Prejudice, Jane Austen
Frankenstein, Mary Shelley
Enormous Changes at the Last Minute, Grace Paley
Fahrenheit 451, Ray Bradbury
Something Wicked This Way Comes, Ray Bradbury
We Have Always Lived in the Castle, Shirley Jackson
The Waves, Virginia Woolf
The Blue Fairy Book, Andrew Lang
The Odyssey, Homer
Started Early, Took My Dog, Kate Atkinson
Olive Kitteridge, Elizabeth Strout
The Scarlet Letter, Nathaniel Hawthorne
Beloved, Toni Morrison

ACKNOWLEDGMENTS

Many thanks to

Marysue Rucci
Jonathan Karp
Amanda Urban
Ron Bernstein
Suzanne Baboneau
Dana Canedy
Zachary Knoll
Samantha Hoback
Elizabeth Breeden
Jackie Seow
Brittany Adames
Carly Loman
Julia Prosser
Nicole Dewey

Sam Fox, Rory Walsh, Drew Foster
Miriam Feuerle and everyone at Lyceum Agency

Sue Standing

A special thank you
Madison Wolters, Deborah Revzin, and Rikki Angelides

With gratitude to my readers

ABOUT THE AUTHOR

ALICE HOFFMAN is the author of more than thirty works of fiction, including *The World That We Knew*; *The Marriage of Opposites*; *The Red Garden*; *The Museum of Extraordinary Things*; *The Dovekeepers*; *Here on Earth*, an Oprah's Book Club selection; and the *Practical Magic* series, including *Practical Magic*; *Magic Lessons*; *The Rules of Magic*, a selection of Reese's Book Club; and *The Book of Magic*. She lives near Boston.

MAGIC LESSONS

Alice Hoffman

Every story has a beginning . . .

For centuries, the women of the Owens family have been cursed: any man who loves an Owens woman will die.

It begins with a baby abandoned in a snowy English field in the 1600s. Gentle Hannah Owens takes the baby in, and as the child grows, Hannah teaches little Maria about the 'Unnamed Arts'. Maria has a gift for them – a gift that may well prove her undoing.

When Maria is abandoned by the man she loves, she invokes the curse that will haunt her family for centuries. Because magic has rules, and they must be obeyed.

SCRIBNER

The RULES of MAGIC

Alice Hoffman

All rules can be broken

From the beginning, Susanna Owens knew her three children were unique. Franny, with her blood red hair, who can commune with birds. Jet, shy and beautiful, who knows what others are thinking. And Vincent, too charismatic for his own good.

Susanna needed to set some rules of magic: no walking in the moonlight, no red shoes . . . and certainly, absolutely, no books about magic.

And yet, despite the warning handed down through the family for centuries, that love will be their undoing, the Owens siblings will break every one of these rules and discover who they truly are.

SCRIBNER

PRACTICAL MAGIC

Alice Hoffman

The beloved classic

As children, sisters Gillian and Sally were forever outsiders in their small New England town, teased, taunted and shunned for the sense of magic that seemed to hang in the air around them. All Gillian and Sally ever wanted was to get away.

Years later, tragedy brings the sisters back together. They'll find that no matter what else may happen, they'll always have each other.

One of Alice Hoffman's best-loved novels, *Practical Magic* is an enchanting tale of love, forgiveness and family.

SCRIBNER